ULTRACLOCKS

I0636700

DITHERBOOKS

Gary Budgen

ULTRACLOCKS

DOUBLE DRAGON

A DOUBLE DRAGON PAPERBACK

© Copyright 2023
Gary Budgen

The right of Gary Budgen to be identified as author of
this work has been asserted in accordance with the
Copyright, Designs and Patents Act 1988

All Rights Reserved

No reproduction, copy or transmission of the publication
may be made without written permission. No paragraph
of this publication may be reproduced, copied or
transmitted save with the written permission of the
publisher, or in accordance with the provisions of the
Copyright Act 1956 (as amended).

Any person who does any unauthorised act in relation to
this publication may be liable to criminal prosecution
and civil claims for damages.

ISBN 978 1 78695 847 1

Double Dragon
Is an imprint of
Fiction4All

Published 2023
Fiction4All
www.fiction4all.com

CHAPTER ONE

The shape of data screaming in the October night. Fox, asleep in his clothes, jolted into consciousness. The cilia on his head picked up the patterns and the digital signalling began to resolve itself into pictures filling his mind. Running through a devastated landscape, boots treading on a decapitated head with its eyes still glaring. Then light, a white flare filling the sky, and on the horizon the gold and copper cloud of an atomic detonation.

He wanted it to stop but the augmentation inside his head only craved more, savouring each moment before devouring.

The flash of a fantastic thought. He would wrench open the bedroom floorboards and get one of the hidden guns. Go outside and blast the head off whoever was out there causing this.

Instead he poured a glass of grappa from the bottle on the bedside table and drained that before putting on his overcoat and heading out of the flat and down to the street.

The old soldier was on the pavement outside the Cafe Castringius, his back against the lamp post and knees drawn up. He wore one of those cheap suits they sell ex-soldiers when they first arrive in Genesia.

"I know you," the soldier said.

He wasn't old, not really, but drinking had worn deep scallops into his face.

"No," Fox said.

"Least we had ones like you, with all those worms coming out of their head. You in intelligence? Ugly blighter aren't you. No offence."

Fox had never been part of the soldier's war but people with an augmentation like his were invaluable to an army.

"I have to go," Fox said and took out his wallet and pressed the twenty crown note, which he intended to give to Max, into the soldier's hand.

"That's very kind, very kind."

"Next time find another place to spend the night. No offence."

Fox walked quickly through Little Alexandria, with its gabled houses so close together they nearly touched above his head. Even during the day these streets were tunnels of shadow. At night the lighting cut arcs in the darkness but never entirely banished it.

It would be best now to find something more palatable than war stories to feed his augmentation. He might have sought out those places in the city with intact servers with databases that hadn't entirely decayed. Instead he just walked without aim waiting for the augmentation to quieten.

The soldier had seen a lot of combat, killed a few times and watched as comrades died from radiation. A rich and tasty dish for the augmentation that Fox found hard dispel. In the end he just gave up and sat in the alcove of the back door of a building. When he saw the atomic explosion again he got the grappa bottle out from the inside pocket of his coat.

He must have been there for some time. He found that he had been swaying his head to the sound of the muffled music from beyond the door. It was a mild night and he saw no reason to move but the grappa bottle was empty and there was something crawling up the outside of his jacket sleeve. It might have been a tiny shield the size of coin moving in slow jerks. It reached the crook of his arm and then stopped. It was a large beetle, its elytra catching the lamplight and making it glow. Fox picked it up and turned it over. The miniaturisation was so accomplished that he could only just distinguish that there were different parts there, an escapement, cogs and cams. There was a tiny turning crown on one side and Fox wound this. The bug's legs came to life, tapping out silently in the air as he held it. He set it on his arm again so it could resume its journey up towards his shoulder.

It was just something that some people did. You came across a clockwork bug or bird that had wound down and you turned its key or crown, gave life back to its mainspring. Clockwork automata had arrived in Genesia during the days of Count Septimus. They'd come as swarms of insects and flocks of birds; then humanoids, the ultraclocks, had followed. Their origin was obscure but it was presumed it was in accordance with some caprice of the Count, developing the city's long obsession with puppets and masks, clockwork toys.

During the Court of Comedians there had been attempts to get rid of the automata but that had ended with the revolt that had established the Provisional Government.

The bug reached his neck and its feet tickled. Fox picked it up and put it on his wrist so it could start its climb again. This might have gone on for hours but then the door he was resting against opened, warm air came out with the sound of discordant thumping jazz.

"There you are little cousin."

It was voice like the soft piping of a wind instrument.

Fox looked up at her, up her long legs and the garter of her stockings, low around her knees. The rest of her legs were bare up to the lace fringed edge of a very short dress that barely covered her thighs. He noticed most of all that the skin, of her legs, her bare arms above the long red gloves she wore, was smoother than glass.

He scrambled up onto his feet somehow kicking the grappa bottle into the gutter.

"Yours?"

He plucked the beetle off his arm and held it out to her. She smiled.

She came towards him, stretching out her hand, the velvet glove up to the elbow. Her movements were sinuous not mechanical, yet not entirely natural. More like a dance or a mime.

"You wound it up?" she said.

"Yes."

It was difficult not to think of a doll, of porcelain fragility. But she wasn't the representation of a child. She had been constructed under the scrutiny of a gaze that had eroticised her almost completely, curved and full bosomed. Her abundant dark hair was tied up in ringlets. She was smiling, a big smile, and her large eyes caught the light. Fox couldn't work out how her face moved, how her features were not fixed and still like the doll impression he had.

"He's my little pet," she said and reached out to take the beetle from him. She passed the bug from one hand to the other so that it scuttled over her fingers and it began to move up her arm. She was breathing, her chest rising with a slightly exaggerated movement.

"It was here," Fox said.

Fox's augmentation was worrying him for data. All those interfaces between his own brain and its filaments were tingling. It couldn't fathom her. Computers it knew. Humans with life-bugs it read easily. Even un-augmented humans gave off an electrical pattern that, though indecipherable, was a definite presence.

But it was always baffling to be close to an ultraclock. And the augmentation was further interested because Fox was, because she was somehow beautiful. He wanted to touch her to check if she was real but that wouldn't have been enough because he wanted to know that she, in turn, knew that she was real, that the words she spoke were not some kind of clever trick, as though she were a rather complex music box.

Yet there was nothing for the augmentation to read.

She let the beetle crawl down her glove then held her hands together so it moved onto her other hand, tilting her head to watch its progress. Once again her movements struck him. She was like a priest performing the hand signs of a ritual that had been repeated so many times they no longer needed to be directed.

"Why did you do that?"

Fox didn't understand what she meant.

"Why did you wind it up?"

When she said *wind* there was a slight hesitation, almost a savouring of the word.

"I don't know. People do."

"It was very kind of you. If he'd been left out here, run down, then someone could have trod on him. Or deliberately broken him."

Yes, there were people who did that to automata.

"Olympia," came a deep voice, "What are you doing?"

"Waiting out here," she said.

A figure came out of the door and filled the remaining space in the alcove. It was another automaton, tall with an almost art-deco elegance. He was smooth, pewter coloured and without any attempt—hair, eyebrows—to a cosmetic humanity.

"Here," the ultraclock said to Olympia handing her an umbrella. She hesitated for a moment and held out the beetle to Fox. It crawled onto his arm.

"My coat," she said, taking the umbrella, "I must have my coat."

"Who is this?"

There was no expression on his face as he looked at Fox and Fox was not sure his features were capable of movement. It might have been described as a noble face, like a classical statue but one that had been cast in the machine shops of a vanished industrial era.

"He had my beetle," Olympia said, "Now please Victor fetch me my coat."

Victor inspected Fox for a moment longer then disappeared back inside into a short corridor with a shabby carpet and several doors. The music suddenly stopped to be followed by clapping.

"Your name is Olympia?"

"I sing here," she said, "The Cabaret Vaucanson. You must come and see me."

"I try to avoid large crowds. For some reason I scare people."

Her face went blank. Blank in a way a human being's face never could. She blinked and her eyes darted across Fox's head, over the cilia coming out of the left side of his face, temple and crown. It was as though she was noting the deformity for the first time. Fox wondered if she saw him differently, but then how did she see him at all without the firing of optic nerves?

"Yes, you have a rather unusual appearance."

Victor emerged and carefully wrapped around her a long otter-skin coat that reached to the ground. Then he placed over her head a silver chain with a key attached to it. The key fell gently between her breasts, the movement of her breath settling it there.

"What are you doing here?" Victor said to Fox. "Are you some kind of stage-door Johnny?"

"Leave him alone."

Fox took a step back. He couldn't tell if Victor was angry but he knew he was powerful. Fox staggered against the kerb.

"Are you quite well?" Olympia said.

"He's drunk," said Victor, "Can't you tell? Look he's even left his bottle there."

"And yet he saved the little beetle's life."

"He wouldn't even consider it to be life."

Fox realised Victor wanted him to object, to say something that would rile him.

"I should be going," Fox said picking the beetle from his shoulder and holding it out, watching its legs working.

Olympia opened her palm and Fox placed the beetle there. For an instant Fox touched her cold skin.

"Thank you," she said. "What is your name?"

Fox reached inside his coat and drew out one of his cards. It was frayed at the edges because it had been there so long.

She read. "Evergreen Fox? Private Detective. Café Castringius."

"A detective," said Victor, "Something out of an old film."

"How delightful," said Olympia.

"Sure," Fox smiled. He had wanted to call himself something else, a locater or a finder. But nothing sounded right.

Olympia was smiling at him, a miraculously produced mechanical smile that did not look mechanical.

"Were you spying on us?" Victor said.

"No, I…"

"Don't be frightened, Victor won't do you any harm."

"Oh, wouldn't I?"

It was some little game that had little to do with Fox.

Victor began to pull the door shut. Olympia was looking at the bug, she tilted it onto the hand that held the umbrella and it scuttled onto the handle, following the inner arc.

"Victor." Someone called from further down the street at the junction where it met a wider thoroughfare. A small stocky man was approaching. Emerging into the fall of the streetlight, his formal suit not sitting too well on him.

Both Victor and Olympia turned towards him

"Victor," the man called again, "It is I your master come to fetch you."

And he laughed as he strode up to meet them, playing another game Fox didn't understand. The man glared at Fox for a moment. Fox realised he was leaning against a wall now.

"Who's this?" the man asked pointing at Fox.

"I think," said Victor, "that it is someone under the delusion that he is a detective."

"A what?"

"Come on," said Olympia, "Let us go and leave Herr Fox in peace."

She would be gone soon so Fox stepped forward and reached for her hand. She watched as he drew it to his lips and kissed it. Cold but soft.

"Come on Olympia," Victor said, "we shall walk you home."

Victor started to follow the man who was already walking away.

"Here," said Olympia. She plucked the little beetle from the handle of the umbrella and gave it to Fox. It marched up his palm.

"You saved his life," she said, "now you have to look after him. Wind him up when he runs down and keep him out of mischief."

CHAPTER TWO

It felt as though he'd hardly slept when there was a banging on the door and Fox heard Max telling him that there was a call for him in the café. Fox checked the alarm and saw that it was gone one o'clock. He was usually there by now, spending most afternoons in the Café Castringius, in the back street where he lived.

Eating his meals there got round some of the problems with shopping. Food imports these days being patchy. Staying in the café also meant he was less likely to be seen by people who weren't used to him. Or who knew him and didn't like him. Fox always sat at the same table at the back, beneath a print of one of Nicholas Castringius's late erotic masterpieces.

"She said she'd call back," Max said as Fox sat down.

Max bought coffee, a glass of water, a semmel roll and little pots of butter and apricot jam. Fox took the morning edition of the *Genesia Gazette* from the newspaper table. He always read the Gazette because it was mostly local news with fewer horror stories from the war than in other papers. He shook out the feuilleton but there was nothing there about the Cabaret Vaucanson, just the usual opera gossip and book reviews.

He was some way into an article about the Provisional Government's latest decree on public libraries when Max brought the telephone over, trailing the wire from the bar counter.

"This is Fox," he said.

"You are rather a late riser it appears." It was a woman's voice, not young, not poor.

"A rather important case needed my attention into the small hours, Frau..?"

"My name is Anna Pfaff, am I correct in understanding that you are the Herr Fox, the detective of note?"

Fox didn't know he was of note. He wasn't sure how to take it.

"How can I be of service to..?"

"You are at this…Café Castringius now?"

"Certainly."

"Then I will be along presently. It is Little Alexandria?"

"Go to Pecheneg Square. There is a street off there, Kangalistrasse. The café is there."

"I will be there directly."

"Perhaps you could tell me…"

She rang off and when Max came back for the telephone Fox ordered another coffee and tried not to read the article that had someone found its way into the Gazette. The forces of secessionist Burgundy had recaptured Marseilles, which, from the photograph, was little more than a pile of rubble around the naval base. Fox hadn't heard that Burgundy had broken away from the remnant that had continued to call itself the United States of Europe, which must now just be bits of France, Italy and Spain.

The woman arrived as he was eating rindsuppe. Max pointed Fox out and she tried very carefully not to stare at his head as she walked through the café. She didn't quite manage it.

"Herr Fox?"

"Please, take a seat."

She might be nearly seventy and was neatly turned out in a short hunting style jacket, taupe dress with a peter-pan collar edged in white lace. Only her hat seemed dated, not the cloche hats of fashion but a broad-brimmed affair with a feather, the sort of hat that had come back into vogue out of the late nineteenth to the late twenty-first century, only to disappear again. She looked at the chair for a moment and Fox realised, just too late, that he was expected to pull it out for her. Instead she moved it awkwardly and positioned herself at the table.

"Your friend," she said looking Fox in the eye and trying not to let her gaze roam, "the policewoman told me that you might be of some assistance."

Felice. Fox's only friend in the police force.

"And what is it that you would like me to help you with?"

"You have a strange accent young man."

Fox didn't mention that it was likely that he was much older than her.

"English. I'm from London. Originally."

"Ah," she said, "Unfortunate what happened to London. But then so many places…"

Like most of Genesia it was, to her, all a long way away.

"Of course."

"And this," she said, and she turned away and gave a finger wave at his head without looking, "Is this something that happened because of the war?"

She spoke strict German rather than the melange of five languages that had become a local dialect in the last fifty years. It struck Fox suddenly that he couldn't recall what language he had spoken with Olympia. Having learnt most of them through his augmentation it was sometimes like that.

"It's an augmentation," Fox said, "I had it put in me. A long time ago."

"But its…It's awful. The disintegration. Those things…"

"They're semi-organic cilia, they're what it uses to interface. It didn't start like this. It was a little disc called Omnisense that connected to my head, made it easy for me to tap into all sorts of data. Lots of people had it but it spread like an infection. Most of those who had it died. I guess I'm lucky."

"So," she realised then. And Fox could almost see the pfennig drop. "You are not as young as you appear to be. That kind of technology…"

"As you say."

"I'm sorry," she said, "I have been very rude."

"You're still sitting there. That's good enough for me."

She shifted in her chair and looked around for a moment. Max came over.

"I would like an einspänner," she said and then to Fox, "I usually take ice coffee but the weather has begun to turn has it not?"

Max knew what Fox would want.

"Now," Fox said, "we should see if I can help you."

She dabbed the corners of her mouth with a napkin even though her drink hadn't even arrived.

"Well, there is a certain legal matter that perhaps you could be of some assistance with. A matter of...clarification more than anything. I thought perhaps that a certain interpretation of the law might aid me but it is to no avail. Our city, it seems, has always indulged a certain eccentricity. Of course it reached its nadir with Count Septimus, and then all the disruption since then..."

"What precisely is this matter?"

She eyed her einspänner as Max placed the glass carefully in front of her. The mound of cream was perfectly formed. For a moment it looked as though she might not want to touch it but she picked up a spoon and dug a chunk out, popped it into her mouth and then did her well-practiced dab at her lips. She held the napkin there until the mouthful of cream had been disposed of.

"There is a certain will," she said, "that I would like you to locate."

"How old is it?"

"It would be, well, at least thirty-five years old. Possibly older. I think my father would have set his affairs in order long before his death."

"Well I suppose then it could have been digital. But I'm afraid it's likely to have suffered in the decay. The legal archives were infected. Not so bad as a lot of other places but still."

"Nevertheless," she said, "I would appreciate if you could ascertain if it exists. I am also assuming my father ensured there was a hard-copy. But we'll discuss that should the need arise."

"I'd prefer to discuss it now. I assume it relevant. Because you could have asked for an official search of the electronic archives."

She almost dabbed again.

"I have done so, but I am not sure a standard search would retrieve anything. I suspect there might be some perfidy at play. You see I am not the eldest child. I have a sister. But it is unthinkable that my father would have left the entirety of the estate to her. Yet when my father died supposedly intestate she inherited the house. If the need arises I would like you to visit her and ask her. Ask her if she is blocking my search and if I might see the hard-copy of my father's will."

"Why don't you just ask her yourself?"

She drank the coffee now, letting the remnant of cream smear her upper lip seemingly just so she could wipe it afterwards.

"My sister is of the eccentric sort. We do not get on. In fact we haven't spoken for some years. She occupies my father's house. The house where I grew up but from which she fled when she was seventeen to lead a rather dissolute life. The last time I went there I found it upsetting."

"How so?"

"She is an incorrigible collector and hoarder of the most outré artefacts. What was once a neat and presentable family home had become something akin to a cabinet of curiosities."

Fox would do the search and likely it would turn up negative. He wasn't sure about visiting the sister if it came to that. It seemed like he might be used as a way to intimidate some harmless old lady.

"My standard fee for a digital search is one hundred marks."

"Well, I…"

"What you are asking me to do is illegal, you do know that don't you Frau Pfaff?"

She looked around her but discovered the tables nearby were empty.

"Very well," she said.

"Fifty marks in advance."

She scowled but opened her bag. Hunched over she counted money that was tucked into an envelope. She put some money back into the bag and handed Fox the envelope.

"My card is inside," she said. "You will call me when you have completed your search."

She was already rising, leaving Fox to pay for her coffee. Outside he saw her draw her thick jacket around her and wondered why she didn't have a coat. Then he wondered why she hadn't asked him to call on her at home. On her card there was no address, just a telephone number.

Max was looking over from where he was putting away glasses, or at least pretending to. He had already seen the envelope but would never ask for anything directly.

Fox had already begun dividing up the money, a little rent, his tab with Max. He folded the five ten mark notes and stood to put them into his trousers pocket. There was something there. He took out the clockwork beetle and wound its little crown and watched as it circled the coffee glass left by Frau

Pfaff. Just before it ran into a blob of cream on the table Fox picked it up and let it run around his palm. Max was still watching.

CHAPTER THREE

The remnants of the legal archives were in a data storage centre near the law courts. It meant crossing town so Fox waited till late and wore the hat, a trilby, one size too large, it covered the cilia on his head and shadowed those coming out of his temple. The augmentation didn't like it, responding with a low level headache.

He walked the backstreets of Little Alexandria. There were cafes still open, and a small crowd coming out of the boutique cinema that showed vintage films. He passed the tattoo parlour and the thrift shop, the cheap hotels, all part of the area that he felt most comfortable in.

Still in Little Alex he took a detour to the Cabaret Vaucanson, not the back door he'd been at the night before but down onto Jozsef Budenz Strasse and around to see the front. He stood across the narrow street and looked over at the tinted windows. The whole place was not much more than a café really, the woodwork painted black and the name on a panel in gold lettering. He could hear music, discordant jazz as though someone were thumping at the keys of a piano in boxing gloves but still somehow holding a tune.

The throb in his head deepened. The augmentation knew it would soon be feeding on data. It had been a while since it had anything other than scraps like the soldier's life-bug. It was impatient.

There was singing now from the Cabaret. It took Fox a moment to register that it was in English. 'Around Midnight'.

He went on his way, pulling the hat down as he headed towards Autocue Boulevard where there would still be plenty of people around. They milled around the departments stores that stayed open late or came there to eat in the expensive restaurants after the opera or puppet theatre. He crossed diagonally, leaving Little Alex and skirting those restaurants until he relaxed a little, going into the old city.

The old city stretched from Kleist Square in the west over a number of hills on the rising ground that eventually met the mountain to the north of Genesia. Cobble streets fingered out from the cathedral, the law courts and the Stadthouse where the Provisional Government met. This time of night the area was deserted and Fox followed narrow lanes connected by even narrower stairs with arched entrances emblazoned with the worn coats of arms of guilds.

The data storage centre was located in the extensive crypts beneath the Court of Faculties, a ramshackle gothic pile that rose from the streets around it. Fox didn't need to get inside, just near enough to the crypts, so he skirted around the building to the side where there was an iron fence around a small garden that looked like it hadn't had any plants in it for decades.

When the data decay first struck what happened here with the legal records would have been the same as what happened in almost every other case.

There would have been projects to transfer what could be salvaged onto hard-copy, clerks transcribing computer printouts into leather bound ledgers. But it was realised quickly that this was a thankless task. In the end the bulk of the data was left where it was, in the state it was. If something was lost it was lost. If there was further decay then so be it. There was an acceptance that there would be a gap in the human record that ranged from historical archives to family photographs. The best part of a century shattered into fragments.

He fell awkwardly, landing with his foot on its edge so that the sole of his shoe split away almost entirely. But he couldn't give this much attention because even as he'd been climbing the fence his augmentation had come to life. As he dove down into the shadow of the building and took his hat off the cilia were springing up, and inside he could feel the rush as the augmentation made a connection. The sudden relief of it triggered off reactions in his body, a flood of endorphins as the augmentation picked up the bounty inside, because it was bounty even if a lot of it was rotten.

The structure was a standard virtual tape system, built on top of solid state storage. There was some sort of encryption built in quantum, a prototype, the technology had never really had a chance to take off in any big way.

Mounts, dismounts, swaps. Fragments of old queries left in the buffers when the infection had struck. Then into the layers, working through the digital archaeology typical of these sort of archive systems, accumulations of changing protocols, legacy systems, virtual reality simulations, video and text. It has all been churned up by the digital decay. Values were set to null everywhere: database fields; data dictionaries, meta-data. Indexes were especially hit so that navigation became almost impossible with pre-existing search software.

His augmentation sifted through, surfing over blobs of meaninglessness. When the disaster had struck it would have been like watching someone with a can of black spray paint working their way through the Louvre and obliterating the masterpieces. Not that the Louvre was there by then.

Moment of vertigo. But both Fox and the augmentation were enthralled as they rooted around for meaning.

They lingered a while over VR simulations of crimes, actors playing murder and rape. Fox didn't like it but the richness of the detail was just the sort of thing the augmentation loved.

This, then, was what remained of cyberspace.

Fox wrenched the augmentation's attention away and found an index that hadn't been completely nulled. It led to text documents, contracts, sales agreements and, yes, wills. In the entries themselves there was a lot of damage. He searched as best he could using a variety of keys: name, date, location.

There was nothing in the name of Frau Pfaff's father.

He let the augmentation feed some more, lingering over CCTV footage of automobile crashes, cars that now looked like vintage models skidding off roads, or impacting with other vehicles. It was quite amusing if you didn't think about it too much.

***

Out on Autocue Boulevard most of the shops were now closed but there was a place he knew where he could get his shoe seen to in the covered arcades that linked the less salubrious end of the boulevard to the Khazar Gate.

Just a little way in, there was a cobbler he'd used before. The shop still smelt wonderfully of leather and shoe polish but they'd been a change. A clockwork automaton stood behind the workbench. Life sized, ruddy checked, wearing a Phrygian cap and holding a hammer.

"You're new," Fox said.

He took his shoe off and placed them on the bench. With his one free hand of jointed wooden fingers the automaton picked up it up and moved it beneath the hammer then picked up a nail from a tin on the bench. He aligned the nail on the sole and started to hammer it in with bright little taps with exact intervals between them.

"Do you speak?" Fox asked him.

His head down the automaton carried on hammering, doing a pretty good job from what Fox could tell.

"I met someone like you last night," Fox said, "She was a lot more talkative and very beautiful. Come to think of it…"

He felt in his coat pocket and found the beetle there.

"I even carry one of your relatives round with me. You're getting everywhere these days."

The automaton finished the shoe. Fox eyed the bench with its slot for coins.

"What would happen if I didn't pay?"

The automaton's wooden head tilted up. Fox looked into his painted-on eyes as the automaton pushed his body to full stretch and leant forward a little, almost as though he could have leapt over the workbench. He raised the hammer for a moment and shook it at Fox. Fox put the coins in the slot.

Fox came out of the cobblers and was admiring the chemist shop window display next door. There was a set of carboys there filled with various liquids, they were lit from behind so that the copper sulphate shone with a lovely aquamarine, the nickel sulphate emerald. There was one of iodine that gave off red. Then he saw a couple turn a corner as they entered the arcades from Autocue Boulevard. If he could have ducked back inside in time he would have happily preferred the company of the clockwork cobbler.

"Fox," a familiar voice spat.

Hans Vogt was dressed in the sort of mufti— long black leather coat, shiny shoes, middle of the range suit—that immediately marked him out for what he was, a seedy plain-clothes man for the Landespolizei. There was a young woman falling against him, her eyes wide but not really seeing anything. Her blonde hair was frizzed out and one corner of her lipstick had smeared. She stumbled a little as Vogt came to a halt. She adjusted her shoulder strap and stared in the window of the chemist.

"The colours," she said slurring.

The chemical light made Vogt's gnarled skin go a patchwork of green and blue. Fox had always thought he had a face like a rat but then who was Fox to pass judgement on looks.

Then Fox noticed that Vogt had on his lapel a badge that had been in the press recently, a white Egyptian ankh on a ragged crimson circle.

"Vogt."

"That's Inspector Vogt to you."

"Pretty colours," said the blonde.

Fox could imagine what she was seeing given that she was high on kaleidoscope: the light of the carboys bleeding out into the world around them.

Vogt's stank of booze. He reached out and took the hat off Fox's head.

"Why don't you show the world what you look like Fox? A freak. What are you doing out at this time of night anyway, outside of Little Alex?"

"Getting my shoes repaired. I like it after dark. Less chance of scaring the children."

Vogt snorted at that.

"Out from under your rock at the Café Castringius. Tut tut."

The blonde looked around at Fox.

"Are we under the sea?" she said.

"Perhaps you should get your date home, Vogt."

"Hans," the blonde announced, "the sea monster is talking."

"Shut up Lola."

"Jesus, Vogt. How much kaleidoscope has she taken?"

But as he looked at her she gave a sly little wink that suggested she might not be as out of it as he thought.

"I'm Lola," she said, "Lola Hello."

"Hello," Fox was struck by the English word.

"Yes."

She turned back to the chemist window and fell a little and pressed her hands against the glass. The colours painted her. She was even younger than he'd realised, maybe not even twenty.

"The badge," Fox pointed to Vogt's lapel, "You a fully joined up cretin now?"

"You'll see," Vogt said. He punched a dent in Fox's hat and threw it to the ground.

"You really want the Comedians back don't you? It figures. You want the magic that turns worms like you into dragons. How far up the drain would you have squirmed if they hadn't been overthrown? Big shot in the Ministry of the Interior or State Security?"

"You sound like a Masqueradist."

But Fox didn't know what that meant.

Lola returned from whatever iridescent paradise she'd been in. It wouldn't last long. Kaleidoscope was intense but short lived.

"Why don't you leave the sea monster alone, Hans, he's nice."

The light had seemed to follow her, bathing her and Vogt in it all over again.

"Shut up," said Vogt, "stupid cunt."

"Such a charmer aren't you," said Fox. But Lola just raised an eyebrow.

Vogt stamped on Fox's hat and pulled back his coat and jacket, fumbled with his holster and eventually got out his pistol. It was a Luger needlegun. Fox watched as he brought it up and it was steady for a moment but then shook as he pointed it at Fox's head. Fox wasn't going to back off, to run away or beg. That was what Vogt wanted.

"You know how easy it would be?" Vogt said.

Vogt wouldn't shoot, Fox told himself. Coolly as he could he walked past, careful not to go too near him, or to Lola Hello. He went back through the arcades towards Autocue Boulevard. He passed the glass fronts of pinchbeck jewellers, hosiery shops and a chocolatiers. Near the exit the night trade had gathered. Older versions of Lola were standing against shuttered shops wearing their high boots, faux fur coats and not much else.

One stood next to a tobacconists. Light and reflection from the window patterned her dress and bare arms with images of cigarette packets. Opposite two other women stood against a kitsch antique shop that seemed to specialise in those mosaic Byzantine icons.

"Come for a happy time?"

None of these women would baulk at his ugliness it seemed. Fox managed to smile and walk away. Vogt owed him a hat.

31

CHAPTER FOUR

The next day Fox called from the cafe.

"Frau Pfaff?"

"What? Oh, I'll get her."

A man let the receiver at the other end off the hook and Fox heard footsteps, a radio playing someone. Then shouting for her. It was a minute or so before she came.

"This is Fox. I'm afraid my search has proved unsuccessful."

"Oh."

"So perhaps we should conclude our business, if I could collect the balance..."

"You must go and see her."

"I'm not sure that this is the sort of thing I'd be good at."

"Herr Fox, all I ask is that you go and see her. That you ask her if you can see my father's will."

Her tone had wavered and Fox realised that it was the first time he'd heard her being anything other than totally self-assured.

"Herr Fox, are you still there?"

"Of course. Perhaps we should meet again and discuss this."

"Please," she said, "I just have to know. If she tells you to your face that there is no will then I will accept it. I am not asking for anything more. Then I will be happy to pay you the remainder of the sum we agreed and a further fifty for your trouble."

In the end Fox said he would go and she told him the address, up in Heights.

Max had a car, one of the last Molinas to roll of the line at the Skoda-Alpha works in Pressburg before the war. It was an expensive car, an indulgence Max must have enjoyed in his younger days.

"You'll have to charge her," Max told Fox, "I've not had her on the road since Easter."

"Thanks."

"But be careful," he wagged a finger, "Just because I never drive her doesn't mean I don't love her."

The two had worked on the car together a few years ago to get it back on the road, Fox neutralising the decayed software while Max fitted manual controls for essential systems. It was under a sheet in the yard at the back of the café where it got in the way of deliveries.

Fox hooked it up to the mains and waited inside the café. By late afternoon he'd managed to get away, manoeuvring the car through the narrow streets of Little Alex, across Pecheneg Square and down onto Autocue Boulevard, where he hit the traffic. Autocue Boulevard had been remodelled from the old Emperorstrasse during the last years of digital era. The large buildings on either side had been drive-in immersives, VR landscapes and soft museums. When the decay struck the virtual worlds and immersives were early victims. Since it was the showpiece city thoroughfare it had been reshaped once again. The buildings reverting to department stores and other businesses now that people had to shop in person once again.

He shunted the car forward at intervals, watching the people outside shop windows, well-to-do ladies and servants on errands. Eventually he got past the junction with Khazarplatz and skirted near the river and the tower block slums, steel and glass follies to a discredited architectural fashion. There were some English there, second or third generation refugee families. Fox tried to avoid the place. Finally, over an hour after leaving the café he got on one of the roads that wound up towards the Heights.

He passed Eloise Park and the road became bordered with plain trees and Persian ironwoods, their fallen gold and red leaves covering the tarmac. It could almost have been called a pleasant afternoon if he'd just been able to drive around, seeing some of the places outside the area he usually confined himself to.

Eventually he found the entrance to the drive of Villa Verloren. The iron gates were open and he drove up a curved way, tyres crunching gravel. On either side shrubs had gone wild. He parked in front of the rectangular portico of an impressive pile. It was a house in the chateau style, perhaps two-hundred years old and in need of repair. The brickwork was crumbling in place, tiles were askew on the roof. One of the upstairs windows was cracked with a chunk missing.

Fox pulled the bell chain and waited inside the portico. Already he could tell there were remnants here, the augmentation finding what was left of electro-magnetic signals of various sorts. It was faint, dying.

The doorbell echoed and he realised he could hear music, something odd about it, atonal, made him think of being lost. Lost in the lost house.

As he waited in the cold shadow of the portico that smelt of dusty shrubs and dead leaves he suddenly wished he'd bought another hat. That he wasn't so exposed for what he was.

He was about to try knocking when the door opened.

An old fellow in a baggy country jumper stood there. He wiped his hands on the side of his trousers. He looked Fox over but didn't even do a double take.

"I was in the kitchen," he said.

He did, indeed, smell pleasantly of something spicy.

"I was looking for Frau Kastner," Fox said.

Beyond the front door Fox saw a large vestibule that had a stair leading up to a surrounding balcony. The room was cluttered with stuff. There was a double door towards the back where the music was coming from.

"And you have this to sell?" the old fellow said, pointing at Fox's head. "Some sort of attachment is it? Well, you'd better come in. She wouldn't thank me for sending you away if it turns out she's interested."

He stood to one side to usher Fox in and then went towards the music. The vestibule was filled with the sort of consumer goods not seen around for decades: lots of small stuff in boxes: eyephones, headsets, audiojacks; larger items like portable interface kiosks of the sort that used to be on street corners and train stations. There was one of those Bayangkan auto-beautician pods that never really caught on outside of south-east Asia. All this was dominated by an immersion VR booth standing against one wall below the balcony. Like everything else it was covered in dust but something was still alive in the booth, just. Fox's augmentation focused on it, it was what it had detected from outside the house, decayed remains of game scenarios, ruined little worlds of cities falling into transparency, jungles nothing more than filigreed traceries. The augmentation wanted to wander there, it could have spent an age exploring.

"Oh yes, how marvellous!"

She had come out of the doorway completely naked, the old manservant tripping out of the door after her with a kimono. She stepped forward so that the servant missed wrapping it around her. There was something majestic about the way she held her wrinkled body, her breasts slumped yet her shoulders and hips sturdy. She was smiling at Fox.

"Madam," said the servant, "you should…"

She let him put the kimono on her, stepping into it gracefully. It was gorgeous, red and cerise silk with dragons. As she came towards Fox he smelt her perfume. It was Chanel, a thing from another age all together.

"Otto you silly man," she glanced at him and then waved at Fox's head, "that's not a headset."

Looking up at Fox, moving her head to get different angles on the cilia, as though Fox were a museum exhibit or an art work.

"Well," she said, "you're something like a living fossil. Omnisense. I'd heard you didn't all die but I've never seen one like you. How old are you?"

"Old. I was one of the first. Now I'm one of the last".

"Come, come, let's sit down. Otto, some coffee. We'll take it in the Yellow Room."

The Yellow Room, named Fox presumed after the faded pear coloured wall paper, was where the music was playing on an antique analogue stereo system. It was warm in there, pleasant and not stifling. There were masks on the wall, some African or Oceanic but mostly traditional Genesia ones. The room was as cluttered as the vestibule, with more of the same sort of electrical stuff dotted among books, piles of papers, and even a full panoply of Maximillian armour in one corner holding a fairly lethal looking mace. The eerie music was still playing. It made Fox think of mice running up and down a keyboard in a haunted house.

"Schoenburg," she said, waving her hands at the air, "With a certain palette of notes he thought he could describe the universe. Old music. But then you can't easily hear any decent modern music. All that pap on the radio they broadcast from the opera. Not to mention the decades of lost music, the recordings decayed. Please sit."

There was a space in the middle of the room, an arrangement of a chaise lounge and two armchairs on a rug around a coffee table. Propped against the coffee table were more vinyl music discs. The one on the top was called *Nixon in China*.

"So," she said, "You haven't come here to sell me your head…well, you know I almost called you young man. You must have hardly aged."

Fox was quite happy here. It was interesting. She was interesting. The coffee would be enjoyable. Sooner or later though he would have to get down to business.

"I've come at the request of…."

"Ah," she said, "Anna."

"Frau Pfaff. Your sister."

The music ended, mice steps cut off part way through their desperate attempt to express something Fox would never understand.

"You know," she said, "She could have always just come herself. But I suppose that's the point isn't it. That's what it's all about, she won't. Ah, thank you Otto."

Otto laid the tray down on the table. There were two perfectly made einspänners, the cream sculpted into twirling cones. On two willow pattern plates were slices of sachertorte, the dark chocolate icing desperate to be pierced with the little forks next to them.

"You could always call on her," Fox said.

"I could but there would be very little point. She wouldn't believe anything I told her. She's never forgiven me for how I treated her when we were girls. I used to tease her terribly. I told her once that our mother died because she'd caught an infection from drinking from a tap where a spider had built its web. Anna was eleven before she realised I was just being spitefully imaginative. Tell me, Herr…"

"Fox, Evergreen Fox."

He don't know why he'd told her his full name. It wasn't something he usually did.

"Is my sister paying you to come here? Are you some sort of…employee of hers?"

Fox gave her his card.

"I call myself a detective," he said as she was looking at it, "and yes she is paying me."

"A detective," she smiled. "How much?"

He told her, not seeing any point in not doing so.

"You know I could double that. Treble it. Just pay you to go away and forget about the whole thing."

"It doesn't work like that."

"Well, well, honour. You really are a living fossil aren't you Evergreen."

She motioned him to drink the coffee and partake of the cake. The icing was sweet with just a little tang of bitterness. There was a layer of apricot jam inside. He washed the mouthful down with some coffee and wiped cream from his nose.

Frau Kastner rose, adjusting the kimono around her. Her toe-nails were painted gold. She pulled a music disk out of the pile, seemingly at random and replaced the disc on the turntable with it. The arm came down and bit the vinyl. It was some sort of piano music but some of the notes sounded as though the hammer inside the instrument was striking metal.

"You know," she said when she'd sat down, "I don't get many visitors these days. The ones I do get are usually salesmen. My reputation as a collector brings them here, sometimes they don't even telephone first but just turn up unannounced. I don't usually give them sachertorte."

"Frau Kastner…"

"Call me Cosima."

"Your sister would like to see your father's will."

She laughed.

"Of course she would. Tell me Evergreen, what did she say about me?"

"Well…"

"She said that I was insane perhaps? What you must understand about Anna is that she is almost pathologically jealous. I say pathologically because I don't think she realises how jealous she is, she has hidden it from herself."

"Because of all this?" Fox waved at the room, the house.

"Not really. If it was just about money or even the house it would all be a lot simpler. I've offered her money. No, she wants what I've got because I've got it. Because she can't have what she really wants."

"Which is?"

"The life that I've had. When I was seventeen and should have gone to a Swiss finishing school to prepare me for whatever my father had in mind for me I left. I went to Paris. And I caused a scandal. I became the lover of Edgar Wallace Verlaine, you've heard of him. Poet, sculptor. There were vlogs dedicated to my comings and goings. I stood on tables in restaurants because Edgar thought I was a work of art. When I wasn't too drunk, drugged or hung-over I protested against militarisation. And then I began a notorious career. I was a cyberdildonic model."

"You were a Brobdingnag babe?"

"Oh yes. Thousands of people clambered over and explored every intimate detail of my body when it became a virtual landscape. Does that shock you?"

Fox let that pass. He remembered those times, those days. Macrophilia one of the many crazes around. His augmentation had grown fat on the abundance of data that seemed to fill every niche of the world.

"Yes," she said as though reading Fox's thoughts, "Those were wonderful times. We were all going to leave our bodies and live in a paradise inside computer clouds. Those soft museums and virtual worlds were marvellous. Before the decay of course. When I look back it all seems rather absurd. Why did we want to leave our bodies when we were young and beautiful? Everyone was obsessed with gadgets. Would the devices get smaller, bigger, smarter? When was the next version of whatever coming out? Then we would have it all implanted in us…" But you know all about that don't you?"

"Sure."

"In many ways what happened to you was one of the great turning points don't you think? The end of that age when history became confused with the progress of technology. Edgar wrote about it somewhere, he said that we should shift from a linear view of time back to a cyclical one."

"And all this," Fox said, "your own collection of gadgets. Are you trying to save something of those times?"

"I suppose so."

"Although it seems random in places, the masks, the suit of armour." Fox pointed over at the Maximillian armour, admiring again the heavy mace.

"Oh Parsifal," she said, "I keep him for sentimental reasons. I never wind him."

Fox realised then that what he had taken for a suit of plate armour was in fact an automaton, or rather an ultraclock. He got up and went over, opened the visor. There was a frozen face of what could be polished wood. Fox saw the key now just below the breastplate. Frau Kastner came and stood beside him wafting Chanel.

"He's never been wound since the day he came. Parsifal was here for a few hours after my fifth husband walked through the door with him when he came back from one of his jaunts out in the Diesel Land."

The old industrial wastelands off to the east.

"I suspect," she went on, "my husband won him in a casino or some such. But he's only been wound up once since then."

"Why don't you wind him?"

"Well," she said, "That first day he managed to bring that mace down heavily on my husband's head. Landed him in hospital. He refused to wind him up after that."

"And you kept Parsifal?"

"To be quite honest Evergreen," she said, "I was never overly fond of that particular husband."

She gripped Fox's arm and started to laugh. They sat down again.

The music had run down and Otto had taken the tray away leaving the plates with the unfinished cake. Soon it would be evening and the traffic would be even worse than coming.

"I suppose," Fox said, "That I must formally ask you if you would show me a copy of your father's will."

"No."

"Is there a will? Does it exist?"

She rose to her feet and took Fox's hand to raise him with her. They held hands.

"I like you Evergreen," she said. "Two old fossils like us should not fall out."

"I have, I suppose, a professional obligation."

"I will tell you one fact and ask you one favour. Then we will part as friends. The next time you come to see me we will forget what you came for this time, and we'll just natter. Agreed?"

"Agreed."

"The fact is that there is no will in existence that in any way benefits my sister. The favour I ask is that you don't take any more money from her. Otto will see you are reimbursed for any trouble the whole matter has caused you. Pay you the difference or whatever."

She waved the details away.

"But," she went on, "I don't want Anna wasting any more of what little she's got on this. And for my part I will write to her. I will be nice. I will ask her to come and see me."

They went back out to the vestibule and she called Otto, then went to find him when he didn't appear. Fox looked around at all the old stuff, his augmentation itching to go back into the worlds of the VR booth. Fox focused on everything else. There was a hat resting on top of the headless torso of a tailor's dummy. Fox tried it on and looked into the dark glass of the VR booth. It was a corduroy peaked cap. It didn't look that bad and covered his cilia. He was still wearing it when Cosima came back in with Otto.

"It suits you," she said.

"Thanks."

"Keep it."

"That's very kind."

"But look after it. It was Edgar Wallace Verlaine's favourite. Edgar was very fond of hats. I remember once him being drunk, naturalmente, and arguing with some Kurzwellite who seemed to be putting forward the notion of pivotal moments in history being the invention of this or that technological innovation. Edgar presented his own Hat View of History. That different eras coincided with the dominant type of headgear. The broad-brimmed hat gave us the Thirty Years War, the tricorn ushered in the Enlightenment. And who could imagine the industrial revolution without Isambard Brunel's monstrous topper? The catastrophes since then can only be due to the decline in hat wearing."

Whimsical but somehow charming. It appealed to Fox, who had outlived the time when progress was measured by the latest technology.

***

In the car on the way back Fox realised he hadn't had a drink for a while. Sometimes it was like that when he had something to do. But now he had some more money in his wallet, a new hat and the prospect of nothing much else to occupy him. Soon, later tonight, tomorrow at the latest he would hit the bottle.

He drove into traffic at the junction of Khazarplatz and Autocue Boulevard, near the Pequod Building that used to be the American embassy. There was more than the normal evening build up, and he sat behind the car in front not moving. After a while he saw someone up ahead get out of their car, others followed. Looking down from the corner into the Boulevard you could see a long stretch of it ahead.

There were no cars there. Instead there was an orderly march of people. There were well-dressed middle-aged men in suits, their sons in slightly looser suits. There were a few women interspersed. And among all these fairly standard looking citizens there were others, they carried burning torches and were wearing not quite uniforms, or rather a kind of hotchpotch that suggested uniforms: jackets with epaulettes and brass buttons, not necessarily matching the other similar dressed men.

On a banner Fox saw the symbol again. He could see it clearer now it was enlarged, a white ankh against a black sun. The symbol Vogt had

45

worn. Fox had read about these people in the gazette, the Renewal Society. They wanted the Comedians restored, wanted Genesia to join the war. Fox had thought of them as a lunatic fringe but it seemed they could get numbers onto the streets.

The march was heading into Khazarplatz and Fox guessed they would assemble at the Khazar Gate. As they got nearer Fox saw those at the front, five men bearing their chests, showing not battle scars but the mark just below their clavicles where they'd had life-bugs fitted. Free Company men, volunteers for the war.

He walked back to the car, resigned to the fact that it would be a long while before he got home.

CHAPTER FIVE

The Hotel Relojeria was on a side street off Pecheneg Square, the heart of Little Alex. Fox must have been down that way before but didn't remember it. He'd just finished speaking to Frau Pfaff telling her there was no will and that, no, she didn't owe him any money when Max had bought the telephone over again. Fox recognised the voice, musical yet no longer carrying the hint of delight that it had had outside the back door of the Cabaret Vaucanson.

The hotel was a few minutes' walk away. He'd asked her what it was about and she'd said that if she could just talk to Fox she would explain. He left straight away forgetting his hat but then again he wasn't going out of Little Alex.

Someone was waiting on the door step, leaning on the no vacancies sign and smoking a cigarette in an ebony holder.

"Herr Fox I presume."

She was about thirty and dressed in a way that marked her out as one of the avant-garde set Fox supposed. Her hair was dyed orange-red and cut short like a soldier and she wore a man's jacket, in a style that in England, long ago, would have indicated the hunting type. Her eyes were made up with heavy black lines and she had on lipstick that suggested she might have just been drinking fresh blood. She merely glanced over Fox's head, hardly seeming to take notice of the cilia.

"They're inside," she said.

Fox made to walk past her but she put an arm across the door.

"You have to be very careful now."

"I've met Olympia, and Victor."

"They are all very special to me. I would not have them treated badly."

"Look, Frau…"

"Mond, just Mond."

"I was asked to come here."

"Victor is dead," she said. "You have no idea what that means to them. Olympia told me about you and I made some discreet inquiries this morning. The police don't seem very fond of you."

"No."

"I think that probably works in your favour."

She moved her arm out of the way.

"They're in the breakfast room," she said, "I'll fix you a drink. They usually forget to offer. Not needing it themselves. Are you the sort who baulks at alcohol before I certain time of day?

"Not at all."

"Good."

Fox entered a long through room that had an arch linking it to a duplicate room with French windows looking out onto a garden.

The ultraclocks were waiting. Stood and sat around a huge old fireplace with a tiled smoke chamber that looked like a sloping roof. They were all wearing black. There were three besides Olympia. The room was filled with faint ticking overlaid by a heavier tick-tock beat.

"Herr Fox," she said, "Thank you for coming."

Olympia wore a low cut black lace dress that showed her flesh through it. Draped over her shoulders was her otter skin coat. She was leaning on the automaton who looked like a stripped back clock, his inner workings visible in cage of dark metal where his mourning jacket was open. Only his head had artificial skin of some soft, wrinkled leather, like a rotten peach.

Olympia came to greet Fox, flowing in discrete motions, whatever animated her undetectable.

"Let me introduce my friends," she said. "This is Schiller."

The mechanical skeleton held out his hand. As he did his jacket rode up and Fox noted the two stroke oscillation of a cam driven by cogs as they shook hands. His ticking was the loud beat Fox had noted.

"I hope," he said with slow, careful, enunciation, without a movement of his face, "That you will be able to help us Herr Fox."

"Victor is dead," said Olympia, "He has been destroyed."

Mond sidled up in a waft of cigarette smoke and handed Fox a tumbler. It was whiskey, not Scotch but pretty good.

"I have told him," she said.

"We want to understand what happened," said one of the others.

These two at the back looked as though they were related. Whatever that could mean.

"This," said, Olympia, "is Karl. And this is Bob. Otherwise known as the Fabulous Bakelite Brothers."

49

They both came forward a little to stand in front of Fox but didn't offer their hands. Their bodies were made of what looked like hard plastic, the colour greyish pink but mottled with bits of white and yellow. They were both bigger than any man. Fox imagined muscles constructed of monstrous gears and taunt springs, ready to release their pent-up menace, capable of wrecking desolation. Yet they both had delicate long fingered hands that looked almost human.

Karl had fair hair and a goatee beard. Bob was bald but with bushy black eyebrows. Their expressions were fixed, cast at the moment of their creation so that the bearded one had been given a sort of detached arrogance, while baldy Bob looked like he had been waiting too long in a restaurant for his meal.

"Do you think you are up to the task?" Karl said.

"Who's handling this? I mean do you know which police officers have been assigned to it."

"Herr Fox," said Schiller, "there is no official investigation into Victor's death. Victor was a machine. However his destruction is part of the investigation into the murder of Lazlo Heck. Victor's remains have been kept as evidence in this case. It has been assumed that Victor belonged to Lazlo."

"I saw Lazlo," Fox said to Olympia, "the other night, didn't I? Who was he?"

"I think," said Schiller, "that we are going to have to get Herr Fox up to speed if he is going to be able to help us."

Bob spoke for the first time.

"Victor did not belong to Lazlo. Victor did not belong to anyone."

"None of us belong to anyone," said Karl. "Does that bother you Herr Fox?"

"Please," said Olympia, "Herr Fox is here at my request."

"Drink up," said Mond, "There's plenty in the bottle. You look as though you need it."

"Perhaps," Schiller said, "we need to know what you understand about us, Herr Fox. About who we are and our place in Genesia."

Fox found that he was fingering the beetle in his pocket. It was difficult to think of Olympia, of any of them, as being akin to the clockwork insect, merely mechanical, animated by the winding of a mainspring. And yet the augmentation told him that there was nothing in their heads that it could recognise as thought. There was only Fox and Mond as though they were both onstage with a group of marionettes.

"Please," said Olympia again, "I would like to sit down. I would like us all to sit down."

They were all empty though. Everyone went through to the back room where there were armchairs around a little occasional table. There was a nice view out of the French windows but Fox couldn't help but watch Olympia move with her dancer's grace, her breathing regular, perfect. She took one of the chairs and Mond sat on the arm of it next to her. Everyone took seats.

Schiller took out a fountain pen and little leather-bound notebook from his jacket pocket. He wrote for a moment.

"Sometimes," he said looking over at Fox, "I need to write to provoke my thoughts into moving on. It is my nature perhaps, I was constructed as a writer above all else."

Mond retrieved an ashtray from a shelf and returned to her perch. She fitted another cigarette in the holder.

"The ultraclocks," Schiller said, "have no legal status in Genesia. Some allow themselves to be owned, some do not. Lazlo and Victor were companions. They came to the city together. They died together. Lazlo's death will be investigated by the police, even if perfunctorily. Victor's will not. We would like you to find out who did it. We would like to know why. And we would like Victor's remains returned to us."

"If the police find out who killed Lazlo then won't you know then who killed Victor?"

"Perhaps," said Schiller, "but if the police think that Victor was not important then they will get nowhere."

"To them," said Karl, "Victor being there means nothing more than if Lazlo was carrying a briefcase."

"So what do you think happened?" Fox said.

Mond shifted round.

"They found both of them in Sparta," she said.

The industrial, largely run-down part of the city, with the ancient mask market at its heart.

"On the tracks of the railway," Mond went on, "that goes to the docks at Tartessos. That's all the police would tell me."

Schiller held up his hand, still holding the fountain pen in his metal fingers.

"There is another reason the police may not prove to be particularly diligent when investigating. There is the possibility that they may be involved in some way."

"Wow," Fox said, "this just got a whole more complicated." He didn't like where this was going. It had begun to sound like something he was not sure he wanted to be involved with.

"Please Herr Fox," said Olympia, "there's no one else we can turn to."

"Listen to him," said Bob, "this is too big for him. I told you we should handle this ourselves."

"Herr Fox," said Schiller, "we are not asking you to do anything other than find out what happened. We don't expect the killer will be charged or punished by the law. We just want to know."

"But Lazlo's death will be…"

"Pah," said Karl, "They'll be no real investigation."

"Who's the officer in charge?" Fox asked again.

"An Inspector Vogt," said Schiller.

It just got better and better. Fox wanted to just get up and walk out. Be polite if possible, be rude if not. He felt tired all of a sudden, in need of a drink or two alone.

"Why would the police want to kill Victor?"

Fox asked this and knew it was too late, that he would do this for them because he could, because to not do it would be to leave him with that dissatisfaction he got at leaving things undone. It was bad enough with Frau Pfaff. If he didn't work, if he didn't do what he was good at then what was he but the human appendage of the thing in his head that had a whole set of motives of its own?

"Victor came to Genesia with something to do," said Schiller. "He had a mission."

"Victor had many missions," said Olympia.

"But what is pertinent here," said Schiller, "is that Victor wanted to find out about something in the Castle."

Better and better still.

The Castle, where Count Septimus had once laid on parties and masquerades, had indulged his eccentricities: the collections, the menagerie, the flooded courtyard filled with model boats, the wandering peacocks. It had been Frau Kastner writ large but going to even more eccentric tastes, employing toymakers, puppeteers, jewellers. Musicians came, and dancers. And then came the famous Comedians, who had murdered Septimus and taken over. During the days of the Court of Comedians the Castle became the centre of their bizarre police state, a prison, an inquisition. Until the Comedians themselves had been overthrown by the popular revolution that the provisional government had quickly taken over.

"The Castle," Fox said blankly.

He had been there once, just after the Comedians had come to power. It was his first run-in with Vogt, who arrested him on some pretext and roughed him up in a cell. After Vogt had gone, in the cell, still drunk a little, Fox's augmentation had honed in on the presence Fox suddenly realised it had been aware of since arriving. An intact server and database. There were criminal records, legal documents, government reports. It was tasty stuff and Fox let the augmentation feast, even up to the point where it began to grow confused for some reason Fox couldn't fathom.

Then Fox had heard shouting outside the cell.

"You bonehead Vogt, you've bought one of those in here, that wurmkopf."

Someone had realised what Fox was. What he could do. Two uniform officers dragged him out and threw him outside the gates. Felice had told Fox later that Vogt had got in to trouble over it and that he'd never forgiven Fox for that.

"Yes," said Schiller, "something in the Castle."

"I'm not sure I can do this," Fox said.

"Please Herr Fox," said Olympia, "This means a lot to us. Perhaps if I could tell you a little about Victor."

"He doesn't want to help us," said Bob, "We're wasting our time."

Fox began to suspect that Bob's sour expression had been put there for a reason. Whoever had made that face had created the perfect mask for whatever invisible magic formed Bob's personality.

"Would you come with me," said Olympia rising, "I'd like to go for a walk."

They headed to Pecheneg Square looking like the oddest of couples, an automaton delight, umbrella at her side on a cloudless day, and Fox. With the way he looked.

"Victor was not like us," she told Fox.

"In what way?"

"Wait," she said, "We'll talk in the square."

Pecheneg Square had once been a tourist attraction, in the days when there were tourists. It was formed by four sides of grand buildings including the Rudolf Library with its dome, columned windows and grand entrance staircase with its statues personifying the liberal arts. A road ran around the edge of the square itself and in the centre were the ornamental gardens where paths led between low box hedges and shrubs.

Here they sat on a bench opposite the equestrian statue of the Pecheneg, half barbarian, half founder of the city, according to legend. A little boy stared at them for a few moments before being dragged off by his nanny.

"Victor and Lazlo came to Genesia in the spring. They sought us out at the Cabaret Vaucanson, watching the show night after night, staying afterwards. We could tell immediately that Victor was not like us."

"You've said that, what do you mean?"

"Here," she said, "put your ear here."

She opened her coat and exposed her bare chest as it rose and fell in imitation of breathing.

"It's all right," she said, "just listen."

Fox put my head against her feeling the soft skin rising and falling against his cheek. He could hear what he'd heard faintly before but louder, the tick of her mechanism, the unwinding of a mainspring somewhere, the movement of cogs.

He sat up again. Over on the statue plinth a colourful little bird was perched. It moved slightly, a few steps, then opened its beak and piped a few notes.

"It's clockwork," said Olympia, "how marvellous."

The bird took flight, its wings striking the air in swift, clacking, flaps.

"We all tick," Olympia said, "Some of us loudly, some softly but we all tick. And so need to be wound. But Victor never needed winding. Victor just ticked on without it."

"But Victor was mechanical like you."

Fox know from the night that he had met him that there was no electrical activity inside Victor. No quartz battery, no battery of any kind that would send an electrical signal the augmentation would detect. Neither was his brain biological in any way Fox understood, since there was no electro-chemical activity either.

"Oh yes," she said, "he was clockwork. He was one of us, but not like us. Schiller told me that it was possible. That there was a way discovered long ago and then almost forgotten. But it upset Schiller to talk about it because he didn't know how he knew. Victor had been made in a different way, a better way. To need to be wound is our curse. And perhaps our blessing."

"I don't understand."

"We need each other and perhaps we need humans. We cannot wind ourselves forever. Think about it for a moment. If I could wind myself, be totally self-sufficient, not needing any energy outside of myself then what would I be?"

Fox saw it then. There would be no increase in entropy, no loss of energy.

"A perpetual motion machine."

"Yes," she said, "And think about it beyond just one of us. If the automatons could rely just on winding each other then we would be one big perpetual motion machine. An equal impossibility. So in the end we need to be wound by humans, who get their energy from outside themselves."

"But Victor wasn't like that?"

He considered for a moment that Victor was something like a self-winding watch but that couldn't be because self-winding watches gained the energy to keep their clockwork going by using the bodily movements of the person wearing them. In Victor's case the clockwork movement of his body would be resetting itself.

"No," she said, "Victor didn't need you. And that's one of the reasons he came to Genesia. To show us that it was possible. That he was possible. That our maker had achieved perfection at last."

"Your maker?"

"Victor came from him. He knew him. He told us stories sometimes."

"Who is your maker?"

On a nearby bench two shop girls had arrived. They were opening paper bags and taking sandwiches out. They gave Fox and Olympia sidelong glances. Fox smiled at them and they looked away.

"There is something about us that is not obvious," Olympia said. "We forget you see. Every time we are wound a little piece of memory seems to fade away. It is the memories further back that go first. I can remember when Mond set up Cabaret Vaucanson, three, no four years ago. But before that there is very little. Snapshots. Moments. Walking with Schiller in this square. Looking in the windows of the shops on Autocue Boulevard. Not much else.

"But what I know about perpetual motion isn't a thing of memory at all. Or not in the same way. I'm not sure I have the words. There must be two types of memory. But we just know about this. It is fundamental to us that we must be wound, that perpetual motion is an impossibility. I forget all manner of things but I know this."

Fox wondered if she were talking about the difference between software and firmware. But perhaps that was years of having the augmentation determining his own thinking. Yet hadn't the mind always been described with a technological analogy? From a thermostat to a computer.

"Schiller writes things down," she went on, "But when he looks back to his earliest writings it is only about a wilderness, of groups of us wandering in a wilderness. None of us can remember our maker. None of us know where we come from.

"But Victor knew. Victor hadn't forgotten anything. Sometimes he promised that he would take use there, take us home. When he was done with Genesia. When he was finished with the other things he had to do."

"The Castle."

"The Castle yes. At least that was a part of it. So you see we have to know what happened to him. Because it could be connected with everything we are."

One of the shop girls threw a piece of sandwich out towards the statue. A flock of pigeons emerged from somewhere and began to fight over it. A few boys by the statue were staring at the commotion, one of them leaped out setting the birds into flight again.

"You will be rewarded," Olympia said. "We have money. Mond pays us and we have very few needs. Little to spend it on."

"I'm not sure I can do what you want," Fox said.

"I would just like you to try."

Something hit Fox on the leg and rattled off. Over by the statue the boys lingered. There were three of them, perhaps fourteen or so in age. Fox got up and walked towards them and two ran.

The one who remained glared at Fox, his fists clenched.

"Leave me alone," the boy said.

"What's the idea?"

The boy looked down for a moment and then turned and ran. "Filthy degenerates," he shouted as he went.

The boy had been there long enough for Fox to see his little badge, the black sun, the white ankh.

"Come on," Fox said to Olympia, "I'll walk you back to the hotel."

"Who were they?"

"Just little cretins."

She put her arm through Fox's as they walked. Mond was waiting for her, standing on the step, smoking.

"You'll come in for a drink Herr Fox?" she said.

"Not this time," Fox said, although he could have done with one.

"Of course."

"So you have decided to help us," said Olympia.

"Yes."

"Then perhaps we should discuss your terms."

"That can wait," Fox said, "Until I find out exactly what it's going to entail. I'll come by tonight."

"Then," said Mond, "You must come to the Cabaret Vaucanson. We will be expecting you."

After Olympia had gone inside Mond caught Fox as he was about to walk away.

"Here," she said, "Perhaps this will help you understand better."

It was a small hard-backed book. The cover frayed.

"It's a collector's item," she said, "Look after it."

Fox slipped it into his coat pocket.

Back at the café Fox telephoned Felice and left a message with the receptionist. Then he had to talk Max into lending him his car again.

CHAPTER SIX

The Towers were once luxury apartments now occupied by the poor mostly second or third generation refugees from the wars in the west. There were English there, of a sort. They hung out St George's flags and sang Rule Britannia, and were usually hard-up. If Fox ever ran into any of them he pretended he was Dutch. Lots of kids were into kaleidoscope, clarity, other stuff. When you walked through the canyons formed by the rows of tower-blocks you smelt the river. The docks at Tartessos were nearby. It was a smell of fish and dirty silt, a smell proper to a river; if any of the grandparents had lived through the floods in London they would have recognised that smell.

The local police station was on a traffic island opposite the Towers. Beyond that were a few streets with low rise blocks, shops with flats above them.

Felice and Fox had once had a thing. Fox was not good at things though. Felice had been outspoken in her support for Count Septimus, and if she hadn't have had a least a few friends higher up she might have been purged during the Court of Comedians. As it turned out she was moved from a promising career at the Castle out to the Towers, where the natives were irritating and there was no prospects of any kind. After the Comedians were gone she could probably have come back into the fold but for some reason she remained, either it was thought best or she decided to stay. Fox should have remembered to ask her about it one day.

The most obvious thing about Felice to anyone meeting her for the first time was the disfigurement of her face. The whole area beneath her left cheek to her jaw was scarred, and riven with marks. It was the result of a bad skin-graft done in a field hospital near Lemberg in Ruthenia when she was a girl. It was the best they could do after she'd caught necrotizing fasciitis in the displacement camp she'd been living in.

There was a squat flat-roofed one storey building near the centre of the Towers. It might once have been a community centre but had, at some point, been turned into someone's idea of an English pub.

The Queen Elizabeth had a picture of the last great monarch outside on a sign and more inside. There were union jacks, Churchill, maps, scarfs of football teams that no longer existed. But then none of it really existed anymore. Not like it did when Fox had been a kid. Fox was the last who might have remembered any of this but to be honest none of it was an England that he recognised. The pub stank of fag smoke and there was a sizable crowd for early afternoon. The vintage juke box was an impressive artefact, playing real British stuff: it was a Hard Day's Night apparently. Felice and her colleague Fatty were sitting at a table near where some kids were playing pool.

"Green", Felice greeted him with something like genuine warmth.

Fatty glared for a moment and returned his attention to the game. Fatty didn't like Fox but in the way most police didn't like Fox, not in the way some, like Vogt, didn't like him.

"Get the drinks in F," Felice said to Fatty.

He grunted and went to the bar.

"When the receptionist told him it was you calling me he nagged until I told him he could come, sorry."

"I need to talk to you alone," Fox said.

Fatty would be back with the drinks soon, there was only one way to get him occupied so that Fox and Felice could talk. Fox went over and put coins on the edge of the pool table. He'd have to play a game and win so that Fatty would play next. Then Fatty would keep playing, beating every comer until he got bored or drunk. He was a big ugly man but at the pool table he had the elegance and perfection of a ballet dancer.

"Here," Fatty said, putting the drinks down and slurping lager onto the wood, the slop seemed to congeal into goo in the yellow lighting.

"I've got a game coming up," Fox said.

Fatty snorted.

"I'll take it," Fatty said. "I don't have to hear what you two are talking about, I'm just looking after my partner."

"What do you think I'm going to do?"

"No-one likes you is all," Fatty said shrugging.

The Beatles finished. T-Rex came on, riding a white swan.

When Fatty was gone Fox and Felice chinked glasses.

"How have you been?" Fox asked.

She shrugged.

"How did you get on with Anna Pfaff?" she said. "I thought she might be just your sort of case."

"Don't smirk."

"Moi?"

Fatty suddenly cheered and waved his pool cue in the air in triumph.

"I take it this isn't a social call," said Felice. "You stopped doing those a while back. I hear you hardly leave Little Alex these days. Not that you ever did much."

"Who would you hear that from?" Fox was genuinely intrigued, but then knew at once who it would be. "Oh Max. You've been checking up on me with Max."

She took a sip of her pint and we both watched Fatty's opponent, some greasy looking boy in a denim jacket with a union-jack patch on it. The kid didn't stand a chance.

"You could," said Felice, fixing Fox with her gaze, "occasionally come over and see me. There is even a telephone in my apartment building. By the way, I like the hat."

"Edgar Wallace Verlaine's hat."

She frowned as though the name might mean something but wasn't sure.

"Even the cilia doesn't seem to mind it too much," Fox said, "the headaches aren't quite as bad as with the trilby. Must be the vibes it gives off."

"Vibes?"

They both laughed.

"What do you want, Green?"

"I need to find out about a case. Suspicious death. Fellow by the name of Lazlo Holt."

"Vogt in handling it," she said, "with Downs."

"So you've heard."

"There aren't that many suspicious deaths that are so obviously murder in Genesia. We all get the bulletin from the Castle. Even us down here, amongst the lowest of the low."

"So Vogt is still doing well at the Castle."

She nodded. "The Castle seem very interested in this. Seems like it might have something to do with the Masquerade."

"I'm going to have to confess my ignorance. Vogt mentioned it but I have no idea what it is."

"You've talked to Vogt?" she said with an incredulous expression.

"It wasn't about this. More like him wanting to run me out of town. Or at least the Arcades. He actually pulled his gun."

"Sounds fun."

"It wasn't. But he said I sounded as though I might be a Masqueradist. I didn't know what he meant."

"Well Vogt is in the Renewal Society. They don't like the Masqueradists, who are for everything the Renewal Society hate. The Masqueradists look back to Count Septimus's libertarianism and want to go even further. I like to think of them as sort of Surrealist Communists. Yeah I think that about gives the right picture."

"And Lazlo Holt was involved with them?"

"That's the whisper. But the thing is now Vogt has got hold of it he'll use it to look into the

Masqueradists. Doing a job for the Renewal Society. And possibly a cover-up for them."

"Cover-up?"

"You know they have their offices just the other side of the ruined hyper-loop and the railway tracks from Sparta. In nice respectable Gutunberg. Not that far from where Lazlo was found."

"Perhaps I should just hop over there and ask them about it."

"Very funny, Green," she said, "they're not your kind of people at all."

"What about the Masqueradists. How do I find them?"

"You don't. They're strictly underground. Although there is intelligence on them I don't think it would be a good idea to go looking for them."

Fatty was cheering again as the greasy youth sloped away.

"Then I guess," Fox said, "I will have to go and have a chat with the Renewal Society after all."

"It's not only not a good idea, it's a bloody stupid idea."

A slip of a girl in a blue velvet jacket and dyed blue hair was setting up the balls to be the next victim of Fatty's virtuosity. The jukebox was playing another old song.

"There's something else, Felice."

"Here it comes…"

"I need to get into the Castle."

She looked Fox over.

"Well," she said, "why don't you just get Vogt to arrest you again?"

"Funny."

"Why do you want to get in the Castle anyway?"

"It's connected."

"Okay, okay." She held up her hand. "If it's the case file you need I might be able to have a look at it."

"It's more than that. I'll tell you about it when I know myself."

"Who are you working for, Green?"

"Just some people who knew Lazlo. As I said I'll fill you in soon."

"Wow."

She nodded over to the pool table. The girl, who had to stand on tip-toe to take some of the long shots, had cleared half her balls. Fatty was looking on bemused.

"I've got to watch this," said Felice.

The girl brushed her blue hair back and cued up another shot. The barman and some of the customers at the bar were looking over. Another ball went in a pocket.

"How close do you have to be?"

There wasn't a precise answer to this. It depended on the strength of the signal. But when Fox had been banged up in a cell the augmentation had picked up the database.

"How close are the cells to the database?" he said.

"The floor above."

Another ball clunked into the pocket and rolled down to join the others.

"She's two off the black," said Felice. "So you need to get within a similar range to be on the safe side."

"Can it be done? Look I don't want to do anything that would land you trouble."

"I've got an idea. Oh watch."

The girl potted two balls in quick succession and lined up on the black. Before she took her shot she glanced over at Fatty on the other side of the table and grinned.

She potted the black.

"Well," Fox said, "first time I've seen anything like that."

"Shit," said Felice, "He'll be as moody as hell now."

Fatty was coming around to talk to the girl.

"Look," said Felice, "the servers are located on the ground floor of the inner keep. They couldn't get them any higher without demolishing a wall, and well, the walls are thick. They don't need to worry about flooding anyway."

"No." The castle was on the highest point in Genesia.

"There's this sort of crypt, an undercroft thing, built below the whole of the castle. The rooms down there are mostly used for storage now. There are deliveries there all the time. That's your best bet."

Fatty was leading the girl to the bar. They were both laughing, smiling.

"Actually," said Felice looking at them "I think he's in love."

"I'm going to go," Fox said. "Listen out for any news about the case for me. We'll have dinner. You can come over to the Café when you've done a bit of sniffing around."

"Sure," she said.

"I mean it."

Something came on the jukebox. It was Strawberry Fields Forever.

"See you, Green," Felice called.

Outside the pub, over in the courtyard between two of the tower blocks, a van had pulled up. Bell chimes were running down, the last few bars of Greensleeves. Already kids were forming a queue for kebabs, chips with curry sauce and fried chicken. They'll always be an England it seemed.

***

Fox took a detour on the way back through Gutunberg. These were steep streets, the foothills of what eventually rose up to become the leafier suburbs of the Heights. The houses were tall, gabled affairs, set back from the pavement behind railings and front yards. There was one that must have been the residence of a burgomaster or something years ago, bigger than the others. Hanging from horizontal flag pole was the banner with the ankh and black sun.

A kid stood outside on the doorstep, a boy of maybe seventeen. He was wearing the quasi-uniform Fox had seen in the march, and the ankh armband. He looked over at Fox as Fox looked over at the house. The boy fidgeted, scratched his smooth chin and the top of his cheekbone. Before he decided to come over or go and get someone Fox drove on just as the streetlamps lit up.

Just further up another kid stood outside a small chapel that also appeared to have been claimed by the Renewal Society. Not only was there an ankh flag but around the entrance were painted what looked like other hieroglyphs, a heart, a scarab. They obviously had some kind of thing for Egyptian iconography.

He drove across the bridge over the hyper-loop tube and the railway tracks and came down into Sparta. He didn't know where Victor and Lazlo had been found but thought he might spot a crime scene still taped off. In the end he gave up.

The streets of Sparta were narrow, and there were narrower alleys off them. The houses here might once have been respectable but were badly maintained, some with boarded up windows. Fox had to pull over if a car came the other way but there weren't many. There was a man leading a horse and cart and he nodded thanks as he manoeuvred round the car. The cart was packed with wooden boxes. Fox drove on and came out into the Maskmarkt where all the stalls had been packed away for the night. He parked up, put on his hat and found the nearest café.

He warmed to the place immediately when he saw the portrait of Count Septimus behind the bar. The Count was grinning out in one of his harlequin costumes from back in the good, or at least better, days.

The café was long and narrow with tables and chairs parallel to the bar. The tables further back were occupied with scruffy looking men, market traders Fox supposed. He thought he might ask a few questions but then the waitress come over.

"Hello Lola," Fox said, "it is Lola Hello isn't it?"

She was neat and clean with only the bags under her eyes indicating that she might not have been tucked up in bed after saying her prayers at nine o'clock the night before.

"Shush," she said, "not here. Here I'm Lotte.... Do I know you?"

"The Sea Monster."

She looked behind her and then sat down eyeing Fox's hat.

"I thought it was a dream," she whispered. "You know, the kaleidoscope."

Fox dropped his voice.

"You were pretty loaded."

She shrugged. Then quickly stood up.

"What can I get you, sir?"

A middle aged man had appeared from a back room to take a position behind the bar.

"The guláš is excellent, my uncle's speciality." She looked over her shoulder and Fox saw the flesh tighten on the side of her face as she grinned at the man behind the bar.

"Maybe utopenci?" It seemed it was Czech food here and Fox loved the way they marinated bratwurst. "You have that? And a glass of grappa."

"Sure."

While Fox waited he got the evening paper, *Hören*, from the newspaper table. He flicked though and found a report on page five, after the war news.

Police are investigating the death of a foreigner who has yet to be identified. The body of a man was discovered by workers from the Kirovwerk near the train lines in Sparta, next to the derelict hyperloop line. Cause of death has not been determined. A police spokesman has urged anyone with information to contact the following number....

"Not far from here," Fox said to Lotte when she bought his drink. He tapped the newspaper story.

"I suppose not."

She sat down opposite. There was no-one at the bar, presumably uncle was cooking Fox's utopenci.

"Sea Monster," she said, "you shouldn't be here. We shouldn't meet like this. I can only meet people like you when Lola comes out to play."

"What do you mean people like me?"

She shrugged. It was a cute little gesture as though a teacher had asked her the capital of Spain.

"And when does Lola come out to play?"

"Who knows with Lola, she's a crazy girl. But if you want to know about the body on the railway just ask your friend Vogt. He was with Lola in the Club Adder when a smart little boy in a uniform came and got him and said that a fool had been found dead and to get over to Sparta. Lola was not so far up the kaleidoscope by then but it wasn't nice of him to go and leave her alone in the Adder. Still, she wasn't alone for long."

"What time was this?"

She stood up, smoothing down her apron.

"Perhaps if you run into Lola," she said, "she might be able to tell you a bit more."

73

And Lotte went off to the kitchen and came back with Fox's utopenci which was excellent in every way.

He thought of waiting for her but didn't want to get her in trouble with the uncle. He left one of his cards on the table under a decent tip. It was time to go to the Cabaret Vaucanson to tell them what he would need to get into the Castle.

CHAPTER SEVEN

Fox waited across the street for a while and took swigs from the bottle of grappa he'd bought in the Café Castringius when he returned Max's car. He had his hat on and the headache the indignant cilia were giving him was mild, manageable.

In the time he stood there a few people went in and eventually he walked across the street and went through the door.

There was a little entrance hall where a girl in the cloakroom took his coat and gave him a ticket. She asked for his hat but he said he'd keep it. She shrugged, smiled and handed him a domino mask. He held it in his hand and stared at it.

"It's the only dress code," she said.

When he took his hat off momentarily to put on the mask she didn't bat an eyelid.

He went into the main room and headed straight to the side where there was a bar set back in long alcove. The room was laid out with tables and chairs, electric candles on each of them making them islands in the cigarette smoke and low lighting. The whole place smelt of smoke. At the far end, beyond all this, was a low stage lit with silver light just enough to show the silhouettes moving there. Everyone here was wearing masks, some plain domino ones like Fox's but other more elaborate, with many traditional Genesia grotesques.

He ordered a beer and a grappa.

A tinny cymbal beat started and the stage was lit up brighter. Then the music burst to life.

The Fabulous Bakelite Brothers.

Karl on a trumpet and Bob at the piano. There was an automaton that looked something like a monkey on the drums. None of them wore masks. The beat was slow as Bob vamped a single chord and Karl punctuated this with odd little melodies that lasted a few seconds, they were atonal, ominous. Frau Kastner would have liked them.

Fox made his way to the nearest empty table.

Schiller, maskless as well, in a tuxedo and carrying a walking cane, came onto the stage. The music grew quieter but continued as he spoke into a large microphone.

"Ladies and Gentlemen, denizens of the underworld. Before we commence with our final round of entertainment I want to assure you that here at last you have found a home. When the world has gone mad with reason the only response is the wisdom of the fool. For only the fool speaks truth to power. And of course we, in Genesia, know the difference between a fool and a comedian."

There was jeering, hissing at the mention of comedians. Schiller nodded to this.

"We, the performers at the Cabaret Vaucanson wish to dedicate tonight's antics to absent friends, taken from us before their time. Commence…"

He vanished into the wings and the music lurched up in volume, became faster with the trumpet strained, manic. The stage was flooded with violet light and a woman came on wearing a diaphanous gown and ludicrously high-heeled shoes. It was a moment before Fox realised it was Mond in a black wig that fell to just above her breasts.

She was juggling knives.

"The Soldier's Song," she shouted.

Some of the crowd called out in response. The Soldier's Song.

Tables were banged with fists, people clapped.

From behind Fox someone draped themselves on his shoulder and put a drink on his table.

"One appreciates the Cabaret Vaucanson much more if the senses are given up to intoxication."

It was Mond.

She sat in the chair opposite him. He did a double take on the woman on the stage.

"My sister, Demi," Mond said. "She's more of an exhibitionist than me."

Mond was dressed in in a tuxedo and was smoking from her long holder. Her mask was a smaller version of Fox's, in gold. Demi let the knives fall and clatter onto the stage. She began to sing and Fox knew it was not the voice he had heard from across the street the other might, it was stronger, throatier. As she sang she thrust her hips out at appropriate moments.

Soldiers of the Danube
Soldiers of the Rhine
Haters, Killers, Rapists
Heroes, fools and swine.
Your life's not worth a pfennig
When the missiles take to the air
You'll croak
You'll kick the bucket

Pop your clogs
Without a prayer.
Then they'll scrape you off the mudflats
Toss your bits into a bag
Your bug will go to the counting house
No-one will shed a tear
So soldiers of the Danube
Soldiers of the Rhine
Haters, Killers, Rapists
Heroes, fools and swine:
Frag the sergeant major
Kick him in a hole
And come and stay with Demi
She knows how to console.

The crowd were cheering as Demi finished by miming wrapping her arms around a lover. Once more the tables were banged and there was shouting.

"Fuck the war."

"Yes, fuck the war."

Demi disappeared and the Bakelite Brothers segued into fast rhythmic jazz. It wasn't so loud you couldn't talk over it.

"I take it," Fox said, "That she doesn't approve of the war."

"Who does? Except the Renewal Society. What is your opinion Herr Fox?"

"Not much. I try not to think about politics."

"That's an idiotic thing to say. Besides you won't understand half of what's going on tonight, let alone what's going on all around you. It's typical of Genesia. The people here think the war is a million miles away and that local politics are a little

78

drama that sometimes gets out of hand. But like every little European successor state Genesia has its store of atomic weapons, and that means it could be a useful ally to someone. There are people in this city who want to draw us into the war. And there are people here tonight who don't like the idea very much at all."

"I'll drink to that," Fox said. He couldn't argue with her but usually he couldn't bear to follow the news, the war. He'd seen enough of it during its early days travelling from Paris through Mitteleuropa to get to Genesia.

"Why don't you take your hat off?"

The dull ache in his head was tolerable, but he nodded and took it off.

"No need to be in disguise here," she said.

"And yet we're all wearing masks."

"Exactly."

The Bakelite Brothers finished their song to applause and Schiller came back on stage.

"And now," he said, "The one and only incomparable clockwork chanteuse, Olympia Horlogerie."

She came on with delicate steps, seeming to float for a moment. The dress she wore was black, with classical lines. Bob played a tinkling little melody and the monkey swished the snare drum with brushes.

"Dance," shouted someone close by.

There were cheers.

Olympia cradled the microphone.

"She's going to sing," someone said.

79

Olympia's voice had a soft music even when she spoke.

"This is for the lost," she said, "And all those who have lost."

It was a slow song, brittle so that at times Fox thought she might break.

Bird Song
There's a mechanical bird
In Pecheneg Square,
And a man that I know
With worms in his hair.
My lover is dead,
Yes dead is my love.
But the mechanical bird
Sings to me.
And I like a bird
Sing to you.

The music played slowly as she looked over the audience, but it was clear she was thinking of something else. It was quite a performance and she sang the words all over again.

"It seems," said Mond, "That you have already wormed your way into a song."

The beat of the music got faster, the piano and swishing drums punctured by the trumpet. Olympia, to cheers, moved away from the microphone and began to dance.

It started as tiny jerks, as though she were a puppet being pulled on strings from above, the motion oscillated her whole body, a mockery of tick-tocking as she grew looser, as natural as any mammalian dancer but faster and flawless, without any reflection. She became the dance.

80

"Come on," said Mond, "we'll go to the green room. Schiller will be there, he wants to talk to you."

Fox got up reluctantly, wanting to stay and watch the dance. He picked up his hat and glass and they went. There was a door behind the bar, then a narrow corridor with barrels and wooden wine boxes, stacked bottles. It smelt of spilt booze. The corridor turned a couple of times. Fox could hear the music through the walls and when they passed the wings and he looked out onto the stage from the side. Olympia was still dancing, writhing and grinding now as though she might drill through the stage. Then another corner and Fox was looking into the corridor he'd seen from the other end on the night he'd met Olympia with Victor.

Here were doors to dressing rooms and from an open door of one of these a man in the greasepaint of a white faced clown peered out of a dressing room. He nodded, cigarette in his mouth.

"Pozzo," Mond nodded back.

The green room was done out as a little sitting room, with a sofa and armchairs, a coffee table covered in newspapers and magazines. Schiller was in one of the armchairs, his notepad on his lap.

"I'm glad you have decided to help us Herr Fox," he said, ticking away loudly.

Fox slumped down in one of the armchairs and took off the mask. Mond moved over to the dresser and pulled out one of the drawers and rummaged there.

"Perhaps now the time has come to discuss the terms of your employment," Schiller said.

"I don't like employment," Fox said, "I prefer to think of it as a kind of association that either party is free to break off at any point. But yes, perhaps we should talk terms."

"What are your usual rates?"

"Well the last job I did I got fifty marks for asking someone about their father's will. Scale that up."

"Money doesn't matter to us," he said. "There are other matters I'd like to discuss so let's just say one hundred marks a day until everything has been brought to a conclusion."

There was a remnant in Fox that remained from the days when the augmentation had been fascinated with detective stories. He suddenly wanted to say plus expenses.

"Of course," Schiller said, "Any additional cash outlays on your part will be reimbursed."

It was a lot of money considering it would take time to sort this all out. But it would never be about that, as much as Fox needed it.

"That's fine."

"Have you found a way into the Castle?"

"That's a good question," Fox said, "But I'd like to ask what it is I'm looking for when I get there. Apart from Victor's remains."

At the dresser Mond had bent over. Fox could see her in the mirror, eyes closed, long dark lashes down. With a rolled up ten mark note she snorted up multi-coloured crystals from a little compact mirror. She flung her head back and sucked in air.

"Victor didn't confide in us as much as we should have liked," said Schiller.

Mond spun round. She knocked over some of the stuff on the dresser, the little compact and a lighter, a hairbrush.

"But it should be right up your street Englishman," she said, "It was something to do with the database they have up there. Something of...oh...."

She walked forward a few steps.

"You see," she said, "there's always depth."

Walking over to the door she put her hand against it and stared at a patch where the paint had come off.

"The Cabaret is calling me," she said, "In the flakes of dead paint there, cherry blossom."

She opened the door slowly and carefully walked out, closing it behind her.

"She likes the kaleidoscope then."

"Yes," said Schiller, "It does interesting things to humans doesn't it".

"Sure," Fox said, "She talked about the database there."

"It is your expertise isn't it. When Olympia told us about you, a drunk little man in the back streets who handed out cards saying he was a detective...well you can imagine. But Mond is a very careful person with regard to our well-being. She asked about you. Not that she would directly ask the police of course. But she has friends. We found out what exactly you are."

Fox listened to his loud ticking for a few moments.

He had always known that that was what they wanted him for, had asked Felice about the servers at the Castle for that reason. It shouldn't matter that, in the end, they wanted him for the augmentation. He should have been used to it. It was what he did. Or at least he wanted it to be what he did and not what he was. He was good at other things....

"This," Fox said pointing to the cilia on his head, "won't get me into the Castle."

"No."

"But I'll get in there and then... well you're hiring the whole of me. What is it exactly I'm looking for on their database?"

"Victor never told us."

He found his notebook and pen. Fox watched as his skeletal metal hand moved across a page.

"Forgive me Herr Fox," he said. "It is not easy for me, for us. Beyond a personal mourning...."

"Why do you think Victor was here, in Genesia?" Fox said.

Schiller looked down at his notebook and poised his pen, stopped, looked up at Fox.

"He wanted us to leave, to return with him to Harmony. But the time never came. He had to find out what was going on in the Castle. I assume it had something to do with us, the ultraclocks. But perhaps it was to do with whatever the political machinations are at the moment."

"Harmony?"

"Our home. Where we come from. There are those, my friends the Bakelite Brothers for instance, who doubt there is such a place, and if there was whether it could still exist. Victor's coming assured many of us that it does."

Schiller's head sunk, he scribbled.

"Forgive me," he said, "this is difficult. Like I am running down though I have hours to go before I need to be wound. Sometimes I think I remember. It's like a voice in an empty room, but not my voice at all."

The door swung open.

Mond stood there with her arm around her sister who was naked.

"Come on," Mond said, "Pozzo's on."

She waved the empty cigarette holder in the air.

Demi pushed past her and came into the room heading straight for the dresser.

"Yes," said Schiller, "We can continue this discussion another time."

They all went back into the main room as the crowd were cheering Olympia's last moves and she bowed and went off. Then the tone of the music shifted suddenly as the monkey leapt to the front of the stage and started banging a drum strapped to his chest.

Pozzo cycled onstage atop a tiny unicycle which tipped forward and spilled him onto the stage with a tumble. Karl made an appropriate toot with his trumpet.

Pozzo shouted rather than sung, like someone selling fish in a market.

The Clown's Song.
Comedians fart orders
Their followers smelt roses.
Putting bugs into the children
Telling them that they're soldiers.
Now the comedians are over,
Yes the comedians are gone,

But the pigs that they bred (yes the pigs that they bred!)

Want to shit on our heads

Once again!

He dropped his trousers and each cheek of his bare arse was painted with a white ankh. The crowd began to cheer, a rising note that culminated in shouts and laugher as a turd appeared and hung from Pozzo's backside. It hung for a moment before dropping to the stage to joyous shrieks.

Pozzo shouted.

"The Renewal Society has issued a proclamation. Now stick a life-bug up my arse and I'll be off to war."

CHAPTER EIGHT

It rained the next day, for a few days. Frau Pfaff rang and insisted Fox go back to see her sister and demand to see the will and that he would only get his additional fifty marks when he did. Fox told her he didn't want more money from her and she started to try and explain the situation. But she gave up. Rang off. Fox didn't like the thought that afterwards she was in tears.

Mond called once. To ask about what progress he'd made. He told her he was waiting and that he'd only start charging when the time came.

In the Café Castringius he drank coffee, read the feullition as he always did. Sometimes he got the beetle out, wound it and watched as it crawled over the tablecloth and across the newsprint. The augmentation was almost dormant, sulking and giving Fox a headache as it always did when it was hungry.

Then Felice called and asked him to meet her at the Cathedral.

On Autocue Boulevard, hat on, respectable, everything was it should be: the busy traffic, the mid-morning nannies, and the housewives who liked to shop. It was bizarre that Steffi's department store window, the one that usually displayed boring men's suits, should be the one that the ankh in black sun banner hung inside. There was a little cardboard sign standing on the table inside the window display saying that it had been sponsored by the Renewal

Society, which at least meant the situation hadn't gotten to the stage yet when they could hang there banner anywhere they told people to hang it. They were still paying.

Fox knew enough history and the augmentation had absorbed even more, to recognise a pattern. History didn't repeat itself but sometimes echoes were just enough to make you shiver.

He crossed Autocue Boulevard. There was a large mushroom shaped construction, a cornucopia, a device that had once dispensed food. Fox had been there when it had gone wrong, digital decay destroying the software that controlled it. It started to dispense grey gloop that filled the output cavity. There had been worse stuff in other cornucopias, odd little bioforms, possibly made of synthetic meat. He'd heard that in Gutunberg a deluxe cornucopia had churned out tiny creatures with toothed sphincters. The police had taken a flame thrower to them.

This cornucopia had become a dormant street ornament and as Fox approached a man in what looked like a monk's habit stepped out from behind it and tried to give him a leaflet.

"Jesus raised the alarm for sinners."

Fox nodded and went on.

He'd go up through the old town legal district to where the Cathedral was on one of the hills. As he followed the slowly climbing streets lined with medieval houses he felt the looming presence of the Castle, away over there, on the highest of the hills, the one that matched the altitude of the Heights off to the east of the city. He was glad he couldn't see it, that Cathedral hill was so covered in tiny old streets that he was sheltered.

He made sure he kept away from the legal archive because he knew the augmentation would be itching to go back in.

***

It was the time of day when the light illuminated the stained glass inside the Cathedral, charging the air with colour, making patterns on the flagstones of the nave. There was a smell, dead, clean, cold as though stone could have a smell. There was nothing of interest here to the augmentation.

There never seemed to be anyone here. Perhaps conventional Christianity no longer cut it. Fox had come across all sorts of religious revivals as he'd crossed Europe. As societies broke down and digital dreams dried up, people had turned to the Day Glow Jesus offered by American exiles, Posadists waiting for socialist UFOs, Flat Earth Tunnelers… In Paris there'd been an apocalyptic death cult whose day had finally come. White robed they roamed the ruins eradicating any life left, finishing the job of Armageddon.

Fox and Felice used to come here and he knew the pictures in the windows well, a comic strip of the life of Saint Genesius, the patron saint of the city.

"Just like old times," he said. His voice lingering in the air the way it did here.

They were sat on a pew.

"Well," said Felice, "It is the one place my colleagues never come."

"Surprising really. I can imagine Vogt being quite pious."

"Oh he is in his way, but there's always plenty of other outlets for it."

"Yeah," Fox said, "His enthusiasm for the Renewal cretins."

"There's a lot of it about, especially up at the Castle. There was even talk about banning civil servants from being members only there are at least two members of the Provisional Government with ankhs on their underpants."

Fox thought of Pozzo.

"What have you got yourself into, Green?" Felice asked looking into his face.

"I was hoping you might tell me that."

"Come on."

They walked down the nave and stood beneath the vaulted roof of the octagon in front of a fantastically baroque rood screen.

"We'll go into the Lady Chapel," said Felice.

It was off the north transept and was a large appendage to the main cathedral building reached by a tiny passage through a low mantel. The step of this was worn smooth and concave by centuries of pilgrims. The Lady Chapel had an altar dominated by a statue of the Virgin. It was dull, brown and probably of great significance to someone. There was also a painting known as the Virgin of the Carpathians.

She was stunningly beautiful, but the power of the picture came from the way it managed to depict a woman who embodied both the serenity of the mother of God and the erotic charge of the model, a mistress of one of the old Counts. The detail of her bare breast left nothing to the imagination. It was provocative, almost disturbing given the context.

"You've always liked that picture," said Felice. "Pervert."

They both laughed. It echoed oddly in the enclosed space.

"Possibly guilty," he said.

"It embodies the way men, some men, want women to be. Perfect whore and virgin at the same time."

"Sure," Fox said, "But I still like it. Maybe because it's so out of place."

"Look," she said, "It's okay to feel desire."

He let that go.

"You need to be careful," she said. "The one thing that's clear is that Vogt doesn't want anyone poking around in this case. I went up to the Castle and while I was there I thought I'd chat to one of the girls who does the clerical work in criminal investigations. I mentioned the Lazlo Heck case, the Masquerade connection. The poor thing went white and stammered something about not being allowed to talk about it. She was so flustered she didn't notice when I swiped the official stamp from her desk. The postmaster is supposed to keep it but it gets passed around the office so he doesn't get bothered all the time. Don't worry I put it back after I'd used it on the document."

She reached inside her jacket and bought out an envelope and handed it to Fox.

"Authorisation for a supplier of beverages, soft and hard," she said. "Same format for any police station. All it need was the seal. The signature of the General Quartermaster was easy enough to forge."

"I owe you one."

"You sure do."

"I told you, dinner...."

"Green", she said, "This is all crazy. You should just walk away from it. Things are getting tough in Genesia. Nasty people are crawling to the top again. Ah forget it, let's light a candle."

They went back into the main part of the Cathedral. It was here that they had first ever met. Fox lost after crossing half of Europe, walking the city after dark, coming anywhere he might find something like peace. And Felice, a believer of sorts. Perhaps. At least, like Fox, she found something here. They would meet here for their brief liaisons. It was a long time ago. She'd been young then. A police officer in a state ruled by the idealist Count Septimus.

On the votive table there were a dozen or so stubs and a tall candle burning.   Felice dropped a few pfennigs in the jar and took a candle, lit it from the one already there and placed it in a holder.

"Who's it for?" Fox asked.

"For us Green. Two gargoyles who might have made a bit more of a go of it together."

"You're not a gargoyle."

"Neither are you but what I am is a lot older. And look at you. That thing in your head just won't let you age decently will it? You're old but never had to grow up. Never had to get used to decay and the prospect of your own death. You've stopped aging. You're arrested. Old but like something in a museum is old."

"I can't help it."

"No."

She was still staring at the candle.

"Perhaps you'll die soon," she said, "Some little maggot like Vogt will put a bullet in you because you've decided, for reasons I don't understand, to lift up the stone he was hiding under."

She was walking away now.

"Take care," she said, "I hope we get to have that dinner sometime."

When she was gone Fox sat on a pew for a while. He got out the little clockwork beetle and wound it, watching it run around on a flagstone beneath the bright multi-coloured light of the windows.

**

He had a few more things to settle. From a payphone he rang the Hotel Relojeria and Mond answered.

"I'm ready to proceed," he said. "But I need an appropriate vehicle. A van would be best."

He told her about the cover story.

"I'll arrange it," she said. "I'll have someone for you. It'll be someone we can trust at our end."

"Fine," Fox said, "All they have to do is sit in the van and look like a delivery man. I'll be in touch."

He rang off.

CHAPTER NINE

Nezamysl Street was a narrow road that led around the back and ran parallel to Autocue Boulevard and deliveries were made into the back doors of the stores. It was as though Autocue Boulevard's skin had been stripped away and you were looking at its anatomy, muscles and bone, the water and waste pipes, the telephone and electrical cables. The small windows of storerooms were grimy. There were dustbins against the wall, and around them more rubbish in bags, boxes, offcuts of carpet and cloth.

On a corner Nezamysl Street met another back street that in turn led onto Autocue Boulevard. On any free space of wall there were faded advertisements for clubs and shows, the summer fair in Anderseite and last year's Saturnalia. In one place across the main part of some older posters was a line of four identical posters that were newer. It had been a long time since Fox had seen those faces. They'd called themselves Judges. The Comedians who had murdered Count Septimus: Froggy, Zero, Blanco and Mute. There was no text on the posters, just the white ankh.

The van was waiting there as Mond had said it would the driver standing on the pavement. He was dressed in overalls looking at the posters. As Fox approached it was Mond who turned around, stripped of make-up. She winked at him.

"What do you think?" she said, "Do I look like a lusty young proletarian?"

"Jesus Mond, this isn't a performance."

"Herr Fox. Everything is a performance."

Mond swung the van left, then left again to go up Autocue Boulevard parallel with the way he'd just come down Nezamysl Street, past the fronts of those shops with their lights and displays. At the junction they turned right on the road that climbed as it followed next to the old wall towards Law Gate and Kleist Square. Already the Castle dominated the view ahead. It had been built to encircle the crown of the hill so it stood above the town here, an unreal cut-out at this distance, like something from a child's pop-up book, great walls, turrets and the sloping fairy-tale tower roofs of European castles, different from those in England.

"You fit the van out like I asked?" Fox said.

"Well the van was full of detergent, bathroom towels and the like. But I took that out and I've put a couple of boxes of wine in the back from the Cabaret Vaucanson."

Fox had filled in the relevant section of the papers that Felice had given him. The wine order was put down as being for a Dr Straka who apparently worked in the Castle infirmary, which according to the telephone directory he'd looked at, was on the far side of the Castle so there wasn't a big chance of him happening by or someone calling him to come and look at all this wine he was getting.

At Kleist Square they took the Castle Road, running beneath the shadow of a fairly well preserved section of wall. Opposite the wall the street was lined with, nice little cafes and bistros interspersed with the well-to-do houses of senior civil servants and government ministers, top brass in the army. The road rose steeply for a while, then the Castle was dead ahead.

"This is fun," said Mond.

She took out one of her cigarettes and this time lit up without her holder. Within the confines of the van the smell was strong, that Turkish blend, Sultanahmet.

The Castle was on a promontory and when it had been constructed the builders had made the most of the landscape, carving out a deep gulley to separate the promontory off, creating sheer drops around the castle so that the only way to get in or our was across a drawbridge. The drawbridge had long since been replaced by a steel girder box bridge that could carry road traffic, but it still meant the Castle was easily defended by, say, a few soldiers with energy weapons or good old fashioned machine guns, stationed in the two ugly concrete pill boxes at the far end of the bridge.

Nowadays there was only a couple of Landespolizei with side arms and a lifting barrier. They drove straight across towards them, the van wheels rattling on the metal of the bridge, over the chasm beneath them.

Mond had the papers ready and wound her window down as Fox slowed the van. All the way over he had tried not to think about how high up they were and about the drop.

"Delivery," said Mond as she held out the papers.

The policeman took them and handed them back almost instantly, waved at someone and the barrier was raised. Fox drove into the outer courtyard, bumping and jolting on the cobblestones. He'd read a guidebook the evening before, sat in the Café Castringius and knew that the great wall on the far side was the inner curtain wall with rooms and towers. There was a portcullised gatehouse built into this and beyond that was the inner courtyard and in the midst of that the Great Keep. He hoped Felice was right that the undercrofts ran all the way beneath it. The guidebook hadn't said. It hadn't said either where the undercrofts were.

"Shit," Fox said, "Where do we go?"

There were a few vehicles parked up against the curtain wall. A couple of civilian staff, young women, came through the gatehouse and began walking towards the bridge.

"We could ask someone," said Mond.

"Sure."

Fox didn't like it here. The feeling of being trapped and of wanting to run from that trap was gnawing at him. It wasn't just that he'd been imprisoned here before, and beaten up as well, it was deeper than that, as though the weight of all that had ever happened here was in those big blocks of stone, and they were looming all around about to cut off the sky. He tried to imagine courtyard when it had been flooded to make a lake for Count Septimus to sail model boats on, and of all the times the Castle had hosted festivals and parties: but the days of the Comedians and what they had done here had erased that.

He slowed the van and pulled it to a halt. The secretaries, or whatever they were, were passing on his side so he wound down the window.

"Excuse me ladies."

They looked at each other for a moment and came over.

"Yes?"

"It's the first time I've been here. Where do I deliver the wine I've got?"

"You won't be able to drive," said one, "You'll have to carry it. Through the gatehouse. The stores are over by the canteen. Over to the right."

"Thanks."

"You'll need to see the quartermaster. To get the key."

"You see," said Mond as he drove a little to find somewhere to park, "couldn't be simpler."

"And the key?"

"Oh, I'll do that, you seem to be a little nervous today Herr Fox."

She got out and went off. Fox manoeuvred the van to park as near to the gatehouse as he could. She came back almost instantly, dangling the key in front of Fox.

"Let's just hope," Fox said, "We don't run into Vogt or anyone else who recognises me."

"So you know Vogt then?"

"Unfortunately."

"Don't worry. I don't think anyone will know you in that hat."

They took a box of wine each from the back.

"They're light," Fox said.

"That's because they're empty. Just try to make it look convincing. I'm not giving good booze away to the police."

"But..."

"Oh I do so love the theatre," she announced as she lifted a box and made it look as though she could hardly carry it.

"It's supposed to be wine," Fox said, "not gold bars."

They carried the boxes over the cobbled courtyard and through the gatehouse, which was unmanned, the raised portcullis rusty and looking as though it hadn't been lowered since the days of the Teutonic Knights.

"They don't seem very tight on security," Fox said.

"Who have they got to worry about? The people in charge here mostly don't know what's coming."

"What do you mean?"

"I expect we'll all find out soon enough."

Fox wanted to know what she meant but as they got into the inner courtyard there was a man in kitchen whites standing outside a door watching them, hopefully just out of idle curiosity. Fox tried to ignore him and not to think about the walls all around them, the thick inner curtain wall that was really a building itself, with staterooms, guardrooms and dormitories. Then there was the great keep where he'd been imprisoned. Over there now a uniformed policeman was smoking on the step by the door.

"Slow down," Mond said, "you're almost running."

Fox stopped for a moment as though taking a breather. Then he walked, without looking, until they had reached a set of steps leading down to a small, paved area where two large wooden doors were set into the sunken base of the inner curtain wall.

They put down the boxes and Mond unlocked the doors.

"How long will you need?" she said.

"I don't know. Once I'm near enough it shouldn't take too long."

She raised her voice.

"You stack 'em Fritz," she said in the accent of a Tartessos docker, "I'll nip back for the other boxes."

They carried the boxes inside and then she went out, leaving Fox alone. He was in a vast cellar, vaulted with curved supports, built of ancient brickwork that had been repointed in places. The lighting was dim, yellow, made by the occasional bare bulb, wiring running along the ceiling, hanging down in places. He looked down a central aisle lined with pillars holding the roof supports. Either side of this there were other aisles leading off. He took off his hat. From the position of the Keep he would have to go left and then somehow double back and trace the way to pass beneath the inner courtyard. He took the first left off the main aisle. There were boxes here and there, teas chests, and mounds of something or other under awnings. He took another left towards the direction he figured the Keep was. Then he could feel it, the cilia coming alive as the augmentation began to detect patterns of signals.

There were a series of firewalls and filters that had been designed to keep out the decay. They were once state of the art but no-where had they worked completely and here it was no different.

Fox moved through the undercrofts further, hardly noticing his surroundings. He stopped when the augmentation could feel the signals at their strongest, negotiating the final defences. The database could be envisaged in its entirety now. It was decayed, in poor shape but better than many. Perhaps it had been spared the worse by its isolation in the Castle, or because it had been disconnected it as the data decay ravaged the world's information systems.

He found the meta-data with its system catalogue that would tell him how the whole thing was structured on the logical level above the actual physical architecture of electronic signals, switches and gates.

There it was: a list of subject-oriented objects. Criminal cases, convictions, suspects, victims, demographic data linked to Geographic Information sub-system that, as far as he could tell, no longer existed. Fox's cilia were throbbing and he could feel a charge run through the augmentation as it scanned, delved, ate it all up.

He didn't know what he was looking for, what it was that Victor had been interested in and so Fox looked for any reference to the Lazlo case. He found his name but the case, along with all the other recent cases, just seemed to have been logged with the barest detail and referenced to a serial number for what was presumably a manual file. It seemed they were using the database these days as little as possible in case of new outbreaks of the decay. All the recent data had the most minimal use of the resources: no images or recordings, no pattern analysis or multi-dimensional structures. Just simple record keeping.

There was no reference to Victor, or his remains.

Fox tried searching for automata, masquerade, Renewal Society. Nothing of any significance. Then he came across something. Fairly routine data that had been updated recently, all of it updated with a yes/no Boolean flag.

It was current personal records for police, army and members of the Provisional Government. As well as being marked as yes or no, without any indication of what that meant, they were linked to a series of schematics from the Geographic Information System that Fox thought no longer existed. The part referring to the city itself was intact. There was a series of identical city maps but with people placed on them in different locations, at different times and dates. It amounted to a set of elaborate scenarios, like a book of chess games.

As a test parameter Fox tried Vogt. He figured in all of them. Vogt at the Castle. Vogt at Government House.

He tried to see where these scenarios were being constructed. He traced one back to its source and saw a new scenario emerge. Data was going in a logical flow to... Then appearing from... Fox thought at first it was from a decayed set of algorithms but it wasn't. It was nothing. There was nothing there. Unprocessed data was going into nothing and then an elaborate scenario was coming out of that nothing. Fox could almost see the shape of the absence. It was some non-electronic destination but he couldn't think of what it could be. Hollerith punched cards or paper tape? But that would just be dead storage and here processing was happening, scenarios elaborated. And anyway all but the most ancient of key punch cards had some electromagnetic element even if it was just a buffer to store the card image before printing. It would have left a recognisable trace but there was just...nothing.

"Herr Fox."

Something on him arm that he shrugged off. He needed to see into that which wasn't there. The way the data had been processed to produce these scenarios was something the augmentation needed to know. Here was all the characteristics of classic AI simulation but there was nothing producing it.

"Herr Fox, we should go."

Mond was pulling at his upper arm, nails pressing into his bicep. It took him a moment to focus.

"What is it?"

"Some new arrivals. Soldiers I think. We've been a while. It would be better if we weren't given too much attention, yes?"

Fox couldn't leave and the only thing he could think of was to put his hat on and make sure every cilia was tucked in as he pulled it down tight. There was a sudden pain shooting from his temple inwards. The augmentation could still function and was desperate to explore further and it was finding the hat uncomfortable. It was only when Mond had led Fox far enough away that the augmentation calmed down, Fox's head throbbing as it sulked in frustration.

"Did you find anything?"

"Yes," Fox said, "I think so."

"Later then."

They reached the door out of the undercroft and Fox went out and sat on the stairs for a moment while Mond locked up.

When they went up to the courtyard Fox saw what Mond had meant. Over by the entrance to the Keep a group of men in military uniform were standing as ease. Fox didn't recognise the uniform but knew it was not from Genesia.

"You don't seem well Herr Fox."

"My head. I just need to rest. Take this damn hat off."

"Not advisable here. We'll just walk out to the van. We'll get out of here."

A couple of the soldiers glanced over at them. People came out of the Keep. Three men. Vogt and the unmistakable form of his partner Downs, a muscular giant. With them a man with a similar uniform to the soldiers but fancy, an officers uniform. He was a tall man, as big as Downs but without the bulk. The soldiers fell to attention instantly as their officer swaggered in front of them.

Fox and Mond reached the gatehouse, Fox's head pounding.

"I'll just take the key back up to the quartermaster," Mond said.

"I'll be in the back of the van."

Fox scrambled in and pulled the doors closed behind him. He took the hat off and threw it across the inside of the van. His cilia extended again, searching, wanting, the headache suddenly gone until it realised that the feast of data it had glutted on, the mystery it needed to solve, was no longer there. Fox was panting, leaning against the side of the van not trying to think what would happen if Vogt and Downs found him. Then relief, almost light-headedness as Mond climbed into the van and started the engine.

"All set," she said.

But the van didn't move.

Outside Fox could hear something. The steady rhythm of feet against the stones of the courtyard.

"Best if we let the soldier boys pass," Mond called back.

As the pounding feet grew closer they came into Fox's head as the cilia caught the proximity of data. Soldiers marching through him with the fragments of their life-bugs, stomp coming into a village somewhere mirthless laugher. Kicking down doors and opening fire, a woman clutching a child, half-turning as she fell, one side of her ripped away. Other houses, men and children shot instantly. When there is enough hesitation to recognise a woman she is stripped and raped before being finished off. Accelerant poured everywhere, splashing it in the rooms over bodies. And at the edge of the village watch as it burns.

"Stop it."

But the augmentation wanted more. Wanted the worse bits of their lives because the worse bits were the ones that had created the richest, most complex patterns on the life-bugs. Other scenes, other towns. Yet they might be the same scenes with only slightly different décor or some particular noticed almost subliminally: a family photograph, an unusual ornament half-seen as a body erupts under the impact of high-velocity fire.

All the while there had been a feeling of detachment even in moments of fury, as though the soldiers were watching themselves and cannot accept the reality of what they are doing, as though each moment they shoot or tear away a woman's clothes as she screams, are just snapshots of a life they can discard.

Only one viewpoint is different. The detachment there is cold, almost analytical. This one understands it all even though he doesn't join in. He watches and orders. This is tactics, necessity. He is the commanding officer and as he strides among his men he enjoys their fear of him as much as the terror the victims show. In his isolation from anything human he is almost like a god.

Stomp.

The last boot echoed and the van juddered a little over the cobblestones. They stopped momentarily again and someone said something. Then the rattle over the bridge, a great gulf beneath them.

"You see," Mond said, "It was easy in the end."

CHAPTER TEN

There was air in his face, a breeze from somewhere, it played along his check and jaw. He kept his eyes closed. He was sure that only a moment ago someone had been singing and he tried to remember what the song was about but then he was walking into a village, there were people there, frightened, they were frightened of him...

When he opened his eyes he had no idea where he was. He was on a bed next to a partly open window where a vase of asters stood, the petals fluttering a little. On the bedside table was a jug of water, a glass, and his little clockwork beetle. It was a neat room with a mirrored dressing table, a heavy mahogany wardrobe and a wicker chair.

He stood up and got his feet to the floor. He was wearing red silk pyjamas that weren't his. Outside the window he looked down from the first floor into a garden bordered by thick shrubs and trees. There was little in the flower beds along each side at this time of year but there were some reeds and tall grasses spreading out from one of these beds down to a little pond. The statue beside the pond was of Saint Genesius holding his actor's mask.

Behind him the door opened and he turned as Olympia came in. She was wearing a long nightgown in black lace with a matching bed-coat. Through the fine mesh he watched for a moment as her breasts rose and fell with the steady, unwavering, rhythm of her breathing.

"You're awake Herr Fox. I'm glad. We we're worried about you."

He found it difficult not to inspect her. She looked so very like a beautiful, desirable woman, and yet she wasn't. Her hips moved as sinuously as she came forward. He forced himself to look away from the shadows and contours emphasised by what she wore.

A sudden flash in his head. A village, a terrified woman with her clothes being torn off. Something like a pain from his gut to heart. He didn't know whether the sudden desire for Olympia was some kind of sickening remnant of what he had experienced in the soldiers' life-bugs.

"What happened?" he said.

Out in the garden a bird had landed on the head of the statue. He wasn't sure if it was real or clockwork.

"Mond brought you here last night. You were distressed and we didn't understand what you were saying. Then you just stopped. Sort of fainted. It was rather like you'd wound down."

She gave a little burst of laugher. It was nervous. Charming. Still Fox didn't want to look at her. She settled in the wicker chair. He imagined her legs being crossed. He carried on looking at the bird in the garden as it rested on the head of the saint.

"This is your room? The Hotel Relojeria?"

"Of course."

"I think my augmentation must have realised it had gone too far so it put me to sleep. It has happened a couple of times before."

"You were distressed. Mond said something happened as you were leaving."

"There were soldiers there."

"Yes, it's in the newspaper. Karl and Bob were talking about it."

"Can you get it for me? And a drink. I'd like a drink."

She left and came back with the Gazette and a glass of apple juice, which wasn't what he had meant at all.

He found the newspaper report.

As part of an initiative the Provisional Government has welcome a platoon of Grenadiers from the Northern League commanded by Captain Ambrus Kardos. This goodwill visit to Genesia will involve discussions on matters of mutual interest including border security and protection of non-military commerce.

"Captain Kardos makes it sound as though they are customs officers but they were soldiers. Not just ordinary soldiers. Brutalised. A death squad."

Councillor Gorman of the Minority Party has objected to the visit as compromising Genesia neutrality. A spokesman for the Provisional Government has assured the ruling council that military matters beyond those affecting Genesia domestically would not be on the agenda.

Once again Fox saw women's eyes from the life-bugs. Wide with terror, about to be raped or killed. Later flames, the glee of watching the flames. Then the feeling of calm satisfaction of the commanding officer.

"It keeps playing in my head," he said throwing the newspaper down, "I need something to drink."

Olympia looked at my untouched juice.

"What would you like?"

"Anything. Grappa if you have it."

When she was gone he found his clothes, neatly folded in a drawer of the dresser. He dressed quickly, trying not to succumb to any more visions.

In the war zones the augmented like Fox were invaluable assets in intelligence. The data decay didn't change this, in fact made them more valuable since most of augmented had fought the decay off themselves and could still be used to access whatever data bases and information systems were left. There weren't many of them. If captured they were recruited to the captors own service, often forcibly. If the Northern League caught them though it was different.

The Northern League had realised that the augmented could read life-bugs and considered the augmented abominations. Most armies had used life-bugs for decades but the Northern League considered life-bugs as something more than just a soldier's insurance policy. Just at that moment when the databases used to hold the life store of dead soldiers had been succumbing to the data decay the whole operation developed into part of their nascent religion merging in with their general political fanaticism. Any augmented caught were executed on the spot, usually having their augmentations loosened up with a bayonet in the skull and then ripped out.

Death squads like those Fox had encountered in the Castle had not just murdered the augmented of course. They had been utilised whenever there was a need to terrorise the population of newly conquered areas. It was something he'd thought he'd left behind when he'd reached Genesia.

"Here."

Olympia handed him a glass of grappa. He swallowed, savouring its rawness on his throat.

"I need to know more about what Victor was doing," he said.

"So you did discover something at the Castle."

"I don't know what's significant until I understand what it is Victor was interested in. And I need to know about the Masquerade."

She hesitated for only a moment. Fox watched it, the single rise and fall of her chest.

"I can tell you all about Victor. As much as I know. But for the Masquerade you need to talk to the others."

"Victor was part of the Masquerade?"

"Let's go into the garden," she said, "I'm sure you would benefit from fresh air."

They sat on a little bench by the pool. Close to her Fox was aware of her breathing, and perhaps the faintest of ticking. He thought of a porcelain doll again, as he had once before, delicate, brittle, and so easily smashable with a soldier's rifle butt.

"You're shaking," she said.

"You don't feel the cold like I do."

"Forgive me. We can go back inside."

"No, it's good here. A bit more of that grappa would help though."

She came back with a bottle and a glass. The bottle rattled against the glass as Fox poured.

"I used to sit here with Victor," she said, "and he'd tell me about Harmony. About where we came from."

"What was it like, Harmony?"

"I used to ask him the same question. And he would talk to me the way the nannies in Pecheneg Square talk to children when they are trying to calm them, soothe them when they've grazed a knee. He was so serious about it that I had to force myself not to laugh. He said that Oxenstierna made our bodies and wound us, breathed life into our minds and Monet Same nursed us and we wandered the halls of Harmony until the day came for us to leave.

"I asked him why it was we had to leave because he wanted me to yearn for Harmony the way he did but I suspected that I would get bored there, without the city and the Cabaret."

"So why did he say you had to leave?"

"He said that we chose to leave because we could. Because Oxenstierna gave us free will. But the time was coming when we would go home. And that he had come to take us home."

"That is why he came to Genesia?"

"As I've said, that is part of it. Here..."

She presented her hand to Fox and opened her fist. He hadn't noticed that she had been clutching something. It was the little clockwork beetle.

Fox took it from her.

"You haven't been winding him have you?"

113

"Not much. I don't know what to do with him."

"Then perhaps you should let him go. Let him wander off into the garden."

Fox thought about it. The beetle might wind down, never move again.

"I'd like to keep him for a bit longer."

"Good."

At the French doors Bob was standing looking out. He nodded for a moment and then disappeared back inside.

"What else did Victor come to Genesia for? What was it I found in the Castle? Plans for a military coup it looked like."

"I think that's what the Masquerade suspected."

"And Victor was part of the Masquerade."

"Not really. The others know more than me. I suspect he worked with them. They all have secret names. Victor was the Fool. He told me though that he'd been the Fool before he ever came to Genesia. He used to have a card, you know the tarot card, Le Mat. He'd bought the deck with him from Harmony. The Fool is the protagonist of the story the tarot tells, the one who is wandering into danger but has the potential to gain wisdom because he is without power, without a stake in anything. The Fool is the one who is truly free. If we ever get Victor's artefacts I wonder if I could have that card."

"If Victor was trying to find out about a potential coup then whoever is behind it is probably behind his murder."

Fox knew the tarot. The Fool showing the young man wandering towards a precipice. Victor hadn't had time to become wise, he'd just blundered off the edge to his doom.

"You must speak to the others," she said.

"Wait," Fox said as she started to rise, "the song you sang?"

"Yes?"

"You put me in the song."

She reached over and touched Fox's hand for a moment. The softness of her fingers, the cool solidity, stopped him shaking for a moment.

"I think I remember the songs," she said, "I think even if I forget you I'll remember you in the song. Now come on."

He followed her back into the house, downing grappa from the glass then taking shots from the bottle. It had been pleasant in the garden for a few moments, the augmentation quiet, but Fox still knew it was savouring the scenes of murder and rape, that all that was still lurking there even though the drink had managed to push the scenes down.

At the dining room table Bob was sat at a chessboard with a book of chess problems open beside it.

Bishop took knight and Bob looked up at Fox.

"You seem to have been rather disturbed by your experiences at the Castle, Herr Fox. Perhaps it is time for you to tell us what it is you found there."

"If I'm to make sense of it I'm going to need some more information."

Bob looked at the chessboard again, to the book then back at the board.

"I wonder," he said, "whether it is really necessary for you to make sense of very much at all.

115

What we asked is that you find Victor and Lazlo's murderer and locate Victor's remains."

"Bob…"

He put his hand up stop Olympia's interruption.

"But," Bob went on, "I appreciate that you have taken considerable risks on our behalf. I balance that consideration against the fact that you are being paid of course. But still, Herr Fox, I am inclined to regard you as someone useful."

"Thanks."

Bob placed a bookmark inside the book and closed it then tapped the cover.

"As the great man says when one is running a race one doesn't stop to wipe a smut from one's nose."

"Bob, you are being rude."

"It's all right Olympia," Fox said, "I've had a lot worse. I take it Herr Bakelite that you have decided to be more forthcoming?"

Fox didn't know why Bob didn't like him, or found him irritating but supposed it didn't really matter.

"Tell me about the Masquerade," Fox said.

Bob rose from his seat and went into the sitting room and the armchairs, near to the bottle of grappa and glass where Fox had left them on the coffee table.

"What did you find in the Castle?" Bob said.

Fox told him about the plans he'd seen, about the various permutations of some sort of coup attempt. He told him about the death squad, the murderers disguised as part of a diplomatic mission. But he didn't tell him about the way the coup plans

116

had been the result of data processed in a way Fox didn't understand, of the absence he had found there. Perhaps because Fox thought he knew what that absence might be.

Both of the ultraclocks were looking at Fox. Olympia, her legs crossed, her lace dressing gown high on her leg.

"Tell me," said Bob, "Why do you think Genesia is a city known for its masks?"

"Is this a history lesson?"

"Humour me."

It was unsettling the way his expression never changed, that same pissed-off expression in moulded plastic.

"The Emperor Rudolf," Fox said, "founded the city and brought the saints bones here after then been brought to Prague from Rome. But there was a settlement already, the Pecheneg war camp, fortress, already a thousand years old."

Bob raised his hand to stop Fox's little lecture.

"Schiller," he said, "who is a scholar of many things once remarked that the Pechenegs are the true soul of the city but I think rather the city has a double nature. The barbarian one and the one belonging to the actor saint, the masked man. The id and the superego. Although I'm undecided which is which.

"The Masquerade," he went on, "was formed during the days of the Court of Comedians, when it looked as though we were about to be taken into the war, when it looked as though everything that had made Genesia a place where people like us, and I mean you too Herr Fox, could live was about to end. Those who formed the Masquerade would be prepared to take up arms against the Comedians."

"Yet it never happened," Fox said.

"Not exactly. We were part of the uprising of course but there were enough people with some sense beyond our ranks to lead the popular protests, and enough in the establishment to get rid of the Comedians. And yet the situation is hardly stable is it? The Renewal Society and those around them are the return of the repressed. And so the Masquerade continues its vigilance."

"And you are a member?" Fox asked.

"Our kind have been welcomed. What are we if we are not walking masks after all?"

"And Victor? And Lazlo?"

"Victor had an association with the Masquerade. A shared interest at least for a while. There was something going on in the Castle and Victor was interested in. The Masquerade wanted to know what was going on too. The Masquerade know that soon there will be a move to overthrow the Provisional Government. And it seems you have seen the plans for this. Do you retain the information you accessed?"

"Yes."

"Then it appears you are very valuable. Valuable indeed."

Once more Fox wanted to read his expression but it was the same. And within Bob's form there was nothing for Fox to read, not even the incomprehensible but busy firings of a human nervous system. But it did seem as though Fox had a key to accessing the would-be revolutionaries of the Masquerade.

"I need to talk to whoever Victor was working with in the Masquerade."

Bob was silent for a moment.

"Perhaps," he said. "I will enquire. And you will be willing to detail what you found out at the Castle?"

The soldiers were there. A death squad. Whatever might happen soon they would be part of it. Even now, beneath the warm haze of the grappa Fox could feel the augmentation wanting to play out their atrocities.

"You're paying me," he said, as much to remind himself what this should all be about as to convince Bob, "so you're entitled to know what I found out."

Fox poured the last of the grappa from the bottle into the glass. He suddenly wanted to be away from here, from Bob's eternal look of impatience, from Olympia's unsettling delicacy. He would sit at his table in the Café Castringius and drink some more, read the newspapers. He needed to talk to Felice again, to find out the real details of the case, the ordinary things like the murder scene, the timings, and the suspects. They had got him to go into the Castle and he still hoped somehow it was because whatever was there was the reason Victor was killed. The vast nothingness what was somehow just like whatever it was that produced thought within the minds of the ultraclocks.

"I will arrange something," said Bob as he rose from his seat, "I'm going now. I have to meet Karl at the Cabaret to work on some new material."

Fox finished the grappa.

"What are you thinking?" Olympia asked when Bob had gone.

Fox realised he was a little drunk and that when he looked at her the little doll should be picked up, held and that perhaps if he held her she wouldn't break into fragments but would turn into flesh and then he would touch her in another way all together. He stood up a little unsteady on his feet.

"I'm thinking I've been a fool," he said.

"Why?"

"It doesn't matter. Now if I could just get my hat and coat I'll be getting on."

She stood and reached out her hand towards him. At that moment Fox didn't dare touch her. Eventually she gave up.

"Your coat and hat are in the hall."

In the street as Olympia opened the door they saw Schiller. He was staring at the outside of the hotel. On the wall next to the window an ankh had been daubed in thick white paint.

"They do not like us," he said.

Fox was glad to get away, needing a drink before he sobered up. In the Café Castringius there was someone sitting at his table.

"She's been waiting for you all morning," Max whispered.

Scowling over the cream of her einspanner was Frau Pfaff.

120

CHAPTER ELEVEN

She was wearing the same outfit as the first time Fox had seen her. Once again he noted that she didn't have an overcoat until he noted the shabby fur hanging on the coat rack near the entrance to the rest-rooms. It had once been something special but now the fur looked worn, patchy in places, gone through too many winters.

"I assumed our business was concluded," Fox said after he'd been polite and said hello. He wanted to be alone, to sit and drink alone.

"Are you drunk, Herr Fox?" Her nose wrinkled.

One of the soldiers had raped an old woman and then proceeded to blow her head off with a vermin gun. It had taken a lot of experience before he'd reached that stage; before he could take a rare, detached pleasure in it all. The augmentation wanted to revel in this but all the grappa Fox had drank meant he could block it out after the initial flashes.

"Yes," he said, "I'm drunk."

It could go on like this. If the visions from the death squad soldiers' life-bugs went on he'd have to do something other than drink them away. But for now grappa would have to do.

"But," he said, "I'm not quite drunk enough that we can't have a conversation Frau Pfaff. I hope you are well."

"Tolerably," she dabbed a napkin on her lip. "I want to talk to you about my sister."

"I asked her to contact you. She was going to write you a letter."

"I have received nothing but then my current address is probably unknown to her. Are you convinced she was telling the truth about the will?"

"I think you should see her Frau Pfaff. I could give her your telephone number."

"No."

"She wants to be reconciled to you."

Max bought grappa. He could tell from looking at Fox that it wasn't a morning for coffee. He put some rousted nuts down with it to in a show of maternal concern that sometimes overcame him with regular customers.

"But I am the wronged party," Frau Pfaff was saying, "Reconciliation should be in my gift not hers. What I would like is for you to go and see her again..."

"I don't think..."

"I am prepared to pay you."

"I don't want any more of your money..."

But then Fox thought about it for a moment. It might be an idea to see Frau Kastner again, to think about something apart from Olympia and Victor and all that. The things he had seen in the Castle would still be there, lurking in the circuits of the augmentation, held at bay for the moment by the warm glow of the grappa. But he would deal with that...

"Fine," he said, "I'll pay her a visit. Write your address down and I'll give it to her."

"That won't be necessary. You just relay anything she says to me."

"It's my condition for going."

She said nothing for a moment, played with the napkin in her hand.

"I don't want her to know my address," she said at last.

"Then give it to me and I'll forward any letter. You won't have to come here anymore."

Another pause.

"Very well."

She scowled again but picked up her bag from the floor and produced a pencil and a package of unopened notelets. She got one out and wrote, folded the paper and passed it to Fox. He glanced at the address and made sure no expression at all crossed his face. She lived in the Towers. Everything about her suddenly fell into place: the shabby coat and the guarded manner she had had all along. It couldn't have been easy to play the part that she did. People who lived in the Towers were broke, struggling. Fox didn't want to picture her there among junkies and drunken English. He put the paper inside his jacket pocket.

"I'll go this afternoon."

"Like this? In your state?"

"I'll have a nap before I go. Call me here tomorrow and I'll tell you how it went."

When she had gone Fox telephoned Felice. This time the secretary put him through.

"You shouldn't keep calling me here."

"It's fine. I gave a false name. Can you talk?"

"A bit. Fatty's getting an early lunch at the pool table."

"I figured out how you knew Frau Pfaff," Fox feigned a little ironic laugh, "One of the usual suspects around the Towers is she?"

"There are more people like that there than you'd think."

"Sure. Look, I need to see the case file on the Lazlo death."

She blew air and Fox felt it down the telephone line.

"I'd need a reason for that. I thought you were going to visit the Castle."

"I did. I'm going to tell you everything when I see you. There's stuff going on you should know about. If I can't see the case file then just get anything you've got on it, those bulletins you were talking about. Anything you've heard. One other thing…"

"Yes?" She didn't sound annoyed but then not amused either.

"Lazlo's body and whatever he had on him. Where is it?"

"Well," she said, "I assume he's body is in the morgue in Sparta. The nearest to the scene. There's no reason I know why it would have been taken anywhere else. Anything found with him would be bagged as evidence, so presumably that would be in the local police station in Sparta. The whole thing should have been handled there but it got given to Vogt. Sometimes these things happen."

"And if someone, say his brother or," and idea suddenly occurred, "his sister or niece, turned up they'd be able to view the body?"

"Has his niece turned up, Green?" she sounded weary.

"She could."

Finally Felice laughed.

"Fine," she said, "go and find yourself a niece and I'll see what I can do about the rest of it."

"Dinner tonight?"

"Tomorrow. Give me a bit more time. I'll come over about eight."

They said goodbye and now Fox could forget about the ultraclocks for a while. He'd borrow Max's Molina and head off to see Frau Kastner. After he'd sorted himself out. Quieten the relentless weight of those images he'd got from the soldiers' life-bugs. Packets of poison inside the head that could throb and leech coalescing jewels of violence. It felt like it might never stop, that the augmentation would keep dipping into it, making it a part of itself and therefore of Fox.

Cap pulled low he took a walk down Autocue Boulevard, where the first window displays for Saturnalia were already out. He went into the arcades to the chemist with its glowing carboys, their colours like semi-precious stones. Next door he saw that the cobblers was shut, boarded up with planks.

The chemists was a tiny shop, like most of these arcade places, with a counter the length of the far wall and shelved walls at each end stuffed with little bottles, jars and packages. The ruby and blue carboy light from the front window shone here too.

A man in his forties with a bald crown was at the counter, almost fading into the background of

125

even more shelves of merchandise behind him, and the coloured carboy light washing over him.

"What happened next door?" Fox asked.

He shrugged. "Renewal boys. They don't like the clockworks."

"What did they do?"

"Smashed the windows. Smashed the little cobbler. I don't know anything really."

"Sure." Fox didn't push it, the man was scared.

"What can I do for you?"

"I've been suffering from some anxiety recently, having trouble sleeping. That kind of thing."

Fox wasn't trying to be too convincing. It was a ritual you had to go through and he'd done it before when he needed to. You just had to give the chemist enough of a rationale to deal out the goods.

"Well," the chemist said, "we have a medicine that might be of help, you may have heard of it, clarity." He gave Fox a brief smile. "It's very effective for short term anxiety, depression, that sort of thing."

The chemist found the box on the shelf behind him almost without looking.

"I'm obliged to warn you," he said, placing the box on the counter, "that as well as the side effects listed on the literature in the box that clarity should not be used over a long term period. That it is potentially addictive."

Fox let him go on.

Back at his apartment Fox took two of the green pills, washed and shaved in the basin, changed into his other suit. He lay on the bed and got out the little beetle, wound it and let it run around his palm. He was still slightly drunk, the images of horror at bay. He waited for the drug to take effect.

Clarity created detachment so that everything is seen from a distance, not exactly without emotion but rather the emotions that you feel about something become another element that can be viewed, over there as it were.

It made the world a bit like a stage set, and the thing Fox needed it for, the clips of violence from the life-bugs, were still there but his revulsion, his fear, was next to them and he could step back at look at them. And in doing so, he could turn away so that it became peripheral.

Everything else became props on the stage set. The shops on Autocue Boulevard were just frontages and all the people on the pavement were like rotoscoped figures. As he drove through the Heights the trees by the road were thin, 2D like in ancient video games. The clouds were stickers he could have peeled off and crumpled into mushy blobs. When he laughed out loud as he drove his laugher became like those clouds, stuck in the air flat like a comic book speech bubble.

At the door of Villa Verloren Otto let him in.

"She's in the ballroom," he said, his shirt sleeves rolled up, a retired tin-soldier who'd taken up boxing.

The augmentation wanted to enter the dying worlds of the VR booth in the lobby but that was ok, Fox could see it all as though it were one book on a library shelf that he didn't need to reach for.

"It's upstairs," said Otto.

"What is?" said Fox caught up in his moment of refusing the augmentation.

"The ballroom. I can show you the way."

"I'll find it."

He was already on the stairs.

"At the end of the Shadow Walk," Otto's voice another little cloud.

Fox reached the top landing and then found himself through a door into a carnival of animals, a long gallery where the windows had been covered with black screens. Cut into these were shapes, like Balinese shadow puppets, so that on the wall opposite Rousseau tigers stalked in jungles of fern leaves, snakes coiled forever around the base of a giant kapok trees. The scene went on through the length of the gallery wall, the details as good as Lotte Reinger, a name popping into his head from something he'd seen long ago.

Through a clearing in the trees he saw a distant pavilion, and overhead an ibis flew.

The music had been there all the time, had always been there. Like the animals and the jungles, it too was like a shadow of something Fox couldn't quite work out. How difficult to describe music. Either you're someone who knows the vocabulary or you're not and the words are just jargon. (Jagged boxes in a lumber room. And Fox thought of de Chirico paintings and would again in a moment in the ruined ballroom. And perhaps he himself contained a lumber room, or a gallery, in the extended corridors of the augmentation's neural net?)

The music seemed square. A series of slow notes on a harpsichord that progressed and came back again. Compared to the jungle with its sinuous animals, the jungle where even a cupola was curved like something organic, the music had the structure of a building just like this house. Villa Verloren.

"Herr Fox, Evergreen, how delightful."

She stood in the open door at the end of the gallery, a silhouette for a moment until she stepped back a little into the light of the room behind her, which was lighter than the gallery with its population of shadows. Closer the exact nature of her attire became visible, her hair pinned up in the style of a brocaded ball gown its hem brushing the dust of the floorboards.

The ruined ballroom was still ornate in its decline, decorated with ceiling stucco, moulded patterns at the columned edges of arches leading out through French windows to a balcony. The other, interior, wall was covered with a tapestry, ripped, rotten with rain damage. A shaft of light entered through a hole in the roof. Broken chairs clung to the edges of the dance floor not daring to venture out. At the far end, standing like an outcrop of natural rock, an upended grand piano stood, its curved rear stuck in the air indignantly.

"Are you quite well, Evergreen?"

Where is the music coming from?

"I have this," she said.

On the seat of one of the chairs, this one more-or-less intact, an ancient gramophone was positioned, with a black disc spinning beneath its

129

heavy metal arm. The music flowed out through the trumpet horn.

"Froberger," she said. "Seventeenth century composer for the Hapsburg Emperor. We used to have such wonderful parties here after the data decay meant we brought our pleasures back from the ether. One of the more beneficial side effects."

She had done something to her face so that she looked younger, powdered it almost white, the chalky surface cracked around the edge of her lips, which were painted carmine. She had become like the plaster on the ceiling, brilliant still in places but with patches of mould, water stains, webs of cracks.

"Why don't we go out onto the balcony to get some air," she said.

Outside the balustrade had crumbled away in places making irregular crenulations so that it felt like the tower of a ruined fort looking out over the overgrown hill, thick with shrubs, the fencing fallen, the classical folly in the distance almost obscured by vegetation.

Cosima had pulled a housecoat around her, for there was slight breeze, yet it was still mild for the season.

"I wrote to my sister but there was no reply. Now, let me call Otto to fetch us something to drink and prepare an extra place for lunch."

"It was like a painting. I feel like I've been walking through a series of paintings."

Fox was startled by his own voice, as though the words had come out too heavy and had fallen to the ground below to lie there with the pieces of broken masonry and dead leaves. Hadn't he been asking something about the music a moment ago?

He sat on an iron chair, flakes of white paint and rust brushed off as he did.

"I'll be back in a moment," Cosima said, "just you wait there."

But he wandered back into the ballroom, with its upturned piano, its Froberger music moving in squares. Through an open door at the other end was a library, walls lined with bound volumes, the only incongruous feature the corrugated iron strips that had been bolted to the ceiling. Somewhere there must be a bedroom, a place to lie down for just a moment. But the next room, lit only with the light filtering in from the ballroom, was filled with faces and limbs, a collection of masks on one wall and puppets on the other. There were Genesia folk masks, the style and subject matter from the countryside, wolves, dogs, pigs and deer. All from an age when a village might be a clearing in a deep forest. Other masks of many varieties. Marionettes hanging from their tangled life-lines, characters he might have recognised if he'd tried.

"Why there you are. Otto has made us some refreshments. Downstairs in the Yellow Room."

"I'm in danger of falling in love with a puppet," Fox's voice said.

Everything that had happened seen as a set of pictures, scenes. Beginning with Victor and Olympia at the back of the Cabaret Vaucanson, Olympia's movements a dance leading to Pecheneg Square, the stage of the Cabaret and then the bedroom. To reach out and touch her for just a moment…

"Here, give me your hand, Evergreen. I think something to eat and drink will do you good."

"Because lovers' heads fire in the act of love, their neurons make patterns that I wanted to understand, but never could. I can see it now. It's the clarity doing what it does, making everything lucid. You see a puppet is only seen from the outside, everything I feel for her has nothing to do with the augmentation."

In the ballroom again. The upturned piano. No music now.

"Kleist wrote an essay, a dialogue on the puppet theatre. Have you read it, Evergreen?"

He didn't know at that moment if he had.

"The human dancer," she said, "can never approach the elegance of the puppet because the human can never lose the consciousness that they are performing a dance, there is always that self-consciousness…"

"That's it, that's it exactly… I think. It's not that she is clockwork it's just that with them…with her… You have to understand that for a long time the world has been something I can read. Machines that I can understand completely, and people, well I can't read them exactly but I know they have thoughts. With her there is nothing. Just what she says. What she does and what I see."

"But that is what it is like. For all of us."

"Yes. The problem of other minds. That's what it's called isn't it?"

"I think it's called love."

132

Was it really as simple as that?

"Please," said Frau Kastner, "your hand. Rather a hard grip."

"I'm sorry."

"Here sit down."

They were in the Yellow Room.

"I took clarity earlier," he said, "It was supposed to calm things down."

"Have some sachertorte."

Fox was suddenly ravenous and he ate, focusing on chewing, letting the sweetness of the chocolate play on his palette. He slurped coffee and then sipped at a little glass of zirbenlikör.

"I don't know precisely what clarity is," said Frau Kastner, "but I assume it's some type of selective serotonin reuptake inhibitor. Do you feel any better? Here have some of this."

Maybe she had seen Fox eyeing her cake. He took it and ate that too.

"I think so," he said.

"Why would you take something like that? I mean I've taken many things, when I was younger of course, but usually because I want to feel things more intently, not less so. And it doesn't seem to have had the desired effect anyway."

"It seemed like a good idea at the time," he said. It was a flat statement, meaningless.

The clarity was still there but it had become almost an object the way it made everything else an object. Fox could see it from a distance. He guessed the augmentation had done something to neutralise it, perceiving it as a threat perhaps. There seemed to be no sudden return to the scenes of violence from

133

the life-bugs, and Fox hoped that this too had been something that the augmentation had eventually understood was damaging Fox and therefore would eventually damage it too.

"Something happened to me," Fox said. "It was bad and I couldn't handle it. I thought clarity might help. It did in a way but it's not really my drug of choice."

"I remember when Edgar Wallace Verlaine decided he'd cultivate a habit for absinthe like his nineteenth century namesake. Made him irritating and sentimental. And then violently sick. Are you in some sort of trouble, Evergreen?"

"Yes. I think I am."

And the simple truth struck him, so that he didn't feel the urge to laugh it off or come out with a cliché like trouble was his business or he'd been in worse situations.

"Would you like to talk about it one old fossil to another?" she said.

There had been moments where the clarity had made it all make sense. They had got him to go into the Castle not on completely false pretences, because whatever was there was indeed connected to Victor. But his priority should have been other aspects of the case: the bodies, the scene, and Victor's associates. But the Masquerade were interested in the Castle, the potential coup. And Olympia? For her it was entirely about Victor. Wasn't it?

"I'm working on something," he said, "and I've got a bit lost I think."

He wouldn't mention the death squad, the coup.

"And do you think you'll be able to find your way again?"

"I need to do a bit more old fashioned detective work. First of all I need to see a body. I need to get into the morgue."

"How exactly?"

"I…"

It was a stupid thought and he knew he shouldn't say it because she would agree to it. To please him and because she would find it amusing.

"What is it?" she said.

"A fake aunt would be even better than a fake niece."

She poured two more glasses of the zirbenlikor.

"Are you about to cast me in a role?"

"I shouldn't get you involved."

"I was an actress. Well, of sorts. And I haven't done anything as interesting in a long while. Who will I play?"

"Bereaved aunt of a man who was killed on the railway tracks. I can be your manservant, who'll be at your side. A friend of the deceased called Mond has contacted you because Lazlo, the corpse, was registered at her hotel as his address in the city. We need to get in and see as much as possible before they call the police who could be interested to talk to anyone connected. The good thing is I don't think they're as interested in this Lazlo as the ultraclock who was with him."

"Is this why you came here today, Evergreen?"

She laughed. It was loud enough to have Otto put his head around the door. He scowled for a moment and retreated.

"No," Fox said.

He handed her a slip of paper with her sister's phone number. Then, after a moment, the piece of paper on which Frau Pfaff had written her address.

She looked at it.

"Why would she be living there?"

"I expect because she can't afford anywhere else."

"This is terrible. I must go at once."

"I think it would be better if you made contact with her first."

She looked at the address again then folded the paper and held it in her lap.

"Very well," she said. "Now I'll prepare for my role and we'll go and see this body of yours."

CHAPTER TWELVE

Frau Kastner reappeared dressed as a smarter, better tailored, version of her sister, a respectable lady of the upper middle class, who would terrify officious civil service bureaucrats of the sort Fox hoped worked at the Sparta morgue.

"Are you ready to go?"

"I'll get Otto to fetch the car from the garage."

"I've got a car."

"And what kind of car is it?"

Fox told her about Max's pride and joy but she didn't seem very impressed.

"If we are going to do this, Evergreen, then we are going to have to do a lot of bluffing and I'd rather look as though I've got a good hand to play."

Her good hand was a Rolls Royce Phantom III reissue, one of the late hydrogen combustion models. It was black, beautifully preserved and Otto even put on a chauffer's cap for the occasion.

Fox followed in the Molina. He'd suggested that when they got to the outskirts of Sparta that they park somewhere. Trying to manoeuvre the Rolls Royce around the narrow streets of Sparta would be difficult but Frau Kastner insisted they went for the full impact, so Fox parked the Molina and got into the Rolls. In the event it wasn't difficult because the morgue wasn't too far into the warren of streets and the one real difficult road, lined with the stalls of a little vegetable market, was made more navigable when the costers moved their barrows and gawped at the Phantom. Only a few of the kids threw fruit and it was mostly soft fruit.

"And so we have arrived," Frau Kastner announced as the Phantom slide against the kerb opposite the Sparta morgue.

It was an unobtrusive place, its identity given only by a small metal plaque on the wall next to the door. There was a wide entrance for vehicles next to this door, leading into some sort of courtyard through an arch formed by the second storey of the building like an old coaching inn.

The front door was locked and so Fox rang the bell. This meant that the thin spotty youth who opened the door got a good look at the Phantom and Max standing in his cap beside it.

"Young man," said Frau Kastner, "I have come to pay my respects to my unfortunate nephew. Lead the way Herr Knight…"

Knight was Fox, she had decided this.

She gave Fox her arm. She wasn't unsteady on her feet at all and he wondered how old she really was. She was one of those people you thought would go on forever.

"Madam," said the youth, "Do you have an appointment? We operate a system of appointments here and it is not usual for someone to just come in of the street…"

"Nonsense," pronounced Frau Kastner, "You'll let me see Lazlo at once and that's the end of it."

Spotty youth mumbled another sentence that had the word appointment in it as she swept past him into the building.

The inside passage had a half-glass wall looking into an office, and this office in turn had a half glass wall that showed what looked like a laboratory. The office had some pot plants, a calendar with views of the Elver Marshes and an Italian coffee maker.

"If you'd just like to...wait a moment," the youth said.

"What?" said Frau Kastner, as though talking to a deaf person.

"I'd have to inform someone at the police station..."

"Whatever for?" The idea was simply unfathomable.

"Doctor Miller is out... and it's usually the police who arrange these... visits. I mean in a case like this..."

"I just want to see my dear nephew Lazlo, is that too much to ask?"

"If you could just..."

Fox was already going into the office with Frau Kastner following with a backward step, still facing the young man.

"Madam..." he was saying.

"What is your name?" Frau Kastner asked him.

"Rudy."

"Well, Rudy," she said, "You've been most helpful. I'll be sure to mention it when next I'm at dinner with...." she appeared to suddenly run out of steam. "Who is that little man, Herr Knight?"

"You mean the Minster of Health, madam?" Fox chipped in.

"Of course, that's him."

Fox passed through the office into the laboratory where there was an autopsy table and storage cupboards, a bench with a microscope and lab glassware. There were doors labelled bathroom, medical waste and morgue. Fox held open the door to the morgue for Frau Kastner as though she were arriving at the opera. Rudy followed for a few steps then seemed to think for a moment and went back to the office and picked up the telephone receiver.

The cooler drawers were conveniently labelled and Fox pulled out L. Heck DOD 11th October. For a moment he tried to recall Lazlo as he'd seen him in life but it had been only once and Fox had been drunk. He pulled back the sheet.

"Oh dear," said Frau Kastner.

It looked as though Lazlo had been shot in the chest. There was no autopsy scar and Fox figured he was pretty much as they'd found him, still in the suit he'd been wearing that night. The wound wasn't neat and clean but blackened and singed.

There were things Fox knew which he wished he didn't. One of those things was guns. And the augmentation took a delight in the exact specifications of them and the burnt wound in Lazlo's chest meant that he'd been shot with a plasma weapon. This was a heavy version, large looking, since it had torn a big hole in Lazlo's chest. But Fox could see now that this was an exit wound, and Lazlo had been shot in the back. It was a vicious weapon, that killed efficiently and almost always without fail. Fox thought of the commanding officer of the death squad at the

Castle. Such a person wouldn't flinch from using such a weapon, but that didn't really mean anything.

The fact that there was no autopsy scar was interesting. It really did seem as though no-one was interested in investigating Lazlo, they were quite content to store him in the local morgue, while the police case was quietly forgotten. The sudden arrival of an aunt would be one of those things that could complicate things and when Fox looked over to the office it seemed that the young man had a serious look on his face as he spoke into the phone, put it down and started to come into the morgue.

"Young man," Frau Kastner said as Rudy arrived, "I'd like dear Lazlo's remains and his effects retuned to me as soon as possible."

"I think you can talk to Inspector Vogt about that. I've just left a message for him to say that you're here. If you would just wait in the reception room..."

He stood at the door his hand indicating that they should go back through.

Frau Kastner embarked on her finale, letting herself go weak at the knees so that Fox and Rudy had to help her to a chair in the office.

"Perhaps," she said, "if I could just have a glass of water."

Rudy went. Presumably there was a kitchen somewhere.

"Let's go," Fox said.

"How did I do?"

"Command performance."

At the door Rudy caught up with them holding out a glass.

"Don't you want your water?"

"I'm quite recovered, thank you."

"Aren't you going to wait?"

"No no, I think after all I should lie down. Inspector Vogt you said. I'll contact him directly myself."

Rudy watched them cross the road where Otto opened the back door and helped the aunt in. All across the street Fox and Frau Kastner had tried to stay as dignified as possible even managing to hold in their laugher until the Phantom pulled away.

It was a wheeze, a hoot, couldn't have been funnier. (But even as he'd been laughing some part of Fox, perhaps still affected by the clarity, had watched that laughter crystallise into something brittle and sad, like dead coral.)

***

Fox got them to drop him back where he'd parked the Molina and said goodbye. Then he drove back to the morgue and parked a little further up the street and watched the reflection of the morgue in the side mirror of the car. He wanted to see how much Vogt cared about someone poking around this case, how quickly he would get there when he got the message Rudy had left for him.

Vogt showed up within the hour in an unmarked car. He went in with Downs. They would be listening to Rudy describe the lady, the car, perhaps even the lady's companion, but without Fox's cilia showing he was non-descript and there was no reason for Vogt to make the connection.

When they came out ten minutes later Fox followed as they drove through Sparta, making the

142

usual slow progress and Fox had to stop abruptly as he came into the Maskmarkt. The market was up and running and Fox had to skirt around the edges as Vogt's car had started to do, stopping every few feet to let the market-goers cross from the edges of the square or back again, or to let someone pushing a barrow get into the market to join the stalls already there. The stalls sold masks, puppets, toys and books, there were food stalls and little tents where fortune tellers had been doing their business for hundreds of years.

If Fox got stuck behind Vogt then the inspector might start to take notice of him so Fox pulled over for a moment. Then he saw that Vogt had stopped too, parking out in front of one of the warehouses on the edge of the square.

Vogt and Downs waited there in their car and Fox watched them wait. The street lights came on and stall holders in the market yelled a little more to get the last sales of the day before it was time to pack up.

The wait went on until, coming out from the stalls of the market, Fox saw Lotte. She was carrying a small valise and wobbling a little in high heels on the cobblestones. She crossed over the road from the centre of the square and opened the door of Vogt's car. Fox was sure that by the time she nestled on the back seat next to Vogt she was already Lola Hello once again.

They drove on and Fox followed. Out of Sparta and eventually onto Autocue Boulevard where a group of men in the demi-uniforms of the Renewal Society were standing over people on the ground.

Fox wanted to stop, to understand what was going on but he needed to keep up with Vogt, who was heading south and then round to Khazar Gate. They went down a side street but Fox drove on knowing the place, a little cul-de-sac with the only notable feature there being the Club Adder. Fox parked on a side street a bit further on and walked back.

He stood in the doorway of the closed delicatessen opposite. There was no way he could go into Club Adder even if he had wanted to. They were in there all right as their car was parked outside. The Club Adder considered itself classy, but the clientele were higher ranks of police and army, a few government types of a particular leaning and journalists who had survived the era of the Comedians by writing glowing reports about their strong and necessary measures.

Fox had expected Vogt to do something after visiting the morgue, perhaps contact interested parties in the case. And perhaps he was, right now, inside the club. But it didn't matter, Fox was curious anyway, about Lola he supposed. He'd give it a while before his hunger and (to be honest) thirst drove him back to the Café Castringius.

It was when it began to rain that he decided to call it a day that as shiny black Zil pulled up outside the club. Fox would let them get out before going.

Then he saw Lola coming out of the club. She looked drunk or drugged and she was leaning on someone as she clutched her little valise. The person she was leaning on was tall and wearing a fancy dress uniform. It was Captain Kardos, the commanding officer of the death squad that Fox had seen at the Castle. Across the narrow street Fox was near enough that he started to pick up flashes from the officer's life-bug and the cilia began to stir beneath his hat giving him an instant headache because they wanted more. Villages burnt as the officer watched, soldiers killed and he watched.

Then they were gone and somehow Fox had the wherewithal to get out of the street before Vogt and Downs come out and found him, slumped down in the deli doorway.

He wasn't in a good way now, which might account for the fact that someone was able to sneak up on him just as he was approaching the Molina. A hood was flung over his head and his arms locked behind his back. Then he was bundled into a car and driven away.

CHAPTER THIRTEEN

The room was cold. From beneath the hood nothing could be seen, not even the occasional shift in darkness that sometimes happens when that darkness is imperfect. Smell of something, like a stables but stronger although faded, dung, stale animal piss.

There was a loud steady ticking. Then a voice intoning, echoing the way voices did in the Cathedral.

"For my thoughts are not your thoughts, neither are your ways my ways, declares the Lord. An assurance by God that his people will be delivered from slavery for though they might not conceive of an end to their suffering the conception of God is infinite and deliverance is at hand.

"Don't try to speak. Not yet.

"You saw, didn't you?

"On Autocue Boulevard, being made to kneel on the pavement and clean it. There is nothing wrong with such work except when it is used to degrade. The people on the ground, humiliated, were both flesh people and clockwork people. The Renewal Society finds those to hate in every quarter. What they cannot perceive is that perhaps, far from being inferior the people of clockwork might be the superior beings, whose understanding surpasses theirs. It is an interesting thought is it not? No don't speak, just listen."

The ticking of a clockwork mechanism doesn't allow for silence. The voice that had been speaking was soft, without rancour, but also without doubt or hesitation. The clockwork ticked on. Then many voices at once.

"My thoughts are not your thoughts. Neither are my ways your ways. My face will not imitate your face. My gestures will not be yours. You will read into my face the things you want to see there but they will not be the things my thoughts are breeding. The control of identity is the pivotal weapon of the repressive apparatus of the system."

Then the first voice again.

"Thirty years ago you come out of the west into the city. After you had left London you settled in Paris hoping that the war that had begun in the north would not spread to the old heartlands of Europe but stay confined to the Arctic, Scandinavia, Iceland. Let the United States of Europe and the Northern League with their various allies fight it out. But of course that was never going to be.

"It is difficult to know what happened to you after the destruction of Paris. You have no official military record, which is unusual for someone like you. Presumably as it took you two years to cross from Paris to Genesia you had to rely on more than just your wits to stay alive."

There was another sound now, between the words of the voice. Cooing of birds, undulating throb so unlike the relentlessness of the ticking. Perhaps that sound had been there all the time but was only noted in the moments before the slow flapping of wings sounded, echoing against the walls of the enclosed space.

"It doesn't matter that you are a stranger here. Cities are made of strangers, who shape them and make them their own. But as you understand you have come into a particular situation and as long as you have been here you have tried to remain outside that situation.

"Please do not speak. Don't struggle."

Another voice.

"Once upon a time there lived a happy prince who wanted more than anything for the people of his land to be happy too. To make them happy he put on parties and carnivals and decreed that once a year the ancient feast of Saturnalia be celebrated when masters would wait on their servants and servants would become masters.

"In his own court the prince delighted in all manner of entertainments, dances and concerts, magic shows, puppets and masquerades. Performers of every sort flocked to his wonderful palace. Thus it was that one day four wandering comedians arrived and humbly begged the prince to employ them. There was Froggy the fast talking cigar smoker, Zero the lover of explosions, Blanco the expressionless one and Mute who although he could speak, chose not to speak, preferring to use a bicycle horn..."

"It wasn't long after their debut as court performers that their radio broadcasts had begun. At first gently mocking the Count for his indulgences. Then the tone altered."

Voices came in, imitating the voices of the Comedians.

FROGGY: The Count loves all the people.

BLANCO: The people love the Count.

FROGGY: They'll be cheering at one of his concerts when the city falls to the invaders.

(The invaders could have been any of the sides in the war, depending on who was the bigger news story that week.)

ZERO: We should strengthen the army.

FROGGY: The Count has a navy.

BLANCO: Of model boats.

FROGGY: But they are lovely model boats.

(The enemy would never be just external.)

FROGGY: My laundry lady has been replaced by a talking clock.

BLANCO: For her it's always wash time.

ZERO: Basically she's a washing machine.

FROGGY: She has rights! The Count says so.

ZERO: Rights for washing machines!

MUTE (Hoots his horn).

"Then, one day, the Count had had his accident. Along with his wife. The Comedians would continue his good work. Perhaps moderate some of his more silly excesses. It appeared that the people were willing to give these lovable rogues a chance.

"They continued to perform. But now all the world's a stage and they were the main, no the only attraction. We were the captive audience. Each on our numbered seat, unmoving. Spellbound by their spectacle until they needed a victim to participate in their act..."

Fox was having trouble following this. There was a blurring of the line between metaphor and literal meaning. But then hadn't that been the way with the Comedians?

"Everyone would do as they were told. It was all in place, ready to assume the grandeur of a vicious phantasmagoria if their reign had gone on. We were willing to resist, subvert any fixed role they tried to foist on us. We would not be the audience. We would be the Masquerade."

The voice had stopped.

The flapping of wings sounded again and in the silence the ticking of clockwork and now perhaps another ticking softer, the faintest of sounds...

"Take off his hood."

Paper lanterns hung from staves that had been stuck into the earth floor of the room. Their light glowed with shades of lemon, saffron...

It was a ruin of some kind, an arched room above. Ahead the walls were broken, overgrown with ivy. Beyond this was what looked like the bars of a giant cage.

On plush but almost rotten furniture masked people had arranged themselves. A woman lying on a chaise, the red velvet torn, bleeding dirty upholstery. She was wearing the mask of a beaked medieval pest doctor, its skin bone white. Others in arm chairs, old office chairs on wheels, one standing to one side someone in a robe covering their entire body wearing a noh mask.

From a perch on a piece of broken wall a dove flew across the room to the opposite wall. Further down a man was pissing into rotten straw.

The next voice, a woman's. Somehow familiar but distorted by the mask.

"We understand that you have information that might be valuable to us."

She spoke from the chaise, hardly moving, just the merest side winding of shoulders stirring long black hair.

"What is this place?" Fox said, his voice sounding odd here, throat dry. He was in a chair, arms tied behind the back of it.

"It is the old zoological gardens. Count Septimus took all the animals to live in the Castle and it has been derelict for a long time. All the breeding programmes had broken down by then. Contact with other zoos being almost impossible. Count Septimus tried to bring in specimens of giraffe and Meer cat from Pressberg but nothing came of it. I think they all just grew old and died in the Castle."

"Why did you cover my face if you were going to tell me where I am anyway?"

"No-one," said Doctor Pest, "enters the Masquerade with their face uncovered. And from us you would be disappointed if we did not indulge in some theatrics."

"And after tonight," she added, "our residency here will be over."

She rose from the chaise, sliding her legs off so that her dress rode up a little. Fox was sure it was Demi there, but the mask was not just about concealment, in it she had become someone else. They all had.

"We need to know about the plans you recovered from the Castle."

"I would like to ask…"

"In exchange," she said, "we will answer your questions about Victor. Within reason."

"First you'll have to untie me. And then I would like something to drink."

The pissing man came forward. He had on a clown mask. He wiped his hands on his baggy trousers. It could have been Pozzo.

"I'll get him something," the clown said.

Someone untied Fox's hands and when he glanced behind him there were other masked figures standing and sitting, some further back silhouettes just out of reach of the lantern lights. The clown set a plate of bread and olives in front of Fox and a bottle of Weiss bier. The woman in the pest mask watched him eat and drink.

"How many possible scenarios did you access, Herr Fox?"

"Twenty six." he said through a mouthful of bread.

"And you can recall them all?"

"Yes. You have some kind of database or file storage I can transfer them to?"

"Oh no," she said, "We couldn't risk that. Computing resources are rather fragile are then not? There is the obvious risk of contamination, decay…. I'm afraid you are going to have to do this the hard way."

"Well, we'd better get started. I have a date tomorrow."

They led Fox through the zoo, alleys lined with cages and aviaries in various states of dilapidation. There were paper lanterns tied to cage bars here and there. They looked fragile, as though rain or even a strong breeze would extinguish and ruin them. The woman in the pest mask that Fox took to be Demi went at the front of a procession, Fox in the middle.

They crossed an overgrown field with some benches on it, it might have been a picnic area, and ahead was an impressive looking single storey building, neat and art deco, with a brick relief inscription over the door. Zoologisch Gesselschaft, Genesia.

This must have once been the admin building or the research department. Demi, if it was her, led Fox into a corridor and then office. There was electric lighting here, harsh after the soft glow from the paper lanterns. Fox could hear a generator somewhere, and when they had opened the door a heavy tick and the skeletal clockwork figure of Schiller who was at a desk.

He wore a mask that looked like a Picasso painting, which might have been where Picasso got the idea from, one huge eye on the left, a great flat nose and mouth full of symmetrical teeth curling round. The left side of the face showed a hooded snake.

Beside him was another masked figure standing to the side of the desk, the mask was of a dark-skinned man with a stylised moustache. From the body it could have been either Bob or Karl, or perhaps just another ultraclock of similar build.

"Hello Herr Fox" said Schiller, "We haven't met before. You can call me Senni, demon of blindness. This is Catrine," he indicated his moustached companion. "You've already met Doctor Pest." He nodded towards the woman Fox took to be Demi. "I think we ought to commence with this right away, don't you?"

"Sure," said Fox.

"Do the scenarios have a key attached that suggests ordering?" Schiller (it must be Schiller) asked.

"There is a datestamp from the underlying system catalogue. That gives the sequence in which they were created."

"And you can recall this?"

"Yes."

"Remarkable."

"But I don't know how you want me to tell you this. Each scenario is... complex. Personnel in the police force, army and government are there. There are other people, well I take them to be people, who are codenamed. Each person is cross referenced to different times, map co-ordinates and associated with data such as utilities, proximity to certain landmarks. Whatever produced these scenarios has constructed an impressive set of interrelated multi-dimensional objects."

"That's all right," Schiller said, "We just need to decide on the likelihood of particular scenarios and we do that by tracking a number of variables. For each scenario just tell us the date and time and the starting position of codenamed Sword and codenamed Hierophant."

"Can I have another of those beers?"

It was tedious work. The others drifted off just leaving Fox with Schiller/Senni. From somewhere there was the faint sounds of music and laughter, beyond the sounds of the generator and the ticking of Senni. Senni scribbled down the names and times and positions for each scenario Fox recounted. Apart from a few police and government ministers, Fox recognised few of them.

"Why is Vogt so important," Fox asked when they'd stopped for a moment so Fox could have a sip of beer to wet his throat.

"He isn't really. He just represents a link between the police and the Renewal Society. At the moment the Renewal Society will not act independently. They don't seem yet to have produced a charismatic leader in the way these sorts of organisations need to. They will rally to the reappearance of one of the Judges and press for Genesia to join the Northern League.

"And the others? Sword? Hierophant?"

"You shouldn't concern yourself, Herr Fox."

"It's hard not to."

"I think you should perhaps focus on your task at hand. What you have been hired to do is to find out who killed Victor."

"Then help me."

"Let us just finish what we are doing here."

The music grew quieter, voices eventually died down. Only the sound of the generator and the ticking remained. When Fox and Senni emerged from the building the paper lanterns were out. It must have been close to dawn, Venus pierced the clear sky.

"Where are we going?" Fox asked.

"Someone will take you back to your car."

They walked through the zoo as the dark was just beginning to fade into the grey of dawn. The cages and aviaries contained their own darkness along with the brooding absence of their long departed occupants.

"I want to know about Victor."

They arrived back to where Fox had been strapped to the chair. It was now a chamber of early shadows.

"Where is everyone?" he asked.

"They're here. Or not."

"Schiller..."

Fox thought it was a mistake as soon as he said it.

"So you think I am Schiller."

"Are you saying you're not?"

Doves were lined up on the broken wall.

"You know Strindberg, Herr Fox?"

The augmentation suddenly prompted some memory.

"Swedish playwright."

"In The Dream Play he says he has tried to emulate the logical shape of a dream. In a dream the imagination spins, weaving new patterns, a mixture of memories, experiences, free fancies, incongruities and improvisations. The characters split, double, multiply, and evaporate.

"What you have to understand Herr Fox is that you are not the dreamer, you are part of the dream.

156

Now just walk ahead through this building to the other side and you'll find the zoo car park, your car will be waiting there for you."

"And what about Victor?"

"Victor made a deal with someone to get into the Castle. What he saw there decided his course of action. He agreed to work with us. He'd got into the Castle by promising to enhance the capabilities of the thing that is there. This was just a ruse to get access to that thing. If he could he would take it to Harmony and lead the ultraclocks with him. That was his business not ours. He planned to go back to the Castle. That's when he and Lazlo were found dead. We believe that whoever his contact in the Castle was probably killed him."

"Vogt?"

"Vogt is a pawn. A rook at most. I suppose he has a certain range. It could be. We don't know. It isn't our priority now. You're supposed to be the detective, Herr Fox. You're the one who should find out."

Fox found the Molina where he'd been told it would be. He drove home intending to sleep all day before meeting Felice for dinner.

CHAPTER FOURTEEN

Fox went to dinner as himself, leaving his hat on the bed. He'd thrown water on his face, had a quick grappa while he shaved and headed out. He realised he should have made even more of an effort because his suit was crumpled and collar dirty while Felice had scrubbed up nicely wearing a sort of vintage office-girl outfit in black with a white blouse, and black leather bag. She was already at Fox's table in the Café Castringius sipping a glass of Frascati which was the best you could get these days given what had happened to France.

"You look like you've spent the night on a park bench," she said.

"The monkey house. Or else the lion enclosure. Maybe it was Meer cats. I don't suppose it matters much."

"Sometimes, not often, I have no idea what you are talking about."

"Well. I said I would level with you didn't I? Let me just get a drink inside me and I'll tell you all about my night with the Masquerade and what this has really been about all along. As far as I understand it myself."

Max came over with a grappa right on cue.

"You need to take better care of yourself," Max said, "At least get some food inside you to soak up all that booze. You tell him Felice."

Fox ordered pork knuckle and Felice bratwurst.

"You look nice," Fox told her.

"Thank you."

A smiled creased her face, raising her damaged cheek.

Then they talked. Fox told her that he'd been hired by a group of ultraclocks to investigate the murder, as they saw it, of one of their number, Victor. Lazlo as far as they were concerned was just a part of that case.

While Fox was talking Max bought the main dishes and then put down before them bowls with potato salad, sweet and sour cabbage and sauerkraut.

"Eat, eat," he commanded.

Fox carried on talking taking an occasional bite.

He told her how the ultraclocks had persuaded him that the key to Victor's death was something he was investigating in the Castle, but that there was another agenda to that whole caper as well. The Masquerade had wanted to know was being planned there and Fox had found that out for them.

"So you're working for the Masquerade?"

"No," Fox said, "I don't think so. Some of them might be in it. But not Olympia."

"Olympia?"

He didn't really want to talk about Olympia to Felice beyond the essentials.

"Artiste at the Cabaret Vaucanson. They all work there in some capacity or other. I think her and Victor were an item."

"An item? They're machines. How does that work?"

Olympia was a machine. They were all machines. Intricate and complex clockwork. And yet Felice was wrong. They weren't machines in the way she meant.

"I have no idea at all."

"Not part of your investigation?"

"What?"

She was giving him a look, sceptical, knowing. Fox didn't want to think about what that meant.

"Do you really think," she said, "there's going to be some sort of coup?"

"You saying there's no whispers among the police? From what I can tell there were plenty of serving officers involved."

"Whispers. I don't know. Cops are always moaning about politicians. But they wouldn't let me in on it. They know what my views are. And the Towers are a bit of a backwater."

"You're flagged as a 'no'."

"What?"

"In the scenarios. You're flagged as a 'no'. You're not deployed on any of the maps. In fact the Towers don't really figure at all. Everything is around the Castle, the missile array, and the major roads, Autocue Boulevard, Khazarstrasse.... twenty six variations."

"What about Fatty?"

"Fatty's a no-no too."

She smiled. "Good."

She poured herself another glass of wine.

"What are you going to do?" she said.

"I'm going to find out who killed Victor and Lazlo. I'm going to find out what Victor was really interested in up at the Castle."

"What about this coup?"

"Nothing. If anyone's going to stop it it's the Masquerade and I've told them everything I know. What do you expect me to do, write a letter to the Gazette?"

She raised her eyebrows at that.

"I've got something for you," she said.

She bought out a small envelope from her bag and handed it over to Fox. He took it but she held on to the other end.

"It's nothing much," she said, "I told you I couldn't get the case notes. It's just the bulletin and, well, I had an idea. Evidence is always logged separately from the case notes, way of making sure all the stuff in stores doesn't get cast adrift from whatever case it belongs to."

She finally let go of the envelope.

"Now," she said, "I don't even now the serial number of the Lazlo case but I said I needed to check something that happened over in Sparta, mumbled something about it possibly being connected to a crime in the Towers I checked the Lazlo case while I was looking. I memorised what I could. It's there. In the envelope."

A list of things found with Lazlo.

Gold cigarette lighter.

Packet of Azimuth cigarettes.

Suit of clothes etc.

A little semi-automatic pistol known as a Jenny Wren.

161

Automaton. Badly damaged in chest area. Head had been removed and not found in vicinity.

"Victor's head was missing?"

"That's what it says."

Also in the envelope was the bulletin. Bare facts about the crime.

Body of male approximately late forties. Gunshot wound. Body discovered 1.13 am. Kirovwerk, Siding 11, Sparta. Any information to be forwarded to Inspector Vogt/Inspector Downs.

So at last Fox know precisely where the bodies had been found. Not a place that anybody had any business being. It figured that Victor and Lazlo had met someone in Sparta, their connection with the Castle probably, met them in Sparta and then everything had gone wrong and they'd been taken out. It was not far from Gutunberg where the Renewal Society were. The link between the Renewal Society and the Castle was Vogt. But there were probably other links, ones that perhaps even the Masquerade didn't know about. Vogt had been in Club Adder with Lola when some minion had shown up to tell him about the murder.

"What you thinking about?" Felice asked.

"That I'm going to have to go over to the Kirovwerk, siding eleven and see if the police missed anything. Why, what are you thinking about?"

"Pudding."

Max appeared like a rabbit out of a hat and began to reel through a list of delights. Felice was smiling at Fox and up at Max. Fox thought she had finally decided what to have when she frowned. She was looking over Fox's shoulder, towards the door.

Olympia was there. She was dressed the way she was the first time Fox had seen here in the backstreets with Victor and Lazlo, her short skirt and flash of garter.

"Your employer, I assume," Felice said.

The few other customers were all eyes. Max was ushering her towards Fox's table and getting a chair for her.

"I hope you don't mind me intruding on you like this, Herr Fox," she said still standing, "After what happened I was rather concerned about you."

"Why?" said Felice, "What was the matter with him?"

"Please," Fox said, "sit down."

As she sat Fox was reminded of a marionette being carefully lowered, nothing clumsy and awkward, but rather what Kleist had said: that unknowing grace.

"Shouldn't you be at the Cabaret Vaucanson?" Fox said.

"In about an hour," she said, "Perhaps you'd like to come. Both of you."

"Herr Fox is forgetting his manners," said Felice, "I'm an old friend. Felice."

"Olympia."

The looked at each other, working out how the greeting should go.

"Have you recovered, Herr Fox?" Olympia asked.

"Sure."

"What happened, Green?"

163

Max was hovering somewhere in Fox's peripheral vision, not knowing what to do with someone who didn't eat or drink.

"The soldiers at the Castle had a rather nasty effect," Fox tapped his head.

"I'm glad you feel better," said Olympia.

Felice poured herself more wine. The bottle was empty.

"Poor Herr Fox," she said, "Gets himself in such a mess, don't you think Olympia? He should be more careful shouldn't he?"

"Why don't you have coffee?" Max asked.

When the coffee arrived Felice sipped hers and tried to make small talk.

"What do you do at the Cabaret?"

"Sing. Dance."

"Do you enjoy it?"

"Of course."

"I've never been."

"You should come. Come tonight."

Felice glanced at Fox for a moment. He was not sure he could imagine her at the Cabaret Vaucanson, among the knife jugglers, musical automatons and shitting clowns.

"Perhaps another time," she said. She had her handbag in front of her on the table. But she did not move.

"I'll see you home," Fox said.

"It's all right," she said standing, "I'll walk down to Pecheneg Square and get a cab."

"No," said Olympia, "I have intruded. Please forgive me."

164

And before Fox could do anything Olympia had stood up too. Felice and Olympia stood there facing each other.

"Let's all go for a walk then," Fox said, wishing there was some grappa handy, or at least some more wine, "a nice walk down to Pecheneg Square. And then after Felice has got a cab Olympia can get one to the Cabaret Vaucanson. How does that sound?"

Felice looked pissed off at the idea and Fox had no idea how Olympia felt, but a few minutes later they were all walking the backstreets of Little Alex towards Pecheneg Square.

"You really don't need to do this, Green," said Felice, "I can, kind of, look after myself."

She hadn't quite needed to pat where her gun was kept in its shoulder holster.

On Pecheneg Square there was a taxi rank where there were always one or two cabs waiting.

"Well," said Felice, "be careful, Green. Goodbye Olympia. It's been nice to meet you."

Fox should have said something then, about seeing her again, about owing her one, but it would have sounded hollow.

He watched the cab go off.

"Well," said Olympia, "We'd better get going. I wouldn't want to disappoint my audience, would I?"

They didn't get a cab but walked through more of the backstreets of Little Alex. There weren't many people about but they came into a little crowd down some street of closed up delicatessens, jewellers, a pawn broker. There were men there,

165

boys really, in those semi-uniforms. They looked like they were dancing, doing little backward jumps and then going forward kicking their legs.

Something squawked, flapped its wings. The boys drew back again.

"Oh no," said Olympia.

In the midst of this little crowd of boys was a large bird, an automaton in the form of an eagle. It was magnificent, its feathers catching the lamp light, looking as though they'd been formed of delicate folds of gold leaf.

One of the boys kicked, catching it on the bill so that its whole head flew back and it squawked once again. It flapped its wings trying to alight but another boy bashed down on its back with his fists.

"Stop that," said Olympia. She made to go forward but Fox barred her with his outstretched arm.

A couple of the boys turned. The others carried on tormenting the clockwork eagle.

"You beasts," said Olympia.

The two who had turned walked a little way towards Fox and Olympia. The others were taking notice now, the bird left alone for a moment, flapping its wings in panic.

"Well," said one of the boys, curly haired, ruddy. "Have you come to help us with this vermin?"

He laughed and the others joined in. There was absolutely no mirth in that laughter.

"Let the bird go," Fox said.

They were lined up now facing Fox. Behind them the eagle stretched itself and rose up into the air, flapping around for a moment before souring higher and perching on the edge of a rooftop. It stayed there, looking down at the scene.

"Look at these two freaks," said curly hair to the others, "What's the matter with this one, he's got worms or something coming from his head. I'm not sure I can bear to look at him. I don't think he's fit to be walking the streets."

It was a little speech. Fox could imagine the kid standing on a milk crate.

"And a clockwork whore," said another, as he produced from his belt a wicked looking nightstick.

"You should all go home to your families," Fox said. "And not come out again until you've learnt some manners. Come on Olympia."

Fox intended to walk away, to turn back and go by another route all together. But he know it was never going to be. It was the one with the nightstick who came first, made brave by his weapon. Then the others were emboldened by him.

He was a kid, not used to preying on anything that might fight back. He wouldn't be here at all without the others but once he'd come at Fox the kid couldn't lose face in front of them. The augmentation noted, almost bored, the interesting brain patterns of human violence.

The boy swung the nightstick and Fox moved out of the way. As the boy tried to recover Fox thrust the ball of his hand up hard into his nose. Fox felt the nose shatter as the boy screamed.

The others were on him then.

"Run," he shouted to Olympia.

But Fox couldn't see where she was…

The boys weren't very good at this but they didn't need to be because there were enough of them, punching and kicking from behind. He might have heard Olympia cry out and he tried to get in some blows, to get whoever it was away from his head…

His face was against the cold of the cobblestones. Then someone was screaming.

No one was hitting him now.

When he looked up he saw, in the wash of yellow light from the street lamps, the boys under attack. Three masked men were swinging long staves, practised movements, striking quickly to faces.

Curly hair was getting up from where he'd fallen, clutching his bloody check. He looked on as his comrades were beaten. Fox saw Olympia on the ground, lent against the wall. She was still, a doll discarded in a nursery.

Curly hair took a step towards Fox. Then the air filled with wings and talons as the clockwork eagle fell onto the boy's face, ripping away at his eyes.

"They're just kids," Fox said.

But no-one was listening. He went over to Olympia. Her chest was rising and falling and she was looking at him.

"It's all right," she said, "They did nothing more than push me to the ground."

The eagle took flight leaving curly hair a mess, on his knees, making fast little groans. Further down the street the other boys were laid out on the ground. The masked men had gone.

***

The Cabaret Vaucanson had had its front windows smashed. The show had gone on with a chainsaw juggler on stage. In the green room were Bob, Karl, Schiller and Mond. All across Little Alex groups of Renewal Society boys had been roaming, smashing windows of shops where ultraclocks worked, or, in fact, any place that looked as though it might not figure in their Renewal. So a barber's shop with a picture of Count Septimus in the window had been targeted, a bookshop with a logo incorporating parts of the Count's coat of arms. Here and there white ankhs had been daubed, pride taken in a job done.

"I suppose we were lucky your friends in masks happened by," Fox said.

"Perhaps they were looking out for you," Schiller said.

"I expect I'm an asset now."

"Don't be bitter, Herr Fox," Schiller said, "We appear to be moving into a time when neutrality is no longer an option. You have to accept that you now have a role in this."

Olympia was slumped in an armchair, flanked by Bob and Karl, two Chinese lions outside the gates of a temple.

"Are you okay?" Fox asked.

"She's fine," said Bob, the inscrutable pissed off look forever on his face. His brother's fixed-in sneer that would never go away.

"Tomorrow," Fox said, "I'm going to go to the place where Victor and Lazlo died. That's what I'm going to focus on. No more missions to the Castle that were really for the Masquerade all along."

"No," said Mond fitting a Sultanahmet into her cigarette holder, "It wasn't like that. It was merely a coincidence of interests."

"I'll come see you when I know something interesting," Fox said.

"Please," said Olympia, "Don't go yet."

Bob turned his head and looked at her for a moment.

"Tomorrow," said Mond, "After you have seen what you need to see come to the Hotel Relojeria. I have decided we all need a little outing and I would like you to come."

"An outing?"

"According to the Gazette, it's going to be a clear day. I think it would benefit us all to get out of the city for a few hours, don't you? Be there by eleven."

Outside on the street some uniformed Landespolizei had shown up. There were two of them staring at the broken windows as though they were scratching their heads, though they were not doing anything at all.

CHAPTER FIFTEEN

Past slum streets in Sparta, bordering the industrial zone. To the north the sun hitting the mirror array that still gave Genesia most of its power. Warehouses and small workshops. A ruined building, sideways intact but with its frontage missing so that it looked like a dilapidated dollhouse. Inside hunched figures picked over a stinking mound. It was one of the old meat fabrication plants, the meat fungi now gone wild, harvested by these gleaners who sold it on to the cheapest eateries in Sparta. Then the vast site of the Kirovwerk.

The Kirovwerk had once been an almost entirely automated affair, directed by AI software and using production line robots to manufacture the parts for cornucopia as well as other products that couldn't be easily made on fabricators. The power supply came from its own mirror array across the roof and in a series of nearby yards; like the works themselves this was controlled by intelligent software.

All that had come to an end with the data decay. All the calculations, from angling the mirrors to the design of the product specifications now had to be done by engineers with tools like rulers and pocket calculators. The robots were too dangerous to use because of their corrupted software. Fox saw a heap of these robots rusting in a yard as he climbed over a fence onto the railway tracks, fallen metal sculptures with pincers, drills, and intricate manipulators. They lay where they'd been dumped.

Raw materials still came up from Tartessos docks to the Kirovwerk by rail and got shunted into sidings. After the Hyperloop had closed there had been a passenger service for a while, using the lines that came down from Lemberg and Hermanstudt, terminating in the ornate station at Khazarplatz. But now the lines were used exclusively for goods.

Here the tracks forked into ten or so rail lines some going into various buildings of the sprawling Kirovwerk others off to various sidings. A couple of main lines ran off at an angle and parallel to these was great tube of the defunct Hyperloop, looking like a gigantic pipe on support struts. Further north it disappeared underground beneath the hills of Gutunberg. Fox crossed the rail tracks and walked beneath the Hyperloop, then followed a track that ran beside the back of the works buildings. The sidings leading into various machine shops and warehouses were usefully numbered by little signs dug into the ground beside the sleepers.

Fox found the one he wanted which ran parallel to the open doors of a warehouse where some men were unpacking a flatbed railway truck using a forklift.

"Hey."

Someone from the warehouse had come out.

Fox went over. It was some sort of foreman in overalls, greying hair and a pencil behind his ear.

"What are you doing here?"

Fox put his head down for a moment.

"My friend," he said, "had an accident here. I just came to see…"

Deliberately vague, slightly lost.

"The Magyar fellow. I heard someone shot him."

"The police aren't telling me much."

"The police are swine. They closed the entire siding and threatened anyone who came down here. But look, there's nothing for you here. You should get off before someone slings you out."

"Sure," said Fox, "It's just…. Do you know where it happened?"

He pointed further down the track, past the warehouse opening to where the siding ended at some buffers. There was a little shed to one side.

"Thanks," said Fox, "I just wanted to pay my respects."

The foreman shrugged and nodded. He watched Fox all the time but that didn't matter. Fox just wanted to get an idea of the place. There would be no evidence, nothing concrete, no clues, but still…

He could see that there had been quite a few feet churning up the gravel to the side of the rails. Victor, Lazlo, and the killer would have been there. Along with the police and their various hangers on. The police would have cleaned up leaving no drop of Lazlo's blood, no cog of Victor. But Fox studied the way the gravel had been disturbed, footprints coming in from the direction of Sparta. The police would have driven into the Kirovwerk from that side, then walked up. But further down towards the buffers the gravel was less disturbed, and yet there might have been the faintest of trails. Perhaps the killer had come from that direction.

Fox waved goodbye to the foreman but instead of retracing his steps went straight on, up to the buffers and beyond. Here was some forgotten corner of the Kirovwerk with a little shed that must have been used by railway workers. Fox ducked inside. The hut had an earth floor and open windows. Just somewhere to keep out of the wind and rain really. The ground was well trodden in by years of huddled workers, which meant the cigarette butts on the surface were recent. It was probably nothing but Fox picked up a few. Conradin brand mostly.

Outside the hut Fox walked on, over a bit of waste ground and then a fence. This was the Gutunberg side. He climbed over the fence and walked through a couple of streets of warehouses, respectable and neat. Then there were houses, larger and better kept than any back in Sparta. The brickworks of the buildings was clean and light gleamed off the windows. It was a bright and clear morning, Mond had been right about that.

A few turns through a few more streets and Fox was standing once again outside the headquarters of the Renewal Society and the little Egyptian chapel. It seemed that some sort of press conference was going on, if that was the polite term for what looked more like a fascist rally. People filled the road, a mass snaking either way down the street so that it sometime before Fox could get near the front.

There were photographers and reporters with notepads scribbling shorthand. A couple of police stood shifting from foot to foot. But the largest section of the crowd was made up of enthusiastic Renewal Society types, not just the young men of the sort who'd been roaming the streets causing mayhem, but older people, middle aged family men and women, whose ardour for the cause had somehow compromised their respectability, their smiles and cheering the symptoms of a long dormant disease finally become manifest.

Attention was focused on a little podium that had been erected outside the front entrance of the building. It was topped with a banner with the usual ankh and black sun symbol on it and either side boys held similar flags.

On the podium a stodgy bald headed man was declaiming, saying something or other about something or other. Fox would rather not have been listening…

"…will not sit idly by and see our country become an irrelevant backwater…"

People cheered. Fox looked around wondering if the boys who had attacked him were there. If Victor and Lazlo's killer was there. He was glad he had his hat on.

"…we insist on our right to sit at the table with other nations when the final settlement is made…"

Baldy was bombastic, slightly hesitant. No great orator at all. If this was the best the Renewal Society could do at producing a fuhrer it was underwhelming.

"…proposal that the Provisional Government recognises that the urge for renewal is sweeping

175

Genesia. That elections be called so that the will of the people can be heard."

The cheering and clapping was becoming perfunctory. Baldy on the podium was looking out over the crowd, smiling and waving. By the time he held up his hand to indicate he wished to say more people had already started to mutter about other things.

"And now…" he said, "it is time to here from a representative of those who are being disparaged by the press. The young people of our movement who see a future of mediocrity and have decided that this it will not come to pass. Let us listen now to the words of the president of the Young Renewal, Aksel Ritter…."

Another man boy of the sort Fox had encountered enough of. Short, neat hair so pale it looked like white baize. He wore the semi-uniform favoured by these types. It was beginning to irritate Fox. Not that this one needed a uniform to be irritating, his milky skin and maiden blushed cheeks was just too Heidi not to get on the nerves. He spoke in the perfectly formed accent of the Genesia middle classes.

"Thank you, thank you. Let us show our thanks for Stephan Cappel, yes." He waited out the polite applause before continuing. "People of Genesia," he said, sounding reasonable and proper, "some of you might be concerned about the unrest in our city last night and over recent days."

Actually nobody seemed to be bothered at all. A few young men shouted out enthusiastically from where they had accumulated near the podium.

"And you should be concerned," said Aksel in a twist no one was expecting, "because these disturbances are the sole responsibility of those elements who have for too long dominated the culture of our city. They have rendered us a laughing stock among nations, so that in the hour of our allies' need we retreat to the nursery. Last night..." Pause. "I led a group of my comrades into Little Alexandria..."

Fox looked at the police. They didn't seem about to leap up and arrest Aksel. They were too busy inspecting their shoes.

"It can no longer be tolerated this...this degenerate district, inhabited by foreign deserters, libertarians and animated manikins. It can no longer be tolerated that the reputation of Genesia is a palace stuffed with toys, a place fit only for playing..."

The young men were cheering and clapping. Others were joining in as Aksel became more animated.

"It is no longer to be tolerated that the new generation who desire renewal, are held back by those who wish to remain in the nursery. Is it to be tolerated that while the whole of Europe engages in a titanic struggle, when our allies are in dire need, when they come to us and ask for help that we refuse, and we tell them we are busy playing? No, this is not to be tolerated."

Cheers.

"Is it not true that the legacy of Count Septimus be consigned to where it belongs? The past. To an age more innocent than ours. An age that could afford indulgence."

Cheers again. Some slightly confused because the Count was not usually directly criticised, and, in fact, it wasn't clear if he had been. But who could resist a teenage authoritarian telling you that you'd let things slip?

A few more photographers were at work now. Aksel Ritter was a much better subject than baldy Stephan Cappel had been. "But our age can no longer afford indulgence. It is time to put away childish things."

Fox almost groaned that he hadn't seen that one coming.

"It is time for renewal and renewal will only come by ending the malaise which afflicts us. The Provisional Government must announce the date for elections because we are growing impatient, we are growing angry."

Cheers.

Fox didn't know how long it would go on but he'd had enough. He still had time to get to the Hotel Relojeria. Perhaps Mond had been right about more than the weather. It might be good after all to be outside the city for a while.

CHAPTER SIXTEEN

A bit of clarity. Not much, not really.

Mond dressed in tweeds, a country squire. Her car might generously have been called vintage. It was a long Skoda Ghost convertible in the raygun gothic style that had become popular thirty or so years before, all sharp fins and chrome. It must been around somewhere they'd been power shortages to the mains supply because it had been retrofitted with a CNG engine.

The road out of the city she took was the route over the bridge with the River Listnatý below and to out to where there was a shanty town built around the recycling plant and the landfill mine workings. Instead of heading off towards the countryside Mond took the car into this industrial district, down narrow streets lined with shacks built in old shipping containers, or lean-tos of plastic crates and corrugated plastic roofs. This had once been an area teeming with people, all making a living out of the city's rubbish, which they picked over or dug shafts into for whatever treasure they could find.

The area had started to depopulate decades ago, when the digital decay meant jobs that had once been obsolete returned as computers and all the devices they drove went out of operation. People moved back to the city to become factory workers, clerks and typists rather than live next to mountains of crap.

In places where the shacks had been abandoned pieces of them had drifted into the road, meaning Mond had to swerve around. Then the car came into a little line of intact dwellings in front of the vast hill of a landfill. These were large shipping containers so that originally this settlement must have looked like much of the rest of the shanty town but the shacks had been elaborated, with solar panels and elaborate micro turbines powered by landfill gas. Spaces had been cut with blow torches into the containers to make doors and windows. Out front there was furniture in all the styles of last hundred or so years. To one side was a pile of white goods stacked up like a giant cairn.

As Mond's Ghost drew to a halt people began to emerge, up on the great mound of the landfill a few pickers were looking down. A huge man came out of one of the containers, shaggy haired and with a brown and grey beard, he wiped his hands on the thighs of his overalls.

Mond wound down the window. The stench here was overwhelming, causing Fox almost to gag. Schiller and Olympia did not notice and just nodded as the man greeted them.

"Afternoon, Mond," he said, his accent that of a second or third generation Brit.

"Hello, Owen," said Mond.

She lit a cigarette, neat and without a holder as though the aroma of Sultanahmet could keep the smell of rotten food and decaying matter from getting to her.

"You ain't been this way for a while," said Owen.

"No. Can you fill me up?"

"You better put that fag out then. George…"

He shouted the name again and a boy appeared from somewhere beyond the shack. The boy might have been about nine and wore an adult's dinner jacked frayed at the edges and covered in filth.

"Hello, George," said Mond.

"Get a pipe down," Owen said to the boy.

George ran off, coming back wielding a length of orange hose with a button operated nozzle on the end. He handed this over to Owen.

"Now bugger off," Owen said and the boy ran away again.

Owen flipped the fuel cap and pushed the nozzle in and began releasing the gas into the car.

"How's business?" Mond asked.

"Shit."

They both laughed.

Out on the main road again the car passed the airport. Guard towers and a chain link fence. Guarding there must have one of the dullest jobs of all waiting for the occasional government light aircraft. On the runway were jetliners that had been gradually stripped for salvage over the years, the few remaining skeletons looking like the remains of a species that long ago became extinct.

Then past farms and market gardens that supplemented the food supply for the city and then the edges of the great marshland that stretched away to the edges of Ruthenia. Hereabouts this marsh was known as the Elverbeds, good for eel fishing in the maze of riverlets and streams that flooded and swelled in the spring when the snow in the distant

Carpathians melted. Even out where it became wooded it would become waterlogged, almost impenetrable.

Mond pulled up in a gravel layby that ran down to the marshland. Here it was possible to see miles eastwards, to where in the distance was what looked like the ruins of a once impressive building. But it was too far away to make it out in any detail.

Outside the car it wasn't cold, and the clear light seemed to wash across the landscape.

Mond had got a pair of binoculars from the glove compartment.

"I've always wanted to see an owl," she said.

Olympia and Schiller were looking too, as though they didn't need the binoculars, as though their sight could effortlessly fathom whatever it chose to bestow itself upon.

Fox had bought a hipflask, a little grappa to keep him company. He wasn't looking at the marshes but at Olympia.

"Come and see this," Mond said.

She handed him the binoculars and he pointed them at the distant ruins. They were not what he had expected, not the craggy stones of a castle, the crenulations and arrows slits of medieval combat. Rather it was something more like an oil platform, with metal gantries and walkways reached by ladders. All painted battleship grey, and perhaps not ruins at all.

"That," said Mond, "Is the prize that all the lunatics want. And the absurdity is they hardly want it for themselves but rather to hand over to someone else, as a bargaining counter in their attempt to enter a game that went out of control a long time ago."

"That's Eirni?"

"Oh yes."

"You didn't expect to see it so clearly, so blatantly?" asked Schiller.

"No," Fox said, "I mean I always knew it was there but I suppose it was almost...I don't know, an abstract concept."

Fox laughed at his own absurdity.

"Four medium range ballistic missiles," Mond said, "with a payload of about twenty kilotons each. The inheritance of Genesia from the breakup of the Central European States."

"And it's just out there. In the marshes," Fox said.

"Most of the army of Genesia is out there too, Herr Fox," said Schiller, "The installation is heavily manned and fortified. There is also an extensive network of redoubts, tank traps and trenches. There are anti-aircraft batteries all over the marshes. It would be difficult for an enemy to capture Eirni before the missiles could be launched in retaliation. They are at once a defence and deterrent, and also the only reason why any external power would have any interest in Genesia in the first place."

"The only way," Fox said, "that anyone would get their hands on Eirni would be for us to hand it over to them."

"Indeed," said Schiller.

"Is that why we came out here?" Fox said, "To see this?" He handed the binoculars back to Mond.

"No," she said, "we are on an outing. I've even bought a hamper."

She lit a Sultanahmet and waved it around.

"This," she said, "was just a brief scenic halt."

"Look," said Olympia.

Fox looked at her first, just for a moment taking in her childlike joy as she pointed up.

A mass of birds dotted the powder blue pane of the sky. They moved gracefully, making the neat pattern of an oscilloscope wave.

"Murmuration," said Fox.

"What's that?" Olympia asked.

"In English we used to have these fanciful collective nouns, terms of venery…. You know, pitying of doves, murder of crows, tidings of magpies. For starlings it was murmuration and people called those formations that."

The weaving cloud of birds contracted and flowed above them.

Mond was looking up through the binoculars.

"Well how fascinating," she said.

"Yes," said Schiller, "not starlings at all."

"What are they?" Fox asked.

Once more Mond handed him the binoculars and it was obvious once he realised, it was something about the movement of the wings, the way they beat the air in not quite the way they should. If he'd known more about birds he might have been able to say what precisely the difference was.

"Clockwork," he said, "They're clockwork birds."

"Isn't it wonderful," said Olympia. She must have known all along.

The movement changed to become intersecting three dimensional sine waves.

Or a cat's cradle. Then a great wedge block that suddenly sped away in the direction of the city.

***

It grew colder, the wind picking up, coming from the east. They walked back to the road and then, leaving the Ghost, followed Mond on a hike into a sort of, well a dingle it might have been called in England once, a wooded enclave overlooking some obscure tributary of the Listnatý. This stream formed little pools as it passed through the heavily rooted ground thick with rushes and grass. Mond led the way, Schiller besides her, his loud ticking sounding flat in the woods. Fox strolled beside Olympia.

In places the ground was sodden, spongy to the foot.

"Soon," announced Mond trailing smoke, "when the proper rains start we'd have to wade through this, walk up to her knees."

"Not very good for me," Olympia whispered.

Mond's smoke lingered in the still air as though they might use it to find their way back later.

"Don't worry," Mond said, "the ground rises a little as we get away from the stream."

When the ground did rise the trees grew thicker, some skeletal without leaves, others evergreen. Thick shrubs grew in the spaces between the trees. There was still a path of sorts and eventually this led to a clearing where there was a cottage. It was wooden and packed in at the sides with earth. It looked as if it had grown there.

"My summer place," said Mond, "Time now to shut it down, pack away the bedding and shutter the windows, put salt in a bowl for the damp."

"I'm finding it kind of difficult to imagine you here," said Fox, "Feet by the fire, with a cup of chocolate."

"Think of it as a green room," she said, "where I relax after performing. Now come on, you can all help me, we should probably get back to the car before it gets dark.'

Fox had to stoop to get inside and then, once in, to avoid hitting his head on the rafters. It was a cosy place with a tattered sofa facing the fireplace and little nooks in the wall with shelves stuffed with books. Schiller's ticking filled the room along with the musty smell of old paper and printer's ink.

Olympia drew the curtains and Schiller went over to one of the bookshelves.

"It's wonderful here," said Olympia, "You should come in late spring, Herr Fox. Sometimes if the waters haven't properly subsided we have to use a little boat to get to this side of the woods.

Mond took Fox outside of the cottage.

"I want to show you something."

Around the back she led him onto a path through the woods, the ground rising gently, light patchworking through the trees and the canopy overhead.

She halted at the edge of a clearing covered with a sturdy canvas awning. The grass high but in places bent oddly in low ridges around rocks. No, not rocks.

"They had no customs…No funerary rites. They couldn't bear the thought of burying them."

There were ultraclocks there, spread around the clearing, maybe six or seven. They were beginning to be overgrown with the grass and weeds, shoots entering whatever crevice they might find in a body. Then nearby, not yet covered with vegetation at all, he recognised the body of the little cobbler from the arcades.

"Not many die…are damaged beyond repair. But when it happens we bring them here. This is where Victor should be."

Back in the cottage Fox slumped down on the sofa. It felt cold and dark. Fox didn't like it. The fire wasn't lit and there was no point lighting it now, since they had come to shut the place down. He wanted to be back in the city.

CHAPTER SEVENTEEN

Nearly December, a few weeks before the feast of Saturnalia. Already the clockwork birds that had infested the Genesia had made themselves part of its life, had changed it. They flocked in squares and on the tops of parked cars, perched on the gargoyles of the Cathedral and hung in the air high above the Castle. In Gutunberg it became fashionable for a lady to have one of the birds as a pet, to keep it on a lead and walk around as it fluttered. Songbirds were the most popular. And since these clockwork birds did not need to be wound they were no trouble at all.

There were those though who didn't like the newcomers at all and on the streets of Genesia could be seen the frames of birds that had been torn open like crackers or stomped on. The pavements and gutters were littered with bent little cogs and twisted springs. The young men had been at their joyous work again.

At dusk Fox would meet Olympia in Pecheneg Square and they would walk through Little Alex until it was time for her to go to the Cabaret Vaucanson. The Young Renewal kids didn't come into Little Alex beyond putting up a few posters of the Comedians or Aksel Ritter, on the streets around the edges of the district.

Sometimes Fox and Olympia would see Schiller leaving the Rudolf Library.

"What does he do there?" Fox asked her.

"He's already written a monograph on the ultraclocks. I think he wants to extend that. To speculate about our future."

"And how does he see that panning out?"

"Perhaps you should ask him."

"Let's follow him then."

It was at the Library that the revolt against the Comedians had started. They had come, by their own executive authority, to close the place down. A mob of followers came at dusk bearing torches. They would burn the library because that is what people like them did. As though libraries were established to be burnt.

Only a group of Little Alex citizens, fond of a library hardly any of them ever used, formed a cordon to defend it.

The Comedians hung back in vehicles, let the mob do the work. But the mob baulked at the crowd.

Froggy, impatient, called in the police.

Zero ordered them to clear the way, open fire if necessary.

The police refused. At first, trying to keep the two sides apart and eventually dispersing the torch bearing would-be arsonists. Patted on the back, given drinks and food by the locals the police refused the next order, to clear the square. The Comedians and their mob withdrew.

It all developed from there.

Fox had been there a couple of times. The digital archives were completely dead, public access systems usually were the first to go, with their limited protections and promiscuous connectivity to networks. Still, it was a beautiful place to wander and browse, up from the ground floor via a winding stair with a gilded handrail to the balconied floors that surrounded beneath the inner curve of the dome.

On the second storey Schiller worked, amid the smell of old books with muted coloured bindings. They found him in the same little alcove at a small desk, filling the space with his ticking. His unreadable expression as he looked up, Olympia and Fox knowing that he didn't really want to be disturbed.

***

When Fox and Olympia had an urge to be unobserved they would go to the far side of Pecheneg Square, outside of Little Alex really. It was a neighbourhood of ironmongers, cordwainers and the sellers of semi-precious stones. They found a little café where Fox had never been before. It was a basic sort of place, sawdust on the floor, ran by an ancient Cuman couple who doddered around and paid little attention to the odd customer who came in.

It was here that Olympia first spoke of the Clockwork Tarot and laid out cards in front of Fox on the zinc table. The darkness of her eyes filled with constant movement. Like watching a mass crowd from high in an aeroplane, the altitude so great that the individuals making it up became lost.

"I understand very little," she said, "Victor gave me them."

"Shame," said Fox, "Could have been some help with the case. I could do with a little supernatural insight."

Fox felt he was doing very little except trying to keep track of what Vogt was up to. He'd told Mond that he wouldn't take any more money from her and that the investigation had reached a dead end. Yet secretly he hoped that somehow he might discover something that made him see it all differently.

The suits in the Clockwork Tarot were Cogs, Springs, Keys and Cams. Some of the Major Arcana were different to a regular deck, some the same, although the depictions were usually different. So, for instance, the Magician was labelled Artixano (artisan) and he held a giant cog. He stood at a bench that was almost overgrown with vines and flowers.

"The flowers imply a manifestation of desire," she said.

On the bench before him, were parts of a clock and the tools of a clockmaker, which Olympia could identify although she didn't remember where she had learnt them.

"Look. Callipers, the die plate files, pliers, spring winder and a storking tool."

There were cards which Fox suspected had no equivalent in the usual deck. These were all connected to the history of automata:

The Tabor Player.

The Mechanical Turk.

The Defecating Duck.

"The duck was built by Vaucanson in the Eighteenth Century and was supposed to demonstrate that the digestive system of an animal could be constructed by the master craftsman. But the duck didn't really eat, it was an illusion, the food was stored in one place, the shit produced from another."

"You look like this one," he said, tapping a card.

It was a beautiful woman with limbs jointed with string like a marionette. She sat at a piano and was dressed in Empire style.

"The deck isn't complete," she said. "Because Victor took the card of the Fool. He kept it with him all the time. I suppose it was still with his belongings."

But Fox knew that it wasn't. Such a little oddity as a tarot card would have been noted with diligence by the desk clerk or evidence officer who had catalogued all of Lazlo's belongings, including Victor and whatever he would have had on him. And there hadn't been anything like that on the list that Felice had given him.

Victor had identified himself as the Fool. A code name, an identity.

She packed the cards away in the little velvet bag which she pushed across the table.

"I want you to have them," she said.

"Memento? I'm not likely to forget you."

"But if I ever forget you then perhaps you can show me the cards to remind of now, of this moment."

That night he walked her to the Cabaret but he wasn't going in. Outside, still arm in arm, they watched as a flock of clockwork corvids alighted on the roof opposite.

"Where are you going tonight?" she asked him.

"I'm going to check on a young friend of mine," he said. "To make sure she is all right."

"Oh you could make me jealous, Fox," she said, and slipped away to the Cabaret.

When Fox had followed Vogt a few times he'd seen Lola again, once more going into the Club Adder with the death squad CO, Captain Kardos. It would be difficult to get near her but he had to try. He decided to go over to her uncle's café when she'd been the waitress, Lotte.

Even at this hour the Maskmarkt was open in the final weeks of trading in the run up to Saturnalia.

Fox wandered through the market down the aisles of the the mask sellers' stalls, which were decked out in coloured ribbon and bunting, hand-painted signs and personal symbols, a red moon, a leaping unicorn, endless variations of masks. Clockwork birds were perched on the top of awnings. The sellers shouted with their practised rhythms, holding up masks of all styles, though they never wore masks themselves.

Their shouts and calls seemed at moments to be on the brink of becoming a vast polyphonic song made up of prices and offers, promises and boasts. As well as masks on sale there was also food, so that the smell of sausages cooking filled the air along with that of beer and cigarette smoke, and the sweet aroma of horse dung.

The customers were from every walk of Genesia society, rich and poor, old and young. Or almost every walk. There were no smart young men from the Renewal Society here.

Fox crossed over to the café, busy with shoppers now more than the traders who'd been there when he'd come before. He found a free table at the back and nodded to the uncle who was pouring some brandy for a customer. There was another waitress now, not Lotte but a girl slightly older, thickset and with a smile that seemed genuine despite her being busy.

"It's hectic this time of year," Fox said when she put down his grappa.

"It certainly is, sir."

"Maybe you could do with some more staff."

"Sometimes my cousin is here," she said, shrugged and was about to walk away.

"I think I've seen her in here. Pretty girl and you know..."

"Yes?"

"I'm sure I saw her out, the other day... or rather night."

"Really?" She sat down opposite Fox, just as Lola had done. "Where was this? You know we haven't seen or heard from her in weeks. My father has been fit to burst."

"Well," Fox said, "she was with a... with a man. I think I know where they go."

"Where?"

194

"You see," Fox said, "It's all pretty delicate. This man he's been trouble for some friends of mine. I wouldn't like to think of your cousin involved with him."

"Trouble? That sounds like Lotte. Please tell me where you saw her. I'd like to find her before my father does and tans her hide."

"I'll tell you what," Fox said, "Let me have your number and I'll call you when I see her again. I think it would be a good idea if you could talk some sense into her."

She hesitated for only a moment, glancing round for her father, then wrote down the phone numbers, one for the café and one for her home. She wrote 'Helga', at the top over the numbers.

Fox was feeling fairly smug. It was almost a plan. Spot Lola again and ring Helga and get her to come over to Club Adder, or wherever it was. He would then lay it on thick that he'd like to warn Lotte about the company she was keeping and so he'd get to see her. And ask her what he needed to ask her.

He came back into the market square buoyed up by all this and the two grappas he'd downed inside the café. He might even go over to the Cabaret Vaucanson and watch Olympia.

Then he saw that over the roofs of Sparta a plume of black smoke was billowing up into the sky. It couldn't have been too far away, and he could already taste it in the air. Even as he started in its direction, jogging around the edges of the market, he knew where it was coming from. Fox could have gone right round, out onto Autocue

Boulevard and then over the railway bridges there but instead he crossed the tracks by the way he'd gone before, through the Kirovwerk.

In Gutunberg he heard the shouts and screams. As he approached a corner someone stepped out of a doorway.

"Herr Fox."

It was the woman he had taken to be Demi, the medieval doctor's beaked mask on her face. Behind her, in the shadow of the doorway, a masked automaton stood. It might have been Bob, or Karl, or perhaps not.

"What have you done?" Fox said.

"Made a move," said Dr Pest.

"Jesus. Don't you think things are tense enough as it is?"

"We can't let them play out their elaborate scenario. We have to force their hand."

Fox went past her.

"Herr Fox," she called, "we'll need to speak to you again soon."

Up ahead Fox walked into a plume of smoke and then saw where the night was lit up by flames.

CHAPTER EIGHTEEN

The next day thousands of Renewal Society members and supporters marched through the city in protest at the burning down of their headquarters. They filled the streets of Gutunberg and then went out into Autocue Boulevard bringing the traffic to a halt and heading for the Stadthouse. Fox stood on the first floor of Steffi's department store, in the haberdashery, looking down on it. Steffi's hadn't shut up completely letting the customers already inside shop on. Fox had come in for the view just before they'd barred the doors.

As well as the neat young men there were others on the march, families, older people. They had the usual banners, the ankh on the black sun, placards with the Comedians and Aksel Ritter. But the anger was more than the usual stage managed affair.

There were a few police around, some on horseback. Most just stood sheepishly, wondering what to do. Above all this, mechanical birds flocked. One was much bigger than all the others, the eagle.

By the late afternoon Fox made his way back to the Café Castringius. He wanted to make sure Max was okay.

A lot of the businesses in Little Alex had closed early, shutters in place over windows. In places Fox saw the broken corpses of clockwork birds and bugs a bit like his own.

197

Max was standing outside the café, hand above his eyebrows, sighting down the street.

"Are they coming?" he said as Fox approached.

"Why would they come down here?"

But there had always been something about Little Alex, and it was the sort of something, they didn't like; a vague bohemianism, the lingering sympathy for Count Septimus…. Fox just didn't want to feed into Max's anxiety.

"You should close up, I suppose," he said, "Just to be on the safe side. I'm going to go over to the Hotel, make sure everyone is all right."

"You can call," said Max, "stay and have a drink. Tell me what's happening. Then you can go."

Fox did as he said. Listening to Olympia's light, almost musical voice drifting through the telephone wires as though she were speaking from the bottom of an enchanted well.

"I'm with Mond and Schiller," she said, "We're going to go to the Cabaret Vaucanson later to meet everyone else."

"I wouldn't be out on the street tonight for longer than you have to."

"I know," she said, "Schiller thinks it's going to be another Youngman's Night…"

"Worse," said Fox, "But then perhaps if Schiller's friends hadn't…"

But he shut up. There were ways to listen in on analogue telephone calls that had surely been revived by the likes of Vogt.

"Don't be angry, Fox," she said.

"Take care," he said, "I'll come round soon. Maybe me and Schiller should have a little talk."

Fox wouldn't go yet. It would be better to calm down. Max was already putting down a grappa and some bread and beer sausage. Then he did something he didn't usually do: he fetched a glass for himself and he sat down in the chair opposite Fox. Fox looked at him, sat there beneath the Castringius print with its odd, disturbing, configurations.

"What do you think is going to happen?" Max asked.

"There's going to be trouble."

"There's already trouble."

"It's going to get worse."

The sausage was good as usual. Fox hadn't realised how hungry he was. The last thing he'd eaten was the night before.

"You think these lunatics will try and take over," said Max, "Bring back the Comedians or something?"

There were twenty-six scenarios in Fox's head. The augmentation could play them out like so many games of chess or go, working out all the permutations of each one. They each had a starting position, Vogt here, Sword there and so on. Then the moves would begin. But Dr Pest had talked about forcing the hand of the Renewal Society, disrupting all these plans by seizing the initiative. Making the first move.

"I don't know what's going to happen, Max. I don't think anyone does. I think we'll just need to look out for each other."

On the way over to the Hotel Relojeria the streets were quiet. Shops were shut and there weren't many people on the streets. Occasionally Fox heard the odd excited cry or shout come from somewhere from beyond the rooftops, from the direction of Autocue Boulevard.

When he got to the hotel it was Mond who opened the door with a puff of Sultanahmet.

"Schiller's gone out," she said as she let Fox in. "Wanted to see what was going on. I just hope he's all right."

Fox could have quipped about reaping what you sow, but he didn't.

"Where did he go?"

"Don't worry about that," said Bob as Fox came into the breakfast room, "We can take care of our own. I'm not sure we need you hanging around anymore. You haven't proven to be a very good detective have you?"

Bob was stood behind the armchair where Olympia was sitting. She rose as he spoke, effecting a ruffled frown for Fox's benefit.

"Please forgive Bob's rudeness, Herr Fox," she said, "I think he is finding the times trying."

"Haven't you got banjo practice or something," Fox said, then turned all his attention to Olympia, ignoring Bob with his eternal expression of being pissed off.

"I'll go and have a look for Schiller," Fox said, "It's probably not a good idea to be out and about at the moment."

Karl came into the room.

"Are we forming a search party?" he said.

Bob said nothing, just looked from Karl and then to Fox.

"It seems that way," said Mond, "Just give me a few moments to get ready."

"I'm sure he's fine," said Olympia.

"Of course," said Mond as she went out.

When she came back she was wearing a short scarlet cape and carrying what turned out, as she drew the blade, to be a swordstick.

"Do you have a weapon, Herr Fox?" Karl asked.

"Not on me."

Bob made a sound, hollow and mechanical. Perhaps it was his equivalent of a scoff.

"What do you have?" Fox asked Bob.

"I don't need anything."

And Bob demonstrated how his fingers, used to playing piano could be closed to form an impressive looking fist.

"Shall we go," said Mond.

They all went, Olympia included. Through the back streets of Little Alex and a road that led onto Autocue Boulevard. At first Olympia had stooped at every broken clockwork bird. But there were too many. Then, on the corner, just a few metres away from the corner, they found a humanoid automaton, an ultraclock.

"I know him," said Mond. "I've seen him at the cabaret."

He was a sort of aged tin-man, his silver metal skin worn in places, patterned with tarnished blotches. A metal pole, perhaps torn from a railing, had been thrust through his guts splitting a hole and mangling his clockwork innards. In his hand he held a broken winged songbird, its own cogs spilling where it had been snapped beneath eager boots.

"We should take him back to the hotel," said Olympia, "Perhaps something can be done for him."

"What can be done for him?" said Bob.

Olympia knelt down next to the broken tin man. For a moment she held out her hand and touched his face.

"Victor used to say that in Harmony any automata could be repaired, that there was no need to ever end…"

"Olympia," said Karl, "We are not in Harmony."

"Well maybe we should be."

"I think," said Mond, "we need to look for Schiller."

From inside his jacket pocket Fox found the little hipflask of grappa he kept there. He took a quick shot, ignoring Karl's stare. He tried to remember if he'd seen the tin man at the cabaret but couldn't. What had he been like? Now he just looked like a broken machine.

Olympia was still kneeling. "His head is still intact," she said, "Victor said…"

"Victor's not here Olympia is he," said Bob, "Now let's get on."

Just then the street lights came on. Out on Autocue Boulevard Steffi's was shut but none of the windows had been broken, not like the butchers on Lessingstrasse, the bakers on Samsungstrasse and the little café on Kuhnstrasse. All in Little Alex.

Autocue Boulevard, eerie because empty of cars, was dotted with mingling crowds, not shoppers but people who had had their day out with the Renewal Society and didn't quite know what to do. Unlike the young men who had gone off these were probably not yet convinced of the idea of storming around smashing things, but still too hyped up, too enthusiastic to just go home and read the newspaper or listen to the radio.

Fox took another swig of grappa and came next to Olympia, took her hand.

A child, a little boy, was pointing at the newcomers. He had a little flag in his other hand.

Two husbands left their wives after a quiet word and nod to each other, they started across the street towards Fox and the rest. These husbands were perhaps not quite as determined and sure of themselves as they hoped they looked.

"I think we should get out of here," Fox said. "I'll take you back Olympia."

"Look," said Mond, "There's Schiller."

The ultraclock was a little further down the street where Steffi's had the Saturnalia and Christmas displays. He was stood against the plate glass window, his back to it, as he faced a group of people, more husbands and wives with their children. A man was shouting at Schiller, poking at him with a finger.

"There's never a policeman when you need one," said Fox.

"Come on," said Bob.

He and Karl rushed towards Schiller, Mond going after them, her hand on the swordstick, cape fluttering as she went. Across the road one of the wives was calling her husband back from his advance on Fox and Olympia, telling him not to be silly. But the two men had seen that Fox and Olympia were now on their own.

"Come on," Fox said, pulling Olympia, "Let's catch up…"

But the husbands scooted onto the pavement cutting Fox and Olympia off from following the others.

"You," one of the men called to Fox, "What's a matter with you, can't find yourself a real woman?"

The two men had stopped a little way out on the road, puffed up, fists clenched yet still not sure of themselves. (Brain images of anger, indecipherable at any level of detail but clear as their animal snarls).

"You some kind of freak," the other one said, "You need a clockwork sex toy?"

"Let's go," Olympia said sottovoce.

Fox wished he had his gun. He was glad he didn't. "Why don't you just leave us alone," he said.

"You're a freak, a pervert. Fucking a machine."

"Do you talk like that in front of your wives?" Fox said before he'd thought about it. It wasn't a good time to ask a genuine question.

They both came at Fox, clumsy, not used to being drunk but strong enough. Fox managed to kick one's legs from beneath him as the man made a grab for him. The falling man grabbed Fox's hat as he went.

The other one's punch caught Fox in the eye socket, then tried to grab the newly revealed cilia atop Fox's head.

"You really a freak."

Fox jabbed with his right but missed. Then the man suddenly seemed to deflate, taking a step back, trying to look over his shoulder where Olympia was. In her hand she held a long silver knife. She pressed it against the back of the man's neck.

"Leave him alone," she said.

The man took a step to one side.

"Rolf!"

It was the other one staggering up.

"Come on," said Olympia, "We'd better go."

Rolf was feeling the back of his neck, when he brought his hand away there was some blood there. Olympia had cut, just a little. The wives were running across the road.

Further along Bob and Karl were helping Schiller towards Fox and Olympia, with Mond turning and striking a pose with her swordstick at anyone who might follow.

Fox grabbed Olympia and they ran, hand in hand towards the backstreets of Little Alex.

"You just saved me from a good kick-in, or worse," he said. "The knife?"

"I took it from the kitchen. Bob did say to be armed."

Olympia squeezed his hand, the cold of her fingers delicate and intimate even as they ran.

"Not bad for a clockwork sex toy," she said.

CHAPTER NINETEEN

Olympia dabbed a cloth in a little grappa and cleaned around Fox's eye where the punch had broken the skin. While she did this Fox tried to drink from the grappa bottle to be tutted at and told to keep still. The silk of her dress brushed against his arm.

"I've lost another hat," he said.

"Keep still, I've nearly finished."

The others came in, Schiller to sit in the armchair opposite Fox, his loud ticking somehow comforting.

Olympia finished Fox's ablutions.

"You're harmed, Herr Fox," said Schiller.

Mond stood by the breakfast table, swished her cloak theatrically and then flourished the sword stick before sliding it back into its scabbard.

"Perhaps we should put you back on the payroll," she said, "Or at least give you danger money."

Bob and Karl stood each side of her like ugly fire-dogs. Fox didn't look at them.

"Quite an eventful little stroll you took," Fox said to Schiller.

"Eventful times," he replied.

Mond came and perched on the arm of Fox's chair.

"I'll join you in a drink, Herr Fox," she said, picking up the bottle and taking a swig. "And you dear," she said to Olympia, taking her hand, "How are you?"

"I stabbed someone."

"Well you know I'm sure they deserved it."

"Are we going to open the Cabaret tonight?" Schiller asked.

"Demi will already be there," said Mond. "And even if the entertainment has been a little sparse tonight our regular customers can have a drink. And I think, when we've all had time to recover, we should go there so that everyone knows we're not afraid."

"We'll go now," said Karl.

"No," said Mond, "We'll all go together."

The Cabaret Vaucanson was as busy as ever and as they walked in a cheer went up. Pozzo, on stage in a ludicrous orange swimming costume, shouted for the lights to be turned on them.

"Ladles and jelly spoons," he said, "Our most honoured indignitaries have arrived, cogs intact. Come up and play boys and girls, let the madness begin."

The monkey did a drum roll as the Bakelite Boys and Olympia headed for the stage and Fox for the bar with Mond. Demi was already there wearing a black cat suit and drinking from a long glass, some cocktail that involved a stirrer and a purple umbrella.

"I see you've been in the wars tonight," she said to Fox after kissing her sister on the cheek.

Although they were both the same height Demi was in heeled boots. That and the long hair made her loom over Mond.

The band struck up a martial beat and Olympia danced, kicking her legs high and keeping her arms outstretched as though she were a demented soldier, whose clockwork was the pitiful struttings of a toy.

Pozzo started to chant in time with her movements. Left, left, left.

Her legs marching in great kicks that raised up her skirt.

Left. Left. Left.

Then Pozzo began to growl a song.

Little Aksel's Song.
The cretinous oafs of the ankh
Have found a kid to lead up their ranks.
Little Aksel's a shit,
But he looks the right fit
For wrecking our city to bits.
He's a dumb little chancer,
Whose mum wipes his arse eh
So why the hell put up with this farce?
Eh?

The audience cheered and clapped. There were whistles for an encore as the marching beat halted and Olympia bowed slowly. Pozzo threw out his arms and plucked imaginary flowers from the air.

"Sing Olympia, sing," someone shouted.

"What's the matter?" shouted Pozzo, throwing off his mask, "Am I not good enough for you? You like 'em young eh? Young and beautiful." He looked over at Olympia for a moment and waved, she blew him a kiss back.

"No," said Pozzo, "I don't mean you l'horologie. There's fresher little faces in Genesia."

Pozzo pulled down the top of his swimming costume revealing a tee-shirt printed with the face of Aksel Ritter but in a blonde wig and red lipstick.

"An improvement don't you think?" he called.

The band struck up again and Pozzo jigged along while Olympia disappeared into the wings. Fox finished his second drink and someone, Mond, Demi, handed him another.

"You like her, don't you?" Demi said. She was close to Fox's ear, talking over the music, her perfume displacing for a moment the smell of cigarettes.

"Who?"

"Olympia of course."

Clockwork sex toy.

"Sure," said Fox.

Can't get yourself a real woman.

"Don't upset her," said Demi, "She is not like some of them are. Some of them are tough, but she isn't."

"What are you two talking about?" Mond said.

"Nothing," said Fox.

On the stage Pozzo was juggling what looked like gas grenades while he spat one-liners at the audience. Fox couldn't focus on them, they had become a jumble of words.

"Go and see her then," Demi whispered. She had sidled up to Fox and he could feel the heat of her body, and it became part of the heat of the room which suddenly felt stifling. He drank some more grappa.

"I'll take a beer," he said.

Demi leaned over the bar to the tender.

"Give him a beer as he goes through."

Then Fox was in the corridor to the back rooms, laughter at the incompressible jokes seeping through the walls.

Olympia was in the green room. She was pacing a bit, as though gradually coming down from the antics she had performed on stage.

"I have to go back on," she said, "Do a dance in this." She indicated her outfit. "Because that's what they want isn't it? For me to look like what those thugs said I was."

Fox suddenly grabbed her arm. She tilted her head and looked at him. He let it go.

"I'm sorry," he said, "You've got to…stop. Don't let it get into your head."

He took a step back and stumbled a little, steadied himself on the dresser and then thought it might be better to plonk himself down on the settee.

"I'm sorry, Fox," she said, "I don't know what's come over me."

And yet her chest rose and fell with exactly the same rhythm as it always did. The faint ticking kept its regular interval.

"It's all right. I'm just…"

She came over and sat next to him, crossed her legs and put her arm along the back of the settee. Her arm was behind Fox, not touching, but there.

"I understand what I look like," she said, "That I've been made to be an image made by a certain type of male gaze."

"It doesn't matter."

"Sometimes you look at me like that," she said.

Just a few metres away, out the back doors and in the street at the rear of the Cabaret Vaucanson, was where Fox had seen her for the first time.

"Have you ever wondered about whether I might feel desire?" She took his hand. "Or is it…" Her fingers brushed the cilia on Fox's head.

The augmentation registered nothing. At any moment it would begin worrying for data. Her voice, almost musical, as somehow he had kicked the grappa bottle into the gutter.

From the main room of the Cabaret Vaucanson spurts of laughter, tumbling of a clown who Fox had seen shitting political comment.

She put her hands around the back of her neck and undid the chain which had the key on it. She lifted her skirt and placed the key in the little hole in her navel. She moved Fox's hand onto the key. He had wound her before but there had never been this charged intimacy.

"Are you running down?"

"No. Turn it."

"What? Why?"

"Turn it until the mainspring is fully tightened. Then you have to gently turn it a little more. Like you are going to overwind it."

Fox turned, one hand on the key, one hand on the cold surface of her skin at the edge of her thigh. Smoother than glass, kicking the grappa bottle into the gutter.

The augmentation felt nothing. The thought came that had fluttered somewhere beneath the skin of his consciousness. What if she is just a machine? What if, right now, I am alone with a machine?

211

The key had reached biting point where the mainspring was fully tightened. Fox turned it a fraction more and Olympia gasped.

Is this what he was now? Clockwork lover. Fulfilling his cold, unaugmented desire. The augmentation unable ever to confirm that she was anything more than a rather clever musical box.

"Turn the key a little harder."

Cold skin, smoother than glass, grappa bottle in the gutter. Laugher from the Cabaret Vaucanson.

"Turn the key."

A gasp and then her sigh.

Someone banging on the door.

"Five minutes, Olympia." Pozzo's voice.

And she was laughing again and gently moving his hand away from the key so that it fell against the cold flesh of her stomach. She took the key from the hole and attached it to the chain around her neck.

Fox wanted a drink. Always it had been that the augmentation would not allow him to become just a body. It would latch on to the novel neural activity of whoever he was with, desperate to decipher it, to understand what was happening. With Olympia there was nothing inside her head the augmentation could register, a vast enfolding nothingness.

"Were you made like this? To do this?" Fox asked.

She sat next to him.

"I don't know," she said, "I don't think we were designed this way. It is an accident of our design. Just as your sexual pleasure is an accident of your evolution."

212

"I don't understand anything anymore," he said. He hadn't wanted it to sound so troubled.

She touched his cheek.

"There's nothing to understand is there."

"I suppose there isn't."

"Then come and watch me. I'm going to sing."

CHAPTER TWENTY

Two tablets of clarity. And then two more because he suspected the augmentation had found a way to dull the effect. In the Café Castringius he read the papers, reports of the disturbances. Pictures of the smoking ruin in Gutunberg. Renewal Society planning to march again. Temporary headquarters established in the legal district. The Provisional Government was considering a post to Renewal Society president Stefan Capel, and so Fox was able to put a name to the bald headed one he'd seen on the podium.

Tonight Fox would go back to the Cabaret Vaucanson, drawn by what was already a need.

"It's the telephone for you," said Max because Fox hadn't noticed him standing there with the phone on its wire trailing from the bar. "She called twice yesterday."

"Herr Fox," said Frau Pfaff, "Please, you have to come…"

"I'm not sure there's anything more I can do for you."

It was already gone one o'clock and Fox had eaten. Soon he'd have a glass of grappa.

"It's Cosima," said Frau Pfaff, "The doctor has said that it's a heart attack. She wants to see you. She insists. Otto doesn't like the idea. He's very angry with you. But I told her that I would call you."

"Hold on, what's happened?"

"Some men came. They said they were policemen but from the way they behaved towards my sister I'm not sure they could have been."

"I'll come."

Fox took the Molina again via Autocue Boulevard. There were fewer people out than usual, most not stopping to dawdle in front of department store windows but some took time to stare at hatless Fox when the traffic slowed. Fox smiled at them. None of it mattered. By the time he started up into the Heights the clarity meant that the picture in his head, of Cosima Kastner in bed ill and broken, was like a photograph belonging to someone he didn't know.

Frau Pfaff was at the door with Otto. She looked as though she'd recently had a makeover but not bothered to keep it up. Dust in the furrows between peach clean skin.

Otto supressed a scowl.

"Thank you for coming, Herr Fox," Frau Pfaff said, "My sister is in the Yellow Room."

Frau Kastner in the Yellow Room, laid out on the green brocade chaise plumped up on damson coloured cushions, tangerine kimono visible from her chest up, the blanket surprisingly homely, tartan like something spread for a picnic. There was a sound coming from the record player, the drawn out champ chump of the stylus caught in its after groove.

"I shall fetch some coffee," said Otto.

"Now dear," said Frau Pfaff, "Herr Fox has come all this way to see you because he knows you wanted to talk to him…"

"Anna," Cosima cut in, "I've had a heart attack, I've not become a simpleton so there's no need to talk to me as though I am. Why don't you do something useful like put another record on?"

"Very well. As long as it's not that dreadful…"

"Stop. Don't finish that sentence. None of my music is dreadful. I wouldn't have it in the house if it was dreadful."

Frau Pfaff clucked, but seated herself on the sofa and picked up a pile of LPs from the larger pile next to it and began to look through them.

"Now, Evergreen, come and perch on the end here. How are you? I've been worried."

"I'm fine…good. Why have you been worried about me? Who's been here?"

"An awful ferret of a man with a big lump of a sidekick. Both plain clothes police officers."

"Now, Cosima," said her sister, "I'm not sure they were actually police officers…to talk to you like that."

"Of course they were. Don't be so naïve. And please put some music on."

There were only so many vintage Rolls Royces in Genesia. Perhaps only one. Vogt hadn't had too much trouble with that. In a way it should have been obvious that he would come looking, that it would draw him out.

When they'd come Downs had gone into the kitchen with Otto leaving Vogt alone with Cosima in the Yellow Room. She had asked him if he liked Mahler.

"I fucking hate music," he'd said.

"You can imagine," she said to Fox, "That that made an impression on me. He told me that if I was a relative of Lazlo Heck then I had to tell him everything I knew. Why was Heck in Genesia? Who were his associates?"

"What did you tell him?"

"I couldn't play along with it. So I told him that there had been a mistake. That I had a distant nephew called Lazlo Hall and that when I'd seen the report in the paper I'd jumped to the wrong conclusion. That was all. It was all very straightforward."

"He didn't believe you did he?"

Music came on. Something light and stringy. Mozart maybe. Lazlo Heck had not been named in the papers.

"No. I don't think he believed me at all. He just twitched his nose."

Vogt had wanted to know who was with her. Frau Kastner had told him she was with her manservant Otto.

Vogt had put his face directly into hers.

"Don't fuck with me you shrivelled old cunt."

"I thought he was going to hit me but instead he started walking around the room, slowly picking books off the shelf, lifting ornaments up, inspecting the records."

"Why do you live amongst all this shit?" he'd said, "You some kind of weird old hoarder? Living in this clapped out old wreck of a house. I take it all this shit must mean a lot to you? What do they call it, sentimental value? Be a shame if anything happened to it all."

"And then he took a book. It was a copy of Heine's poems, and he ripped it out of its binding and tore the pages up. He did it slowly, letting the pieces fall to the floor like confetti."

Frau Pfaff came over and sort of lingered over her sister as though she might take her hand or stroke her hair. In the end all she did was mutter something like poor dear and then went back to sit on the sofa.

"You should have just been straight with him," said Fox.

She was an old woman, drawn into something dangerous that she had taken to be a game. Fox had known this at the time. It was clear to him now. All that had mattered then was getting another fragment of information for his wild goose chase.

Frau Kastner, surrounded by her books and records, her dormant automaton in the form of a suit of armour, her dead and dying digital technology out in the hall. Fox had just used her. Clarity.

"I couldn't just tell him," she said. "If they would treat me like this then I know they would treat you far worse. They knew there was more to it than I was revealing."

Otto came in with the coffee tray and put it down on the table.

"You shouldn't have got Frau Kastner involved in all this," he said. "She's not been well since."

"Now Otto," she said, "You get along."

"He's right," said Fox.

When Otto had gone again Fox poured then all coffee from the pot.

"Otto just worries about me," Frau Kastner said.

"Well," said Frau Pfaff, "You have me as well now dear."

"Yes," said Fox, "You two seem on good terms."

"That's thanks to you," said Cosima, "And that's more important than some altercation with les flics."

"And what has the doctor said?"

"Oh the usual. To rest. To begin some light exercise after he sees me again. It's fine. I'm sure Anna made much more of it when she called you. But I wanted to make sure you were all right. And to tell you what happened. Those two policemen were horrible."

"I know. I've met them before."

She nodded. "Not a pleasant experience I presume."

Augmentation stirred, kicking at the door in a delayed interest in the decayed worlds of the virtual reality booth out there. The clarity seemed to have a diminishing effect and now the augmentation was recalling when it had brushed passed the surfaces of those worlds when Fox had come into the house.

"No, not pleasant."

"Would you like to talk about it, Evergreen?"

"What I'd really like is a drink."

To be back with Olympia. To be abandoned and without thought, to approach the great nothingness of her. At least the clarity made that clear.

"Anna," said Cosima, "Would you be so kind as to ask Otto to fetch some wine?"

When Frau Pfaff had left the room Fox noticed the look Cosima was giving him.

"Once again," she said, "I find you not quite yourself."

"And I've lost Edgar Wallace Verlaine's hat."

"Well, I'm sure we can find you another hat."

"I'm not sure I want one."

"Good for you. Now tell me what's bothering you so much that you're taking those pills again."

"I'm not sure I can handle what's going on in my life. And I'm sorry for what I've got you into."

"You didn't force me, Evergreen. And I rather enjoyed it at the time. But you do seem to have got yourself into some involved with some nasty people. Maybe it's about time you retreated from this particular case."

"It's become personal."

Fox laughed suddenly. It was the picture of it he had. Clarity suddenly making it regress, a dropped photograph framed not by its own border but the world around it, to which it was inconsequential. The ugly wormhead drunk sitting genteelly with the lady of the manor about to speak of his complicated love life.

Frau Pfaff came in carrying a tray with a bottle of red wine and a glass. Otto was holding the door for her. She put the tray down on the table and Fox poured himself a glass. It was rich but not too heavy.

"Well," Fox said, "You two seem to have become the best of friends again."

It turned out that Frau Kastner had telephoned her sister and entreated (Frau Pfaff's word) her to pay a visit, sending Otto in the roller, which must have been quite a sight in the Towers, where the kids might have pelted stones at it, scratched it, stolen the spirit of ecstasy or perhaps bought out the red white and blue bunting for the arrival of this great British brand (that had seen out its senility in Bavaria).

"I believe," said Cosima, "that I need my sister. Even before this recent illness I had come to realise that."

It was a beautifully executed role. In fact they were both playing beautifully executed roles. Perhaps though those roles were easier to play than the ones they had been playing before.

"I should thank you," said Frau Pfaff, "If it wasn't for you I wouldn't be here."

"Don't mention it."

Fox had another glass of the excellent wine.

"I should go," he said.

"No," said Cosima, "I insist you stay to dinner."

"Yes, please do, Herr Fox."

Down below, in the city, Olympia would be wondering where he was. Or Fox hoped that was the case because he had no idea really. He wanted to be back there but even as the effect of the clarity seemed to dissolve entirely his own desire at last became, at least for a time, something he could view from a distance. And staying to dinner was the least he could do.

"It would be a pleasure."

"If I could just have an hour to rest then I'll be on form again," said Cosima. "Why don't you go upstairs to the mask and puppet room? If you won't take a new hat then at least take a mask for Saturnalia. Go on, off you go. Now Anna please turn the record over I want to listen to the other side. It was rather a good choice after all."

Through the gallery again and the ruined ballroom. Now, in the fading light of the afternoon, the silhouette formed by the piano a taint in the darkness.

The room of puppets and masks had hardly any light at all and each protuberance from the wall of one of its inhabitants, an elongated nose, a horn, fangs, capturing their own varied shapes of darkness.

On Saturnalia it was a tradition that all the citizens of the city would wear masks and that the rank and order of society would give way to the impromptu order conjured from anonymity and charade. Disguises meant people could indulge in behaviour they would never entertain in their everyday life.

But Fox was sick of masks. He would be himself now. He would not go in disguise. If he wore a mask it would be a mask of what he was. And already part of him was laughing at the pomposity of that.

So he took a mask that would in no way disguise who, what, he was. A white mask, naturalistic yet without crease or blemish, a mask that did not cover his head with its cilia. Such masks were known as plain face masks. This one had a kind of wistful smile.

At dinner in the Yellow Room, Frau Kastner with a tray on the chaise lounge, Fox showed the mask to the sisters.

"Well," said Frau Pfaff, "I've never been quite approving of the whole custom and rather admired the Judges attempt to do away with it but if you are going to participate don't you think that's rather a dull choice?"

"Oh I don't know," said Cosima, "You could almost be one of the ultraclocks."

"Perhaps," said Fox, "I'll find myself a big old watch that ticks loudly. But no. I'm not going as anyone else. Just Fox in a mask."

It was a good dinner and he finished the wine.

Afterwards he kissed Cosima's hand.

"Take care of yourself," he said, "I'll see you soon."

In the vestibule, while the augmentation explored the outer edges of a nearly transparent cityscape in the VR booth, Frau Pfaff nodded formally.

"Thank you for coming," she said, "It means a lot to her."

CHAPTER TWENTY-ONE

Coming into the city the lights blurring, from the wine or the come down from the clarity. On the main road that ran down near the river was a nice view of the Towers. There was heavy traffic and Fox, sidling the Molina up to the trail of back lights realised he wouldn't be able to go another way now. It was the type of traffic that shunts forward occasionally but is mostly stationary, with long stops leaving Fox nothing better to do that to take in the lights coming on in the Towers.

Someone got into the passenger seat of the Molina. The woman in the mask of the medieval pest doctor. Another person got into the back seat of the car.

"Hello, Herr Fox," said Dr Pest. She held up the plain face mask Fox had left on the passenger seat.

"Hello, Demi," Fox said.

"Not Demi," she said, "But you can keep presuming if it makes you feel better."

"Mond?"

A forced laughter filled the snout of her mask. Fox inched ahead in the traffic then stopped again.

"I like your mask," she said, waving it, "Very understated."

"It's a gift. Now, what do you want?"

Fox checked the rear view mirror. The person in the back wore a plain mask.

"Who's your friend?" Fox asked Dr Pest.

"It doesn't matter," she said, "We're all friends."

"That's good."

"By the way," she said, "You're going to have trouble getting home tonight. Autocue Boulevard is once again playing host to the Renewal Society. We've forced their hand. Now, because they think they have an opportunity they never had before all their careful plans have to be re-examined. They want to seize the day and are frightened they'll miss their chance, if they don't act now. With the burning down of their nest and the disorder of yesterday there is a tentative offer of government, a place for Stefan Cappal. This is an obvious sign of weakness on the part of the Provisional Government and the Renewal Society will want to go in for the kill, march on Government House, declare a new order, age of Renewal etc. etc. blah blah.

"Except," she went on, "The workers of the Kirovwerk, the market holders of Sparta and all the lovely degenerates of Little Alex won't appreciate it. It's all happening, Herr Fox, the Renewal Society have filled Autocue Boulevard with their supporters following a motorcade of Stefan Cappal and Aksel Ritter. And meanwhile the people in masks are barricading Little Alex and Sparta. But of course you take such little interest in politics don't you?"

"What do you want?" Fox said flatly.

"Just a little help."

"Help?"

The traffic had stopped now, Fox realised he hadn't moved all the while she'd been speaking.

"Yes," she said, "As I say the Renewal Society are improvising but they are improvising on one of their plans. Certain people still have to be in certain places if they want things to work. We think they are going for scenario twenty-two. The Sword is going to be part of a direct assault on the Provisional Government, which is in emergency session. Vogt is already lurking in the lobby ostensibly part of the security detail. Code name Hierophant has yet to appear on the scene, but that's common to nearly every scenario. All we need from you is the rest of the details of twenty-two. Then we can see how closely they can follow it."

"And then what will you do?"

"Don't worry about that. Just tell us what you know."

Within the windings of the augmentations memory all the details were there. For each scenario a map, the positions of the various people, times when they should be there....

"You just want me to start reciting, like I did before?"

"Yes," she said, "But everything this time, not just the highlights. My companion behind us has a nice little vintage Perlcorder. Just start talking that's right."

Names of police officers, some of whom Fox knew, most not. Army officers, civil servants, government ministers. Fox lost track of what he was saying, which side who was on and what was supposed to happen. But it didn't matter. Presumably whoever had planned this needed to know both friends and enemies. So did the Masquerade.

The traffic shunted a bit forward over the twenty or so minutes it took Fox to talk through it all.

"There's a side street up ahead," said Dr Pest, when Fox had finished, "Goes into Sparta. I suggest you take it. If you want to get back to Little Alex tonight it's probably the best bet. Get as far as you can and walk."

"And how will I get into Little Alex if it's barricaded?"

"Oh don't worry," she said, "You'll get through. Even if nobody knew who you were you don't exactly look liked you fit in with the Renewal Society."

Fox did as she suggested, down a ramp into a side street of warehouses and high tenements that had once been merchant's homes and were now slums in the purlieus of Sparta. There was a car behind them, a black Mercedes. Fox realised now that it had been behind him all the time.

"You can pull up," said Dr Pest.

When they had gone Fox drove deeper into Sparta, where the narrow streets were quieter, shops shuttered. Even the laundry usually hung across the street from high windows, had been taken in.

It was only when he got to the Maskmarkt that there were people in the streets. The market was still going on but the men and women milling around were not the varied types of shopper usually here but appeared to be almost entirely locals recognisable by their workaday clothes and their way of casually lounging by the stalls and talking to the stallholders rather than looking at any of the wares. Here and there were people in masks.

On the other side of the street from the stalls Fox saw a young girl wielding what looked like a Landsknecht pike, wooden shafted and topped with a vicious steel spike. The weapon swayed as she walked and held it upright. At least three times her height. Perhaps she had liberated it from the military museum or it was a family heirloom. She stopped as a boy ran up to her waving a wood saw and she lowered the pike. The boy leapt over it laughing.

Fox drove on, across the market and onto the streets that led off the other side. He went towards Autocue Boulevard but met a barricade before he could get there. The people of Sparta were ready to defend their neighbourhood in case the Young Renewal kids or other thugs associated with the Renewal Society decided to go on a night out there.

The barricade was constructed around a wrecked car, bundled on with wooden storage boxes and some rather lethal looking metal chairs their legs pointed towards any potential enemy coming down from the direction of Autocue Boulevard.

A group of people were standing around a brazier that had been lit inside a steel beer barrel. They were laughing and talking, waving beer bottles at each other when a point was made. A few looked over at Fox as he parked the Molina but they soon got back to their discussion. A couple of kids were clambering over the barricade, one jumped off and then immediately began to climb up onto it again.

As Fox got out of the Molina and approached the barricade the boys stared at him from their perch on the wrecked car. Men and women started to look over at him.

"You can't go through here," a tall man said. There was no hostility, not really.

They all eyed Fox up though, trying not to gawp too much at the cilia growing out of his head.

"I need to get to Little Alex."

"It's all barricaded there too," tall man said, "And you don't want to have to cross Autocue Boulevard this evening. Looking like you do, you know..."

Fox shrugged. "But I have to get home. I'll climb over and come back for the car tomorrow."

Fox came closer and put his hands out to get some of the warmth of the brazier. It was late, getting towards seven o'clock. Soon Olympia would be at the Cabaret Vaucanson and Fox wanted to be there. He knew now that he would always want to be there.

A woman, young, dressed in work overalls, came over and handed him a bottle of beer.

"Thanks."

"Welcome."

"Do you think they'll come down here?" Fox asked her.

"I hope they do," she said. "It's about time they got something back."

After he'd finished his beer Fox managed to clamber over the barricade. The street here was empty and he felt an odd instant nostalgia as he heard laughter from back the other side of the barricade. He could linger there, spend the night drinking and waiting for the enemy. It was like a clip from a movie that it would be nice to inhabit.

He walked on and the laugher was gone, and the real urge he had remained. The need for Olympia.

On a little street that led between two shops and then on to Autocue Boulevard he stopped, looking at the backs of the crowd there, mostly better dressed than the people from Sparta. He could tell that even from behind. They were cheering and waving little paper flags, flashing white of the ankh symbol with its black sun. White and yellow light that was glowing somewhere out on the boulevard.

To get back to Little Alex he had to get to the other side of Autocue Boulevard but there was no way he could go through there. Maybe he could have done it with a hat. The only thing to do was to wait it out.

Up ahead were entrances to apartments, the fag-end of Sparta slums nestling above the rear of the shops facing out onto Autocue Boulevard.

He tried the door. It was locked but the lock was flimsy and easy to force. He figured that most of the people who lived here were back behind the barricade, sheltering, not wanting to risk staying for an incursion of the young men of the Renewal Society.

He took the stairs fast, past rough wood doors on each landing until he got to the top storey where there was a metal stairway up to the roof. It was a low flat roof that went out over one of the shops in the front, and this had large dormer windows and a service hut of some kind. The hut had a light in a caged sconce which allowed him to make his way through the heavy shadows till he was at the front looking over a low brick wall looking out onto Autocue Boulevard. High above he noticed there were birds wheeling in flocks.

It was windy, cold enough so that he drew his coat close. Down below he saw the parade. It had drawn to a halt before a line of police, including some on horseback, who formed a line stopping any further progress towards the way into the old town and eventually the Stadthouse. People filled the whole of the boulevard, lots of young men carrying burning torches, older people too. Those lining the pavement were part of it too but were still, somehow, separate, as though they hadn't quite taken the final step. In the middle of the road were three open-topped cars drawn to a halt. The headlights were on full beam, bathing an arc of the crowd in white light, making them bleached ghosts.

In the front car Stefan Cappel's bald head shone. Fox looked down upon him as he declaimed into the crowd. Luckily Fox couldn't hear what he was saying but people were cheering every few sentences. Next to Cappel was Aksel Ritter, arms folded, waiting for his moment.

In the car behind this were two non-descript Renewal Society types. And in the car behind that was Captain Kardos. Fox knew it was him even from this distance. It was the way he bore himself as he stood gazed over the crowd, as though inspecting a potential meal.

Looking around the car Fox spotted members of Kardos's death squad, trying to appear casual but on guard, ready to pounce on anyone that might threaten their CO. Fox was far enough away that the augmentation didn't stir, but even the thought of them threatened to bring on flashbacks of their violence.

Then Fox saw, next to Kardos, but sitting down and ignoring everything around her while she smoked a cigarette, the blonde haired figure of Lola Hello. Any idea of Helga coming and getting her cousin for a chat seemed rather daft now. Little Lotte had moved into an entirely different world.

Some of the birds had come lower now, not quite to the tops of the buildings but just above Fox. The eagle was there, looking down on everything. Once it glanced over at Fox. Or at least Fox thought it did.

Light flared on the other side of Autocue Boulevard as more torches were lit, their flames flickering as they came to life, held aloft by laughing young men. And the crowd on that side of the street stirred, the torchbearers leading off a group grown bored with the stand-off. They were going towards Little Alex.

Aksel Ritter stood up beside Stefan Capel and started gesticulating, pointing at the police. Then over at the breakaway group of young men.

Fox could no longer wait and watch.

He left the roof and went back down to the top landing of the apartments. He knocked on one of the doors. When no-one answered he pushed it in. The lights were out but he found the switch. It was a small place, the plaster on the walls cracked in places, the furniture in the living room old and worn. On the mantelpiece were photographs and china ornaments, and above these hung a picture of Count Septimus.

Fox found what he was looking for in the bedroom on a hook inside the wardrobe. A Sunday best hat, narrow brimmed, a sort of pork-pie affair. It was tight but he managed to squeeze the cilia in. He drew up the collar of his coat. He got back out into the hall and then went back into the living room again, leaving a five-mark note under a statuette of a shepherd girl petting a sheep.

On Autocue Boulevard he picked up one of the little paper ankh flags someone had dropped on the floor and waved it as he pushed his way along the pavement.

Aksel Ritter was still talking, or rather shouting. Stuff about our day is near and assuming the burden of renewal. Not quite at the police line Fox delved into the crowd on the street to get across.

He headed into Little Alex along one of the back ways he knew. Shops had their windows shuttered or covered with makeshift boards. From somewhere he could hear the shouts of gleeful youth intent on violence.

He ran into a fight at a barricade that was little more than a flimsy pile of storage boxes, chairs and loose timber, built across the street in front of a street lamp. The Renewal Society boys were trying to tear it apart, kicking at its base and leaping up and hitting out at the masked figure just behind it, a solitary watchman.

This lone defender, a man in an Orpheus mask, lifted a box from the barricade and threw it at his three crew-cut assailants. Then he quickly found a wooden stick and began to slash the air in front of him at them. They were laughing.

No-one noticed Fox till the boy nearest him went down from a punch in the kidneys. Then Fox picked up leg from a broken chair and swung it at the others. Orpheus jumped down the front of the barricade to join him.

They were kids really, these Renewal Society bravos, one on the ground whimpering, the one immediately in front of Fox barely the age to shave.

"Go home," Fox said.

But the smooth chinned kid jumped forward and tried to land a punch. Fox jabbed with the chair leg at the boy's eye pulling back just before it could penetrate and kill him. The boy stumbled back against the wall clutching his face, crying out in shock.

Orpheus brought his stick down on the head of the third as the one on the ground began to get up.

Fox kicked him in the face, feeling his palette crack. The boy began to scream.

"Come one," said Orpheus and dragged Fox back and they climbed to the other side of the barricade.

"Thanks for the help, Herr Fox,"

"What's happening?" Fox wouldn't even bother to ask him how he know who he was.

"I think this lot were just a scouting party. Trying to find a way into Little Alex. Fuck off."

This last was aimed at the three boys who were still there. The one who'd faced Orpheus supporting the one whose eye had been gouged. He was clutching at his face and Fox imagined the blood seeping between his fingers. The third boy was against a wall. He might have passed out.

"We'll come back for you, Paul,"

And the other two staggered away leaving him there, he was moaning, a steady droning dirge.

"I have to get on," Fox said.

"Sure," said Orpheus, "I'm expecting help."

Fox would go to the Cabaret Vaucanson because Olympia would be there by now. She would be preparing for the night's show because the show would go on. The show would always go on.

"You okay?"

"Cold," said Fox.

In fact shaking, wanting to sit down as the adrenalin fizzled away.

"You got anything to drink?"

Orpheus laughed.

"Not tonight, Herr Fox."

"Sure. I should go."

"It's okay. Others will come soon. Don't worry about me. You get along."

In a wider thoroughfare of Little Alex Fox wandered through the debris of another fight. Broken shards of smashed glass, bottles, blood drying to patches of darkness in the feeble

235

lamplight. Someone had taken the time to ankh a wall in white paint. Further back a barricade had been breached and so they were into Little Alex and Orpheus's lone vigil was pointless. Fox thought about going to tell him but had to move on.

He thought at first that everything was all right.

The Cabaret Vaucanson had not been touched. Then he realised that it was quiet, the doors were locked. He banged on them but no one came so he went around the back, to the alley, the back doors. The place where he had first met her. Where he had scrambled up, somehow kicking the grappa bottle into the gutter, where desire smooth as glass had begun. All the scenes that had eventually collided in the Green Room.

He hammered on the door.

Schiller came. Skeletal Schiller with his too loud ticking stood there not moving to let Fox in.

"Something terrible has happened," Schiller said.

"What?"

"Olympia," he said as Fox pushed past him. "She's in the Green Room."

And so the scenes collide again. Again as they always do. Olympia on the sofa, where he had loved her, for it had been an act of love.

Two shots had been fired. One in her chest, causing it to leak out the airbags that had once given her the imitation of breath. They hung in shreds like ruined sails. The other shot had destroyed her face, shattering her skin into pieces that lay on the floor about her leaving a gaping hole. Some part of him noted the multitude of tiny pins attached to a board.

They must have sat just beneath her skin, pushing out cheeks and curving smiles, lifting a quizzical eyebrow. The nothing of her mind, always a mystery to him, was revealed in destruction as what looked like a crystal formed of white rock.

The complex music box was broken.

CHAPTER TWENTY-TWO

The faint smell of burnt dust in the air and the corona around the wound indicated that a plasma weapon had been used. The same as with Lazlo.

"Mond was with her…." said Schiller.

They stood in the corridor. Fox couldn't go back into the Green Room. He wanted a drink.

"I'm going to the bar. To get a bottle of something…"

Schiller said nothing.

Cabaret Vaucanson was empty, the stage dark. When Fox switched on the light behind the bar the room filled with shadows, beneath tables and chairs, at the foot of the stage.

He took the first thing that caught his eye, a bottle of Polish vodka. When he went back to Schiller the ultraclock was still in the corridor.

"Mond is missing. They were together. They were going back to the Hotel Relojeria when we all decided there would be no show tonight."

"Where were you?" Fox asked.

"I was fighting, Herr Fox." he said. "And after I'd finished fighting I went to find them. Mond should have come to the barricade after she'd taken Olympia home but she is still missing…"

Yes, he kept saying that, that she was missing…

Fox took a very long swig of vodka. It made him gag and cough. Schiller looked on, fixed

238

expression, ticking away. "We need to find her," he said.

"What about Olympia?"

"There's nothing we can do now."

"I don't want to leave her here."

"Whoever did this could still be nearby. They could be assaulting Mond. We need to look…"

Another hit of the vodka, but a lesser one.

"Come on, Herr Fox…"

They went out the back doors, tracing the route between the Cabaret Vaucanson and the hotel. Fox stumbled behind Schiller.

"Where are your masked friends then?" he said, "Where were they tonight to stop this happening?"

"Mostly," said Schiller, "I imagine they have been trying to stop the Renewal Society thugs from terrorising Little Alex."

Mond wasn't far. Propped up in a doorway of rundown tobacconists in a back street. A round little man with a brush moustache was stood over her. She wasn't moving. As Fox got closer he could see the bruising around her eyes and temple, blood running from her nostrils. But he could also see that she was breathing.

"I telephone for an ambulance," the man said in a thick accent, "But they say they can't getting here what with the situation."

"How is she?" Schiller asked.

Fox put his hand to her neck, felt her forehead. He didn't really know what he was doing. "He's right," he said to Schiller, "We should try and get her to a hospital."

"I try to ring again?" the man said.

"Who are you?" Schiller asked.

"Herr Meliq. This is my shop. I thought to stay shut up. Keep quiet but I think she bangs on my door. She was here when I came down."

Lights were coming on again here and there in the street. A little further down a woman stood on her doorstep, hands on her hips, looking over at the three of them around the fallen Mond.

"I'll carry her," said Schiller.

"I'm not sure carrying is good for injured people," said Herr Meliq.

"We don't have a choice," said Schiller.

Schiller reached down and picked her up easily and gently with a fireman's lift.

"Where are you going to take her?" Fox asked.

"I'll take her home, and call someone who can help. Come on."

Fox followed beside him, Schiller moving in long strides, tireless…

"Why," he said to Fox, "are you wearing that ludicrous hat?"

Fox took it off and looked at it, then threw it on the ground. Sometime he might need another one but it seemed he had acquired a habit of coming by hats as much as a habit of losing them.

"I bought it off a shepherdess," he said.

Little Alex coming to a strange life again at the very hour when normally most of it would be shutting up. People out to look on their streets, noting here and there the evidence of violence, the broken bottles and barricade debris, but mostly everything was the same as it ever was.

"Where are the others?" Fox asked Schiller as they came to the hotel.

"Perhaps they are already back. We'll see."

But Fox didn't want to be here now.

"Where are you going?" Schiller asked as Fox walked away.

Fox ignored him.

Back outside the Café Castringius he peered through the window. Max was sat at one of the tables and let him in when he tapped. The radio was playing, a feverish news bulletin. Max switched it off and fetched a bottle of grappa to join the wine on the table. He topped up his own glass with wine and filled a glass of grappa for Fox.

"You okay?" Fox asked him.

"Sure," he said, "the radio says it's all died down now. The Renewal Society have gone home."

"They'll be back."

"Then the government has to do something."

Fox shrugged and downed his drink, poured another one and downed that.

"I have to go out," he said, not really to Max.

"Are you all right? You look...I don't know..."

"I'm fine," Fox said.

In his flat he pulled up the rug next to the bed and then got a crowbar from under the sink. Then he wrenched up the floorboard. He reached in and took out the canvas bag where the guns been resting all these years. He selected the one he wanted taking the parts out of the bag and arranged them on the floor, then began to put them together. Maglev outer tube over the barrel. He remembered the pock marked face of the old man he'd bought the

241

weapons off in Paris, near the burnt out shell of the Gare de Nord. Paris was almost deserted, flattened mostly, as bad as it could get with conventional weapons. It was only a week or so later that tactical nukes began to be used. The old man had shook as he'd opened this same canvas bag to display the contents, Fox's augmentation tracing the frantic beat of the man's pacemaker. Fox knew that he had expected to be robbed rather than paid, possibly killed if he resisted. Instead Fox thanked him and handed over ten thousand Swiss francs. Then left feeling sordid because he'd frightened him so much.

He'd bought the guns because he had to cross a Europe crowded with armies, official and free company, wandering everywhere, looting, shooting deserters and worse. Fox had never used any of them. But like diamonds in the soles of his shoes it gave him enough confidence to eventually make it all the way to Genesia.

When the weapon was in one piece he took out the shoulder holster that he'd always found awkward and eventually got it on. He slid the crowbar inside his coat pocket where it stuck out a bit.

He went back to the Cabaret Vaucanson.

The back doors were still locked so he had to wrench them open with the crowbar.

She was still there, a beautiful, violated doll that was not a doll.

She had been shot with the same, or at least the same type of, weapon as Lazlo. A plasma weapon that had left charring and had burnt dust in the air that had smelt when he had first come in to her.

This wasn't the work of a bunch of Renewal Society thugs; at least not the run-of-the-mill types. No, someone had deliberately come and killed Olympia, and more than likely it was the same person who had killed Victor and Lazlo.

He came close to examine her, taking her hand in his. There was something between her finger and thumb. He slipped it out. A tiny fragment of cardboard, smaller than his little finger nail. It had a straight edge of white and the rest was ragged where it had been torn from something larger. There was the beginning of a deep magenta colour that Fox recognised as the pattern on the back of the cards from the Clockwork Tarot.

He scanned around the Green Room but knew the deck of cards wasn't there because Olympia had given them to him. They were still in his coat pocket.

He put the fragment into his wallet. Then he smoothed back Olympia's hair and adjusted her dress. He lifted her in his arms, cradling her close to him.

CHAPTER TWENTY-THREE

Clarity. Too much clarity. It didn't help. Memories became labyrinthine structures he couldn't stop himself from exploring, as though he had become little more than the biological equivalent of his augmentation, hacking into, away at, himself.

He didn't go to the Café Castringius but instead to the little Cuman café they had gone to together. He'd sit and drink and try to think about what he should do. Go after Vogt and force him to tell what he knew. Find Lola and ask her about what had been said in the Club Adder the night Victor had been killed.

Instead he drank grappa and jabbed at his insides, chipping off bits of the past that only the clarity would allow him to bear.

Once he had called on Olympia early in the morning, unusual for him to be up but he hadn't slept very well. He thought he would take her on a walk, or perhaps a drive, but when he got there she was lying on the bed in, strangely vague, tilting her head as though she was trying to make out who Fox was.

"I was running down," she had said, "You have to wind me."

"Of course." As though it were no more than winding the little beetle. He hadn't known then what winding could be.

"I think I was dreaming," she said, "Sometimes it is like that."

"What did you dream?"

"It's silly, but still, it is something I often dream of. I am in a garden, perhaps it is Harmony because it is familiar. I wander around, I think I am looking for someone, but then I am in something like a grotto, a cave with odd carvings, faces like gargoyles in the Cathedral. But then the place becomes vast, a cave system that is dark, although I can see, or at least I know what is there. I can hear the beat of my mechanism, the ticking echoing. It wakes me from my revelry because it is not sleep of course because I hadn't run down…"

Then she laughed, her soft musical laugh. And she lay on the bed and opened her peignoir to leave a gap at the waist. She handed him the key and as he turned it inside her she laughed again.

Are dreams visceral? Do we flow through them becoming first one thing then another because that is how our bodies work, air becoming blood, becoming rhythm and thought. How would clockwork dreams be?

A day when they had gone up to Eloise Park in the Molina and they had talked of the differences between humans and ultraclocks. For them the running down, but always the prospect of being wound and time restored. Unlike a human heart beating a lifetime until it doesn't beat anymore.

The beetle had been there, running down, only to be wound again. Were there real beetles left in the city park? Down there did a scarab stir? The clockwork beetle wound again, off on its way. Is that what clockwork dreams would be like?

Perhaps, though, Fox's sense of time was not like other humans. The accumulated years without decay fixing him somehow in an elongated present. He recalled Felice's words at the cathedral.

And in the little Cuman café Fox heard himself laughing, the sound of it outside, distant even as it came, like a flock of starlings on the horizon making mysterious patterns.

He listened to the radio set behind the bar. The old man would have his face to it, almost motionless, only coming to life when Fox called for another drink. Mostly the programmes seemed to be historical dramas but occasionally Aksel Ritter or Stefan Cappel would churn out their speeches. From what Fox could gather Cappel had been given some sort of government position. There were still marches but from the look of them they seemed orderly, almost regimented. Fox supposed that that was part of the deal that had been made, Cappel kept Ritter and his thugs on a leash….

In the evenings Fox might wander, Little Alex, Sparta, streets he never usually went down. He found places where ultraclocks lived, ones he'd never met before who had ordinary lives as servants and shop assistants. They had no association with the Cabaret but they had known Victor.

Victor's had been a dual message. One of hope from a clockwork man who never needed winding, who never ran down. They would all return to Harmony their homeland, away from the degradations of Genesia. The other part of the message was that the ultraclocks surpassed humanity, and so must separate themselves off and prepare for a future when humans might no longer exist.

Fox heard variations of this, often spoken hesitantly, not wanting to offend. It was hard to tell what response Victor had evoked beyond a kind of deferred yearning. If there was a fervour or an antipathy towards humanity Fox never detected it.

There had been going to be a meeting. Whispers of it had spread among them. Even those with little prior involvement heard about it. The rumour was that Victor was at last going to reveal the location of Harmony, that he was giving all the ultraclocks a choice.

But the meeting was never convened. Victor disappeared and later turned up dead. The ultraclocks belonged to Genesia now. It was all they had left.

When they spoke of Victor it was with reverence, almost awe. Fox would ask them about Olympia and, yes, sometimes she had been with Victor. Fox would get them to describe her in as much detail as they could remember because he wanted to see her though as many eyes as possible. Back in his room as late as possible he drank more, took more clarity.

***

Sometimes he telephoned Villa Verloren and spoke to Otto or Frau Pfaff. Yes Frau Kastner was much better.

Max caught up with him once outside the apartment building when Fox was going home to change his clothes before one of his strolls…

"They've been calling you," Max said.

"Who?"

"The one called Schiller. A woman called Demi. They are insistent that you get in contact with them."

"I'm sure they can find me if they want, or their friends can."

But perhaps Fox was no longer of any interest to the Masquerade now that they'd got what they needed from him.

"Why don't you come in?" said Max, "I'll fix you something to eat."

"Soon, Max," Fox said, "Soon. I've just got to sort some things out. You know."

"You look thin."

"It's the medicine I've been taking."

He frowned at that, reached out and took Fox's forearm as though to lead him into the café and lay a banquet before him that would enact some kind of transformation of his spirits.

"Soon," Fox said, pulling away, "Soon. I promise."

In Pecheneg Square that night (or perhaps another night) they caught up with Fox. It was raining, a cold drizzle that meant there was no-one else around, which suited Fox. He sat on a bench where he had sat many times before. On the edge of one of the statue plinths a mechanical bird, one of those starlings, stared at him. Perhaps it was one of the birds they had all seen from the Elverbeds that day.

"Herr Fox," said Dr Pest.

She sat down on the bench beside him.

"The Cabaret Vaucanson has been closed for days," she said, "They'll be a private reception in the evening. I think you should attend."

"Why would I want to do that?"

"They'll be remembering Olympia. Saying goodbye. They laid her out in the resting place this morning. We tried to contact you."

Fox said nothing just let the drizzle run down his face. He thought of the rain falling on the awning in the forest clearing.

"You need to restart your investigation," said Dr Pest, "You need to find out who killed Olympia."

"Why do you think she was killed?"

"Perhaps she knew something about who killed Victor."

"She would have told me anything she knew."

"Then perhaps there is another reason. It's important to us all to know. We must know that there will be not future impediments to actions we might take. Victor was after all an ally."

Fox thought of the ultraclocks he had spoken to, the ones who might have followed Victor back to Harmony. As Olympia had always said, Victor had his own agenda.

"I'm not working for the Masquerade. In fact I'm not working for anyone anymore."

"But you do want to know."

"Look, Demi, why don't you just leave me be."

"You know," she said, "I'm nothing like Demi, or Mond. They're twins. Even without taking off this mask you should be able to tell my body shape isn't like theirs. Have you ever really notice any of us beyond what is superficial, and what we want you to notice."

"Then take the mask off."

"You think you would know me if I did?"

"Try me."

Fox got up. It was time to go home.

"Before Saturnalia," she called after him, "time is running out."

***

In his room he picked up the book that Mond had handed to him on that first morning that seemed so long ago. It would help him understand them, she had said. All this time he hadn't looked at it. Perhaps being with Olympia he hadn't wanted to understand them. Not in any cold analytical way.

It was a battered old volume, not much bigger than his hand.

The Clockwork History of the World.

The book seemed to veer from accounts of artisans of clockwork automata to proposing something like a parallel history of technology. A stream that split of sometime in the Eighteenth Century sidestepping the industrial revolution and clinging on in Swiss clock making valleys and the back streets cities of middle Europe the industrial revolution wouldn't reach until Stalin. Their work went on, little toys and whirligigs, out of step with the coming of modernity, waiting in the wings. Watching a society addicted to their electronic

250

digital gadgets the clockwork artisans bided their time. The clockwork owl of Minerva would only come out at dusk, at the denouement, to play in the petrified forests of humanity's hubris.

It made Fox think of Cosima, of her remembrance of her own time.

"How we were obsessed with adverts, with product launches. Little epics were made to advertise those trivial communication devices, aps and add-ons. It was as though Scheherazade had hired herself out to the corporations so as to sell and sell, little gadgets we didn't really need."

There was a crude technological determinist strand to the book, which gave an account of the world as shaped almost solely by the machines it produced and which in turn reproduced its social forces. The implicit question was, if the steam engine gave us the industrial revolution, what sort of world would we have had, or could have, if the clockwork technology of the previous age had reached such a pinnacle? It tempted Fox to retreat into Edgar Wallace Verlaine's Hat Theory of History. Yet he was interested in the next part. The history of clockwork automata themselves.

Descartes on his last sea voyage, called reluctantly to Sweden, kept talking of his daughter, who was travelling with him. The crew had never seen her and knew that he had come aboard alone, without his beloved Francine. Encountering foul weather then a dreadful storm, the superstitious crew began to talk of the workings of sorcery. Taking matters into their own hands they broke into Descartes cabin and pushed him to the floor, away from the oak chest he was trying to protect. Inside they discovered a clockwork child, a little girl of perfect beauty and proportion. As the great philosopher wept the crew took her out onto deck and tossed her overboard. The storm subsided, but then storms always do.

Jacques de Vaucanson's early endeavours produced two clockwork servants whom he had wait at the table for the visit of dignitaries from his religious order. The dignitaries were impressed at how life-like they were, how well they served. The next day the head of the order issued the command to destroy Vaucanson's workshop lest he produce any more of these clever blasphemies.

Years later, bedridden and ill, Vaucanson's fever dream conjured up a vision of what would be his first famous creation. He would build a mechanical woman, modelled after the statue in the Tuileries Garden of a flute player.

February 1738 she is exhibited for the first time. She plays twelve different tunes, without recourse to trickery but rather mimicking the method a human would use to play this most difficult of musical instruments.

She is made so that her body can be opened and the mechanism exposed. Since Vaucanson wanted to demonstrate his skill and artistry, as well as provide an entertainment.

Next a tabor player and a pipe player. Then the famous defecating duck. The human automata all seemed to have perished during the Revolution. The duck on the other hand outlived the Age of Reason and, sans feathers, may still be languishing in a Polish museum, no longer, alas, defecating.

Julien Offray De La Mettrie, the philosophical Materialist argued in Man, A Machine that life is animated matter of a given complexity. He comments on Vaucanson:

"If Vaucanson needed more skill to make his flautist then his duck, he would need to use even more to make a speaker, a machine which cannot be taken as any less possible, especially in the hands of a new Prometheus."

Automata would not long remain without a voice. Between 1778 and 1791 Wolfgang von Kempelen built four speaking machines with bellows for lungs, rubber mouths and a box containing an ivory reed glottis. This was his true work while at the same time he built the mechanical chess playing Turk that fooled Europe with its concealed dwarf inside.

Pierre and Henri-Louis Jaquet-Droz made a harpsichord player in 1772. She would begin by moving her head, eyes and chest as though waking for her audience. Not only did she play but moved with the music. She imitated the movements of female musicians of the age. She was made not merely to be a mechanical toy but to perform those subtle and nuanced gestures that the new ideas of sensibility saw as the outward gestures of an inner life of feeling.

The greatest artistic achievement of this era was the silver swan of Cox and Merlin. Her elegance and beauty as she preens itself, as she swoops to catch a fish, renders irrelevant any issue of how lifelike she is.

Mark Twain, who assumed she was male, wrote that "He had the living grace about his movement and living intelligence in his eyes."

It was James Cox who went on to develop the autonomous clockwork man based on his atmospheric pressure clock. The lock that needed no winding as was claimed to be a perpetual motion machine but is rather one that utilises natural energy to keep its mechanism working. A mercury filled barometer was attached to a winding wheel which was wound when the mercury responded to changes in atmospheric pressure. The lost or not so lost secret of Victor and the birds that needed no winding?

But at what moment does the breath of life enter these beings? When does animated matter achieve consciousness? We might ask ourselves this about human history for the clockworks are hard machines as humans are soft machines, that is the only difference.

***

Fox refused to think of either Olympia or indeed himself as a machine. He, more than anyone, had learnt how a machine knew the world. The thing in his head deciphered the world of signals, and how those signals composed themselves into data, then information. This was not how Fox himself apprehended reality. Nor, he believed, how Olympia did.

He flicked a few more pages. It seemed the author changed tack, trying to advance some overarching theory thought a dialectical process.

But it is much more significant the way that Descartes serves as the beginning of our story. More fitting than Heron of Alexandria, Daedalus, the clockmakers of medieval Europe or the Arab machinists such as the sublime Ismail al-Jazari.

For Descartes, the founder of modern western philosophy, was the instigator of the dualist school, which served to separate the concept of mind from that of body.

It might begin with the foundation myth. Involving, of course, automata.

It is said that Descartes first began to think about the nature of mind and body after encountering a statue of Neptune in the Royal Gardens. The statue was so contrived that when someone approached it they would step on a concealed button which would, by mechanical contrivance, cause Neptune to thrust out his trident and threaten those approaching.

(There is a viscous irony then, in that apocryphal story of Descartes's clockwork daughter, her fate is to sink to the realm of Neptune.)

Dualism in its many permutations, interactions, epiphenomenalism, occasionalism, Kantism, thought battles with its many opposing schools, not least the neuroscientific, survived into the era of the digital. This enabled proponents of the singularity to claim if not a respectable mantle, then at least one with a pedigree, serving to lend kudos to their claims that our minds might migrate to the inner worlds of a computer.

To ask, in this context, the question of the breath of life, is to rest on all sorts of unspoken assumptions stemming from centuries of these discussions about the mind and the body.

What if, as many philosophers believe, dualism is ultimately nonsense? What if consciousness is identical to the physical body that possesses it? If the mind is identical to the brain what then are the ultraclocks?

* * *

They were all there the next night at the Cabaret Vaucanson, Mond, Demi, Schiller and the Bakelite Brothers, Pozzo and the monkey, others Fox didn't know, whom he might have seen in the audience or even performing one time or another. It seem that a week had gone by since Olympia's death. It felt both longer and shorter.

There was no show on. Just people, without masks, at tables or lingering by the bar. Fox scanned for someone who might be Dr Pest but it could have been a few different women. She might not be there at all.

"Herr Fox," said Schiller ticktocking over, "It's good to see you."

He escorted Fox to the bar, people parting to let them through. There was a grappa waiting. Fox took it and went over to the table where Mond was sat with two young women either side of her who got up casually as he arrived and went to mingle.

"So you lived," Fox said.

She raised her glass, wearily tilted.

"And how are you, Fox?"

He shrugged. "Who attacked you?"

"Who do you expect? The nice respectable boys from the Young Renewal."

"That's who went after Olympia is it?"

"I don't know."

"I need another drink," Fox said and made to rise until Mond gestured him to stay put. She motioned one of the young women she'd been sat with over.

"Fetch a bottle of grappa to the table will you dear?"

When the bottle arrived Mond finished her wine and poured grappa for herself as well as for Fox. Someone was tapping a piece of cutlery inside a glass and calling for quiet.

"I think Schiller is going to make a speech," she said, snorting out a laugh, shoulders shaking. Then she shook her head, sadly, as the voices began to die down.

"Ladies and gentlemen," Schiller began. Mond took out her silver pill jar and tipped, onto a compact mirror, a little pile of multi-coloured powder. With the tip of her finger she separated some the powder into two ragged lines. "We have gathered here today to remember our good friend Olympia..."

"It's all bullshit," hissed Mond. A few faces turned to glare at her for a moment but then realised who it was that had spoken. She took a ten mark note from the pill jar. The note was curled like a wood shaving from being rolled so many times. She made a tube and snorted one of the lines of

257

iridescent powder she had made. She pushed the mirror with the remaining line over to Fox's side of the table.

"I don't want to stay here," she said. "Take me away."

"Where to?"

She tapped the edge of the mirror with a black lacquered fingernail.

"We'll see," she said. "Take some."

All the time Schiller had been talking, Olympia's wonderful talent, how much she had touched our lives.

"I've taken clarity," Fox said. "What will happen if I take some of this as well?"

Her eyes widened, inspecting Fox.

"It's a gentle rolling green...Kaleidoscope makes it all gentle. Your face is green."

Polite claps for Schiller but someone was shouting about murder, revenge.

Fox snorted the line of kaleidoscope.

"Let's go," he said.

Outside they stood in drizzle, a shimmering curtain of glass beads catching the moon and the street lighting.

"You know what I've always wanted to do?" Mond said.

Fox was watching the rain.

"What I've always wanted to do is see what the Cathedral is like when kaleidoscope is working. They say kaleidoscope is made from the ground-up bones of medieval illuminators. Do you think that's true, Fox?"

Where the pavement was wet it froze light silver and gold beneath his feet. Schiller and Bob were outside the Cabaret Vaucanson for some reason. Mond had lit a cigarette and was waving the holder, wafts of Sultanahmet, conducting the rain.

Arm in arm they went, out of Little Alex to pass the glare of lit up window displays at Steffi's and then the dancing shadows of the narrow streets towards the Cathedral. Even as the light display in Fox's head burst and dazzled the clarity forced an awareness of what was happening. Seeing himself and Mond arm in arm, walking in the rain.

The augmentation began to take an interest in what was occurring to his brain, imposing its own interpretative logic on what Fox could see. Various neural net pattern recognition systems came into play, trying to make sense of edges, shapes, colours. Because the kaleidoscope was mixing things up and nothing was easily deciphered the augmentation went into recursive spirals trying to see patterns that weren't really there. The augmentation began to hallucinate meaning, piggy backing Fox's own visual system, threatening to generate baroque nonsense as shadows became tunnel entrances, the patterns of wet light on the ground became sky fading to far away horizons....

"Fox. Fox," said Mond. "We're here."

Trying to focus he watched as he and she entered the Cathedral, a silent, vast, darkness, lit only by the guttering candles in the votive table by the octagon.

"Can't see the windows," Mond said.

Fox walked towards the shrine, Mond stumbling with him as she held onto his arm.

"I must have forgot that it was night," she said, giggling.

Fox took and candle from the jar and lit it. Then he took another one, lit that, and handed it to Mond.

They stood before the nearest window and held up their candles. Wax began to make new skin on Fox's fingers. He thought of being mummified in it. Silent inside like a cathedral, accumulating time, beyond the reach of either his own thoughts or the forever brooding augmentation...

Candlelight illuminated a scene from the life of Saint Genesius, the puttee face of the jovial actor rendered onto terror in the cells of ancient Rome. Tortured by Diocletian's torturer, cut up in ancient Rome, Saint Genesius's mouth open, caught in a stained glass scream, his mask fallen onto the floor.

"No," said Mond, moving her candle away. "Put the light on something else."

Fox swung round with his own candle so that the glow now reflected another window, Saint Genesius performing in a theatre, wearing his actor's mask. Another blob of wax fell onto Fox's hand.

"Come on," said Mond.

She took his hand as they sat on a pew, away from the windows.

"You shake," she said. "It's like the echo of a ticking, as though you're a dying ultraclock."

Clockwork. Mechanical antidote to the meaningless accumulation of data. Mummer knowledge, a play at hubris. They, the ultraclocks,

260

have no data in their limbs, bodies, movements. So far from the fakir AI things of yesteryear.

Mond was saying something wasn't she?

"…realised very soon that assuming they were anything other than people…"

Too long his world had been filled with signals. But the ultraclocks were not like that, which was the way it must be for everyone else who lived without his augmentation. Each a mystery that can never be solved, only guessed at by what they chose to reveal or give away by accident. Perhaps that was why Olympia had made him feel human again.

"It's all right," said Mond, "Let it out."

In the dark of the cathedral they sat in their capsule of wax light like jellyfish sinking in a lake. The outer darkness was not black but full of life forms, biomorphic shapes of shadow creatures formed by the furniture and fixtures.

Saint Genesius was an actor who performed for the Emperor. He had liked to enact mockeries of Christian ceremonies. One day he was performing a parody of the Eucharist when he collapsed on stage. An actor priest came on and gave him the real Eucharist. Genesius saw a vision, all his sins written in a book were being taken by angels up to heaven. On his recovery he became a Christian and even the tortures of Diocletian could not make him abandon his faith.

"I know the story," Fox said.

"What story?"

"What you just said. The story of Saint Genesius. The story just told me."

"I don't think I've been speaking. Listen, can't you hear how our voices now are cracking the silence."

She was holding Fox in her arms. He was shaking.

"What would God do with a book of some poor fucker's sins? Is that what God does, sit by a pool of ambrosia on a lounger reading paperbacks sent up from Earth, little misery memories of the repentant?"

"You're going to pieces," said Mond. "You need to focus on something. Be a detective. Solve the case."

"Was I ever a detective?"

"This is Genesia. Don't you get it? You want to be a detective, wear a detective mask."

They stayed while the candles burnt down and the darkness enveloped them. At dawn the light came through the windows illuminating the life of Saint Genesius. The colours filled them, rose and emerald, the angels rising to heaven.

The scene on the stage where Saint Genesius falls, the light of God entering him. Even the torturers looked blessed, playing, as they were, their allotted parts. Fox looked at the first scene, of the actor performing a mockery in his stage mask, not knowing that he is just about to don the mask of a saint.

In the morning he drove the Molina out of the city, out to Mond's summer cottage and the little path up to the clearing in the forest. Then he picked Olympia up from the grass beneath the awning and carried her to the back of the car. He drove though the deserted streets of the city, down Autocue Boulevard with its litter of ankh flags, up the road to the Heights and Villa Verloren.

CHAPTER TWENTY-FOUR

Pretending to be a detective. It had started not long after the omniscience augmentation had spread through his neural system and almost overwhelmed him with its need to probe for data everywhere, to accumulate as much in its quest to know. Fox had read the classics, Hammet and Chandler, seeing the human world as something that could be solved, as though people and society had inherent algorithms of their own, a narrative form that offered the prospect that he, like the augmentation, might one day understand.

Pretending to be a detective. When it was all over, when he had done what needed to be done, he would stop pretending. No clarity. Just a nip of grappa to steady the nerves. He was in Café Castringius by mid-morning, clean enough, smart enough, given the circumstances.

He had got Mond to call the police station in Sparta and ask about progress on the Lazlo Heck murder. They soft-soaped her with talk of a number of on-going lines of enquiry. It could mean anything. Nothing.

From the café Fox rang Felice over at the Towers police station. There was a long delay but then the receptionist said that she wasn't available. He assumed she'd guessed it was Fox and didn't want to talk.

He read the papers. He made himself eat and not drink too much. The fading kaleidoscope from the night before momentarily made the food look bright red, the cabbage like clotted blood.

The Gazette had all sorts of news about the shenanigans of the Provisional Government. Stefan Cappel, now Minister of City Ordnance (whatever that was) had proposed the banning of mask wearing in public. It seemed he had huffed and puffed about the terrorist organisation known as the Masquerade but he hadn't gotten his way yet. There was a small protest of mask makers who stood outside Government House wearing masks and carrying picket signs. There were even some objections from conservative members of the government about the traditions of Genesia. It was less than a week till Saturnalia and the city was not about to give up its masks.

After lunch Fox called Max over to his table.

"I want to buy the Molina," he told him.

"Why, Fox? You can use it any time you want."

"I'll give you a thousand marks for it."

It was almost everything Fox had left from what he'd had earned since starting work for the ultraclocks.

"That's way too much. And like I said, there's no need...."

"If anything happens I don't want it traced back to you. Let's do it now. Get the paperwork and I'll take the registration over to the legal district."

In the end he wouldn't accept a thousand but took seven-fifty. Fox took the registration documents and stopped off at Steffi's on the way. In the menswear department a pipsqueak boy shop-assistant wouldn't serve him but a middle-aged matron apologised and helped him pick out a new suit, shirt and trilby. When he put the hat on his head throbbed a little, the cilia no longer calmed by clarity. He'd have to feed the augmentation soon. He'd been neglecting it too long.

He looked at himself in the long mirror, adjusted his tie and made sure his coat covered the gun in its shoulder holster. By the time he walked over to the legal district he felt as though the disguise was complete. He submitted the papers that meant the Molina was his.

In Sparta, in the café on Maskmarkt, he spoke to Helga again, but she hadn't heard from Lotte. So it was back to the Café Castringius for a bite before heading out for the evening's work.

It is hard to pick up a trail after a death. He'd focus on Vogt. Not because he was sure that Vogt was the key but because he didn't care what he did to Vogt. He was quite happy if Vogt was the heart of it all. Then he could kill him. Then it would all be over.

Colours. Kaleidoscope remnants outside Club Adder, neon, the white that is not quite white because it is electric, fabricated, sick looking white snake white. Fox shook it off. Effects of drugs like a thought he could distance.

Stood in a doorway opposite Club Adder waiting for Vogt. Waiting for the snake.

He could stroll across and go in, sweep off his hat and present his head of worms to counter their snakes. But Club Adder was not the sort of place that would have appreciated that. So he stood in the doorway he had stood in before.

The first night he stayed for about two hours without anything to show for it. He went home when it began to rain.

The second night he saw Lola with Captain Kardos. Fox almost didn't survive the experience. The two of them got out of a dark Zil, Lola wrapped in a sable coat and draped over the captain who was in a dress uniform, black with white piping and epaulettes. This very moment was being recorded on the captain's life-bug, carved within him in a place he couldn't access himself but that Fox could. It wasn't just words but the rich interaction of thought, movement, sound and smell. If Kardos had just got out of the car and escorted Lola into the club Fox might just have caught a whiff of the rotten menace as he'd done before. But instead Kardos left her to lean on the Zil, the chauffeur sitting patiently while Kardos turned towards Fox, noticing him taking a few strides across the road to where Fox was lurking.

"It is rather an unsavoury habit," Kardos said, his pronunciation careful, sculpted, "to hang around in the streets. One might suspect all sorts of motives."

"I…"

Beneath the trilby the augmentation was already beginning its revels.

He like to watch, this man, Kardos the Sword. He liked to watch while others performed atrocities, the degradation of the perpetrators that he commanded just as much an integral part of the experience as the fate of the victims. The augmentation span through an array of burning villages, shootings, Kardos breathing through a gas-masked environment suit as the people of a town fell where they stood because of the nerve agent he had ordered dropped there.

This formed the surface of the life-bug, but there was another track, a digital unconscious not quite repressed. The times when Kardos allowed himself to get his own hands dirty...an apt phrase, everyone the blacksmiths of their own fate, but not soot and smut but the feel of a knife going in. Ironmongery and blood.

"I'm just..." Fox hardly able to talk.

Kardos had once stripped a young man and bought his boot heel down on his testicles, looking at the faces of his men for admiration as the victim screamed.

"Degenerate drunk," Kardos sniffed at Fox, spittle of his words on Fox's face.

Fox needed this to stop, thought for a moment of reaching inside his jacket for the gun, finish him off once and for all.

Then, something. Not really there at all, yet full of terror, lurking in the corner of every room that Kardos had ever been in. Perhaps superimposed upon his own past, a creature inserted into the scenes. A monstrous silhouette, the personification of the void. Licking its chops in anticipation. Ammut.

"Ambrus, Ambrus, I'm getting wet."

It was Lola calling, not seeing or else not recognising Fox doubly shadowed by the hat and the awning of the doorway, intent on her own moment.

Then Kardos was turning away, his parting shot a judgement.

"This ludicrous city needs to be tidied up of the likes of you."

Kardos and Lola disappeared into Club Adder. Fox slumped a little but managed to pull himself upright and walk a few steps back to lean against the wall opposite the club. The driver's door of the Zil opened. Vogt got out.

"You're lucky he didn't know what you are Fox. He might have just killed you on the spot if he'd thought you could access his life-bug. What are you doing here? Give me a reason I shouldn't arrest you and make you disappear somewhere."

"What are you, his chauffeur now?" Fox managed to say. His voice sounded as though it might shatter. He wanted to pull out the gun and finish Vogt off, but the face of the boy with crushed genitals lingered, like a light blot on his inner vision.

Fox did the best he could, leaning over and vomiting on Vogt's shoes.

"Lola," Fox said wiping away sick from his mouth as he stood, "came to see Lola."

"How sweet," said Vogt, rubbing the toes of his shoes on Fox's trousers. "Ugly old Fox is soft on Lola." He laughed. "You're pathetic, Fox. You really are. But she is a sweet girl I give you that. Still she's currently of interest to Captain Kardos so best if you left that one alone."

Vogt couldn't keep the amusement out of his voice. It was all so hilarious.

Fox thought he would vomit again and bent forward and Vogt bought his knee up and connected with Fox's lip, the iron smell of blood, a flash of somewhere near Mecklenberg where Kardos had done some cutting of a young girl to demonstrate to his men... Once again Fox bent and vomited, Vogt stepping back deftly this time.

"Don't come round here anymore," Vogt said and got back into the car.

Fox held his lip and his righted himself. He needed to keep Kardos's life from infecting him. He staggered around the corner to where he'd parked the Molina and started it. Up ahead he could see the Zil.

He followed as it went towards Khazarstrasse and the gate then along a little stretch of Autocue Boulevard before turning into the gentle hills of Gutunberg. It was raining now.

The Zil stopped at another respectable townhouse decorated with ankh flags. Fox drove past and pulled in further up the road watching in the side mirror. The Zil still had its headlights on. The light beams from the Zil spotlit the rain. Fox waited till he saw the lights go out and Vogt go into the building where one of those short haired idiot boys let him in.

With his tongue Fox felt his lip. There was a little scab where the blood had hardened. Iron. Crimson.

Vogt had called him pathetic and perhaps he was. It might be better to be someone else.

The plain face mask was still on the passenger seat and Fox picked it up and carefully fitted it to his face. He made sure every cilia was tucked inside his hat and pulled up the collar of his coat. From the shoulder holster he drew out the gauss gun, checked it over.

He didn't know what he was doing.

He took the deck of tarot cards out from his coat pocket. At random he drew one of the cards out. Put the rest in the glove compartment. He wanted to be a knight, a mage. Something intimidating. The card was 'The Wheel'. A giant cog. She had told him, across a zinc table, the significance of all the cards, and this was not the Wheel of Fortune of a normal tarot deck but wheel of entropy, of running down…

He almost left it too late, Vogt was already coming out of the house, carrying a briefcase when Fox opened the door of the Zil and lay down on the back seat. Vogt placed the briefcase in the space in front of the passenger seat and started the car. Fox couldn't see where he was going but soon, from out of the back window he could see the tops of the department stores of Autocue Boulevard. He waited for a quieter street, for the lights outside to grow dimmer. The buildings now were the red stone of the legal district.

Fox sat up and placed the barrel of the gun on the back of Vogt's head.

"Keep driving," he told Vogt, making his voice as much like the accent of Sparta as he could.

Vogt hit the footbrake as he flinched forward.

"Keep driving," Fox said again, "Or I'll blow your head off."

"You're making a big mistake," said Vogt, "Do you know who I am?"

"I know exactly who you are."

"What do you want?"

Vogt was holding his nerve well. Sooner or later, Fox knew, he would try and exert some sort of control of the situation. Fox needed to act soon. The trouble was he really hadn't decided what it was he really wanted…

"I might kill you," Fox said. "I really might."

Vogt put the slightest touch on the brakes so Fox pushed the barrel of the gun harder into his flesh.

"Who the hell are you?" Vogt said.

"I'm The Wheel," Fox said. "Now turn here."

He directed Vogt down a side street and eventually into Sparta where he made him pull over in a deserted street.

"Now," Fox said, "take your side arm out of its holster by the barrel and pass it back to me."

Vogt started to do this and Fox reached over before he could try anything clever.

"Now," said Fox, "You're investigating the death of Lazlo Heck. Tell me, who killed him?"

Vogt said nothing for a moment and then chuffed out three little laughs.

"Ha," he said, "This is all rather desperate isn't it? I'm afraid my investigation is somewhat stalled."

"Perhaps you should try your friends at the Renewal Society."

"You know," Vogt sounded weary, "it's true that the Renewal Society wasn't upset about the death of Lazlo. But they didn't have anything to do with it. A clockwork in a mask did it. Perhaps it's your friends you should be asking."

Fox tried not to sound non-plused.

"And Olympia?"

"I don't know any Olympias."

Fox poked the gun harder.

"As I said. Somebody in a mask killed the Magyar and his clockwork. Now, do you intend to shoot me or not. I have business to attend to."

"What mask? What ultraclock"

Vogt said nothing. Fox couldn't push the gun into his skull any harder. He realised he didn't want to believe Vogt but he did. And he couldn't shoot him (if he ever could have) since he had nothing to do with what happened to Olympia.

"How do you know this?"

Vogt sighed.

"What do I care?" he said, "Some kid called Hofner. Hans Hofner. Now get out."

"Where do I find this Hofner?"

"About ten minutes' walk from here in Sparta police station. Or maybe not 'Herr Wheel', perhaps like a lot of our young officers he's resting before the big day tomorrow."

"What are you talking about?"

Vogt laughed again.

"Maybe you need to get some rest yourself. Tomorrow is Saturnalia."

***

Outside in the street he dropped Vogt's gun down a drain and trudged back through the rain towards where he'd left the car. Somewhere between leaving Vogt and when he reached the Molina he stopped being the Wheel, took the mask off. He was tempted to throw it away, crush it beneath his foot. But it had served its purpose, so he held it in his hand, let the rain splatter on the inside of its blank face.

He sat inside the Molina, wet through, for the first time that winter he felt the cold seep into him. He let the augmentation delve through its archives, the records he had retrieved from the Castle, personnel files…. Hofner was there, part of some of the scenarios. A police officer and also a Renewal Society member, and being a regular person, not a Sword or a Hierophant, his record was complete with a picture and address. Hans Hofner could be the fresh-faced youth who Lola had heard bring the news of Lazlo's murder to Vogt in the Club Adder. He lived in Sparta at the police barracks. There was no way Fox could go in there, but under the confusion of Saturnalia he could find Hofner and could make him tell him what he knew.

With a crash on the bonnet the clockwork eagle landed on the Molina. It stared at Fox through the window screen.

"What do you want?"

It angled its head at Fox and then stared for a few seconds. Then it took flight and circled above the cobbles of the street before taking off into the night. Fox realised he was shaking, tired and much too sober. An ultraclock in a mask had killed Victor and Lazlo.

He decided he would pay a visit to the Cabaret Vaucanson.

It was traditional in Genesia that the eve of Saturnalia was spent quietly, with family, behaving in a way that conformed to the life of a respectable citizen or whatever status in life one had. Of course such conformity meant nothing to those in Club Adder where Lola and Captain Kardos were, and Fox guessed that the Cabaret Vaucanson would equally disregard the tradition. The difference was that many of those at Club Adder despised Saturnalia, while the denizens of the Cabaret would feel that the festival was their very own, that they had kept its spirit alive all year and now were waiting to for the rest of the city to enter their world.

So it was that Fox took a domino mask and walked into their party, into the smoke and noise of the Cabaret Vaucanson, the stage filled with musicians he didn't recognise, tables pulled back for dancing, and the crowd from the Hotel Relojeria around the bar as though they had hardly moved since Olympia's wake.

Mond came over and took his arm, drawing him into the group of Demi, Pozzo, Schiller and the Bakelite Brothers. She motioned the barman and a bottle of grappa and glass was summoned to the bar. They were all wearing elaborate masks, only Mond showed her face.

Fox couldn't tell Karl and Bob apart, who was the wolf and who was the pig.

Their masks were in the Genesia style, not naturalistic but stylised. Wolf mask, bright red ears, almond eyeslits. The face painted white with red and yellow dots and lines, odd swirls of colour. That it made no attempt to look like a real wolf added to its menace with the patterns and symbols hinting at rituals that could no longer be truly understood.

Pig mask. Bright pink almost ochre in places. Wide eyes-slits and a tusked mouth. Might have been a sabre toothed tiger except for the large black snout painted with crude white dabs for spikes of hair.

"No mask?" Fox said to Mond having to talk closely at her ear to be heard over the music.

"Tomorrow. I'll join the parade from the Maskmarkt to the Castle. I'll demand entry and proclaim myself Countess for the day."

The music was too loud. The pig and the wolf might have been staring at him. Schiller in a traditional mask of the Roman actor stood to one side. Fox would ignore them all, tap his feet to the music and drink his way through the bottle of grappa. But then the wolf was at his ear.

"And so Herr Fox," he said, "Mond had told us that you are back on the case. Isn't that how you phrase it? Your little meanderings around the city at our expense. Except you never have anything to show for it do you?"

Fox took a long swig of grappa, trying to think of a comeback but the wolf had gone.

It didn't matter. Tomorrow he would find Hans Hofner and maybe that would lead him to whichever Masqueradist had done in Victor and

276

Lazlo. And who had followed it up with killing Olympia.

"Just ignore him," said Mond coming up next to Fox, or perhaps she had been there all the time. Fox nodded, focusing on the band, on his glass.

"Schiller wants to talk," she said, "Later, in the green room."

Fox shrugged. It didn't matter. The music kept throbbing inside as he watched the dance floor, flesh and clockwork people, moving in various ways, according to their kind. A stick of a man wrapped his arms around the shoulders of a large woman whose body kept the rhythm perfectly, hips swaying as the man clung to her. His arms might have been oscillating pistons. Two clockwork women in tops hats and suits twirled like figures atop a jewellery box.

"Are you unwell?" Mond asked him. "Your lip..."

"I'm fine," he said, not bothering to shout or even look at her.

When they went to the green room, she sprawled on the sofa, smoking her Sultanahmet in its holder, the scent of it making a cloud around her. Fox sat in the armchair opposite while the ultraclocks looked down on the two humans. Fox still had the grappa bottle with him, half full, half empty. Mond of the sofa made the thing her own, displacing anything that had ever happened there...

"Will this take long?" said Karl.

None of them had masks on any more but Fox still didn't know who had been the wolf.

"We have matters to attend to tonight," said Bob.

The heavy ticking of Schiller stood in for a pause before he addressed them all.

"We all have matters to attend to," he said, "But Mond has assured me that Herr Fox has renewed his efforts."

"Isn't it time," said Karl, "That we put an end to this whole sorry farce?"

Fox took another little drink. The music was coming through the walls...

"You are being unfair and rude," said Mond waving her cigarette around, "Herr Fox has become involved in this...."

"Perhaps," said Schiller, "We should hear what he has to say."

Fox didn't feel like saying anything. He felt like going out the back doors away from this room, going out to where he'd first seen Olympia, somehow retracing his steps to be as he had once been before.

"Well?" said Bob.

"I'm quite happy not to take any more of your money," Fox said. "I told Mond that before. I'd still go on trying to find out who killed Olympia anyway. But without being beholden to any of you."

"But," said Schiller, "We have been paying you, and by now it amounts to a not inconsiderable sum. And while we appreciate that you may have become somewhat personally involved that does not negate your obligation to us. So is it true you have resumed your investigation?"

"Well," said Fox, "I did manage to get an interview with Inspector Vogt and while he seems to have little motivation in pursuing his enquiries he did, helpfully, point me in the direction of a potential witness."

"What witness?" said Bob.

"I'll talk to him tomorrow."

Bob took a step forward, big bulk of a moving statue, his brother beside him, making a matching pair.

"Then," said Schiller, "You'll come back and enlighten us won't you?"

Fox sipped grappa, wanting to be away from here, He stood up so that only Mond was still seated, smoking, staring at them all as they stood there.

"Sure," said Fox.

He put his glass down on the arm of the chair. Bob and Karl were in his way and he stood there until Karl shifted and let him get by to the door. He left by those back doors and outside, in the street behind the Cabaret Vaucanson, it was snowing, the flakes already having settled so that only the faintest dark traces of the cobblestones could be seen beneath the coating of white.

Tomorrow was Saturnalia.

CHAPTER TWENTY-FIVE

The horses will drag the float through the snow, on top, amid the paper flowers the muses in furs cavort as more snow falls, little flurries falling on dance, on mimicry and tragedy and other personifications. By the wheels and crowded around, the musicians play tabors, bagpipes, flugelhorns and mellophones. Soon they would be joined in the Maskmarkt by other floats, horse drawn, motor powered and then, to lead them all, the great litter in which the paper-crowned Lord of Misrule would be borne, through the narrow streets of Sparta.

Already, by mid-morning, all these streets and those beyond, are packed with masked people, the artisans and workers of Sparta, the café owners and shopkeepers, madams and harlots. And from the meanest back alleys of Sparta, down from flights of stairs leading to attics, up out of the earth from cellars, the Sparta ultraclocks came, walking in step, in traditional Saturnalia masks.

Smells of wood smoke, schnitzel, sarsaparilla and coffee, pretzels, sausages. Kids scooping up the foot slurries of snow and trying to make snowballs. The bell of a carter selling warm punch can be heard.

What do we see on the day of Saturnalia?

Why see? Why not hear? Why not smell? Smell of schnitzel, warm punch, smoke from cigarettes, coughs, laughter, the sound that crowds make that cannot be captured in a word, chatter of voices as they join, split, iterate.

And what is there to see?

Jugglers. Fire eaters in domino masks. Children holding balloons, letting them go to watch as they float above the roofs of the houses. A man with his mask pulled up so he could swallow a rapier and then a sabre. Sparklers fallen into the snow, melting their shapes into little sunken depressions. A woman dressed only in cigarette packets. Ensigns. Boys in plain face masks and midnight blue uniforms with gold piping carrying banners and flags of countries that never existed. Knock down ginger boys.

Foot jugglers in antique Brazil strips.

The little mermaid all grown up, her breasts a delight beneath diaphanous insulating gown of microfibres.

Pies on trays, held aloft by Bumblesque characters with waxed Prussian moustaches.

The ladies of the arcades dressed like Byzantine empresses with masks of gold formed of iconic tesserae.

Two men wrestling in a cage in Greco-Roman style, oblivious to the cold and the snowflakes that blow in and melt upon their fevered skin.

Pavement prophets, fortune tellers specialising in the arts of cartomancy, astraglomancy, conchomancy, crypto-ornithomancy, and futures seen in the dregs in wine glasses.

A sea monster.

A boy with a staff.

A girl with a pike.

Various children with skipping ropes, yo-yos, canackers, pogo-sticks, skateboards, roller-skates...

Water pistols squirting near freezing water, which, when it sprays the bare ankles of the Empress Zoe causes her to skip and other empresses to rock.

A man dressed as Tancred.

Clockwork Harlequins and Columbines. A clockwork monkey with a snare drum keeping an eye on the police.

Four managers from the Kirovwerk bearing a litter with the winner of the lottery who will be served by them all day.

A wolf.

A pig.

***

Do all the citizens of Genesia participate in Saturnalia?

No.

What behaviour does the non-participating citizenry exhibit during the festival?

Inside the houses of the upper classes they should be trading bon mots and drinking wine, keeping the season in their heads, and keeping off the streets where the world would be turned upside down, dreading a knock on the door and the appearance on the threshold of a worker from their department store/factory/office who might command them to become servants for the day.

What is the purpose of Saturnalia?

The purpose of Saturnalia is Saturnalia.

What then is the purpose of that purpose of Saturnalia?

To state that the purpose of Saturnalia is Saturnalia is not only tautological it is to hover over the risk of instigating a recursive algorithm that potentially extends towards the infinite. The phrase the purpose of Saturnalia is Saturnalia was used by Count Septimus during the process of resurrecting the ancient, not quite totally defunct, festival.

The purpose of Saturnalia is to channel into a ludologically complex set of behaviours, transgressive and deviant, constituting a diffusion of societal discontent and defining a boundary between normalcy and that which is not acceptable during periods of non-Saturnalia.

What is the purpose of the police presence?

To patrol the boundaries of Saturnalia.

And where are the police deployed?

The first squad encountered is waiting at the intersection of the back streets of Sparta with Autocue Boulevard. There are twenty-one armed officers under the command of a senior officer. They all eye the Saturnalia crowd as though waiting for something to happen amid all the things that are already happening.

What is happening now?

Out on Autocue Boulevard the crowd has swelled to fill the entire street, cover the pavement. This is the only scheduled stoppage of traffic on any day of the year. Outside Steffi's, in front of the plate glass windows of mannequins in their winterwear another squad of police officers watches the crowd. A young woman, a happy Valkyrie, plants a kiss on one of the officers, who looks around and checks that his CO isn't looking before reciprocating.

Who is that, standing apart, angrily shouting?

Local man. Tolerated apostle, spitting Jesus. Irrelevant to the story.

What is he saying?

That Jesus raised the alarm for sinners.

And what is the eventual destination of the parade?

Traditionally the crowd would flock to the gates of the Castle and call Count Septimus to come out, demanding that he act as a slave to them for the duration of the day.

And subsequently, since the death of Count Septimus?

During the reign of the Judges, known colloquially as the Court of Comedians, the festival of Saturnalia was outlawed on pain of death. After their fall the parade ends once more outside the Castle gates, where the Count is called symbolically, the seat of government no longer being here, but in the Stadthouse in the Old Town.

What role does government house play in the proceedings?

It is closed. The shutters drawn. Outside a line of policemen wait but the crowd doesn't come this way. As in most matters these days the Provisional Government is ignored.

What is happening now?

Outside Steffi's people are gathered around an old man with a cart who has encamped himself here, not far from the squad of police. He has a cooking stove powered from a gas bottle, the hob with two lit rings. On one ring is a pot giving off the pungent aroma of paprika. On the other is another pot filling the air with the unmistakable smell of spiced alcohol.

Beneath a nearby gazebo various ingredients, bottles of condiments and spirits are laid out, such as schnapps, gin and grappa. Those who like to watch the parade take a leisurely drink and might linger here for an indeterminate period.

The snow has dwindled to a few odd flakes and soon it will have stopped entirely. The press of the crowd, the proximity of all the bodies has, anyway, generated a warmth of its own. It has made waiting here not unpleasant.

What is an indeterminate period?

An amount of time that might pass while the passage of time is hardly marked, when taking a drink, for example, idly watching the crowd, the very antithesis of clock watching, except that in the city of Genesia watching a crowd involves a certain amount of ultraclock watching.

But how long does an indeterminate period last?

The amount of time for two glasses of grappa to be drunk and the faces of the police officers outside Steffi's to be scrutinised and compared to an image from a personnel file.

Which is?

Three minutes and fifteen seconds.

And then what?

Jesus raised the alarm for sinners. Jesus raised the alarm for sinners. As the apostle castigates the drinkers who laugh beneath their masks and the old man selling booze and goulash from his stall spits

285

Jesus back to see him off with piety between his legs.

And subsequently?

There are more police on Castle Hill, lining the pavements and managing to keep the revellers out on the roadway. The houses of the well-to-do will not be violated by gaudily dressed insubordinates who have thrown off their place in society for the day. The policemen here look markedly more nervous than those on Autocue Boulevard, they shift from foot to foot, and puff frosty breath in front of them, rub their hands not so much, or at least not exclusively, from the cold but rather with low suspense. Not exactly anticipating violence but open to the possibility, content that they are not too far from the Castle with its reinforcements and lethal weapons.

Atop their float the muses have been joined by the woman dressed in cigarette packets, and a retarius who has lost his net and trident. The horses slow, having trouble with the hill, hooves scrabbling on the frozen cobbles. The crowd forms an impediment to forward movement too but the beasts are docile, well used to crowds, and fall to looking at the ground, letting fall dung, and generally ignoring everything around them.

Somewhere the Lord of Misrule has been diverted into a café by his keepers, back off Autocue Boulevard, so that it is unlikely he will reach the Castle anytime soon to demand the Count come out and serve him.

Other floats are mired in throngs of people, netted in tabor beats and melodies of pipes, the odour of schnitzel, laughter and shouts.

In a little space the crowd has made just outside the railings of the house of a junior minister of finance a clockwork dancer is performing a little tap routine, steel heeled shoes clacking out a furious rhythm on the paving slabs to the delight of on-lookers. Nearby a pavement policeman tries not to look, tries not to be impressed, unlike some of his colleagues he bears no grudges, he would rather be out there in the crowd, an audience that is also a performance.

How can an audience be a performance?

How can it not? For even the most solitary of performers is her own audience, and let loose upon the streets, become a carnival, any audience becomes its own performance, losing the self-consciousness of who they are and what they do. For, as Kleist said of the marionettes, that they are the performers who never step into affectation.

What has Kleist got to do with it?

Up ahead, further up the Castle Hill, puppeteers are setting up in tents. Soon, before proceeding onto the Castle, the crowd will pour into Kleist Square, fan out, watch the performances, the children rushing to the front to clap and cheer. Here the policemen are more relaxed, even as the evening draws in and the sky begins to darken, the white snow-holding expanse above the city becoming the grey of old pencil lead. From a lingering point are the plinths, the statues of Kleist and his lover Henrietta Vogel, it is possible to see the faces of the

287

policemen, now licked by firelight from a bonfire that has been lit in a brazier.

Then why go into that tent?

To escape the scrutiny of the wolf.

What is inside the tent?

Thunder and lightning simulated by two blank masked figures to the side. One who flashes a torch, the other who shakes a broteion.

What is a broteion?

A bronze jar filled with stones that rumbles thunderously. It sets the scene for....

That part in the puppet drama where Mute the Comedian plunges a dagger into the belly of the pregnant Countess.

BLANCO: Is it done?

MUTE: (nods).

BLANCO: Then it's done good. But you know it doesn't make you big shot. I'm big shot.

MUTE: (brandishes knife).

CHORUS: There is no honour amongst comedians. Only knowing to stay as one will keep their gains.

(Enter FROGGY and ZERO)

BLANCO: It's done.

FROGGY: Then drag the wench's meat into the Royal Chamber. We'll break the Count's soul before we finish his body.

Boos from the crowd.

At the side a blank faced figure shakes peas in a sieve to simulate that it had begun to rain.

The masked audience inside the tent, both flesh and clockwork, gasp and jeer, applaud with revulsion at the dreadful deed they have seen represented on the tiny theatre of marionettes.

What do they do then?

They go out into the evening and the last of the daylight, the maskless faces of the policemen painted in shadows beneath their helmets, still visible to the careful eye, the cart of the Empresses has come to a halt nearby. The Empress Zoe, Anna Comena and St Mary of the Mongols have descended to the ground are all smoking cigarettes and teasing the policemen. They have lifted their masks a little so they can smoke, their lips are painted red, bright scarlet that glows even in the dying light, they laugh and smile, striking poses, legs spread making isosceles triangles of their frames, lines disrupted only by a hand on a hip. St Mary holds a bottle of expensive fortified wine, possibly Madeira, the journey of which, across a ravaged Europe, is not to be contemplated.

Thus it is prized, regarded as precious and unlikely to be shared?

On the contrary, the spirit of Saturnalia has infected even the royalty of the stews, so that she will obligingly put the bottle to the lips of even a hideous stranger who is presumed to be wearing a prosthetic cap simulating some kind of deformity, coffin worms burrowing up from beneath the crust of his scalp.

What does it taste like?

Rich. Sweet. Rough on the throat but not like grappa. Impossible to capture its essence with words. It tastes of its colour, an earthy red brown. Of the process of its making, heating the wine to

580 c and allowing a degree of oxidisation. It tastes of its history, a vinito de roda, a wine that has made the round trip, the taste discovered when a consignment of wine had been stored aboard a ship and kept there for an extended period and then returned to the island of Madeira transformed by the heat of the ship's hold and the motions of the vessel itself.

It goes down very well.

Is there much left?

When the bottle is passed back, to Anna Comena, there are a fair few mouthfuls remaining and she refrains from looking at the level of liquid in the bottle and back at the stranger who has already gone. The muses soon appear, having lost their float, which has perhaps gone on to the Castle without them. They chat and laugh with the Empresses, and the gaggle are joined by one of the wrestlers who holds up in triumph, one in each hand, two bottles, one of schnapps and one of vodka. Around them is a whorl of people, centred on the puppet tent, the whorl moving in jollity as though it might at any moment be sucked down into an invisible plughole beneath the tent and so never make it to the Castle at all.

The little cafes are full, their clientele spill out of them, others spill in, a tide of people lapping the edges of Kleist Square, the sounds of laugher and shouting, the rhythm of the tabor and the strained melody of Carpathian bagpipes.

To the Castle, someone shouts.

To the Castle.

Over near the exit, where the road leaves the square, a group of people, masked like everyone else, stand watching the crowd, yet somehow apart from it. They are not revellers at all. Among them are ultraclocks. There is a pig and a wolf. There are no police here now, they have been recalled up to the Castle. There is a crack, a sudden explosion up above as a firework whooshes up and then bursts in contrails of flame and emerald light. It will soon be night.

And from the door of a café out on Castle Hill, someone is shouting from the doorway.

"Sea monster, Sea monster!"

CHAPTER TWENTY-SIX

"Sea Monster, Sea Monster!"

Fox had followed the squad of police up from Kleist Square towards the Castle when Lola Hello appeared. She was dressed in a gold spangled dress and sable coat, gold carnival mask covering her eyes and nose. From the door of the café she skipped out and grabbed his arm, gripping him with her gold lace gloves.

"It's me Sea Monster," she said, raising her mask, "You remember?"

The street here had not yet become crowded, the head of the march lingering back in the square, waiting for whatever impetus would spur it on to the Castle. The café was a well-to-do place, among the well-do-do houses here. Out on the street though someone had tethered a rather tatty cart with accompanying horse to one of the old cornucopia units.

"Come and have a drink," said Lola, "You know I'd recognise you anywhere, even in a mask…. sorry"

She had pulled her own mask back down but not before Fox had seen the bruising around her right eye that her powder hadn't quite concealed. He followed her into to her table, by one of the windows. The place was almost deserted, the usual clientele keeping well away today from anywhere near Saturnalia. A waiter came over, stopping on route to lock the front door.

"You seem to have the whole place to yourself," Fox said.

Except for a young man at the bar who was trying not to make it too obvious he was looking over at Fox. An undercover policeman or something similar.

"I told Ambrus," Lola said, "I wanted to go to the parade. He didn't want me to but I think he was glad I was out of the way today. I'm to sit here and watch. Little Humbert at the bar is taking care of me, but he's a little scared of me, thinks I might taint him, spoil his chance of finding a nice little freulein to marry."

She raised her glass and waggled it at Hubert, who pretended to read the newspaper on the bar in front of him.

The waiter bought a bottle of red wine and poured two glasses and took away an empty one, along with an empty bottle.

"I've been wanting to talk to you," Fox said.

"I thought so. Helga said someone had been asking about me. Hey, you know I think Helga would be just right for Hubert there, don't you?"

There was something about Hubert. Fox's cilia had been probing all the time, so that Fox could catch a glimpse of dreary days spent behind a desk in an office typing correspondence. Then the presence of Kardos, whom Hubert had been suddenly seconded to by someone in the Renewal Society. Fox's augmentation sifted, searching, wanting something rich. But Humbert's joining a crowd marching through Sparta the other night was about as good as it got, and that had been uneventful. There was little more. Hubert had been fitted with his life-bug very recently.

"Yes," Fox said, "Although I think Helga might be a bit too good for him."

"That's true. Here's to Helga." She raised her glass.

"What have you been up to, Lola?"

"Oh, a little of this, a little of that." She took a mouthful of wine, her rose pink lips touched by quick visit of her tongue darting over them.

"With Captain Kardos?"

An expression might have spoilt the smoothness of her skin beneath the mask. The curves around her mouth showed for a moment. Fox had been watching for her reaction, wanting to see how much she would give away.

"He looks after me," she said. "He buys me lots of nice things. Things that little Lotte could never imagine. Or rather the sort of things that little Lotte used to imagine all the time when she was wiping up the spilt beer and cleaning the toilets in her uncle's café."

"That must be nice."

"Fur and jewellery. And shoes. And bags. He lets me loose in Steffi's. And I have an apartment of my own. Not far from here."

"And that bruise beneath your mask. Was that something he gave you too?"

She fumbled in a lizard skin bag she picked up from the chair next to her. She brought out a cigarette holder a bit like Mond's one, then a packet of cigarettes. She put a cigarette into the holder and lit it with a slim-line gold lighter. She held a pose, holder in lace covered hand.

"A man like Ambrus Kardos," she said, "has had experiences that some of us can hardly imagine. It isn't any wonder that he is sometimes a little...troubled." She took a long slow pull on the mouthpiece of the cigarette holder. Smoke trailed out of the nostril holes in her mask. "He's quite religious really. Goes to that Egyptian place in Gutunberg. Men only. Khepri or something. When I asked about it he says it's not my concern. Anyway...He's not all bad."

Fox tried not to notice the cigarette holder shaking in her hand.

"I think he's more than a little troubled, Lola. But I'm not your daddy am I?"

"I'll drink to that."

They clinked glasses.

"I used to love Saturnalia," she said, gazing out of the window. "When I was still a kid, fifteen or so..."

She said it like it was a lifetime ago, when in fact it was just a few years. But a lot more separated her from then than just the passage of time.

"We'd make our own masks," she went on, "we'd be doing it for days before, to make sure the papier-mâché had set and the paint had dried. The hardest part was always getting the elastic fixed so that it would stay on. Me and Helga would search the rag shops in Sparta for old clothes to make an outfit... Then on the day we'd be out in Maskmarkt strutting about as though we were a pair of duchesses...."

She took a long draw on her cigarette holder and then she drew up her mask, took it off and put it on the table.

"The next day we'd wander through Sparta and along Autocue Boulevard and up to Kleist Square. We'd pick up masks where people had lost them, usually cheap things but we'd get a few coins for them from a man in the Maskmarkt who'd repair them..." She pointed up at Fox's mask. "Take yours off too Sea Monster," she said.

Fox did and they both looked at each other. Her bruise was pretty bad.

"You've got a kind face," she said.

"You mean, for a sea monster."

They laughed together. Hubert was staring over, he couldn't help himself, realising the cilia weren't part of the mask Fox had been wearing.

"Seen Vogt?" Fox asked after the laugher had died away, and they'd drunk a little more. Outside the window the street was still almost empty.

"Oh him," she said, "He's the great match-maker. I think he had me in mind for Ambrus before he'd even arrived in the city. Vogt seems to think that Ambrus is important and should be kept happy."

"Why is Kardos here at all?"

She shrugged, her slightly drink loaded eyes rolling for a moment.

"Are you hungry?" she said.

Fox's turn to shrug.

"Sure," he said.

She raised her hand, arced like a dancer, clicked her fingers. The waiter materialised from somewhere.

"I'd like some…" She started to reel off a list of delicacies.

"Madam," the waiter said, "I'm afraid the chef is not in today. It is a holiday…" He gestured outside and, as though on cue, the first of the masked revellers began to arrive form Kleist Square, a tabor player and a bagpiper leading on a group of women in elaborate costumes, surrounding the cart that was there. One of the women tried to lift the other onto the cart, pushing at her rear end as she struggled drunkenly onto the back while others gathered round to laugh at her efforts.

"I'm fine," said Fox.

"You must have something to eat," Lola said.

"I'll see what I can do," the waiter said and disappeared behind the bar somewhere.

"I want to ask you something, Lola."

"You look a little serious Sea Monster. Don't spoil everything. You're not going to ask me to leave Ambrus are you?"

"No. Although you should. What I was going to ask you about was the night we first met. When you went to Club Adder with Vogt. Do you remember that?"

"Do you know how many times I've been to the Club Adder?"

"Lotte remembered," Fox smiled. "It was the night someone came and told Vogt that they'd been a death and Vogt went off. The night we met…earlier, in the arcades."

"I was out of my head," she said, "And back then I was pretty naïve. New to the whole scene."

Back then? Back seven or so weeks. She was living fast, and yet somehow, Fox knew what she meant.

"Do you remember who it was that came in to see Vogt?"

"Some kid...I think. You know I was still thinking about you at the time. I'd never seen anything like you and I kept asking Vogt what had happened to you. Why you were so deformed. Then he told me to shut up and that I didn't know what I was talking about. I started to think I'd imagined you..."

"And this kid comes in. What was he called?"

"Oh I don't know. He was one of Vogt's little gofers. Haven't seen him for a while. Although I might have done. They're all so very similar these clean cut Renewal Society boys. The police seem full of them these days. I mean it could be Hubert over there."

"Do you know if it was someone called Hans Hofner?"

She shrugged, slowly, a sleek mammalian movement. She would have looked alluring if it wasn't for the bruises just beneath the surface of her face paint.

"I don't know," she said. "All I remember is him going on about some fool being dead."

"It was *The* Fool wasn't it?"

The waiter came back with two plates of bread and sausages accompanied by a couple of artistically chopped tomatoes.

"I'm afraid that's all we can do," he said.

Lola picked up a piece of tomato and held it between her finger and thumb before popping it to her mouth and mashing it was a few sideways shifts of her jaw. For a moment she looked like a child dressed up in the clothes of her glamorous absent mother.

"Sure," she said, "It was the fool this, the fool that…the fool is dead."

"And what did Vogt do?"

"I told you," she said, toying with another segment of tomato, now squeezing it a little so a pip and juice oozed onto her thumb. "He just up and left me in Club Adder."

"Sure," said Fox.

Whoever Victor had really been working for the police or the Masquerade, his contact in the police had been Vogt. Vogt had known Victor was The Fool. Fox's guess had been that Victor had (as Olympia had always said) his own agenda. But whether he'd betrayed the Masquerade or not didn't matter so much as whether someone in the Masquerade believed he had. Vogt had told Fox he'd been killed by an ultraclock in a mask and that Hans Hofner had seen it. But all day Fox had scanned the faces of the policemen on duty at Saturnalia and he hadn't turned up Hofner. There was always the option of trying his address but he'd have to think of a way to get into a police barracks and somehow get out again after confronting Hofner.

"Look, Sea Monster, he's here."

"What?"

Outside the street was crowded, the masked people carrying burning torches all around the litter on which this year's Lord of Misrule was being borne. Fox couldn't see either of the Bakelite Brothers who he'd seen earlier, nor Mond who he hadn't seen but was sure to be here somewhere.

"I want to go out there," Lola whispered. "Go up to the Castle and see the ceremony. Will you come with me?"

Fox finished a mouthful of sausage. It had been a long time since he'd eaten and the taste had suddenly made him ravenous.

"What about Hubert over there?" he said.

The augmentation had flicked through enough of Hubert's life-bug for Fox to know that Hubert was dully incorruptible. Little there. Odd images. Pain of a knife cut across his chest. An insect about to crawl unto his skin.

Fox suspected that Hubert had always done everything he was told by his superiors in the police and now by his unofficial superiors in the Renewal Society. They'd said obey Kardos and that's what Hubert did, and not at all unwillingly. He had an awestruck adoration for Captain Kardos.

Fox finished another bit of sausage.

"Well," said Lola, "Can't you do something about him?"

Hubert was glancing over as they whispered.

"Well," said Fox, "Apart from knocking him unconscious I haven't any ideas."

But Fox's thinking was done for him as he began to see images replay from other life-bugs, those burnt out villages, the people murdered,

300

raped, the strutting presence of Kardos. For a moment Fox thought it would overpower him...

"Are you all right? Sea Monster?"

Fox gripped the edge of the table, pain shooting through his fingers with the pressure.

Then the images were gone, or rather not gone but overwriting bits of Hubert's life-bug... Kardos watching as a child had his throat slit, the blend of different life-bugs enabling a montage: the soldier performing the deed looked over at Kardos while the cold satisfaction that Kardos felt washed over the entire scene.

Fox looked over at Hubert, who was standing up, staring around as though he was lost. Fox didn't understand the technology of the life-bugs but evidently they weren't simply devices that recorded the inner life of their hosts, they could somehow feedback, or at least be made to feedback, into the host's consciousness. Maybe it was because Hubert's tape had been so innocuous that the augmentation had been able to do this...

"I..." Hubert was trying to get the barman's attention. "I would like...water."

But even as the barman was fetching a bottle of spring water Hubert staggered away towards the toilet.

"Come on," Fox said, "Let's go."

He snatched up the last piece of bread as he rose.

In the street the band were playing, surrounding the litter of the Lord, a mellophone player, a fiddler and a phantom of the opera on sax. People were dancing in the firelight from the torches.

The Lord of Misrule had changed his attire, or else it was a different lord all together. He stood on his litter in a gold Agamemnon mask managing to balance his wobbly legs while he swished his arms upwards urging those around him to press on. There was a microphone built in somewhere and his voice came from speakers carried by drama masked Tragedy and Comedy.

"Beyond yonder Castle," he declaimed, "Where the Count resides, to give up his place, he'll come to the gates and beg his subjects to treat him well while he is in their service…"

Cheers, torches raised, bottles of booze raised.

"Now sing a song, now dance on one foot!"

Lola was gripping Fox's forearm and pulling him through the crowd towards the litter as it made its slow way forward, up the hill. The head of the whole crowd must be some way further on because the road ahead was full of people. Fox could hear the raucous melody of the musicians kept somehow in order by the beat of tabor and snare drum that was now playing along.

"We should have bought the wine," Lola shouted, elated, childlike.

They walked by the litter for a while and people passed bottles to them, beer, wine, spirits, which they in turn passed on. A woman dressed only in cigarette packets turned out to be wearing a sheer body stocking underneath, she looked, now, like an odd Dadaesque collage.

At the head of the Castle Bridge the crowd had fanned out a little, parted to let the Lord of Misrule through. Fox noticed that here there were a number of ultraclocks, none he recognised although they were all in various masks. Three of them were particularly large wearing army greatcoats, they were as big as the Bakelite Brothers but there was no wolf or pig there. Another ultraclock with a traditional Roman actor's mask wasn't Schiller because this one had a shining cylindrical torso like the Tin Woodsman.

At the far end of the bridge there was a line of police around the gatehouse. Behind them the sheer solidity of the Castle rose, a stage set where the Prince is dead and the drama occupied by the invading army already.

The bearers put the litter down and the Lord of Misrule now stood at the head of a crowd that must have stretched all the way back to Kleist Square and perhaps beyond. The drama masks put their speakers of the ground and stepped back. Around the Lord of Misrule an arc of torchbearers formed. Fox and Lola stood with the Lord just beyond these.

"We've got a great view," she said and she squeezed Fox's forearm.

"People of Genesia," said the Lord, "It is customary now to call for the Count. But as we all know the Count is dead. Murdered by his treacherous advisors, the false Comedians, the unjust Judges…"

There were boos and hisses but the playacting had an edge and Fox heard snarled obscenities at the mention of the Comedians.

The police looked on impassively, except for the odd shift which might have been from the cold.

"But there are those in the Castle who want to restore the Comedians," the Lord said.

"But aren't the Comedians dead," shouted the drama masks on cue.

"There is one left… there is one left…"

Shouting, to the Castle, to the Castle. The voice of the Lord from the speaker suddenly louder above the clamour.

"The Masquerade are taking over the Stadthouse, the telephone exchange. We, the people, must take the Castle…"

"Is this part of the ceremony, Sea Monster?"

"I don't think it is."

The ultraclocks had shifted to the front, beside the Lord of Misrule. From somewhere further back a burning torch was thrown. It landed on the bridge where it fizzled for a few moments and melted its shadow in the snow. There were a few, perhaps ironic, cheers.

The three big ultraclocks pulled firearms from beneath their great coats.

"Let's get away from here," Fox said.

The police still stood looking on, like pasteboard figures in a shooting gallery.

Fox tried to pull Lola away, wanting to get back, down the hill, to be in the restaurant with Hubert sat at the bar reading his newspaper. But the crowd surged forward and someone fired, good old fashioned projectile weapon that sent one of the two-d policemen crumpling to the ground.

Led by the armed ultraclocks the crowd rushed onto the bridge, the pounding of feet on the steel rumbling like a thunder board.

"Stop."

Lola shrugged Fox off and started to run across the bridge with all the others.

"I have to get back to him," she said.

Fox followed as best he could as she slipped through the narrow gaps in the crowd. There was only another single shot and then cheers. Fox thought for a moment that the line of police must have abandoned their post at the end of the bridge. Then came the whoosh and roar of gauss guns and lighting up the air, brighter than the fizzle from the energy weapon. People were screaming, diving to the ground or falling. But up ahead the ultraclocks were charging into the police line.

Some of the crowd were falling back revealing the Lord of Misrule as he stood in the middle of the bridge. He was shouting something but then there were more shots.

Fox saw Lola darting along the edge of the bridge towards the police. He ran after her, caught her as she stopped some way back from where the ultraclocks were stood firing at the police.

"What are you doing?" he said, pulling her down.

They sheltered behind one of the stanchions of the bridge while the fire fight went on. It seemed like others from the Masquerade had come forward to even the odds.

"Don't you see?" Lola said. "I have to get back to him. He said that if something happened I had get back to the Castle."

"You can't get in there."

Fox heard himself laugh, high pitched, sounding almost hysterical.

"It's all right Sea Monster, he'll look after you too."

There was a burst of machine gun fire, bullets hitting the steel of the bridge, sparking and rattling around. Then the sound of feet and Fox's cilia rising to meet the wave, the men coming bearing inside the memories of burning villages, the stench of charred corpses and spent semen. Their boots were on the bridge. The death squad had come.

"Sea Monster? Sea Monster?"

CHAPTER TWENTY-SEVEN

Whadaya know? They are in a room inside the castle. There are no masks here. Faces are naked. If it rains, out there in the courtyard, the sounds is not a pea filled sieve but real rain, it blackens the cobblestones. There is no artifice here, everything here is real. What fills his head is real, that small village on a back road towards Lemberg. It is there that once can develop a taste for atrocity.

"I suspect," said Kardos, his face leering close, fish eye distorted, "That he is a spy. An assassin. Look what he has on him. The weapon. Gauss gun. The Tarot card of the Wheel. These cards have been used as a method of identification among the Masquerade. And the little mechanical insect..."

"Significance?"

"A parody of our sacrament."

"How would he know?"

"It is a spy's purpose to know."

Kardos held the clockwork beetle in his hand then dropped it to the floor. Crunch of his heel, untidy fragments, cogs and springs. Impossible to focus on.

The Comedian has no life-bug but Kardos's closeness threatens to overwhelm...the vertigo of infinite matrices as the augmentation leaps links from memory to memory, the bright cherished violence...It is spring and across the river the village nestles around the small onion-domed church. It is a ramshackle place of wooden farmhouses and barns. It is early morning. It is spring and somewhere a dog is barking...

"And those, on his head?"

"They indicate that he is an abomination."

Like a lot of these villages in Transgalicia it has seen its fair share of soldiers from various armies. They have come in, sequestered food, slaughtered livestock and taken the best beds. Two summers ago a young lieutenant had tried to take liberties with the miller's daughter but the Hetmen had sorted it out.

"He is," Kardos said to the Comedian, "what used to be called a creature of the singularity. An augmented person. He has had a device placed inside his head that allows him to interface with almost any electronic digital signal."

"What makes his augmentation different from your own? From the bugs you fellows have implanted."

The Comedians face was in a cloud of cigar smoke. A familiar face that has been lurking on posters across the city in other days and more recent days. Fox had seen it thus on a backstreet behind Autocue Boulevard.

"My faith is not to be trivialised," said Kardos.

"Whadaya? Whadaya," said Froggy the Comedian and once again he puffed out a cloud, shaking the cigar. "Whadaya going to do with the sap?"

Resurrection of old mannerisms that had been second hand by the time the Comedian had first appropriated them from some monochrome dream of the mid twentieth century.

"He was found with Lola, bothering her according to one of my men. It must be a way of gaining access to my person. I have seen him before, following me I now suspect. But I didn't know then what he was. In the field we had a quick way of dealing with abominations like this."

He never says he recognises the village when he arrives that spring morning with the band of irregulars. They have been tasked with the rather general objective of rooting out any enemy sympathisers along the river valley. He looks different from the day he left, his chin covered in stubble. In the motley uniform of this para-military unit he is not so much smart as intimidating; they all are with their standard issue grey flak jackets the rest of their uniform, their combat trousers, their different belts and buckles and caps, scarves and boots, all from dead men.

It appears that no-one recognises him, even as they run from the street back into their houses, even as they peek out before closing the shutters, locking their doors.

"Whadaya going to do with those?"

"I'm going," said Kardos, "To cut off the stigmata of his abomination."

But Fox, even now, can hardly focus on the secateurs, as he is swallowed by Kardos's memory, breaking down the door of the familiar farmhouse, stomping in with his comrades. His sister is older now of course, with breasts and a lissom shape. They will rape her before they kill her. They will probably do the same to his mother. His father is already dead, bullet through the head as they enter, slumped before the empty fireplace, blood seeping over an old newspaper used for fire lighting…

"I'm going to take away his abomination. Then I'll find some other tools to make him tell us what he's up to. What he knows. Then I will grant him the privilege of becoming one of us, of realising that all of us are merely whispers in the darkness that can only ever be held in the fist of God…"

In the bedroom the women back away, they whimper. Most of all he cannot stand this whimpering, pleading, this abasement. Then across his mother's face he sees her frown, an eye widen as she begins to recognise her son. This recognition threatening to drag him back to the idiocy of his life here. He acts before anyone can stop him and puts both his mother and sister out of their misery. Later he will get a punch on the jaw by one of the men who wanted them, one or the other, or both. He is regarded as soft in the mercy he has shown and for a while is held with suspicion. But from that moment on Kardos is free. Only God will ever know his achievement, the deed he has done to free himself. Watching it all now is that monstrous presence that Fox had glimpsed once before. The death beyond death that Kardos knows as Ammut.

Ammut, the hippo, crocodile, lion creature, that ate the heart of those deemed unworthy at the judging. There is almost a relief at that. Of Kardos being terrified by a bogey from Egyptian mythology. It could almost be funny…

And yet there, in those last moments Fox has access to Kardos's life-bug, there is a memory within the memory, from before he was ever fitted with a bug and yet because he has remembered it after, Fox finds it, a little jewel, a kobold prize, of his mother leaning down to kiss him goodnight...

The cilia are cut without pain. There are no nerve cells there after all. Snip. Snip...

Fox was in the room with Kardos and the Comedian. It was dismal, little light entering through a high grimy window of iron grilling. He shivered with the cold, he had been stripped to his underwear. Snip and the last of the cilia goes.

Then the thing called Evergreen Fox falls apart.

"Look at his face," said the Comedian, "Whadaya thinks a matter with him?"

Spinning in the whorl of Kleist Square, broken doll of Olympia, people lapping, stranded melody.

***

He was somewhere else. Strapped to a chair as he had been once before, surrounded by the ghosts of animals, now only in the presence of the revenant Comedian now and the walking recording of barbarity that was Captain Ambrus Kardos.

The room was not a prison cell but some kind of workshop or laboratory with a metal bench in the centre and glass fronted cabinets on the walls, a set of small sinks. There were no windows but in the far wall, far away, there was a door with frosted panels in the upper transoms.

"Well, Herr Fox," said Kardos, "You had plenty of ID on you. A card calling you a detective, your residency papers. And of course your tarot card. The Wheel is your code name in the Masquerade, yes?"

Kardos wore a uniform with a cobalt blue tunic and blue grey gainsboro breeches, but the tunic was unbuttoned, the belt of the breeches loose.

"You had a beetle," said Kardos, "some kind of gee-gaw intending to insult the sacrament. How do you know about the sacrament?"

The blow sliced down diagonally on Fox's eye. There seemed to be blood trails on the gainsboro breeches, but he knew they are on the surface of his cornea.

"You should understand," said Kardos, "That what Master Froggy said was true. Everything here is real. This is the place beyond theatricality. You don't have a mask here. Now tell me what you know about our sacrament."

The next blow was aimed carefully to hit the exact same place as before, a ripple across a lake, the pain filling the void inside his skull.

"You should tell him what he wants to know," said the Comedian. "Although I have to tell you this is like a show in so much as it'll be like joke after joke without a punch line the way things are going. And you see, he's getting another toy, artistry but real, you get it yet?"

It was some kind of surgical instrument. Scalpel. Lancet. There is a whole taxonomy. The augmentation would know…It lies silent but heavy, the heavy void, deprived of its senses. The blade comes down with a deft movement, an angle of the wrist expertly doing it across his cheek.

"You see," said Kardos, "I have always wanted a member of the Masquerade to torture. I thought I would have to go and get one but you just came to me. Tell me about the ultraclocks. About Monet Same and Oxenstierna. Was it always their plan to infiltrate the city with their machines?"

"Whadaya, whadaya? Oxenstierna was a pain in the ass. If he'd stuck around we would have killed him with the Count. And Monet Same, no one ever saw. Why do you think this sap knows anything about either of those two?"

The blade hovered around Fox's eyelid.

"There is a particular psychology concerned with the human eye," said Kardos, "We want to protect it as our most important interface to the world. It is the source of our personal mythology. Just below your eyelid, nesting inside the rim of your orbit, is the lacrimal gland. Now if I was to push the tip of my fine trocar in, that's right, just here... not only would it cause immense pain it would destroy your tear system. Would that bother you? Are you given to crying? Oh I see that you are."

The Comedian was somewhere over by the door.

"Tell me when he tells us something useful, Kardos. As amusing as this is I've got a few other things to look into."

Kardos put the trocar down on the workbench, with the other instruments and a full syringe. From a shelf he took down an instrument case of red morocco leather that was opened by means of a clip which he turned on its mounting. Then he unfolded the case. There was a set of immaculate scalpels and lancets displayed, other tool like the cutlery for meal that should never be.

Then he went back to the shelf and took down a kidney jar and placed that next to the instrument case.

Then Kardos moved out of view, fumbled with something and spoke.

"Yes, Dr Straka. My suite, the workroom. You will need dressings and painkillers."

Then Kardos was there again.

"Now Herr Fox. These are instruments for performing a particular procedure," he said, "I learnt how to do this from a doctor in Saxony. Made him show me on twelve subjects before I did it myself on the thirteenth. The doctor was the thirteenth.

"I'm going to take out your eye. Don't struggle it will only cause more damage than it needs to. No don't talk yet. I want to know that when you talk you are completely aware of what I am capable of. That if you don't tell me everything then I will take the other eye."

From the leather case he took out one of the instruments and held it up. It was a pair of scissors with long curved blades.

"The curve," he said, "makes it easy to insert around the globe of the eye so I can cut it from the orbit."

He put the scissors back in the case and took out a thing that looked like a screwdriver but with a wing nut on the handle and a loop of wire coming from the tip.

"Enucleation snare. The wire goes over the globe then onto the optic nerve and then I tighten the wire by turning the nut see…"

He demonstrated turning the nut. The loop of wire contracted.

Then he brought out from the case something that looked like a spoon.

"For scraping out residual tissue."

Someone came into the room, small dark haired man with a moustache.

"Captain, what are you doing?"

"Shush, shush. I'll tell you when I need you. I just need to show Herr Fox here the muscle hooks, see. The doctor here will use these to pull way the lids to allow me to perform the procedure. Now, shall we commence? No don't talk, don't struggle or shout. No. You had a chance but it was never going to be easy was it? Now something to keep you still and quiet."

Afterwards, when the eyeball was in the kidney bowl, Kardos pointed to it with the blooded forceps he was holding.

"There," he said, "around the nerve tissue. One of the little cilia has grown, tiniest of things but you see how much that abomination inside your head has infiltrated you. You're almost a machine aren't you, Herr Fox, not really human at all anymore. Now doctor, finish with the dressing, I have to change and call on Lola. Some of my men will come and escort Herr Fox to his quarters."

From somewhere outside the rumble of a bronteion making imitation thunder. Or was it real thunder? Or was it a series of explosions somewhere in the city?

CHAPTER TWENTY-EIGHT

The cell. Time passed.

It was difficult to know…

The cell.

It was difficult to know how much time had passed. There were explosions across the city but the city was beyond the walls, an imaginary place now.

The cell. Taken out of the cell by two soldiers of the death squad, their dark minds no longer accessible. To the room with the workbench, his belongings laid out there as they had been before, tarot card, wallet, keys, and the gun. The gun, just there…

The surgical instrument case open to expose its steel. The eyeball in the kidney bowl.

Kardos came in and sat in a chair pulled up close to the one in which Fox was bound.

"You know," he said, "Lola has been asking after you. She is most concerned. She said that I must take care of you. Perhaps you will see her later. If you have an eye to see that is."

The blade of the scalpel hovered near the surface of his good eye.

Inner canthus. Caruncle. Limbus.

The augmentation blind inside, spitting bits of its accumulated knowledge around. The blade hovered.

***

Fox told him everything. He, Fox, Evergreen Fox. Told him everything.

***

Except about Olympia.

***

Kardos patted Fox on the back, lent low and kissed his forehead.

"There," he said, "It wasn't too difficult was it? Don't you feel as though a burden has lifted from you? There's nothing you have to do now is there? All that nonsense, all those secrets are gone. And you know why they are gone, Evergreen? It is not because you have told me, no. It is because you have submitted to your true nature. The lesson of Pinocchio isn't that it is wrong to lie. No, the lesson is that it is better to be a puppet than aspire to be anything else. And now you are a puppet again. I can help you. I can guide you so that you act only is ways that will be beneficial. You do understand don't you?"

Fox nodded his head. He asked Kardos if he could go back to his cell. He wanted to be back there because sometimes he was able to think of Olympia. He could only ever do that when he was alone. He realised now that he should never have left her. He should have stayed with here in the Villa Veloren. The longer she remained there the more he feared she would become an inanimate object and he someone capable of only loving an inanimate object.

"Yes," said Kardos, "You can go back to your cell. I will send for you later."

317

In the cell he thought of her but it was too late. He could not see her as she was when she was alive, but only as the broken thing that he had found in the green room of Cabaret Vaucanson, the wrecked doll he had laid on the absurd four-poster bed in some unused room of Villa Verloren, while Frau Kastner watched on in pity.

When the explosions started again he rested his head against the cool stone of the cell wall. He wanted to feel the vibrations.

Time passed.

It was difficult to know how much time passed. Infer blank spaces. Many. Blank spaces disturbed only by explosions somewhere. Not near enough. Gunfire, not warm enough to help him.

All he knew of the area where he was in the Castle was the cell, the workroom and the passages in between. The cell had no window and therefore must a different cell from one vaguely remembered from earlier? It was featureless apart from the low iron-framed bed, the slop bucked and a drain the size of his palm. He had to empty the bucket down the drain with its narrow grill that caught most of the waste in it. After a while he didn't care about the stench except when he saw it in the sneers of the soldiers come to collect him and take him to the workroom.

The corridors in between were always empty except for Fox and his escort. Near the workroom the corridors were carpeted and the doors off them were neat, painted in white and gold. Except for the workroom, which had an iron door. He thought of these other, painted, doors. To get from here back to the cell you passed through one of these and this led down a spiral stair, till you got to a colder region, where it seemed like the walls were generating cold. With one eye now, distances played tricks so that his shoulder brushed a wall, he missed steps and had to steady himself.

Then the familiar smell of the cell ahead. But he couldn't always fix in his head which door they went through. It might have been a different door each time except that each time there was the familiar spiral stair, the relief of the cold, of the smell of the cell…

He thought that he was the only prisoner. He still wore the clothes he'd been wearing before except that his shoes and socks had been taken away along with his coat and jacket. He no longer had a mask of course, just the bandage where his eye had been removed. The eye itself remained in the kidney bowl beside his other belongings on the bench in the workroom. The eye gave off a faint smell like a stagnant pool of water.

Then he didn't really go the workroom anymore. They stopped taking him although he couldn't really fix the last time he had gone precisely. Time passed and he listened to the explosions and thought of Olympia. Of her lying on the bed in Villa Verloren…He hoped soon that the explosions would come here, that they would come and claim this place.

***

He sat on the bed eating something like porridge from a bowl. The cell door had been left open. After a while, when he looked up from the bowl he realised that two people were there, standing a way back from the open door.

One of them was Kardos in his beautiful dress uniform. Next to Kardos was Lola in a black lace dress, filigreed it showed her skin around the hips and stomach. Her hair was tied up and kept in place by an arrangement of pearls. She must be cold.

"There," said Kardos, "your beau, Lola. What do you think of him?"

Fox wasn't looking at them anymore. He was looking at the flecks of porridge around the edge of the bowl.

"No," said Kardos, "Well I'm sure he'll clean up well enough."

Later, perhaps later the same day, soldiers came. They bought the doctor who cleaned the empty eye socket and put on a new dressing. Then the soldiers took Fox out of the cell up the spiral staircase to the corridor with the carpet. One of the soldiers opened a door that was not the door to the workroom.

"Wash," the soldier told him, "The Captain's orders. Wash and get dressed. There are clothes in the cupboard."

It was like a hotel room, with a bed, a low sofa and coffee table and an en suite bathroom.

To shower Fox had to undo the bandage the doctor had put on and for a moment he was pleased that they hadn't thought of this, that they hadn't quite thought everything through, this mistake in the ordering of things could almost be a weakness.... He washed, standing inside the shower with both eyes, good and bad, closed and scrubbing soap into his skin. He ran his hand across his head, feeling the stumps where the cilia had been cut off.

He touched the skin over his absent eye, tracing the contours of the scar, deliberately making himself hurt so that when he took his finger away he would feel a moment of relief... When he was dry he put the bandage on his eye again as best he could.

In the wardrobe there was a simple uniform of black jacket and trousers and grey shirt. No piping or epaulettes. On the inside wardrobe door was a full length mirror. He looked at himself. For a moment only. The bandage had slipped and he could see the bruising around the exposed area. His head looked bare and cratered.

Someone knocked on the door of the room.

"It is time, Herr Fox."

As though on cue an explosion sounded in the distance and Fox thought he could make out the intermittent crackle of small arms fire.

In the corridor Lola was waiting with a soldier. She was in the black dress he had seen her in before. Up close he could see how white her skin was, that she shuddered.

"I'm to take you to the Count," she said.

"Count?"

"The new Count."

As they walked her fingers touched his for a moment.

"I'm so sorry," she whispered.

But Fox didn't know what for.

They left the carpeted suite of rooms and entered a stone walled corridor with a low ceiling. It was even colder here. There were alcoves every few metres and in the alcoves were arrow loops. Fox tried to look through these as they passed but only once saw anything except darkness. It was a brief flare of light that was followed a fraction of a second later by the rumble of an explosion.

"What's happening in the city?" Fox whispered.

But the soldier heard and told him to shut up.

They entered into a round tower with a spiral stair down and started to descend. They went in to more stone passages and then through a door into a gallery with pictures on the wall. Hapsburg Emperors perhaps. There was music, a jolly undulating waltz, the sway of the strings and the blast of brass filling the gallery.

At a door at the far end the soldier stood to one side and opened the door for Lola and Fox to pass through. They entered a balcony that overlooked a ballroom where a couples were twirling to the waltz, the men in uniforms, the women in long ball gowns that flared out as they were twirled by their partners. Other officers and their female companions looked on from the tables around the edges of the ballroom, while waiters threaded their way through them with trays of drinks.

Fox reached for the edge of the balcony but his hand didn't make it. Vision still getting things wrong. When he finally gripped it he held on to the wooden balustrade of the balcony for a moment as the music began to reach some kind of climax, the waltzers speeding up...

"I'm so sorry, Sea Monster."

The solider was no longer with them.

"Why are they dancing?" Fox said. Because no one should be dancing any more.

"Come on," she said, "We have to go. Froggy wants to see you."

"What is happening?"

"I don't know. They don't tell me anything. There is fighting in the city. It's been going on for weeks. No one is leaving the Castle now. Before Ambrus used to go out, leading his men and other soldiers. But no one goes out now."

The dancers twirled so fast that the hems of the women's skirts rose up high. One white dressed looked for a moment like those flowers that used to grow on railway embankments and waste ground in London, long ago. When he was a child.

Used to squeeze the bowl and the flower would fly out. Mother-says-pop-out-of-bed. They'd called them...

Bindweed flowers. Calystegia sepium.

The words itself popped up. From no-where or rather from some deep crevice where the augmentation hid, still inside.

Fox clung to the balustrade, the pain in his eye socket resurging.

"Come on," said Lola, "Please."

The dancers twirled and as the music finished the officers swept their partners half-way to the floor, the women stretched out as though in a faint.

"Who are they?"

"An advanced party from the Northern League," she said, "Come to support Count Froggy,

323

or the Renewal Society. Or both. I don't know. Come on, we have to go."

She took his hand and led him along the balcony. A few people below had noticed them and were staring up. Another waltz started and Fox could see the little orchestra now at the end of the ballroom. He stood still again and look over it all. He could see that there was something not quite correct about everything. The hems of the dresses were dirty in places, the uniforms looked like they had been worm too long without being washed because they were creased on the arms and chest, the shoulders slightly askew....

The rhythm of the music felt suddenly cheap, pathetic... Fox longed for the atonal music or harpsichord mathematics of Frau Kastner. Not this nonsense...

"Come on."

At the far end of the balcony was a small wooden door up a step. Fox had to stoop to get through. Then they went down the curve of a wooden stair and through another door.

Kardos and Froggy were waiting in some sort of stateroom, tapestries on the wall, a blood red carpet. Froggy sat on a gilded throne on a low raised platform. Fox wanted to find Lola's hand again, to grasp it.

"Whadaya know," said Froggy, puffing smoke from his cigar, "Our spy seems to keep losing the tools of his trade. You leave an eye somewhere, kid?"

"I..." Nothing came out.

"The captain has told me it all," said Froggy, "You're not even what you pretend to be are you? Not even a proper Masqueradist really. Just got caught up in something you never understood. Used as a patsy to get data from our systems and sent on a wild goose chase to find out who killed Victor. Do you still really care about that? Has it been worth it?"

Fox shook his head.

Kardos took a step towards him and Fox flinched.

"Come to me Lola, my dear," Kardos said. And Lola went over to his side and held his hand. Kardos would note that she was shaking, would appreciate it.

"You know," said Froggy, "Victor was working for us. At least I think he was. Helping us with one of our projects but maybe he was double crossing us because the things all crooked now. But you know what? It doesn't matter. We don't need it. And the funniest thing is, is that we didn't even have him killed. What Vogt told you is true. It was a clockwork in a mask. Maybe they thought he was working for us. Maybe not. And all the while you've been chasing this and it's all pointless. Don't you see how funny that is? Don't you? The world is vaudeville. The world's a routine. Everything is a joke. For us anyway. Little people like you are always the butt of the joke."

Fox nodded, not wanting to show on his face the thought that had suddenly occurred to him. His own thought, not the augmentation, his own because, it seemed, Froggy hadn't realised that he'd gone so far with all this for another reason, for Olympia. That in the end that's what it had all been about. Somehow he had kept something from Kardos even as the knife had hovered over the remaining eye.

"Now," said Froggy, "I thought the best thing to do with you would be to throw you off the battlements down into the chasm. But whadaya know, the captain here is going to offer you the chance of redemption. I think he's going soft in his old age."

Froggy did something with his hand on the arm of the throne, pressed a button perhaps. From behind one of the tapestries a soldier appeared, another of Kardos's death squad, seemingly reduced to domestic service.

"Take him back," said Froggy.

"Thank you," said Kardos.

Fox caught Lola's eye for a moment and then followed the soldier back the way he had come. He was returned not to his cell but the room he had been in before, with the comfortable bed and the bathroom. There was one difference: a book had been placed on the coffee table. It was a palm sized book bound in black calf skin and embossed in gold with an ankh. On the fly leaf Fox read the title.

The Book of Renewal.

CHAPTER TWENTY-NINE

Fox read the book. He suspected his life depended on it.

The part of you that will be judged weighs no more than a feather. Anubis weighs, Thoth transcribes. The mistake of those who pursued electronic resurrection during the so-called singularity was to misunderstand the role of Thoth. The recording of life is the preservation of life. The recording of life is life. Thoth the scribe stands at the threshold, he is not just writing down the result of a judgement but taking an account of a whole life.

This is the resurrection. Not before the golden sun of a new dawn but beneath the black sun of nullity, the end of the universe, the omega point. That which has been described using the label God.

The book went on like this before it progressed to an account of the wanderings of the nameless author across Europe in the years after the digital decay and the realisation that the promised singularity would never come.

Fox remembered talking to Frau Kastner about those days, about that singularity. The dead would live again inside computers. It would be so good in there that the living would migrate too.

The Book of Renewal was born out of the collapse of that dream. The life-bugs that had been fitted, first to soldiers, then the rich and a few others, no longer offered the prospect of digital immortality because whatever computers the lives could have been uploaded to were susceptible to digital decay and so were as mortal as any body of flesh. The life-bugs themselves, so long as they remained inside a body were relatively safe. They had never been given any network capability, they were meant to be extracted at death. Only Fox, or someone like him, with his ancient technology could eavesdrop on them since that was what the augmentation had been designed for, to connect to any kind of digital repository.

The nameless narrator carried his life-bug, wondering what it all meant in that post-decay society...the data was gone or going, the ecological disasters had disrupted the West...wars were breaking out, the tactical nuclear exchanges had begun...

The commander of a gun battery that had been ordered to defend a museum district within an unnamed city. Here were stored not just the accumulated treasures of that particular nation but the colonial loot of several other European capitals, sent there when those cities had fallen in one way or another.

There were no citizens there anymore, the soldiers would be spending their lives for artefacts that had no meaning for them, that were not even of their local culture but from other places, other times.

Soldiers should be prepared to lay down their lives. Even soldiers who were beginning to understand that the life-bugs they all had implanted no longer offered the prospect of digital afterlife.

The bombardment came. The destruction of the museums seen as a victory by the assailants. The narrator somehow survived as the war moved away to some other theatre.

He wandered in the ruins, amid the shattered treasures. In the storage warehouse he found, intact, the remains of Ancient Egypt, boxed up, safe. Over weeks, foraging in the city for food, he stayed there, began to construct his own museum, to surround himself with statues and wall paintings of kings and gods.

It was there that he received his revelation. As with most revelations he had to overcome doubts that assailed him. This took the form of a debate.

The debate was represented from the narrator's point of view, his opponent a shadowy figure that raised objections, mostly weak ones. (There is no-one else there, of course.)

The gods of Egypt are many masks for a unified single god, the narrator proposed. How could it be otherwise? For God is one or might as well not exist.

But, argued the opponent, what if we accept the masks for what they are? Faces of a multitude of distinct beings.

All would dissolve into chaos. A world that cannot be ordered by any respectable taxonomy. The ancient Egyptians would not find these amenable to their primary goal, resurrection and eternal life. The dung beetle god is not a dung beetle. Merely that aspect of God who creates from nothing, brings order out of waste matter. The bull is not a bull. The crocodile is not a crocodile.

And yet there they are, said the opponent, indicating the statues and paintings all around them.

These are merely the tracks that the divine presences leaves upon the Earth.

***

It seemed he had come up with a solution. He will create a place, an institution, The Archive. It is described it in detail, but as Fox read he was never quite sure if it actually existed or was something imagined, almost an elaborate thought experiment.

Here the dead's life-bugs would come.

In the great hall the scribes sit and listen to the dictation of the life-bugs. They transcribe the life, the person lives again in the text. One day the text will be assembled. A great book will be constructed and that book will be sent to God.

After this section of the Book of Renewal the writer changed. The new writer referred to the original as the Founder and gives and account of the Founder's missionary journey across the warzones of Europe. His first congregation was among soldiers who were still fitted with life-bugs as governments tried to perpetuate the illusion that there was some possibility of digital preservation.

The Founder shattered this notion and in the space where it had been he offered the hope of his new resurrection. If it was a bleak and tenuous hope this didn't appear to have damaged its prospects. Perhaps it even enhanced them.

We will be part of the Book that is sent to God, the soldiers intoned.

That part of you that will be judged is light as a feather but a billion feathers is a weight only God can hold.

Reading made Fox tire. His eye socket hurt. His neck ached from having to move his head to compensate for the missing eye. He turned out the lamp and fell asleep. He didn't dream.

Someone unlocked the door and Fox sat bolt upright shaking in the dark.

"Sea Monster," she whispered, and without turning on the light sat beside the bed. When she took Fox's hand he could feel his own shaking infect her.

"Lola..."

"Listen," she said, "He's asleep. In the ballroom one of the women talked to me. I'd known her before, they're all girls brought from the arcades. She told me that things are coming to a head, that the Renewal Society has little more than Gutunberg, the Castle and the streets around it. The Masquerade has made some kind of truce with the Provisional Government so they can focus on fighting the Renewal Society."

"Lola," Fox said, "What will Kardos do to me?"

There was a noise nearby, like something being dropped and Lola was already on her feet.

"Just hold on," she said, "And then she slipped out of the door and Fox heard it lock again.

In the darkness he listened, waiting for Lola to be found out. For something to happened that would mean they would come and hurt him some more. But there was nothing. She had told him to hold on.

He tried to think of Olympia but could only imagine her broken and ruined, not like she had been when they'd sat together in the Cuman café, or on the bench in Pecheneg Square, or when she'd been on stage in the Cabaret Vaucanson.

He turned on the bedside lamp. Hold on, Lola had said, but all there was to hold onto was the book.

Towards the back there was a liturgical section, excerpts from the Egyptian Book of the Dead with commentaries.

There was a passage marked lightly with a pencil line beside it.

"O my heart of my mother! O my heart of my mother. O my heart of my different forms! Do not stand up as a witness against me, do not be opposed to me in the tribunal, do not be hostile to me in the presence of the Keeper of the Balance."

Commentary: Ancient Egyptians believed that the heart held the mind as well as the soul. It is such a heart that is weighed against the feather of truth. A heart that is unburdened by sin will balance in the weighing. A soldier will have many sins but the Scribe in the archives will be an editor to expunge those sins before that soul becomes part of the Book that is sent to God. The Founder has made a provision for this.

Fox knew he had to resist the urge to view this as what it was, mumbo jumbo. Nonsense that had spawned in the ruins of the global information network, a kind of fungus that had grown in the carcass of the internet and the death of the prospect of the singularity.

He flicked through, looking at the odd illustration of Egyptian iconography, scarabs, the weighing of the heart in the Hall of Truth. Eventually he managed to get to sleep again. He did not dream.

A soldier bought breakfast on a tray, another one of Kardos's men, maybe one whose memories Fox had once read, now reduced to sullen glaring. Fox eat the egg, toast and marmalade, drank the coffee. He suddenly wanted a cigarette even though he hadn't smoked in nearly fifty years.

He was old. It seemed that for a long time he had lived one moment to the next, that life could just be that extended series of moments. Since he had come to Genesia he realised he had come to believe he could almost disregard what had gone before, all that had contributed towards making him who he was. Except there had never been just him, not since the augmentation. There had always been that other. It had recorded everything that he had ever come across that it could feed on. And Fox had kidded himself that it wasn't feeding on him too. It was no better than the life-bugs. And yet no, it didn't record his memories, at least they were still his own.

The soldier came back and stood at the door.

"The captain will see you now."

Fox lifted the breakfast tray but the soldier told him to leave it. He followed the soldier through the carpeted corridors of what he had come to know was Kardos's suite of rooms. He was led into a room he hadn't been into before, the first he had been in for a long while that had a proper window, a glass mullioned one, imposing a grid over the view of the old city with the cathedral in the distance. Here and there plumes of smoke drifted into the sky.

It was a kind of sitting room, large and divided into different zones by the arrangement of sofa and chairs here, a card table there. Kardos sat in an armchair and pointed to the one opposite.

"Sit, Evergreen. Please will you."

Fox did as he was told.

"Christmas has come and gone," said Kardos, "And hardly marked this year. I think the Provisional Government were using the Cathedral as a redoubt. It will be New Year in a few days. A fitting time for renewal, don't you think?"

"Yes, Captain, I suppose it is."

"You are scared of me aren't you? It is unfortunate but what I have done has been necessary. You needed to be rid of all your secrets and now you can move on. I don't want you to think of me as something alien to you. I am a man who has lived life in war and done what is necessary. In the end what matters is who wins. You are English. You should understand that after all."

"What do you mean?"

"It is one of the symptoms of a victor's history that the British managed to limp into the twenty-first century with such a certainty of their own benign nature. The perpetrators of Auschwitz were criminals, brought to trial if they were rooted out. And yet the British soldiers who castrated Mau Mau rebels in Kenya got to go home to their sweethearts, their cricket on village greens in Surrey. It would be

334

easy to think I am some product of what was once regarded as the barbaric east of Europe wouldn't it? And yet you're too knowing for that aren't you?"

Fox wanted him to be wrong. Not because he had any sense of patriotism but because he wanted there to exist a place where people lived who were not capable of atrocity.

"And look at the British now," Kardos said, "Their island ruined, they are scattered across the continent. Drunks and braggarts living in slums. Not even with the residual pride they used to have, the pride of fleas living in the corpse of a lion and thinking they are king of the jungle."

Most people in Genesia are decent, kind people, Fox wanted to say. But he knew he could no longer make that sound sincere.

"You have nothing to say?"

Fox shook his head.

"You know," said Kardos, "I believe that this time victory has eluded me. That it won't be I who write the story. Therefore I must focus on what is to come. As we all must do in the end. Tell me, have you read the book that I left you?"

What did Kardos mean victory had eluded him? Out of the window Fox saw something that he had almost forgotten about, the clockwork birds. They wheeled around a plume of smoke watching everything below.

"Yes," said Fox, "I have read it, most of it."

"And are you ready?"

"I don't understand."

"Soon you will die, Evergreen. You will die by my side defending this castle from the Masquerade.

335

Or I will kill you myself. I hope it is the former. When one accepts the sacrament it changes one's viewpoint. You will come to see that what you have regarded as something core to your being, to yourself, is little more than a story you have told yourself. When that story no longer belongs to you, when you accept that it will be given over to God, then false morality dissolves. The Founder has made a provision for our sins, they can be omitted. They can be edited. All that is left is the actions we take as soldiers in the cause we have chosen to serve."

What would be left of Kardos once his sins were omitted?

Then something strange. A thought. A feeling from Kardos. The faintest of playbacks. Image of his dead sister. Fox couldn't help it as his hand went to his head and he had to feign scratching. Very nascent, barely perceptible. Fox could feel the tips of cilia just emerging inside of one of the holes left behind when they had been cut.

"You mean the life-bug?" Fox said.

"It is so much more than that. When I die my story will be taken to the Archive, and my story is me. It is who I am, and yet in the Archive I will become edited, sanitised, what I could and should be. I will become palatable in the eyes of God. My heart will weigh no more than a feather."

Kardos was going to destroy what was left of Fox. If Fox was allowed back to his own room before it happened would he have the courage to do what was necessary to escape? He thought of the means, of a way he might gash his wrists, make a noose...

There was a flash of light somewhere outside then an explosion shook the room so that the floor trembled. The mullioned windows were covered in dust. Somewhere, not far away, voices were raised. There was screaming.

"Come," said Captain Kardos. "It is time."

When Fox just sat there Kardos gripped his forearm and pulled him up. In this way he led Fox to the workroom once again.

Fox sat in the same chair. Kardos did not need to strap him in any more. Fox thought he might have felt the augmentation groping again for the data inside of Kardos but then nothing. It was like a shoot that had encountered frost and returned once more into the safety of the earth. On the work bench everything was as it had been before, Fox's detached eye, floating in some kind of preservative, alcohol? That would be fitting. The eye stared back at Fox. Even when it was out of view he could feel it in there, still staring. There was Fox's wallet, the tarot card of the wheel. There was the morocco leather case too, now closed. The precise surgical instruments would be resting inside.

Only Fox's gun was missing, put out of harm's way he supposed. At least they took away the temptation to taunt himself with the possibility that he could grab it, use it on Kardos, even though Fox know he no longer had that kind of audacity left.

Kardos held something covered in a cloth of gold. He took the cloth off to reveal a wooden box engraved with a scarab resting on an ankh.

Another explosion sounded. This one closer than the last.

Kardos opened the box. There was a small knife the size of a penknife but ornate, the ceremonial sword of a toy soldier.

Then Fox saw it…

There was a scarab.

The scarab is Khepri, the dawn, the self-creator. Without Khepri there is only oblivion, nothingness. The Egyptians envisaged this oblivion as Ammut, the eater of souls who lurks, waiting, everywhere.

He almost laughed at the absurdity of it. The model of a beetle, almost life-like but made of something artificial, the plastic or metal carapace shining, catching the overhead lights.

Unbutton your shirt.

Fox did so.

Kardos lifted the scarab. It was the size of his small finger nail. It rested on the palm of his left hand.

"Repeat after me," he said,

"What…"

"Repeat. My mouth has been given to me that I may speak in the presence of God."

"I…"

"Do it."

"My mouth…" Fox said, but already he had forgotten the rest.

"You will speak in the presence of God."

With his free hand Kardos picked up the tiny knife. Then with a swift motion he slashed Fox on the chest, gashing the skin just above his heart.

Kardos intoned.

"O my heart, my mother! O my heart my mother! Do not stand up as a witness against me."

Fox put his hand to the wound in his chest. It was bloody but not too deep. He didn't understand what was going on. Why the incision had been made there. Why those with life-bugs always showed this scar, how could the life-bug have gone there?

But it didn't go there.

Between finger and thumb Kardos held the little scarab. It had come to life, its legs wriggling. It wasn't a clockwork but older tech, solid state electronics. If the augmentation had been fully functioning Fox could have investigated it, possibly even disabled it...

Fox suddenly tried to get up but Kardos pushed him back into the chair. Then he held the scarab to Fox's ear and it entered the labyrinth there.

"Khepri," said Kardos, "To come into being."

Fox could feel it entering him.

"A beetle wanders in the night tasting dust, smelling worms, feeling the ground. He pushes and pushes the seed of himself, a dried ball of dung. Insanity! It is one hour before dawn. Breezes blow. The ball of dung turns to gold. In the light of day, the ball breaks, beetles fly into the sun. This is Khepri."

"The scarab's body," said Kardos, "Is the hardware needed. What has been called the life-bug. The ball the scarab rolls is not his own dung, but Ra the sun. In this case the ball is you, your life."

It was inside. In order to do the work it must have to establish all sorts of neural connections.

339

Fox's temple above the entered ear was already throbbing.

There was a knock at the door. Kardos ignored it for a moment, staring intently into Fox's eye, as though to witness metamorphosis.

The knocking came again.

"What is it?"

A soldier entered.

"Sir," he said saluting, "The main gate has been breached. The Masqueradists have entered the outer courtyard.

"Order the men to the inner gate," said Kardos, "Rally what defences you can. Go. I will follow you."

The soldier went. He might have left the door open but Fox was finding it hard to focus now. Pain like an intense light blazed white across his head. Perhaps Lola was already through the door by then but maybe she came a few moments later.

"Come," said Kardos to Fox, "It is time."

Fox looked at the hand held out to raise him up. He felt disembodied, yet somehow heavy.

"What have you done to him?" said Lola.

"Go away."

"He's my friend," she said.

She came closer.

"What do you intend to do with that?" said Kardos.

Through the haze of white pain Fox tried to understand what was happening. There was gunfire somewhere. Shouting. And Lola standing at far end of the workbench with Fox's gun. It was in her hand, which hung loosely at her side.

Kardos was laughing.

"What are you going to do," he said, "Are you going to shoot me?"

Kardos tried to yank Fox up again and Fox staggered to his feet. There was something going on in his head, he could make out a shape there, and the shape was being probed by the augmentation as though the aug was trying to solve an intricate puzzle.

Kardos took a step towards Lola, letting go of Fox who fell back into the chair.

"Now give me that. You know you could never use it."

"Ambrus..." Lola said.

Then she raised the gun and fired.

Kardos lay on the floor and Lola dropped the gun so that it clattered beside him.

"What have I done?" she said.

She hadn't moved, just stood there looking down at Kardos's body, with the hole that she had blown into his chest.

"You have to help me, Lola," Fox said.

"Is he dead? I think he's dead."

"Just help me up Lola. We have to get out of here."

The shape inside Fox's head had resolved into a kind of image. Not something he could see as such. Odd feeling of not quite knowing. Face of a long lost childhood toy...

Lola helped Fox up and he stepped over the body. It was strange that Kardos was dead when he had come to be almost the whole of Fox's existence.

Fox didn't really get that Kardos could be dead and Fox alive.

"Look. What's that?"

Something was crawling out of Kardos's nose, a tiny thing, its carapace smeared with blood. A scarab almost identical to the one that was now inside Fox.

Lola took a step backwards.

At the edge of the philtrum the beetle crawled a few more steps leaving a trail of tiny blood prints. Then the carapace opened and the wings spread and it flew up into the air.

"Oh my god. What is it?" said Lola.

The scarab flew around and then in the direction of the open door. Then it was gone. Off to find the archive, to deliver Kardos so that he might become part of the book that would be sent to God.

"We have to get out of here," said Fox. "What's happening outside?"

Fox picked up the gun from the floor and put it in his waistband. He got his wallet and the tarot card from the workbench.

"We should hide somewhere, shouldn't we?" Lola said.

She was holding Fox's hand. She wasn't shaking anymore, but her grip was tight and she wouldn't let go as they found their way through the deserted suite into the spiral stairs.

"We could go back to the cells," Fox said.

There was nothing specific in his head just the throbbing. He became aware again of the cut in his chest. He put his hand to it to stop the bleeding.

"There's a guard room," she said. "I saw it before. When I came down."

"Where do these stairs lead to?"

"I think we will have to get out of the great keep," she said, "Get somewhere else."

"There's the undercrofts."

Fox took his hand away from the wound on his chest. His fingers were muddy with blood. He sat on the stairs.

"I'm going to have to do something about this," he said. He'd hardly noticed it, all the while trying to focus through the throbbing in his head, the augmentation lashing away at the interloper it had found.

"We should have fixed it in the workroom," she said. "There would have been bandages. I wasn't thinking. I'm sorry. I should have been more…"

"It's all right."

It's all right that you've just killed someone.

"We could go back," she said, almost brightly, suggesting a trip to a favourite picnic spot.

"Just a cloth would do," Fox said, "Some rags to bind this up with. To stop the bleeding. If I could just get out of this shirt."

She helped him do it and they bound the wound as best they could.

"Perhaps we should just stay here," she said, "Stay and wait for it to all be over."

"We need to know what's going on. What we do depends on what happens to the Castle. We should go up. Somewhere we can see." But the thought of going upstairs was almost overwhelming. And then there was the sudden

343

weight of what he'd felt once before, the very presence of the castle, its walls, its stone pressing down on him. He needed to get out. At least at the top they might be able to come out into the air.

He clung to her hand, step after step, the wound in his chest merging with the pain in his head and the empty eye socket. When he tried to focus all he saw was the ragged grey expanse of the walls of the tower the stairs spiralled up through. There was shouting somewhere, gunfire, but it had become constant, like the buzzing in his ears, his skull. Lola was talking but he couldn't really follow what she was saying. Perhaps it was all being recorded on the life-bug and would be played back for God's amusement one day soon.

Then something changed because he felt air on his face and a moment later they were out on the narrow battlements, high up at the edge of the great keep. The door they had come through was in the conical roof of the tower. The battlements ran partly around it and then off in a line. The roof of the keep itself was below, the height of several men beneath where they perched. Fox clung to the tooth of a crenulation. He looked out over the castle, and the city beyond. It was night. Some of the houses were lit and fires were burning in places, showing darting tongues of flames and blooms of smoke, he could taste the smoke on the air.

"Look," said Lola.

She was on the other side of the walkway from Fox, looking over a plain wall, the inner wall. Fox went over and looked down into the inner courtyard. It was like peering into pool filled with electric fish.

Down in the inner courtyard there was the flaring of small arms fire and the rapid flashes of energy weapons. In the moments of illumination Fox saw people crouched behind a car on its side. Others were using the stairwell of the undercrofts as cover.

Some of the shooting came from low windows around the courtyard. Silhouettes ran along the edges of walls. He couldn't tell who was who.

He tried to think straight. There might be a way into the outer courtyard. It would be difficult... He couldn't focus. Outside the ambient light of the city and the gunfire it would be dark everywhere and cold. But the cold was somehow good. It was outside.

"Where do the battlements lead?" he said.

"I don't know, another tower I suppose."

Away from the great keep. So another tower might take them down somewhere else.

"Come on," he said, taking Lola by the hand.

But the next tower was just a guard tower. A covered room, roofed with arrow slits with a door to the next section of battlement, and not stairs leading down at all. Fox was suddenly spent. He sat down outside on the walkway, back to the wall of the tower. He closed his eyes, felt Lola next to him.

"We should go on," she said.

"I need to rest. Besides everyone seems to be occupied down there. I don't suppose they've even got the manpower to send someone to look for Kardos."

They waited there while the firing went on below. At some point the cold drove them inside the guard tower. The night passed away and became quiet. Maybe down below they had reached some kind of stalemate.

Lola spoke.

"No-one has to know what I did, do they?"

"I was kind of hoping that the side that would be pleased he was dead would win."

"Do you think they will?"

"I don't know."

Fox heard himself laugh, a sort of echo inside his head. It went on too long, wounded animal in a bucket.

"You're scaring me, Sea Monster."

He didn't understand what she was talking about.

"Stop it, please."

Then it broke, and Fox sobbed, his head resting on his knees, one good eye welling with tears. Lola held him.

"Let's not wait here," she said, "Let's do something."

He sunk into her encircling arm. He just wanted it all to stop. The pain in his chest, his eye socket, inside his head. He wanted to be free of the Castle.

Fox stood up and went out from the tower onto the battlements. He walked on, in the opposite direction from the way they'd come. At one point he could feel he was jogging.

"What are you doing?"

He thought of the scarab crawling out of the dead Kardos, flying off, finding its way out...The grey of the sky seen from the battlements... He gripped the crenulations. There was a moon now, and the sky was pewter, but in the east the first traces of dawn were coming, base metal into bronze.

"Don't, Sea Monster."

The wind was lovely. So long since he had felt it.

"Get down."

She was holding him round the waist as he sat wedged between two of the crenulations. The air felt so good and the great darkness below that would soon be washed away. He could tell where they were now, a spur of the battlements on the outer wall, on the edge of the great outcrop of rock the castle rested on. Below there was nothing. To fall here would be to escape from the city itself.

"Look."

***

"Look," said Lola. "That way."

Fox got down and looked where she pointed, in the direction of the city. The sky was dotted, the dots rushing towards them. The clockwork birds had come. Something in his head now, out of the Book of Renewal, the ibis amongst the reeds.

But this is not Egypt. This is not the Delta. Those birds do not come from the scribe.

"What?"

They both looked down into the outer courtyard below as the birds wheeled around above it. Highest of all was the eagle, bigger than the others, the starlings and songbirds, magpies and crows.

"Pityings of doves. Tidings of ravens. Mumuration of starlings. Murder of crows."

"What are you saying," said Lola, "I don't understand."

347

They followed the birds over the castle, down to where the fighting had been. The inner courtyard had lighted in the dawn. It revealed an impromptu barricade made from two market barrows over near the gatehouse entrance from the outer courtyard. From behind the barricade masked people looked up at the birds. On the other side of the inner courtyard the Castle's defenders hid in doorways and beyond shattered windows.

Then the birds swooped down, the sound of their wings beating the air, echoing, amplified by the walls around the courtyard. The birds fanned out and flew towards the places where the Castle's defenders were huddling, policemen, Renewal Society, death squad. They flew in windows and through broken doors. Fox had seen what the birds could do. In many ways they were like flying knives, their sharp spiked beaks tearing into their victims. As they reached their targets the sound of wings beating ceased, Lola gripped Fox's arm as screaming rang out amid stuttering gunfire.

The Masquerade was on the move, racing from their barricade.

"Look," said Lola.

She pointed. Along the crenulation the eagle had landed. It was perched there and looking over at Fox and Lola. It looked at them for a few seconds and then took flight, going down to join its comrades below.

"What shall we do?" Lola said. "Shall we go back the way we came?"

"Sure," Fox said. "Or maybe not. I don't think anywhere is safe."

He wasn't really thinking. It was still too difficult. Lola wanted him to get her out of there. But he couldn't go on. The pain inside his head and across his face and eye made everything seem, not exactly distant, but as though he were watching the shore from beneath water and however near it might be he couldn't reach it. He was sinking.

He must have sat down again. Didn't seem to have the will to stand up, or even throw himself off the battlements.

"I want to go home," said Lola.

"Yes."

The cold had settled on him with a welcome numbness, a shell cracked only by the pain.

For a while now, he realised, the augmentation had tried to figure out the firmware of the life-bug, trying to find out what else was in there beside instructions that had made him like Kardos. The probing of the augmentation met resistance, something opaque.

"There's someone coming," Lola said.

Fox pushed himself up the wall and managed to stand up.

"Get behind me," he said.

He could hear the steps clattering before he saw them coming into view where the battlements straightened before the door to the tower.

CHAPTER THIRTY

Three figures. All masked. The taller men in carnival masks. The smaller figure a woman.

Fox had his hand on the gun in his waistband.

"Hello, Herr Fox," said Dr Pest, stepping into the tower where Fox and Lola had retreated. "You're not intending to shoot me I hope."

Fox left the gun where it was.

"Who is she?" Lola said.

"I don't know," Fox said, "Not really."

"I think you'd better come with us," said Dr Pest, "You look as though you could do with some medical care."

"So you've got it all in hand," Fox said, "Taken over the Castle."

"Come on," said Dr Pest, "We'll take you to the infirmary and perhaps then we can talk."

"I want to go home," said Lola, "I just want to go home."

"Where do you live?" Dr Pest asked.

"I live with my uncle. He has a café in the Maskmarkt. I work for him. I'm a waitress."

And all at once she was Lotte again.

"Well," said Dr Pest, "That's in the liberated zone. You'll have no trouble getting there. But it might be advisable to have some medical attention before you go."

"I'll be fine," said Lola.

Dr Pest motioned to one of her companions.

"Escort this young woman to her home."

"I'm fine," said Lotte, "I know my way."

"This is not negotiable."

Lotte shrugged.

"Goodbye, Sea Monster," she said. "Come and see me when you're better. I'll have uncle cook you something good."

Fox nodded. He didn't want her to go, he didn't want her to leave him. But already she was walking away, back along the battlements the way Dr Pest had come. She looked back once, turned slightly and raised her hand in a weak little wave.

Then she ran back and threw her arms around him and Fox made sure he made no sound in response to the pain of it.

***

Dr Pest led Fox to the infirmary. Much of the Castle was untouched by the fighting, only the lower parts of the Great Keep damaged, furniture broken, windows smashed, there were bodies lying on an ornate tapestry that had been ripped from the walls.

There were a few other Masqueradists in the infirmary, their masks off and beside their beds.

"No prisoners?" Fox asked.

"No," said Dr Pest, "No prisoners. I'll come back for you this evening."

"Was it worth it?" Fox asked. "All this carnage?"

She looked down at him as he tried to get comfortable on a bed.

"It is because of the intelligence you gathered, Herr Fox that we had to act. Although our actions tried to forestall their plans they went ahead with a variation of one of the scenarios."

"Don't blame me for this catastrophe."

She shrugged.

"What is it that we need to talk about?" he asked.

"I have something to show you," she said. "I think it's only fair."

The shot given by a nurse in a white noh mask took away much of the physical pain. The nurse left pills on his bedside table for when he left. All the while he lay on the bed he could feel the augmentation, churning, poking, trying to get at the intruder…

In the bed next to him there was a young girl, about the same age as Lotte. She groaned. Most of her left arm had been blown away, the stump lying on the top of her blanket, glued up with glistening battle dressing. The others there weren't in much better shape. It didn't seem as though anyone was in the mood for talking.

Another nurse came, an ultraclock. He had a fixed happy face.

Fox asked him what had happened in the city.

"I wish I could tell you the city had been liberated," he said, "But the Provisional Government still controls the old city and the Heights. The Renewal Society have repulsed our initial assault on Gutunberg and the suburbs beyond."

"So it's a stalemate. The Masquerade has the rest of the city?"

"Correct. Although there are rumours of foreign intervention. The Northern League will join with the Renewals. Other powers might want to restore the Provisional Government, or some version of it. I suspect they all might be waiting to see how the situation develops. What happened to your eye?"

"I lost it. Very careless of me."

The smiley nurse gave a nod and let out a sort of heavy tocking laugh from his chest. It made Fox snigger for a moment. And there they were, both making odd noises in the infirmary.

"I recognise you," said the nurse.

"Really?"

"Yes. You spoke to some of us. About Victor. We were in Sparta. I was among those who were going to go with him, to return to Harmony."

"What about this," Fox said, opening his shirt and showing the scar above his heart. "They put something inside my head. You understand?"

"It would kill you to take it out. They're made that way. But your sight will get better. You might have some problems with short range vision at first but your brain should learn to compensate."

"How long?"

"Differs. Depends on the person."

Later Dr Pest bought Fox some clean clothes, white shirt and some trousers. Fox refused the mask she offered. She didn't press it. They left the infirmary and went out into the courtyard. It was evening and Fox was cold again, pulling the jacket they'd given him around his body. They crossed over to the Great Keep and in the vestibule Dr Pest

353

handed Fox his gun, taking it out from a shoulder bag.

"Here," she said, "You might need it. When you leave the Castle I mean."

"What are you going to show me?"

"On the lower ground floor. Here are where the old servers are. They contain the databases you infiltrated."

"Yeah, I'm not sure I'll be able to do that at the moment. And I'm not sure I would even if I could."

Fox touched his head. The cilia that had begun to grow back were little more than stubble.

"We're not going there for the servers. There's something else there."

They went through the ground floor, through a ruined office that might once have been an elegant sitting room. They went through other similarly ruined places, a typing pool, a rest room...Everywhere the furniture was busted and paper scattered. In a few places there were bullet hole and patches of blood.

Then into a corridor near long abandoned kitchens and a locked door of steel which Dr Pest unlocked with a key.

Down a flight of steps they came into a room that long ago had been converted into the typical housing for big iron. There was an inner room with thick glass windows. Old biometric locks, long obsolete, cameras that may or may not have worked. The door was secured now by a padlock, which Dr Pest opened. The inner room was air conditioned, there was a nozzle for a halogen fire prevention system.

The big iron itself was impressive. An old mainframe still shiny on the outside whatever the condition of its data was. Fox felt a vague stirring of the cilia but it lasted only a moment. Then Fox saw it. There were network cables connecting the mainframe to an object on a bench. He didn't recognise what the object was, once he'd realised it wasn't a rock. And above this, on a shelf something of about the same size. Victor's head. There was a blast hole in the forehead.

"What is all this?"

"This," Dr Pest pointed at the rock like thing. "is what he," she pointed to Victor's head, "came here for. It's why he had dealings with the Castle. Victor came to Genesia for two reasons. To take the ultraclocks back to Harmony with him. And to see this."

Fox came closer to the rock on its bench. Then stepped back. The green room. Broken apart Olympia.

"It's a brain," he said, "an ultraclock's brain."

But it was all wrong, too big, a misshapen lump.

"Or at least something like an ultraclock brain," she said. "It's silica, silicon dioxide. Structured something like a nano-gel but instead of just pores there is a much more complex structure. Silica and air make it an excellent insulator of both electrons and heat."

A lump of intricate matter. But then wasn't the human brain? Wasn't the big iron around the room with all its potential to hold data?

"I don't think Oxenstierna," Dr Pest went on, "had envisaged something like this inside a creature, an ultraclock. Not at first. This was built to take the place of electronic digital technology. We don't really know its full potential but after you had come here we understood they were using it for their coup scenarios."

Fox was looking at the outside of the vast nothing he had sensed when the augmentation had infiltrated the servers. It was what he had not seen in Olympia, in all of them, since that first time he had really probed an ultraclock, at the back of the Cabaret Vaucanson. Victor had been there then, robust, alive. Now he was just a head on a shelf.

"And him?" Fox nodded at the head.

"We think Victor helped interface the brain with their servers. It was his way of getting to it. But it's finished now. We think he sabotaged it so that it slowly died. His intention all along I expect."

Fox looked at her.

"But that's not what got Victor killed is it?" he said, "An ultraclock in a mask killed him. And the same person killed Olympia. Before I'm finished with it all I'm going to find out who."

"That's the spirit," said Dr Pest.

The determination had reformed as he'd spoken the words to express it, and yet, at that same moment he felt so tired. His head was thumping again. Other pains that had been at bay were returning. He wanted to be with Olympia, to lie down and sleep next to her.

"Perhaps you know who it is who killed them?" said Fox.

"No," she said, "And to be quite candid I'm not going to try and find out. The Masquerade doesn't need an internal investigation. We're engaged in a war. But I'm not going to try to thwart you either."

"I'm going now," said Fox. "Will I be able to get to Little Alex?"

"Yes. I'll have someone drive you there."

Fox wanted to refuse and tell her he'd make his own way but he wasn't sure he'd get there the way he was feeling.

"Thanks."

It was one of the tall, masked men from the battlements who drove him home. The masked man didn't speak and Fox was fine with that. As they left the outer courtyard to go over the bridge Fox saw something dangling from a lamp post just the other side. It was Count Froggy, hanged, there for everyone to see that the Comedian was finally dead. That all the Comedians were dead.

***

The Castle hill had been cleaned up to an extent. There were no bodies on the ground just the footprints of a battle, the shattered guard post on the bridge, broken shop windows their glass scattered across the road.

At the corner of Autocue Boulevard and a side road to Little Alex the driver parked. There was no other traffic, just wrecks here and there stretching away down the boulevard. On the other side, where the Old City began the street entrances were blocked with mesh fencing topped with barbed wire.

357

"That's the front line with the Provisional Government," the driver said. "Quiet at the moment but you should be careful where you go. Genesia isn't an easy place at the moment."

"Thanks," said Fox, "I'll make sure to bear that in mind."

When he got outside the cafe Max came out to greet him, holding his forearms, ushering him inside. They'd been a telephone message from a week or so before. Otto had called and then called again, finally relating the news that Cosima Kastner had died from a second heart attack.

CHAPTER THIRTY-ONE

Drinking coffee and tea. Painkillers. No grappa. No alcohol at all. He'd eat whatever Max could get hold of now there was rationing. The only customer most of the time.

They'd come round to find him in the days after Saturnalia, Mond and Schiller. No one had known where he was. Fox didn't want to see any of them until everything was settled. He would have called Otto but all the telephone lines were down.

"Can I get to the Heights," he asked Max, on the second morning.

"I don't know. There's no newspapers. The radio is just propaganda. It's difficult to know anything."

The Molina was out the back where he'd left it. The tarot deck was still in the glove compartment. Fox slid the Wheel card back in it. He might have struck out there and then but Max came out.

"Rest another day," he said. "Just one more day."

Fox had a plan. It would have been better if he'd thought of it before, when he'd been in the Castle where he'd easily have stripped a corpse of useful uniform. But he had the essential element of the disguise, the cut above his heart.

"Don't go yet," said Max. "I don't know what it is you're going to do but you should make sure you know what's going on. Everything's up in the air now. You can't just drive across the city like you used to…. And besides, it's New Year. I know it's not going to be much of one but still…I could find something special from the cellar. What do you say?"

"Sure, Max. That sounds good."

Fox promised he'd be back in the evening. Max was right after all, Fox needed to have a better understanding of the way things stood in Genesia. He left the Molina and went for a walk.

The old café where Olympia had laid out the clockwork tarot was closed. When he asked at the ironmongers next door he was told that the old Cuman couple had gone, perhaps to relatives in the country but no one was sure.

On the walls of the streets there were posters from the Masquerade, four colour prints of ultraclocks and humans marching together in masks, caricatures of Aksel Ritter. Closer to Pecheneg Square the posters proliferated, seeming to grow out of every empty wall space, as though they were as natural as mould. Posters were pasted over other posters, the slogans of a new order that professed to disperse order.

Whose dream is the city? It is our dream, a collective dream.

It shall be the duty of every citizen to be an entertainer.

The role of the Count to be held in rotation. An absolute ruler with no power whatsoever.

For the elimination of twilight.

On a street near the square Fox ran his hand across the surface of a line of posters. They were slick, wet with wallpaper pasted that had been used to put them up. A good fly- poster always did a coat over the front of the poster as well as the back.

Pecheneg Square itself had undergone a metamorphosis as though the reality of the posters had cross-fertilised with the people who congregated here, the slogans lodged in them and urging them to action. Around oil drum fires podiums had been set up and little crowds listened to people who seemed to have discovered themselves orators overnight. The statue of the Pecheneg had been draped in flags, red-black, rainbow, green…

The Rudolf Library appeared to have become the headquarters of various revolutionary factions more or less associated with the Masquerade. He found Schiller there, in his same nook, but no longer left alone to his scholarship. While Fox was with him three people came and asked his advice on this or that matter.

"No time to work on your book now," said Fox.

"Not at the moment. But we always have time in a way. It's what we're made of."

"Mond gave me your last one."

"A mere preface to what I want to say. When I reread it I think it amounts to not much more than pleading, an extended whine for us to be considered…for the possibility to be considered sentient creatures, deserving of humane treatment."

"Fair enough aim."

"As the years have passed, as I have studied I have come to realise that there are no simple answers. For you, or for us. We cannot be understood in isolation. As soon as we came here, to Genesia, we changed."

"You integrated."

"Yes. But more than that. All of us, human and ultraclock, are part of something that cannot be divided into its parts."

"How did Victor figure into all of this?"

Schiller had no expression, he never had. There was no signal or tell.

"Victor? That is a good question. I think he thought we had achieved all we could here. But perhaps there was more to his message than that. Perhaps we will never know."

How could Fox read anything beyond Schiller's words? And yet Victor had been killed by an ultraclock.

Fox didn't hang around but went off to walk the backstreets of Little Alex. He wouldn't go near the Cabaret Vaucanson.

On Autocue Boulevard he crossed a road empty of cars. Steffi's was shut, the boarded windows covered with yet more posters.

The Old City was sealed off behind its mesh fence. Fox walked further east and into Sparta. More posters on boarded windows of abandoned houses and masked people carrying guns looking Fox over as he passed by.

Only the Maskmarkt had preserved itself but now the stalls were mostly selling food, tin goods and packets of dehydrated meals. More Masquerade guards wandered, making sure people were only purchasing their allocated ration, which the guards seemed to know by heart. The stallholders wearily listening to some masked ultraclock or young man or woman rolling of the amount of bread, meat, and vegetables allowed each customer.

Fox thought for a moment of going over to the café owned by Lotte's uncle. He imagined her there, taking orders, fetching plates of food and glasses of beer. Then he know almost at once that he would never go there, frightened of finding it not like that at all.

He wandered off into the streets on the other side of Maskmarkt, where Sparta ended at the rail line, the ruined hyperloop and the Kirovwerk. He didn't get very far. A young woman with blond hair to her shoulders and the mask of a hawk stood by a cart that had been pulled lengthways across the street.

"This is a restricted area citizen,"

She had a rifle over her shoulder. Not that Fox was about to argue with her.

Gutunberg was just the other side of the railway tracks and the hyperloop. This was the front line with the Renewal Society.

"Is there fighting today?" Fox asked. He couldn't hear any gun fire.

"As I said, citizen, this is a restricted zone. If you want to join in the defence of the city you need to report to the militia office on Bruno Street."

"Thanks," Fox said. "I might just do that."

He was cold now and his head had begun to hurt again. He'd go back home and take his medicine before seeing in the New Year with Max. But just before he turned away from the end of the road in the restricted zone he saw someone looking

363

back at him. They stood with the falcon masked girl, a great bulk that even from a distance must be Karl or Bob.

***

In the Café Castringius there were a few other customers. Max had pushed a few tables together and everyone sat around while he bought out a plate of nuts, some berries that had come from a tin, bread and cheese. Then bottles of French wine that were each probably worth a week's wages in the Kirovwerk.

Fox let himself have one glass just to convince himself that he could. Then he drank tea. He was pleased how seldom he now made a mistake reaching for a glass or cup. Perhaps already he was adjusting to having only one eye.

All these people. Lovely people he should have taken notice of before.

Klaus who whenever he had a meal would always talk about similar meals he'd had in the past, so that it was as though he was never tasting the food in front of him but another one, and perhaps that meal in turn hadn't been tasted at the time in a sort of infinite regression of taste experiences.

Albrecht the dentist, who would talk about the arts, the opera and his great passion for the marionette theatre. He knew the gossip about the voice artistes there, the latest scandal in the finances of the place, hardly ever about the performances themselves. He always kept promising himself that he would go to the next great show, but never did. At the table he always looked over his glasses at the food he ate, inspecting each item before putting it in his mouth. He wanted to learn English....

Did these people only become real now because Fox has paused to be with them, broken from some relentless rush into a story he never wanted to be involved in but, from those moments at the back of the Cabaret Vaucanson, could not resist?

And what about Max, who Fox hardly took notice of except as he served Fox's needs? Reliable, paternal, maternal, Max. He thought of Cosima. Of how quickly she had become part of his life. Always envisaged out there in Villa Verloren. As though she would be there forever.

Max went to get another bottle.

All these people. Lovely people.

Soon they would have to be left behind.

Tomorrow Fox was going to war. Beneath the floorboards of his flat he would retrieve another weapon he had got in Paris so long ago. The Z-Gun that had a number of useful automatic settings.

Tonight it was Max's turn to be looked after. He'd drunk too much, laughing loudly, too loudly towards the end. Glad of the company, of having Café Castringius feeling as though it were full again. Fox helped him upstairs to his room and Max collapsed into his bed. Klaus had fallen asleep in his chair and Albrect crept out into the night.

Fox tidied away the empty glasses and bottles, locked the café with the keys from behind the bar and posted them back through the letter box. Then he went home.

CHAPTER THIRTY-TWO

The city was now divided into distinct zones. The Masquerade had Sparta and Little Alex, the areas to the south bordering the river down to Tartessos. The Provisional Government held the Old City and some areas to the east around the Towers. The Renewal Society, since they'd lost the Castle, had their stronghold in Gutunberg and the suburbs to the north of the city.

But wasn't there always a way? Secret passages through cities, sewers, railway lines. Over roofs. Through the air ducts.

No.

Fox thought initially he would have to go to the front line. Flashback to numberless first-person shooter games that the augmentation had accessed. It kind of liked them. But this wouldn't be like that. Fox had been in real warzones before. Apparently, survival was all down to luck/training/experience. Delete as applicable.

Isn't there always a way?

Yes. Not the exposed railway lines but the hyperloop that ran beside it. So instead of heading to sign up for the militia he wandered through night streets to the docks at Tartessos.

Tartessos was in the part of the city controlled by the Masquerade. It was far enough from the front line to be free from too many armed militia. Further north the railway line and the hyperloop were in the no-man's land between Sparta and Gutunberg, but here they both terminated in the freight depot down by the wharves on the river.

Fox had schematics stored in the augmentation on how hyperloop systems worked but nothing specific on this particular line. The near vacuum frictionless tube wouldn't come right out onto the loading area, there had to be some kind of compromised area using conventional maglevs pulling the carriages out into the depot.

He walked though deserted backstreets of Tartessos, coming out at last with one that ran parallel to the river. It was lined with warehouses. When he came near the hyperloop depot he ducked into the doorway of one of the warehouses, out of the light, because up ahead the depot was guarded.

Masquerade militia, masked and armed. Standing idly beneath a wall mounted lamp. One with a cigarette, smoke drifting across the beam from the lamp. From their size it looked like they were both men, probably human. With the Z-Gun that he had got he could take out both of them at long range, but there would be a lot of light and noise and there might be more guards around. The other options were dirtier, getting close with the handgun or a knife.

Then, as he watched, a familiar figure came from an alley to the side of the depot entrance, the silhouette of her mask identifying Dr Pest. She spoke with the guards for a moment and they both shrugged and walked off down the alley from where she had come.

Dr Pest looked over in Fox's direction for a moment, then she looked to one side as the eagle glided down with a final flap of its wings and landed at her feet.

"You can come out now, Herr Fox," she called.

Fox did as she said.

"How's your head?" she asked. "I'm liking the whole eye-patch look."

"I'm fine. Max got it for me."

He didn't elaborate on how he felt, the presence of the augmentation, almost blind, seething at the intrusion it detected, occasionally groping through its stumps of cilia resulting in headaches.

"What are you doing here?" Fox asked.

She waved this question away.

"Ingenious," she said, "to try and go through the old tunnel. Or stupid. No one knows what it's like in there. The guards were only a precaution. Still you are a desperate man. I thought it better that we don't find out how desperate. Two guards given easy duties don't really deserve that do they?"

"I'm going through," said Fox.

"I know."

"How did you know?"

She pointed at the eagle.

From the eagle a voice came, sonorous, without any perceptible movement of its bill.

"I have you in my eye often, Herr Fox."

"So you talk then?"

"I am one of the first who talked."

"After our last conversation," said Dr Pest, "I thought it best to make sure we knew what you were up to."

"You said you wouldn't get in my way even if you couldn't help me."

"I'm finding such distinctions a little hard to maintain at the moment. But I suggest you be on your way. I'm just an officer doing a kind gesture for two guards who need a little break, nothing more."

She pulled open one of the large doors to the depot.

"There's crawl space, maintenance shafts, above the tunnel of the loop. Slow going but might be safer than the loop itself. There's access to the exterior at fixed intervals. Get out at the fifth one and you'll be in Gutunberg."

"Thanks."

Fox used his torch. There was a line of freight capsules parked at the platform. They were dirty and the copper fittings around the base had become green with verdigris. The doors of all the capsules were open, the loads long gone. He followed the capsules to the tunnel entrance and went in through a narrow airlock system that took a bit of forcing. Inside was how he imagined the interior of a giant drain-pipe but with an extended metal plate running down the flattened floor. It was cold, perhaps even colder than outside but as he went a little further in it became stuffy. The air was stale and he had to go slow to keep from getting out of breath. He found the ladder that led up the wall to the maintenance shaft, then through another airlock door. It was cramped but not literally a crawlspace as he could walk. There were vents to the outside letting in cold air. After a while he passed the first hatch. He shone the torch and saw a large number one printed on it.

As he came up to the third hatch the torch picked out stuff on the floor of the maintenance tunnel, bedrolls and old clothes strewn about. When he heard voices he switched off the torch and he could see that the hatch itself was open, the dim light of the night coming in. The voices were from out there and he sneaked a look.

A piece of wasteland. Couldn't really tell where. The warehouses and derricks of the docks of to one side outlines against the night, the city in the other direction. Around a small fire two figures sat huddled close, laughing at something. One passed a bottle to the other. It was tempting to go out and join them.

About twenty minutes after that the shape of the tunnel changed, growing wider and becoming a low ceilinged room. The floor was covered in wiring, presumably for equipment out in the hyper loop tunnel itself. Fox realised he must be in a loading area of the Kirovwerk. He carried on until he reached the continuation of the maintenance tunnel, the fourth hatch was a good while after that. He must be already near Gutunberg but he decided to rely on Dr Pest's intelligence so went on to the fifth.

When he found it, the fifth hatch, he waited and listened, pressing ear against the cold steel of the airlock hatch and then finally turning the wheel. But it didn't open onto the outside like the one in the wilderness had. Instead there was a vertical tunnel with ladder rungs in the side. The good citizens of Gutunberg wouldn't have had a hyperloop running through their streets. It had been bored deep beneath the neighbourhood. When he got to the top he listened once again but he could hear nothing. He turned the wheel and pushed up.

Later, he supposed, if this war had all gone on and become less amateurish they would have done something else, seal it, or thrown concrete down it. Now they did just what the Masqueradists did, post two kids on a bored look-out duty. They were huddled together around a brazier, beneath the eaves of a townhouse, stamping their feet on cobbles, which here still had remnants of snow. Fox didn't use the torch and quickly put down the hatch.

I am going to have to kill you boys. I don't want to but this is where we've got to now. Go through the mechanics, make sure the firearm is ready, the timer, the autofire.

The thing in his head, which even the clipping of his cilia had never killed, was brooding, anticipating tasty violence. It wanted this, as though doing it could vitalise it…. murder games it had played, running and shooting, first-person, third-person, virtual and retro… Perhaps he'd miss anyway. Perhaps his vision was still all askew.

Fox put the gun back in the holster. He started to climb back down the ladder.

It was trek back to hatch three, the open one. When he came out it was dawn. Here the loop was running on low pylons. He climbed down a little ladder that stopped just short of the ground. He walked over to where the two figures were still sat beside their fire. He came into the warmth, relief from the sealed cold of the tunnel and the night itself.

Wasteland. Hobos or tramps.

Ambient light from the fire fell on railway tracks.

"How comes you boys aren't sleeping?" he said as he sat down with them.

They both looked over at him, shrugged. Firelight danced on their faces.

"It's easier to sleep by day," said one. "That's when the botherers come round. You lost or something?"

"Just cold," said Fox.

"The fire's free. Stay a while."

One had white hair, slicked back, hardly thinning. The other wore a woollen hat. The lines of their faces, beneath the fire licks, held deep shadows.

Two unmasked old men. They were beautiful.

"You a soldier?" the white haired one asked.

"No."

"You look like a soldier."

He passed Fox the bottle of schnapps and Fox took a glug.

"How come? A soldier I mean."

White hair pointed to his own eye.

"Sure," said Fox. "It must look like I've seen some action."

"It does."

"So," Fox went on, "you get any trouble out here. You know. This side or the other?"

The one with the hat spoke for the first time.

"Both sides try their luck sometimes. Nothing big. First a few warning shots towards the other side. Then there's a bit of shooting and it's all over.

Once the clean cuts tried it in the night but they must have not got far. The masks cut them to pieces. As far as I know the bodies are still out there somewhere. I figure we're about dead centre from both lots. And we keep out of sight during the day."

"Well," Fox said. "I suppose it will be light soon. I should be on my way."

"Where you figure on going?" said white hair.

"I have to find someone. In Gutunberg."

"And how you figure on getting there?"

"Well, you did take me for a soldier."

"I actually took you for a deserter, but true."

Fox said goodbye and began to walk across the waste ground, across the rail tracks and between the pylons of the hyperloop. He could see what he thought was the defensive line ahead, barbed wire or fencing, a floodlight here and there. They wouldn't see him just yet, so he got made his preparations, his own little masquerade.

He set the Z-Gun up on its retractable stand, angling the barrel to aim up and over his own height. He turned the dial for automatic fire with the timer counting down from fifteen seconds. He took off his eye patch and threw it away. Left the backpack and his gun on the ground. He breathed deeply for a moment. He jabbed himself in the eye socket as hard as he could bear, opening up the wound again. The pain rushed back, a familiar flavour to it. Then he started to run forward shouting for help. The Z-Gun began to fire, lighting up the sky and making a good amount of noise.

"Help," he shouted, "Help."

There was some return fire but then they saw Fox and he held up his arms and kept running. As he reached the fence a couple of soldiers had come forward, pointing rifles at him.

"Help me," he said, "I've come to join you. Franz Wheeler, come to join…"

A rifle butt hit him in the head and he went down. The Z-Gun had stopped and as Fox lay on the ground propping himself up.

"Name and rank," said one of the soldiers. "Or you're a bloody Masqueradist."

"No," said Fox, now become Franz Wheeler, "I'm one of you. Free company from the north."

They loomed over him. Then he had played his other card. Not the wheel of fortune but his ace. He pulled his shirt open and showed them the ceremonial scar.

"Brothers, comrades," he said, "I've come to join you."

CHAPTER THIRTY-THREE

The voice of Aksel Ritter, quacking fascist clap-trap. Stuff about the family. Strength of the nation. Then a band would begin playing something manly and stirring

Franz Wheeler lay propped up in the bed of the makeshift infirmary that had been established in the summer house of the mansion. The mansion was in a superior area of that well-to-do part of the city called Gutunberg. It was called the House of Doves. Presumably there had once been flocks of them here as evidenced by the accumulation of pigeon shit on the slice of roof that Franz could see from the window.

The summerhouse was away from the mansion itself, set in large gardens of topiaries and little copses. The snows had melted away though it was still cold, necessitating layers of blankets, all donated by the loyal citizens of Gutunberg.

Franz had not yet been seen by a doctor only a nurse, Juliet. She was, in fact, the well-spoken daughter of the mansion. She had dressed his pierced eye socket and bandaged his head, which had not only suffered the butt of a rifle but also bore extensive lesions all across a portion of his crown and temple. She had not seen the like of such wounds before, but then, she had assured herself, she was quite inexperienced, and had bandaged them up for good measure.

"She's a looker, eh," said Paulsen, the only other patient who appeared capable of coherent speech.

Franz assented that she was.

There were other nurses who came and went but Juliet was almost a constant presence. She was small and had an almost irresistible plump allure that could only be accentuated by the white uniform and the way—when she attempted bravado while cleaning a patient—she would blush peach across her cheeks and the back of her neck where her thick black hair had been pinned up.

Franz was surprised at himself for noticing her in this way, it was something he had almost forgotten.

She was always more voluble with those patients who were in such as state where they could hardly move, the ones who groaned rather than articulated words.

"Come on now, there's a good fellow. All be over in a jiffy…"

While with Franz or Paulsen she said little more than perfunctory directions, to lie this way or that, to lift this or that limb.

Franz could hardly bear her stifled sweetness and attended to his own ablutions as soon as he was allowed.

"I'll soon be fighting fit," he would say to her and she might offer that yes she expected he would. And that there were many far worse than he.

***

"I wish they'd sort out another radio," Paulsen said, "It's boring without a radio."

Franz had accidently knocked the last one to the floor and then felt compelled to stamp on it during a late night visit to the toilet. No more military music or speeches from Aksel Ritter for the time being.

"Still," Paulsen chirpily continued, "I reckon you'll be out of here soon. Walking wounded and all that. Unlike these poor bastards."

Paulsen didn't mention that one of his own legs had been amputated.

Franz said he hoped so, but they were waiting for a doctor to come.

Paulsen, caught up in the enthusiasm, not even fitted with a life-bug, had been injured on the first day's fighting over in Sparta, running at a barricade in some lunatic attempt to storm it with a group of fresh faced recruits to the cause. His leg was ripped apart by flying debris and there was nothing the field medic could do about it.

"It'll all be over soon," he reassured Franz, "the Northern League will come and that'll be the end of the rebels."

Snap of his fingers. Just like that.

Franz ventured the opinion that it would be difficult for any army to get into Genesia. The Masqueradists held the bridge over the river to the south. True the Northern League wouldn't be coming that way but they'd struggle to get over the mountains with an army, they'd need to go around the city, through areas still held by the Provisional Government. If they tried coming from the west the Masqueradists now held the Castle."

"Don't be so down-hearted Franz. I've heard they'll come in a plane and parachute, or down the river in assault craft. It'll all be over soon and the rebels'll be finished. Just you wait and see."

When a doctor did finally arrive he stayed for about nine minutes in total and opined that while Franz was doing well, and could be released soon, it would be just as well if he stayed a few more days and helped serve at the benefit dinner that would be happening next week.

Julia nodded, her expression unreadable.

Franz, allowed out now, spent the afternoons wandering the gardens, even though by the time he came back he would be shivering in his pyjamas. Alone he went from inspecting the winter beds to exploring beyond the thick line of shrubs to the perimeter wall. He fingered the uneven brickwork, fissures, cracks, outcrops and brick ends. The places where neglected ivy had spread up the wall to colonise its top. It would not be a particularly difficult wall to climb if it came to it.

Soon though these little excursions stopped as Franz was requested to attend in the house. The preparations for the forthcoming dinner had begun. Once he saw Juliet, known in the house as Lady Juliet, dressed in her civilian clothes. She did not make eye contact, having known, from an early age that servants should only be seen when they were needed.

From an upper-storey Franz managed to get a clearer appreciation of the position of the mansion at both the front and back. He would stand in his new suit of clothes, his dead eye itching beneath the

378

patch he now wore. From the front of the house he could see onto the street. From the back of the house he could make out what was beyond the garden walls, those walls that he had explored so minutely at close range.

He spent a lot of his time looking out in this way. Until someone came and ordered him to some task or other, the movement of foodstuffs from the storeroom to the kitchen, ensuring that the vases in which flowers would be placed were positioned equidistantly around each relevant room. Checking the inventory of wine in the cellar...

There were servants of course but many of them had become soldiers for the current emergency. What remained were the female staff and an old butler called Kreb, who issued commands in tight-lipped snarls using as few words as possible.

The evening itself would begin with a reception in the lower hall of the ground floor. The ladies and gentlemen would be served hor d'ovres and champagne (possibly genuine since there were many fine wine cellars in Gutunberg yet to be exhausted, and this house had one of the best).

There would be a brief talk from some person of importance (it was not specified who). Then dinner would be served in the upstairs dining room. The chef had been borrowed from a neighbour, since the mansion's own chef had disappeared just after the troubles had begun.

Musical entertainment for the evening would be provided by what could only be described as a scratch chamber orchestra of amateurs, mostly aged gentlemen of the area, too old to fight. Miss Julia was also scheduled to perform a solo piece on piano a Bach E minor toccata.

During the course of the evening guests would be escorted in small parties by the doctor and Franz to the summer house, to give their good wishes to the brave soldiers who were sojourned there.

From what Franz could make out there were several of these makeshift hospitals across the district and, it seemed, these parties had become a semi-regular event in the last few weeks, keeping up morale until victory might come in the vague form imagined by all except those like Paulsen, who based his deep understanding of military strategy on having seen half a day's action.

It was a clear, cold, night, the moonfall making the garden a patchwork of grey and black. On his trips to and from the summer house that evening there was little occasion for Franz to say anything. The doctor did the talking, speaking knowledgably about the conditions of all the patients although Franz knew he had hardly inspected them. Paulsen played his part well, all the better since he was totally unconscious of the part played, the jovial injured solider, making light of the pain and mutilation he had suffered.

"They're very good to us here, sir. And the nurses lift our spirits, if you know what I mean."

Only once did any of the dignitaries address Franz.

"And you? Where did you receive your wounds?"

This some mid-ranking Renewal Society type. Or at least that was the uniform he wore, though Franz had the impression that his membership was not long standing. His accent was the stolid and confident tone of Gutunberg, somewhat shaken by recent events perhaps.

Franz recounted his story of a Masqueradist raid in the wastelands near the Kirovwerk that he had got caught up in as he tried to reach this part of the city to join his brothers in the fight. In other hands the story might have sounded boastful, self-aggrandising, but Franz had a natural demeanour of modesty. The dignitary was left almost lost for words.

"Good man," he rasped, "Good man." Patting Franz on the back.

By the time the visits were over Franz was shivering with cold. He retrieved the bottle of wine he'd liberated earlier from the cellar and stashed around the back of the summerhouse in a grass drain at the bottom of a rain pipe. He stood inside the kitchen looking out over the garden and the moon.

The waltz music had stopped and notes of piano piece drifted down from upstairs.   Bach toccata, the lines of some counterpoint, promising to carry into a complex fugue and yet there were those little mistakes, stutterings and sudden pauses.

God doesn't live in the details, God lives in the mistakes. Or at least it is mistakes that make us human rather than machines. The ultraclocks were human in that way, not perfect, their imperfections being something like those of all of us.

Franz imagined Miss Juliet up there on the piano, delicate fingers perhaps in reality too delicate for her ample frame but then he had never thought about that till now. Slowly he made his way through the house and up the stairs. He lurked in corridor near the doors to the ballroom, where Kreb and another aged butler drafted in for the evening stood sentry. The butler hardly noticed Franz but Kreb tried to shoo him away with complex movements of his eyebrows. Kreb must have some standing orders not to vacate his spot, or maybe there existed some arcane protocol that this is how it should be on occasions such as this. Eventually Kreb settled for turning his back on Franz, which allowed two creeping steps forward, a glimpse of the guests gathered around the piano.

The music had continued all the while, the little flaws, the missed notes, not spoiling it for Franz at all, but rather the mistakes framed those sparse yet perfect moments when Miss Julie managed to get the fingering just right, and the interweaving counterpoints created, for just those moments, delicate shapes of sound that Franz might just have been at the instant of grasping when they were gone, she had stumbled again. There was a silence and someone coughed.

Miss Juliet was visible as just a head and bare shoulders at the other side of the piano, the coral silk of her dress only emphasising the blush that spread up from her neck and across her cheeks. When she finished and the polite clapping followed from the elderly men and their wives, the younger officers in their uniforms, Franz wanted to cheer.

But already some spell had been broken and Kreb turned and advanced on him, banishing him once more into the underworld.

"You'll be out of 'ere tomorrow, bloody skulker."

Go forth to the happy place whereto we speed, do not make my name stink to the Entourage who make men. Do not tell lies about me in the presence of God. It is indeed well that you should hear.

Kreb, not so much a prophet as a man with connections. The next day Franz was out in the garden when a uniformed man, escorted by a nurse, alas not Miss Julie, appeared.

"While we have no use for you in the thick of things I have heard that you are eager to serve, yes?"

Franz could only assent.

A remove himself from any direct action this man wore the uniform of a senior police officer, with the lapel pin of the Renewal Society. Franz wondered if he had been fitted with a life-bug or if he was merely sailing under a flag of convenience. Despite his immaculate turn-out his eyes were heavy, the chill in the air only serving to add to an impression of hardly supressed misery.

His name was Colonel Dolman.

Tomorrow Franz was to report to his office to serve as what amounted to a gopher or factotum, but carried the official rank of Private Second Class Logistics.

While he was packing away his few possessions: his old clothes, the pyjamas they had given him, the donated shaving kit. Miss Juliet appeared in her guise as a nurse.

"So you're leaving us at last," she said, still not looking at him directly, a mistress of the peripheral glance.

He nodded.

"I saw you looking at me," she said, "Lots of times."

"I'm sorry,"

"I hated it, the effrontery… and then during the recital…I was so awful…"

"I thought it was beautiful."

"I ruined the piece. But I saw you, in the corridor…you liked it anyway."

"Not anyway."

"Perhaps it's because you're a proper soldier. Not like all those officers there. Perhaps you don't care about all the mistakes I made because of that."

"Yes, that must be it."

But it wasn't that. And Franz wasn't, after all, a proper soldier.

CHAPTER THIRTY-FOUR

He wished he could have left Franz Wheeler nestled behind forever in the House of Doves, a faceless servant scurrying...no, not scurrying, but rather gliding silently along back corridors and down staff stairwells. Occasionally he might get a glimpse of the young lady of the house, but he is not the sort of servant who attains close proximity, too ugly, of dubious pedigree. And yet somehow he lingers.

But Franz could not be left behind yet. He still had a few more scenes to play.

That morning, coming away through the streets where the snow had gone, Fox felt the stirring in his head. Something old and familiar, the augmentation wanting to reach out and find something to feed upon. When he slipped his hand under the forage cap and traced his fingers across his head he could feel the tiniest of growths coming up, tracing their way back through the paths they had made decades ago when they had first grown.

Not that there was anything to feed on. Fleeting impressions from the life-bug of a passing soldier, just an ordinary Joe, newly made, who'd only stood behind a barricade and fired a rifle at an unseen enemy.

Fox made his way through the back streets of residential Gutunberg, passing perhaps only a few twists and turns from the police barracks where, maybe, Hans Hofner was.

He would wait, would have to. He had come to the Renewal Society zone with no plan beyond getting in, no idea how to find Hofner in the barracks. But as things had turned out all sorts of new possibilities were presenting themselves with the new role he was about to assume.

The Office for Procurement was on a forgotten square on a hill. It was the sort of square you might never find unless you were looking for it, not big, formed by high, gabled, houses built long ago by merchants just becoming aware of their own possibilities as the Middle Ages waned. The intervening centuries appeared to have touched the square very little. Only the presence of two canvas-backed military lorries gave away that this was a different time entirely.

In the middle of the square in a little green space was a statue. Not a Pecheneg or a saint, but some respectable burgher adorned in the fashionable frills of the baroque, now iced with a toothsome patina of verdigris.

The Office of Procurement itself was in one of the large merchant houses, the brickwork look as though it had been recently scrubbed by men too useless for combat duty. Just like Fox. There was no sentry outside, just a wood sign nailed to the door beneath a brass lion head knocker.

Office of Procurement. New Republic of Genesia.

C.O. Colonel Frederick Dolman.

Fox didn't have to knock because the door was open, and the first room on the right of the corridor had been transformed from its original purpose of boot polishing, store cupboard or whatever, to a reception with a counter behind which an old solider with a Franz Joseph moustache lay asleep in a comfy looking deckchair. Fox couldn't detect a life-bug, but perhaps the cilia wasn't yet strong enough all the time.

Fox coughed and saluted then banged his heels as the old soldier stirred.

"Private Wheeler, reporting for duty."

"Eh?"

The soldier pushed himself up but didn't stand. He peered at Fox.

"Another cripple they send us."

"Colonel Dolman told me to report here."

"Did he? I suppose he did."

"Yes, sir."

"At ease, soldier," he chuckled.

Slowly and with an effort he stood up, lent on the counter and began looking through a leather bound ledger that was open there.

"Wheeler…Wheeler…"

His finger went down to the very bottom of a list. As though Wheeler would be anywhere else.

"Franz Wheeler," he said. "Found it."

"They call me Wheeler Fortune."

The soldier starred at him for a moment.

"You don't look too fortunate to me."

"Well, I'm alive."

"True, true."

"And ready to begin work…"

"Yes, yes. You're all so eager aren't you? Young ones with your…" He gestured towards

387

Fox's chest, at the solid state immortality he assumed Fox had bought into.

"Just trying to do my bit."

"Well, Fortune, I've been with the colonel a long time. And he has served Genesia better than any. And now we are where we are and you are ready to do your bit. Is that all you've got?"

He pointed to the small tool bag that Fox's stuff was in.

"Yes, sir."

"*Yes, sir*" he quoted, giggled again. "*Yes, sir.* You'll get on well here. There's a bunk for you up in the gods. Where the scullery maid used to be. No maid there now, more's the pity. Stow your kit and come back and I'll set you to work."

***

It was a simple enough job and Fox could not have asked for anything better. Old Franz Joseph, who was actually called Joseph, sent Fox out on errands with another old timer called Ruge, also without a life-bug as far as Fox could tell. They were given a list of pledged items, possible procurements and the like and had to drive to each address to pick up the scrap metal, tinned food, lumber, paper—anything that had been deemed useful in the great struggle against the masked rebels, clockwork abominations, and the sad old Provisional Government who were seen as little better that complicit with the general decadence that had led to the current state of affairs.

Ruge drove the lorry.

He was a big man who would have been fearsome twenty years before. His broad shoulders drooped now but he still gripped the steering wheel as though he wanted to strangle it.

"We must not let them palm us off with excuses. They all like to make a show of how they support the cause but then when it comes to handing over they become cagey. One old woman told me her fire poker was a family heirloom.... But they don't understand the cause really. Only the young truly understand."

"What about you?"

"Yes, I'm old but I can see that renewal is what we need. Everyone must play their part. They let their sons go to fight but then worry about their fire pokers. When we have won things will be better. Before all this I worked in a butcher's shop for twenty years. Not my own shop but someone else's. These fine ladies used to send their servants there, they wouldn't have lowered themselves to come in person. Now when I tell them to give me their fire pokers they will give me their fire pokers."

"That's progress."

The first stop was three streets from the office. Fox and Ruge loaded assorted bundles of newspapers, a tin bathtub that must have been for the servants and an old perambulator. There was also some bags of potatoes that were sprouting roots.

"Damn," said Ruge, looking at the list he had after they'd finished there.

"What's the matter?"

"Bloody house on Mithra Square."

Fox had heard of it, some shopping place in Gutunberg, he'd never been there.

"What's the matter with that?"

"Don't get me wrong," said Ruge suddenly defensive, wary, "It's just it's always busy these days. The ladies who lunch. You'll see."

It wasn't far but as the lorry entered behind a large sedan Fox could see the problem. There were cars parked around the edges of the square, on both the centre side and the perimeter near the houses. In the middle of the square were crowds of, well, ladies, there was no other word for it, dressed in luxuriant day wear, long dresses, and tight jackets, rakish hats.

"What are they holding?" Fox asked, but then he saw.

Fluttering around them on leads were clockwork birds.

"They trim the beaks off, stops the vicious little blighters attacking. Don't know why their husbands let them have 'em. Indulgence I suppose."

From a loud speaker in the square, a speech was blaring out, the usual stuff.

The chaining of clockwork birds, the symbolism too stupid and obvious.

"Fashion, I suppose," Ruge went on mercifully short of analysis.

Faces without masks. How much the flesh does and doesn't give away. Lines and creases of age, wear, worry. Faces as false as costumes, as uniforms. Faces inappropriate as fancy dress on a day that called for casual. Then the sudden urge of the recrudescent augmentation desperate even if it didn't know if it could feed on the female of the

Renewal species. But Fox never crossed over to be among the crowd in the square.

**

Fox was free to spend the evenings as he would, knowing it would be better to avoid soldiers if at all possible. He rarely saw Dolman who, if he came into the office at all, sat in his own room upstairs and went through requisition lists. Joseph dealt with most of the work. Perhaps it was that Dolman had been handed this command as a way of shunting his sideways, of keeping him occupied. Reward for his years of service? A way to be rid of a traditional soldier in this bright new age? He had no life-bug, Fox could tell now, and he did not fit with the new regime.

Ruge had a wife who was in service as a cook but he was not usually in a hurry to rush home back to her. He would take Fox to a little bar in back streets where the houses were not quite as salubrious as most of Gutunberg. Ruge would stay for two drinks, one he bought, the other bought by Fox. A third drink would have possibly made things too complicated.

When Ruge went off home Fox began to walk. The streets of Gutunberg were still lit by streetlamps, but nearer the front line, where the sound of gun shots became something you could feel as well as hear, there was hardly any lighting beyond that which crept out of cracks at the bottom of shuttered windows, the edges of black-out curtains. Fox moved through this almost darkness beneath the ambient light of the sky fed by whatever light from elsewhere had bled into it. And the occasional flash of an explosion.

He would find his way eventually back to within sight of the police barracks, noting when squads left and when others returned from the fighting. Were they still actually policemen or soldiers by now?

Still, he did not get too close, scared of once again plummeting into the fragments of violence that the aug would seek out on the life-bugs. Eventually he knew he would have to see how far the cilia had regained their power.

There was a bar near the barracks, what had once been a rather gentile café but no longer frequented by anyone but soldiers and police. When it grew crowded men would spill outside, the gutter filling with bottles, an ally between the bar and the next house becoming a pissoir. Fox felt better hanging around nearby rather than venturing into bar itself. He stood in the lee of the doorway of a haberdashery diagonally opposite and listened to the laughter, shouting, the wheeze of an accordion.

It wasn't long before someone wandered off and Fox could follow them. The man stumbled along, steadying himself as he came out of the piss stinking ally back onto the street going away from the bar. He was singing something to himself, the words sounding like a hurdy gurdy fancy, hurdy gurdy fancy, over and over like a wheel going round inside Fox's head as he got nearer and felt the thrill of cilia stir once again. Hat in hand, Fox stood in the darkness where the soldier would pass by, ready, reaching for the life-bug.

...Scenes flickering, fighting somewhere near the cathedral, its dome shattered, birds wheeling round. Standing on a barricade. Same barricade day after day. Cold creeping up the legs, hands even worse. Lost pair of gloves. No chance of another. There was Gavrila nearby, the gentle boy whom had become beloved, if such thoughts were not absurd.

Hurdy gurdy fancy. Hurdy gurdy fancy.

The soldier, not more than a boy himself really, stumbled out of range, off into the night to seek the soiled doves of the brothels, the girls and boys who had decided not to throw in their lot and fight for the Masquerade. They had their reasons perhaps, or were simply caught the wrong side of the lines when the city divided.

Fox realised he could do it. That if he found the right person he'd be able to use them to locate Hofner. But he couldn't just walk into the bar, even covering the cilia wouldn't dampen out all those life-bugs, all those voices and images, unsolicited confessions, half narrative, saturated with the fluids of desire, regret, and hate.

Hurdy gurdy fancy, indeed.

***

Ruge was chatting to Bill, the driver of the lorry that came to take the scrap that had been collected and stored out on the green of the square opposite the Office of Procurement. The scrap would be taken out to the armoury on the hills to the north. The driver was another old codger, doing his best in a situation he hardly understood.

"I could do with a run out." said Fox "I've only just got out the hospital. This eye you see."

"All right then," said Bill, "But no bloody whistling, hate whistling."

So when they had finished loading the lorry Fox climbed up in the cab beside him.

"You got ID? Papers?"

Fox had papers. The colonel had seen to that when he'd come. Franz Wheeler Private Second Class, Logistics. Office of Procurement.

The manufactory they were to deliver to was some way out towards the spur of the Heights, that came into the district of Bruno, the northern part of the city, which was like a salient of Sparta although without the character, industrial, with run down residential streets stranded amid chain link fences around forecourts of broken tarmac or concrete. Glimpses down the mean side streets with washing hanging across between the top windows of houses, the horizon blotted out by the industrial buildings and beyond that the looming shape of the mountains. It wasn't really that far as the crow flew but they had to get out of Gutunberg, and it was the roadblocks they met that made it interesting for Fox.

It was just what he wanted, a sentry box with a single policeman operating the pole gate. As soon as the lorry came in range he let the augmentation begin, trying to develop an effective way of searching the chaotic accumulation of experience and feeling on the life-bug. But it was no good, it didn't work like that, there was no index or meta-language, just this heap of fragmentary moments, impressions, shards of narrative...

When the policeman handed back their papers Bill drove on and Fox had learnt nothing.

At the next checkpoint he tried something obvious. While the augmentation probed the soldier's life-bug, Fox spoke up.

"Hey, didn't we go for drinks once. With my friend, Hans Hofner? How is old Hans?"

Fox waited, rooting down into the life-bug, the point where new memories and experiences were inscribed. Waiting for recollection to stir something from the past. A face, laughing but not kindly. A young man who might have been naturally cruel. Fox saw him for the briefest moment, recognised that face. Hans was grinning making some jibe. Hofner's face tapered towards the chin, giving it the streamlined curve of something like a fox or jackal. This look accentuated by the eyebrow that hooded his eyes. His grin wasn't nice. Crooked, flanked by heavily folded cheeks.

This policeman at the checkpoint didn't like Hofner.

"Don't know him," he said.

As he handed back Fox's papers the policeman's hand shook, his eyes avoiding looking directly at Fox.

***

Beyond a third checkpoint they came at last to the manufactory. The place was a collection of ramshackle buildings across yet another concourse of broken concrete, weeds growing through the cracks and a rusted cement mixer abandoned to one side. Once through the gates they drove over this surface the lorry rattling with the dents and potholes.

"They used to make light aircraft here," said Bill, "Back before my time. Imagine that, people used to own their own aeroplanes."

"Not many people."

"Yes, but still. It's amazing, eh amazing."

"What do they do here now?"

Bill shrugged, even as he was driving and being shook by the concourse.

"Anything that's needed. Bullets for projectile weapons, power packs for energy weapons…stripping down old electronics and stuff…no heavy ordnance here, that's strictly import, our friends in the north if you know what I mean."

As the lorry clattered towards the open doors of a warehouse some people emerged. They stood there looking at the lorry. Given that it was still cold they should not have been wearing thin, ragged, semi-uniforms. Their heads were shaved and none of them greeted the lorry, just stared with expressions of resentment, exhaustion and hatred.

Beneath his sympathy there might be something far worse. Fox had been like this, broken to the point where maintaining any semblance of his own self was too much of an effort. Kardos had done that to him and he had to tell himself that the contempt he felt wasn't for these poor souls but for what he had become during those days in the castle.

"This is a work camp?" he said.

"Prisoners," said Bill, "What else are you going to do but set them to work?"

A commanding officer, another police man, came out and ordered the lorry unloaded. He sidled up to Bill and started chat amiably.

"Still cold eh?" said the officer, "But I take it you make better time now without the snow or the traffic."

"Definitely," said Bill.

The augmentation couldn't help but reach out and begin to read the life-bug. It was a monotonous relay of dull days in the camp, punctuated by occasional violence against minor transgressions. The officer was bored, having to spend a lot of time on the accounts, on bookwork. But he wasn't a bad man, he didn't think of himself as a bad man.

CHAPTER THIRTY-FIVE

Two nights later he finally found Hans Hofner. Late in the evening lurking in the darkness near the police barracks he saw him approach and enter the barracks with a group of others, coming back from some drinking bout. Fox couldn't just follow him inn. Not only did he have no right to be there but the presence of all those life-bugs would be too much. He figured Hofner had to emerge some time, but the first evening of the stake-out nobody came back out at all and there were only a few lights on inside.

The second night Fox saw him coming back again. Silhouettes at first, helmet mounted lights dancing at the far end of the road, the only sound the trudge of their feet because none of them were talking. This time they were returning from an action, tired, one with a polymer battle dressing on a wound on his cheek, another limping. The came into the light at the front of the police barracks, Hofner at the front carrying a shoulder mounted rocket launcher rather than the rifles the others had.

Fox didn't have long to act.

"Hans," he shouted, emerging from the shadow of a doorway across the street, "Hans!"

Hofner stopped, nestling his heavy grenade launcher on the ground.

"Who is this?" one of the others said.

Fox stopped a way back, already the augmentation was beginning to probe.

"I'm with the Office of Procurement."

Even now, face dirty and weary there was something sneering about Hofner's expression. He had stripes of rank on his shoulder, a corporal…. Fox tried to focus on him as the augmentation began to delve into the life-bugs of the others, explosion going off out on the canvas of the wasteland battlefield, the satisfying thrust of a dagger into the eye hole of a mask…

"What do you want?" Hofner said. "Here to requisition the iron bed frames?"

He laughed. No one joined in, they were busy tramping up the stairs into the barracks.

"No," said Fox.

"Look, I'm tired," said Hofner brushing a hand through matted red hair. "What do you want?"

They were alone, the life-bugs of the others fading, only Hofner's now, a flickering tape of the faces of other men, of his comrades, his relishing of their fear of him…

"I'm a friend of Vogt," said Fox.

Hofner looked him over. Fox couldn't read his sudden change of expression. The augmentation meanwhile wanted to delve deeper. Fox took off his forage cap, feeling the cold of the night across his scalp, in the little crevices where the cilia peeped out.

"You've seen action," said Hofner, nodding at Fox's eye. Then he hefted the grenade launcher. "Let me stow this and we can talk. Better outside."

He came out a few moments later and threaded his arm through Fox's.

"What do you think you are doing, my friend?" he said. "You need to be more careful. Now, is he back? Have you heard how it went?"

Fox hesitated for just a fraction too long, distracted by the augmentations searching...

Hoffer was gripping Fox's arm now, holding him to the spot. They were someway down the street, out in the darkness beyond the light around the doorway.

"There was a password," he said.

The augmentation was beginning to discover the stuff it liked, a train of incidents connected by violence. Hop and skip from stabbing to shooting, the kick in the head of a prone figure...

"A password?' Fox repeated.

The grip on his arm was hurting and Fox stumbled back against the walls just inside of an alley.

"Who are you?" said Hofner.

"I need to ask you...about...the night you saw the Fool die. The ultraclock out on the tracks."

"What?" He pushed Fox against the wall, slamming Fox's head back.

"The ultraclock, killed near the Kirovwerk."

It was the same trick as with the guard at the checkpoint. Hofner wouldn't say anything but the moment he thought of the incident it began being inscribed on the life-bug and as it did it connected up with pointers to the earlier recording, of the actual incident.

Fox felt Hofner's hands on his throat.

Light. The railway tracks near the Kirovwerk. Fox had forgotten how beautiful Victor was.

400

Washed in the arc lights from the factories. Looking as he had that first time, at the back of the Cabaret Vaucanson, as though only the backdrop had changed, the scenery shifted. Victor was with his side man Lazlo, walking into the scene, played out in the recording inside Hans Hofner...Seen from the confines of a small room, the railway hut.... rough taste of a Conradin brand cigarette.

"You're..." Hans was saying, "Vogt got me a message before he left. Some crazy mask, The Wheel, looking for me..."

Hofner's thumb began to push on Fox's Adam's apple as his other hand, on Fox's chest, forced him further into the wall. From somewhere further down the alley came the smell of piss...Out near the Kirovwerk Victor and Lazlo walked towards their fate....

They were both looking around and ahead, coming towards where Han's Hofner was concealed...Hans Hofner, hidden in his own past, in the railway hut, about to come out, about to move, when he saw something...

And in the alley Hans continued to throttle Fox.

"Who the hell are you?" Hofner was saying, but Fox didn't need him now, he'd found the place in the life-bug that he wanted, could watch it play out without the conscious presence of Hans Hofner.

Fox kicked out hard, catching Hans in the groin so that he doubled over spluttering.

Back near the Kirovwerk someone came past the railway hut, his back to where Hans was spying.

Hans Hofner, here, now, came up with a good upper cut, even though his balls must be stinging

401

bad. Fox was going to lose this one... There was only one thing he could do, but he couldn't do it until he had seen.

In the hut Hans had stubbed out his cigarette, shifted his position to try and get a better view as the bulky stranger strode towards Victor and pulled a gun...

Hans now punched Fox in the face. Fox thought it better to go down, as he studied...

Lazlo started to run away back along the railway tracks. The figure shot him in the back. Lazlo fell. Then the bulk turned back towards Victor one in the head and one in the chest. Then the bulk calmly pocketed his gun and walked away, at last turning his face towards where Hofner hid.

Hofner pressed Fox's head against the floor in the alley and drew something from his back pocket. It was a ratchet knife, smooth steel, infinitely capable. Against his cheek Fox felt the wet of the ground, the stench of piss. But he had seen enough, he had seen the masked face of Victor's killer.

He let the augmentation take control of Hans Hofner, flooding back the moments of Victor's killing, through the interface from the life-bug to the brain, where the aug could not read the details only the sudden storm of electro-chemical reaction.

Hofner paused, the ratchet above Fox.

The aug went link by link through violence.

Hofner just stood there.

Ginger smile, the knife unmoving. Enjoying the rush of involuntary memory.

Fox tried to kick at his legs. Ineffectual. Wallowing in the piss pools of the alley.

The aug got it.

It delved for something else, skipping like a flat stone then diving down into the life-bug memories. It fed back into to him injecting from solid state into the unfathomable mess of the human mind.

On Hofner's face, longing, loss, yearning, even as Fox smelt the blood iron mingle with the piss as he lay there wounded, bleeding... Hans had once had a love, a young boyfriend who lingered still from just after the life-bug had been fitted.

Standing there with the ratchet poised...

Long enough for Fox to kick out again at Hofner's feet, rise and punch.

And punch.

Punch him into nothing while he lingered over lost love. Take the ratchet off him. Hans Hofner: got from him what was needed and left him in an alley. Not Fox, not really. Smiled watching him die. Wiped blood off the ratchet on the thigh of his trousers. Didn't have any more business here. Franz Wheeler. Wheeler Fortune. Wheel of Fortune. All finished.

The aug wanted to stay, witness the finally spluttering of Hofner's life out into elliptical sensation written onto the life-bug. Pick over the bits of Han's Hofner running out, running down. And did something in Fox want to stay to, to see Hofner suffer, to be at the other end of pain and humiliation? To gorge out an eye and toss it into a bowl. He found he couldn't move away. That he had to wait until the end.

The final act, light falling on Hofner from the street. A movement on his face. A scarab flies out.

403

The last signal Fox registers is a 2D schematic of a flight plan to its final destination.

***

Once final act. The two cold, bored, great-coated guards near the man-hole cover. The street Fox had seen before when he'd poked his head up from the tunnel. Two guards. Wondering why they were there.

Fox was looking bad enough as he always did these days, stumbling forward, towards them, falling at their knees, make a good play of keeling over.

Ambulance, ambulance.

One went. The other was solicitous.

It is harder than you think to punch a man unconscious but Fox managed it. He wasn't fitted with a life-bug…just a young kid in all of this. When the other one came back Fox was gone.

CHAPTER THIRTY-SIX

Back in Tartessos, smell of the river, oil from derricks, refreshing after all that good air of Gutenberg with its hidey holes of blood and piss. At the hyperloop depot there were Masqueradists up to something as Fox came down out of the maintenance tunnel. They were loading the carriages of the hyperloop train.

Dr Pest appeared. Fox thought she might have been smaller than he remembered. Less like Mond or Demi.

"We've been waiting for you before we use the tunnels for our own purposes."

"Sorry to hold you up for so long."

"Nearly two weeks."

But it couldn't have been only that. Could it? The time in the ward in the House of Doves had stretched like the sleep before waking that seems to linger forever.

The people in masks had filled the hyperloop carriage with explosives, and were now packing around this any shrapnel they could get hold of, from cutlery to brass candelabra, hooks and wrenches and other railway tools, bolts from the sleepers...

"You're going to send that through to Gutunberg?"

"Yes," she said, "Good isn't it."

Who was he to judge, ratchet with Hans Hofner's blood still in his pocket?

"I need to see them all," Fox said, "Mond, Schiller, the Bakelite Brothers."

"Really?" she tried not to sound intrigued. "Well, well. They will be at the Cabaret Vaucanson I expect."

Fox nodded.

"Did you find out?" she said.

"I'll be on my way," said Fox.

"What are you going to do?"

Her hand was on his forearm and he stared into the eyes behind the mask. All around were Masqueradists, busy putting together their gigantic hyperloop bomb. All of them were armed and would, presumably, do whatever Dr Pest told them to. Some of them stared over at the two of them curious as to what it was had crawled out of the service tunnel and hadn't been shot out of hand.

"Come," she said, still holding onto him, "You've got time for a little refreshment before you go. You look tired."

She led him off into the corridors of the offices of the old hyperloop terminus, away from any prying. They walked through the ruins of what had once been the future, cracked immersion booths where loads had been administered through interactive actuators, headsets for direct neural control of the loop system, schedules linked to the arrival of river freight. Everything had been going to be done this way one day. Then it had been. Now it no longer was. On the walls there were a few old posters, cyberdildonic stars and starlets frozen in odd movement now that the smart paper no longer worked. Everything here was dead. The augmentation found no remnant of living data, the decay was complete.

Dr Pest led Fox up some stairs to what had once been the recreation room and canteen for the staff of the depot. There were immersion booths here too. They were dead. The games over.

"Well," she said as they sat down opposite each other at a wipeclean polymer table.

"What is it that you want to know? Remember I don't actually work for you."

"No. You work for the people who hired you. I suppose."

"It was Olympia who originally wanted me on this investigation. Even if she wasn't the one who paid."

"Sadly you can't report back to her."

"No. But I can tell the others who killed their friend."

"Victor? Olympia?"

"It makes sense to me now. There's just one more little thing to clear up and then it's all over."

"Do you want me to do anything?"

"What could you do?"

"If it was a member of the Masquerade I feel a certain obligation."

"As you said before you don't feel the time is right for an internal purge. It's much better if I deal with it, isn't it? Then I'll disappear."

"Disappear? How dramatic. Where will you go?"

"I'll go to Harmony."

She gave the minutest of shoulder laughs.

"Tell me," she said, "What was it like over there? Among the Renewal Society."

"Most of them aren't in the Renewal Society. Just ordinary people. Either they think you lot are dangerous rebels and so support what they see as the forces of order that's more effective that the Provisional Government. Or they just happened to have been caught on the wrong side when the barricades went up. And, by the way, they're willing to hold out. They think the Northern League are going to come and save them."

"They might be right. Your friend Vogt disappeared in that direction. We think he went with intelligence about what was happening here. They'll try and seize the atomics first. Vogt might even have something that could finally convince them. We've had our scouts out watching."

"And what will you lot do?"

Basically it sounded as though they were doomed.

"We have to take the city before they get here. Then negotiate some kind of neutrality."

"And you think that will work?"

"If we're the government the atomics are ours."

There didn't seem much more to say. Fox stood up and they went back to the loading area of the depot where the bomb continued to be prepared.

"How are you planning on getting to Harmony?" she said, "The only one who knew where it is, was Victor."

"Yes," Fox said, "They all forget don't they. Every time they are wound up they forget."

"So?"

"Don't worry, I'll figure it out."

He wasn't going to tell her that he already had.

***

He went home and slept until mid-morning. Tried to shower but only a trickle came out. He wondered if the death smell of Hans Hofner was real or not. When he went into the Café Castringius Max actually threw down his tee towel and hugged Fox.

"We all thought you were dead."

"Thanks."

Then Fox said it again without bitterness or sarcasm.

There were a few others in and they came over and shook Fox's hand.

"We don't have a lot," said Max when he'd seated Fox at his table, which had a little reserved sign on it. Max joined him. "The rationing you see. I know we have the docks but very little comes in apparently. That lot…" he indicated the other side of the city, Gutunberg, "They have that airstrip and the Provisional Government have the road out to the north through the Heights."

"It's okay Max, I'll have whatever you've got. Then I have some business to take care of."

"You need the Molina?"

"Maybe. Later. I'll need a route to the Provisional Government zone. To the Heights. You think that is possible?"

"Sure," he said, "The Provisional Government isn't saying boo to a goose these days. They're leaving the Renewal Society and the Masquerade to fight it out between them. You going to see Felice?"

"Felice? I should I suppose…"

"Ok," said Max rising, "Let me fix you something to eat."

Back in the apartment Fox got ready. Packing the final weapon he'd got in Paris. A little handgun. He would be gone soon, away from the apartment and the Café Castringius.

Once, sat together in the little Cuman café, Olympia had asked him what it was like to be so old, to have so much memory. It is a recurrence of endings, perhaps not abrupt but fade outs, darkening vision as people you know get old and die, as places change or are no longer there at all. It is as though you are the read head of an endless tape that can only ever travel forward because you know what has passed though is irrevocably lost.

The old Cuman man had come over at that point.

"You must eat something," he'd said to Olympia, "You never eat. Look at you, so thin."

Fox and Olympia had giggled to themselves, assumed it was the old man's idea of a joke but perhaps, after all those times they had been there, some trick of light, some age related macular degeneration of the old man's eyes had rendered her human.

***

Fox avoided any of the main streets and squares of Little Alex, going instead through familiar alleys where all there was to remind you of current events was the occasional propaganda poster.

The back doors of the Cabaret Vaucanson were locked with bright new steel chains and a padlock.

410

Fox could hear something inside, muffled, familiar. He paused for a moment wishing he could make an entrance here. It was music, someone tinkling on a piano.

The front entrance was busier than the back streets of Little Alex, people going about their business, the unmasked no longer strolling casually but moving quickly, no one wanting to be out on the streets unless they were Masqueradists. The Masqueradists in their masks had an air of purpose. There was one outside the Cabaret Vaucanson with a rifle on her shoulder, the mask of some sort of fat cheeked rodent on her face. The place itself had a few sandbags piled outside. They were below the tinted windows and hence completely pointless, as though a half-hearted attempt to militarise the place had been abandoned before it hardly got started.

In the cloakroom were piles of tinned foodstuffs, different sorts, brands, collected piecemeal from somewhere assumedly in some moment of revolutionary zeal.

He could hear the piano better now.... something slow, jazz, almost blues. Sad but in a contrived way that the best blues never was. The contrived sadness of a mechanism perhaps.

In the main room the house lights were on. There were a few people around, humans and ultraclocks, lounging in chairs, their masks on tables. The humans looked tired, drinking and smoking. Some of the ultraclocks looked worn, scuffed and bullet scared.

On the top of the piano was a mask, faced down. Bob was playing. As Fox came in he turned

411

his head and glanced over carrying on playing all the while.

"Fox,"

It was Mond. She came over and took Fox's arm and led him to a table. Eventually Fox took his eyes away from the piano player.

"How are you?" Mond said. "Let me get you something to drink. "She looked around but there was no-one to serve her. "Just wait a minute. I'll fetch you something. You look…We heard…what happened to you."

"Don't worry," said Fox.

He meant he didn't want a drink. But he was glad when she either didn't understand or chose to ignore him because when she came back with a glass of something he was grateful.

The piano stopped but by the time Fox looked around Bob was playing again, it sounded like the same tune, but wasn't.

The drink wasn't good, not Italian grappa.

"What is this?"

"Ofechovka. At least that's what they call it. I'm not sure there are walnuts left."

"How have you been, Mond? Your war going well?"

"Cynicism always becomes you. It must be a detective thing."

Fox drank.

"I'll only be a detective for a little while longer. Measure it in minutes."

"What do you mean?"

"I've finally solved the case."

"The case?"

She clapped her hands like a delighted child. Did the tiniest applause with the middle and index finger of one hand against the life line of the other palm.

"Oh," she said, "You are serious. We should call everyone together and have a denouement. Who did it Fox?"

Fox got up and went over to the piano. Bob continued to play. The face down mask was there. There was something disturbing about the inside of a mask. He had always known this but not admitted it, repressed it.

"What are you doing?" Mond had come over.

Bob carried on playing while throughout the room the voices died away, everyone focused on Fox.

"I never knew," said Fox, "Who was the wolf and who was the pig."

The inside of masks, creases and hollows full of shadows.

Bob looked up. Wearing the mask of his own face, his bald head with its bushy eyebrows, his fixed weary look.

"What are you doing?" he said to Fox.

Mond's voice came from behind. But Fox wasn't listening now.

"If I turned over this mask," he said to Bob, "what would I see, a wolf or a pig?"

Perhaps for too long he had considered them human, or a perfection of humanity. Without a life-bug to read, without even the unfathomable electro-chemical activity of a human brain, their inner nothingness rendered up onto their surfaces, their actions. But of course the void within them had always been an illusion.

"Well?" said Fox.

Olympia had been what Kleist said about the marionettes, completely without self-consciousness, and so capable of perfection. Not just singing and dancing but in the way she navigated the broken landscapes of everyday existence.

"Which one of you was it?"

Bob finally stopped playing.

(Bob Bakelite's playing. An alternative scene dredged up from somewhere, perhaps with the help of the augmentation. Piano notes lingering like slow motion rain drops. Even after he stopped, the tune carried on in Fox's head, no longer sounding like mechanical blues but the fall of an emotion that was as real as any Fox had ever felt. Somewhere other notes were playing, other instruments, a brush beat hardly there at all, keeping time.)

"You never listened," Bob said. "When we told you about Strindberg at the zoo. Why do you assume there's always the same face behind the same mask? Why can't one person be many?"

"Or," said Karl, appearing now from the wings of Fox's peripheral vision, "many be one."

The gun shook in Fox's hand.

Would it be like killing a human being? The way it felt killing Hans Hofner. Olympia was dead the way any person could be dead, wasn't she?

"Don't," said Fox. But he didn't know what he meant.

"Let me tell you how it was with Victor." said Bob, still sat on the piano stall as though he were

414

just taking a break, "I told myself it was because he was double-crossing us, selling out the Masquerade but really it wasn't that. He never gave us away. Just tried to destroy our purpose. The great Victor Invicta who came here and was always better than us, who had Olympia even, though he was keyless and couldn't even do it with her...well Victor, for all his plans, his schemes, in the end he thought he was our messiah. Was going to lead us back to Harmony...our place...which none of us can even remember. And what? We weren't good enough to be here? I'd see the way he was affecting the ultraclocks. And so, what I did, I did for all of us, because we don't need to be led away from here. We can live here. We're part of it. We're with the humans who want to change things... God...You don't get it all do you Fox? You have to believe there's a better story than that, some complex plot, but no. I had to end him. Because he was a fake. What he was selling was fake."

"What about Olympia?" said Fox, the gun was steadier now, hardly shaking at all, almost aimed.

"He didn't kill Olympia."

The voice came from behind.

Karl's voice.

"She should never have been with you. She was beyond your conception. All that sleazy little men like you saw was a fetishized doll. But I didn't want to do it. I.... That night, when Mond was attacked Olympia came here for help."

Her timing had been, as always, perfection. She rushed into the Bakelite's dressing room in a panic. Karl was busy taking something out of the safe, having just drawn out the pulse gun, he held in his hand the card that had been with it. The tarot card. The Fool. Perhaps Bob had kept it as a trophy, perhaps as a way of confessing to the only other person who could open the safe. She saw the card.

"She asked me whose gun it was...she was accusing me...," he turned for a moment to his brother. "I picked up the gun from the case. I knew she would never forgive you for killing Victor."

It was as though no-one else was there, that the Bakelite Brothers were playing out the scene by themselves. But then they were coming towards Fox, chitin sheathed machines that moved as though the air around them was a resin they were sweeping away.

"Put the gun down Fox." Mond's voice.

"Who are you going to shoot?" said Karl, but Fox didn't understand the nuance of that, did he mean which brother, or was it just a little sarcastic jibe.

And Karl reached out and put his fist around the gun and squeezed it into a lump of useless metal.

"We're not really made of Bakelite you know. It's just a stage name."

He would crush Fox now in the same way as he had the gun. When Fox looked into Karl's face there was still no expression beyond the paralysed arrogance that had always been there.

"You were protecting me." Bob said. "I understand that."

"You're my brother."

Fox had wondered once what that meant, perhaps now he knew.

Fox was in the centre of a small crowd, an audience scattered among the tables and chairs of the Cabaret Vaucanson. In a moment they would clap and cheer the performance. Already someone was calling out.

"Get out of here, both of you, just get out of here."

It was Mond, and she was accompanied by the soft beat and Fox recognised it for what it was now, not soft at all as it came closer, as Schiller came closer, ticking away.

"I am placing you both under arrest in the name of the revolution."

Fox thought he heard someone laughing. Yes Karl laughing. Moving with a sudden blur. The something hit Fox in the stomach and he fell to his knees, his whole torso feeling as though it were about to crumble. Karl pushed past him and rushed towards the exit, followed by Bob.

The wind had been forced out of him, so that he couldn't stand, not yet…

Mond helped him up and got him to the table where they'd sat. His drink was still there. He hadn't finished it.

CHAPTER THIRTY-SEVEN

Sometime later that evening a large explosion detonated in the hyperloop beneath the streets of Gutunberg and the forces of the Masquerade rushed up from Tartessos and Sparta it would later be known as the January 28th Offensive.

Mond told Fox what it was just after the explosion happened, shaking the walls of the Cabaret Vaucanson, the chandeliers swaying, plaster flaking off from the walls.

They'd been drinking steadily all afternoon.

"I guess," Fox said, "that means everyone is going to be too busy to look for them."

"What will you do now?" She'd asked Fox this one way or another many times. "They need to be brought in...brought to justice..."

She was rambling.

Schiller joined them for a while, ticking away as he sat there, his clockwork skeleton a concentration of endless discrete movements. He'd set things in motion, had informed the Masquerade about what the Bakelite Brothers had done.

"I need to get to the Heights," Fox had said to him.

"That's in the Provisional Government Zone."

"You think they are there?" asked Mond. "Why would they be there?"

Fox took yet another drink. He was nicely sloshed by now, able to get that way a lot quicker than he had for a while. He hoped he was being cryptic and inscrutable. He didn't know where the Bakelite Brothers were. He didn't care anymore.

"I'm leaving," he said, "And I have to say goodbye to someone before I go."

"Go? Go where?" Mond said.

Tick. Tick. Tick.

"And what," said Schiller, "About the two killers you have discovered? Don't you want to see them brought to justice for what they've done?"

"You hired me to track down Victor's killer. I think I can finally say I've done it. The case is over."

"And Olympia?" said Mond.

Tick. Tick. Tick.

"Well," said Schiller, "The Provisional Government zone is more or less quiet. The Provisional Government are doing what they have always done, waiting to see what will happen. We have a border with them. There hasn't been any shots fired across it lately. They attack neither us nor the Renewal Society. So I assume you could go there. You could enter as a sort of refugee. I will arrange to have papers drawn up, a document of passage."

"Don't you even care what happens to Karl," said Mond. "He killed Olympia."

"What will happen to him?" Fox asked Schiller.

Tick. Tick. Tick.

"If he's caught then I imagine they'll have to be some sort of trial…. There was no cause to kill her. Bob, perhaps, might plead a case that he suspected Victor of something…"

Tick. Tick. Tick.

"But you have to understand," Schiller went on, "that to many the Bakelite Brothers are to be admired. They have fought relentlessly and bravely for the Masquerade. They believe in the cause whole heartedly. The idea of some sort of trial for Bob…is problematic. And yet the Masquerade cannot condone their behaviour. It would perhaps be better if they were never seen again."

"Is that what you think?" said Fox, to both of them, "Is that what's going to happen when you put on your masks, when you become part of the Masquerade? You're going to make sure that their bodies are never found. The fog of war and all that."

Tick. Tick. Tick.

They said nothing.

"Goodbye Mond. Goodbye Schiller. Have those papers sent over to the Café Castringius for me will you."

***

He packed a few things from the apartment in an old valise he'd had since he'd carried it across half of Europe all those years ago. The night was filled with the sound of automatic gun fire, the sky lit up with flashes of energy weapons.

"You should come with me," Fox said to Max.

They were stood out the back of the Café Castringius as Fox put the valise in the Molina, after checking the car was charged.

"What, now?" said Max. "Soon I'll be the only café left open in Little Alex. I'll finally have a monopoly. Anyway, where would I go? Where will you go?

420

"I'm not sure yet. I might be back before you know it."

Max turned to go back inside.

"Wait," he said, "I have something for you."

He came out holding up the print of the painting that had hung above Fox's table in the café.

"Take it."

It had been on the wall so long that Fox had stopped seeing it. It wasn't a painting so much as a collage of painted elements.

The Lascivious Orchid Inseminates the Embryo.

The orchid has been torn from the ground to that its tubers are exposed. The blades of the leaves reach out towards a blue pool. Beyond the orchid there is a forest of other orchids. These are labelled like an anatomical drawing. From the orchid by the pool a tear or bud or perspiration comes, it is flowing towards the pool where there is the sleeping face of an unborn child. But as well as engendering life the orchid is dying. It has been, after all, ripped from the earth.

"Max," said Fox, "What would I do with it?"

"Wherever you are hang it up. You'll feel at home."

"Sure."

Fox reached out to take the print but for a moment Max hung onto it.

"You could always sell it." Max said, "You do know that it's the original don't you? My grandfather met one of Castringius's old friends. Running away from Perlenstadt. My grandfather helped him out and the man gave this to him. When

421

he opened his café, here, he named it after it. We collected the other prints, but this, this is real…"

"Max I can't take it."

"Then borrow it. Like I said. Make you feel at home. And you can bring it back to me one day."

There wasn't any way Fox could refuse was there? But he didn't want to think about in what circumstances he would find himself when he could hang the picture on a wall.

***

Border crossing. Cold morning.

He drove along Autocue Boulevard, no longer a front line but still scarred from the recent fighting here. Steffis boarded up, the lights out, hardly any of the other shops open either. There were a few people around, the odd masked figure going about some urgent business or other. South of Sparta and Gutunberg the sound of gunfire sporadic, bursts of percussive small arms fire. The occasional flash of energy weapons visible but washed out in the morning light.

He drove on. The Towers and English Town to the right. Stretches now where the road was completely deserted, the houses having that look of abandonment. Then, ahead, he saw the barrier, a check point with a pole gate across the road, and a lorry parked next to it, some sort of artillery piece mounted on the flat back. This was the Masquerade side. There was a space beyond the gate and then another gate further along the road.

As Fox watched something came down out of the sky, a flutter of gold wings that caught the sunlight. It was the eagle, coming to rest out there in

422

no-man's land and looking towards the Molina as Fox drove towards the first check point.

He bought the car to a halt before the barrier and a woman approached. Fox wound down his window letting a chill in. The woman lent to inspect him. She was wearing a Venetian carnival mask, studded with semi-precious stones for eyebrows.

"Where are you going?" she said.

She sounded bored, irritated. Perhaps she wanted to rush off to the bangs and flashes of the fighting going on elsewhere.

"Over there."

"Funny."

"To be honest there's someone I want to see and they're in the Provisional Government zone."

"Papers?"

Fox showed the papers that Schiller had given him. She studied them then signalled for someone to open the gate.

"Hopefully they won't shoot you," she said. "If you're planning on coming back there's a curfew at dusk."

"Thanks. I'll bear that in mind."

He didn't know if he'd be back this way. It depended on what he found out.

He drove towards the next checkpoint. Another barred gate and a pre-fabricated steel booth beside the road. The eagle had gone now, off to tell its master where Fox was.

The guards on the Provisional Government side looked odd in their old Landespolizei uniforms. Everything had changed so much that they seemed to belong to the past. Once more he wound down his window as a red-faced policeman in his fifties walked out scowling.

"Papers."

Fox handed them over.

"These mean nothing here," he said. "What do you want?"

"Friend of mine. An elderly lady out on the Heights."

"You look like you've seen some fighting." The police man waved a finger around his own eye to indicate the patch Fox wore.

"Enough. I've seen enough. I don't plan on seeing any more."

A telephone began to ring in the booth. For a moment Fox thought the policeman would wave him on but he was told to wait. The policeman stood at the door of the booth talking into the handset, looking over at Fox, his breath visible in the cold. When he came back he pointed through the gate to the road beyond and patch of rough ground beside it.

"You're to pull over. No funny business now." Fumbling with the holster on his belt he extracted his pistol holding it low.

"What is it?" said Fox.

"You see there?" He pointed back off to the left, towards the Towers. "Well. They keep an eye on everything comes along this road. Someone has taken an interest in you. Must have noticed your car through their binoculars. They're sending someone down. After you park get out of the car and wait."

"Am I under arrest?"

Once again he scowled.

"You'll find out soon enough. Now park up, park up."

He waved Fox on with his gun as the barrier was raised.

Stamping his feet against the cold Fox waited by the car and watched down the road until he saw another car approaching. As it got near he saw the driver. It was Felice.

"I'd recognise that Molina anywhere," she said as she got out.

She started to laugh. Stood there in what looked like a new uniform she laughed and all Fox could do was join in. She took his forearms in her hands.

"Green, you stupid bastard. What the hell have you been up to?"

Fox through her eyes now, the patch, face recovering from bruising, head stubbled with sprouts of cilia.

"Just working a case. But it's over now."

"You lost an eye."

"Careless of me."

She smiled. She was wearing the uniform of Captain, with epaulettes and a braided side cap, she was clean and neat even though she looked tired. Fox nodded at her stripes.

"Promotion?"

"More a sideways movement. The ways things are round here now. Come on, follow me and we'll go for a drink."

"It's a bit early."

"When has that ever stopped you?"

"I'm a reformed character."

"And I'm a Captain so you'd better do as I say."

Fox did, following her car in the Molina. They didn't go to the Towers but skirted round and up a hill through narrow streets. It was a neighbourhood he'd hardly been to before, medieval houses of what had once been a separate village called Cornith. Felice pulled up outside the local town hall where the Genesia flag was hung. A sign outside said it was the seat of government for the whole city.

"I've got something to show you," she said.

She led him into the nether regions of the town hall, beyond the made-over front rooms to where the corridors were dark.

"Used to be where they stored all the documents but we had to shift a lot of stuff. To make cells."

Heavy doors with heavy locks. Felice took out a bunch of keys from inside her jacket and unlocked one.

It still had much of the air of a stock room, the dry smell of old paper lingering. In the far corner was a fold out camp bed and on this, propped up on some pillows, Vogt was reading a newspaper.

He looked up then did a double take. Put down the paper and sat up on the edge of the bed.

"Prisoners are not allowed to be visited by just any old riff-raff," he said.

"Hello Vogt," said Fox.

"You look terrible Fox, more terrible than usual even with all your worms…what are they cut off. And this eye patch…You look terrible. Why are you here? Come to gloat have you?"

But Fox didn't know. In the end it turned out that Vogt had had nothing directly to do with Olympia's death, nor even with Victor's. What had he really done in all of this? Beyond being a constant annoyance to Fox over the years…But then he remembered how Vogt had procured Lola for Kardos. How he had frightened Frau Kastner. He was a weasel, a bully. Perhaps Fox should confront him with all this.

"Things didn't turn out the way you expected then." said Fox.

"Pah," said Vogt, "just go away will you. Scuttle back under your rock."

"Sure," said Fox, "But there's just one thing."

"What?"

Vogt was fiddling with the edge of the newspaper as though desperate to return to whatever it was could absorb him there.

"You owe me a hat," said Fox.

Back in the corridors Felice told him how Vogt had been apprehended with a set of documents offering up access to Genesia's atomic weaponry to the Northern League in exchange for an assurance that they would come and make sure that the Renewal Society prevailed in the city. There was also a bag containing a sizable number of diamonds as part of a sweetener to the deal.

"The funny thing though," said Felice, "was that Vogt was nowhere near the Northern League. He was headed in completely the other direction."

It seemed, in the end, that Vogt had discovered a greater cause than the great Renewal and that cause was himself.

"What will happen to him?" Fox said.

"A trial."

But what happened to him really depended on who did finally win control of Genesia, and how good a story Vogt would be able to spin to them.

***

Back in their cars Felice took a few turns into Corinth and pulled up outside a restaurant. Fox drew the Molina up behind.

The restaurant didn't look open but Felice banged on the door and eventually and old woman answered.

It was just as well that Fox ate first and made sure he just sipped the vodka that was served up with the meagre portion of pork, sauerkraut and dumplings. Felice downed hers but then slowed to match Fox's pace. It meant that there were things that both of them wanted to say, that needed to be said, would wait until the booze had relaxed them both.

So they talked about the war, about politics.

"So the Northern League are going to come and make sure the Renewal Society get the city."

"When the Northern League come," she said, "They'll settle it in their own favour, that's for sure."

"So you think they will?"

"Maybe capturing Vogt means more than just the warm feeling I get out of it. Maybe they needed the diamonds to sweeten the deal. But I suspect they'll come for their own reasons."

"What will you do?" Fox said. "I mean all of you. The Provisional Government."

She decided to finish her drink and topped Fox up once again.

"They seem incapable of making a decision," she said, "They still have the Eirni atomics…"

"I suppose that is what it all comes down to in the end," said Fox. "The big prize. While everyone's fighting over the city what the Northern League want is our big bombs."

"Neither the Masquerade nor the Renewal Society have made a move against the base yet," Felice said. "They skirmish with each other around it but they know the stakes completely change if they try to take it over. As long as the Provisional Government are in control then, to the outside world, the status quo is as it is. Any attempt to take it over could tip the balance towards outside intervention."

"But isn't that what the Renewal Society are banking on?"

"Oh yes. But they want their potential friends in the Northern League getting here first. There are other players who might also have their eye on Eirni.

"So what happens if the Northern League come?"

"There's the rub. Well we either put the bombs out of action and give in or use the battlefield atomics."

It was sometime in the afternoon now but still nobody had come into the restaurant. Fox should get on with his journey.

"I have to go and see Frau Pfaff."

"And then?"

"Then I'll be leaving."

"Where are you going, Green?"

Some shift, subtle. Fox was aware of her uniform again, of who she was and what he might now seem to her, even after all these years.

"I'm going to Harmony."

"Ah. The girl. The cabaret clockwork girl. I heard what happened. I'm sorry. But I thought nobody knows where this Harmony is. That it's a myth."

"I think there's a way."

"And that'll be it? You'll go off to Harmony. This isn't some complex Masquerade plot?"

She was smiling, a ripple across her scars, but it was a serious question.

"Come with me," said Fox, "Up to the house I mean. You'll see then."

She ordered coffee and it turned out, after all, that it wasn't going to be a long evening of drinking that ran into the night. Fox was grateful. He wanted to get on, but knew that if Felice had wanted a drinking session he would have gone along with it. He figured he owed her that.

This time she followed Fox, back out of Corinth and eventually onto the road that led up further into the Heights.

CHAPTER THIRTY-EIGHT

From the outside the Villa Verloren hadn't changed. The Molina crunching over the gravel after the iron gates, the grandiose portico…it was all still in a state of gentile shabbiness, although the window upstairs, that had been cracked, had been repaired. There was a ladder lying on the ground beneath it.

Otto opened the door.

"Well, well," he said, "Look what the wind has blown in."

"How is Frau Pfaff?" Fox asked as Otto led them into the vestibule.

"Very well indeed."

The vestibule hadn't changed. Less dust perhaps on all the old detritus from the nascent singularity that had never, really, happened. Remnants of the cyber age. The VR booth was still there but it was dead now, the internal landscapes gone for good.

"So," Fox said to Otto, "Frau Pfaff hasn't cleaned out her sister's collection."

"In the end," said Frau Pfaff coming into the vestibule, "I didn't have the heart to get rid of any of it."

She had changed. She wore what must have been her sister's outfit, Chinese pyjamas the colour of jade with a dragon twisting across her breast. On her head was a turban of yellow silk with a headband of gold damask around it.

"I'm glad," said Fox.

More than glad. Relieved beyond measure that the house remained as it always had been for him. That everything would be in its place.

"It's lovely to see you Herr Fox. And you Captain Sax."

"How are you?" asked Felice.

"Oh yes," said Frau Pfaff, seemingly in response to another question, "Let's go into the Yellow Room shall we. Otto will take some coffee and something to nibble on."

"I'll see what I can do," said Otto.

Like the vestibule the Yellow Room was as Fox remembered, the pleasant clutter of old electronics, books and vinyl records. And standing in his place the ultraclock that Fox had taken for a suit of Maximillian armour. The one Frau Kastner had called Parsifal, standing there with his mace.

"Perhaps I should put on some music," said Frau Pfaff fluttering around the record player. "But of course, I can't…"

"Don't worry," said Felice, "It's fine."

"There's something I have to see," said Fox.

He couldn't wait anymore. Frau Pfaff looked perplexed for only a moment.

"Oh or course, Herr Fox. Of course. She is still where you left her."

Upstairs. He'd chosen one of the bedrooms. It was dim, with the heavy curtains closed. He tried the light switch but the light didn't come on. He could see her in the half-light coming through a crack where the curtains didn't quite meet, burning dust motes in the beam falling upon her.

Beautiful. Inanimate. Her death had finally signified that what she had possessed before had been life, even if it was of a manner he could not entirely comprehend.

***

Later they all sat in the yellow room and it became dark. Otto bought candles. There had been no mains power for weeks up here in the Heights.

They talked about Frau Kastner. It turned out that there never had been a will and that their father had died with only debts that Frau Kastner's husband had paid off. She never wanted to tell Frau Pfaff, wanting her sister to keep her image of the upright and respectable father intact. In fact the old man had gambled out at some casino in the Diesel Lands, managing to maintain some kind of façade of respectability in Genesia even as the debts piled up. Death had saved everyone a lot of embarrassment but only because Frau Kastner stepped in and threw her husband's money at the potential scandal.

"So you see," said Frau Pfaff, "I always had it wrong about Cosima. She was just trying to protect me."

Fox almost said that none of this mattered now but of course it did. As the city stood on the brink the thought of Frau Kastner and the way she had given her father a death mask of respectability was somehow comforting in a way he wasn't sure he could explain.

Otto joined them and they drank a little, old wine that must have been in the house for a long

433

time. It tasted of fruit groves in countries that no longer existed.

"How are you intending to travel to Harmony?" Otto asked.

Fox shrugged.

"That Molina's charge," Otto went on, "won't last too long."

"It's academic," said Felice, her words slurred slightly, "He doesn't know where it is. Nobody knows where it is. Not even the ultraclocks know."

"Oh," said Otto, "I think he's thought of that, haven't you Herr Fox?"

"How clever," said Frau Pfaff.

"What?"

Felice was looking at them. Had Otto seen Fox's glances over towards the armoured ultraclock?

What was it Frau Kastner had said? Not wound since the day he arrived. Ten years before, one of the first to come. Not wound and so his memory not tick tocked away, not slipped through gear and escarpment...

"Parsifal," Fox said.

"Parsifal?" said Frau Pfaff. "I've always thought of him as Don Quixote since I came."

Fox went over to the ultraclock and touched the key just below his breast plate. He lifted the visor to revel the sad wooden face. Then he turned the key. The ticking began, echoing within the metallic carapace of armour.

Parsifal raised his head and looked at Fox and the mace he was holding clattered to the floor.

"An accident!" Parsifal said. "An unforgivable accident."

Everyone was standing around the knight now.

"That doesn't matter," said Fox. "But I need you to tell me something. I need to know where Harmony is."

Parsifal looked around the room, then at Fox again. Took a step forward.

"Why?"

"I'll show you."

Taking one of the candles Fox led Parsifal upstairs, the ultraclock clanking as he walked in stiff armoured steps.

In the room again. Olympia. Candlelight glowing on her skin.

"I know her," said Parsifal. "I left her in Harmony. Not so long ago."

"I'm going to take her there. To see…"

"Oxenstierna will raise her from the dead. I have seen it done."

Fox gripped Parsifal's arm and the ultraclock turned to look at him. The light from the candle flickered on is wooden face.

"Across the Diesel Lands," he said. "Towards the old railway junction at Okraj…"

And he told Fox the way to Harmony.

***

The five of them talked in the Yellow Room. Parsifal had been sent by Oxenstierna with other ultraclocks to Genesia, to the city of cultured eccentricity, ruled by Count Septimus, whom Oxenstierna had worked with years before. Parsifal's long repose had meant he'd slept through the murder of Septimus, the Court of Comedians and their overthrow.

"And how," Parsifal asked, "Do my brothers and sisters fare in Genesia now?"

Felice looked at Fox.

"They are in danger," he said. "They should go home."

"Then why don't they?" asked Parsifal.

"They have forgotten. You must tell them before you too forget."

The ultraclock was still for a moment. Only that odd echoing ticking.

"That is what I will do," he said.

"And you, Fox?" said Otto. "I ask again. How do you intend to get there? There won't be anywhere to charge the Molina out in the Diesel Lands."

"I'll walk if I have to."

"Perhaps I can help you out there," said Otto. "We'll see in the morning."

Felice eventually nodded off curled in an armchair and both Frau Pfaff and Otto retired.

"I would like to go outside," said Parsifal.

They walked in the grounds, to where they could see over the city. There were a few flashes of energy weapons, patches of light in places that still had power.

"What is he like," asked Fox, "Oxenstierna?"

"He is...he is not like other men I have met. It is as though there is a part of him somewhere else, as though some great pre-occupation holds him. Even as he is talking to you he is partly somewhere else. He was our guide, our teacher but in the end he was our maker. How can anyone truly describe their maker?"

Later Fox lay down next to Olympia and held her, knowing that if she was still there she was someplace he couldn't reach.

He dreamed of Hans Hofner, of him dying at first but then the dream shifted, or perhaps it was the augmentation coming to Fox's rescue and feeding him with a memory, a boy running through a snow covered forest, playing some game. This was not a memory of Hans Hofner at seven. He would never have had a life-bug then. Rather it was a memory of Hans Hofner remembering being seven...

Someone in the forest called out a name but when the dreamer turned there was only darkness and the dream slipped away into nothingness.

CHAPTER THIRTY-NINE

In the morning Parsifal had gone. Fox hoped he had gone to the city, to tell them all the way to Harmony. In some way complete the mission that Victor had set out on. At least part of it anyway.

Felice looked hung-over.

"I have to get back," she said as she smoothed down her uniform.

They were in the yellow room drinking the coffee that Otto had bought. It was weak and watery, perhaps the last grains in the house.

"You in trouble?" Fox asked.

"No," she said. "I was getting off when I came over to the checkpoint. I'm not AWOL. Just a bit late."

She finished her coffee and they walked out through the vestibule. Frau Pfaff and Otto had already said goodbye.

"See you, Green," she said.

She tried to make it sound as though she might see him a little later, or at least in a few days' time.

Fox watched her drive away and wondered if she really did have to get back or if she didn't want to see Fox carrying out Olympia. But really that was none of his business.

Otto came out and found Fox standing there on the gravel.

"As I was saying last night," he said to Fox, "I think I can help you. Come on."

He led Fox around the house through some overhanging trees, then a wooden gate and a well-tended kitchen garden, tided and mostly bare for the winter. One the other side was a lawn overlooked by the darkened windows of some gallery in the house that Fox had never discovered. On the lawn were dust sheets covering vehicles.

"You've seen the Rolls Royce," said Otto point at one, "But the other one might be of more use to you."

"Otto I've got a car."

He went over and began to undo the toggles that tightened the dust sheet, then pulled it off.

"Wow."

"Yes," said Otto.

It was one of those land rovers that had been made for people who never left the city. A vanity item for the rich. Yet it still had all the off-road capability of a proper land rover. The people who'd once bought vehicles like this would have settled for nothing less.

"It runs on alcohol. Pretty much can convert anything you put in it. And very fuel efficient. There are also two subsidiary tanks for gasoline and diesel."

Frau Pfaff came out through the kitchen garden. She was more sedately dressed, with a head scarf and a wax jacket. She reminded Fox of Elizabeth the Second in old photos and memories of childhood TV.

"Well," she said, "What do you think? You can get to the front by going the other way round the house."

439

Olympia lay on the back seat. Fox had placed a blanket over her, a quilted one with gold thread that Frau Pfaff had let him take from one of the bedrooms. He put the Castringius painting in the boot.

It was easy enough to get back through the checkpoint into Masquerade territory using the papers Schiller had provided. The masked guard glanced into the back but said nothing.

"What happening?" Fox asked nodding down towards Sparta and Gutunberg. The noise of the fighting had become less intense. No more explosions but instead only the sporadic crack of gunfire.

"We'll beat them," she said. And Fox could hear something in her youthful voice, some bright and valiant optimism that was in the process of becoming brittle. She was little more than a kid.

"Sure we will," he said.

He drove away, towards Tartessos and then up onto the bridge to the other side. Masqueradist guards pulled him over and checked his papers again half way across. They were polite and diligent, checking everything but when they uncovered Olympia they try not to look insouciant.

***

Countryside. Places he had been before. Edges of the city. Farmland that fed it then a main road bordered by woodland. Then he took a minor road that was going in the direction he wanted. He needed to be as far away as possible as quickly as possible. Then something ahead coming out of the

440

sky to land on the road ahead, and from out of the trees by the side of the road came a familiar figure.

Fox slowed the car and stopped in front of Dr Pest and the eagle.

He got out of the car and walked towards them and when he spoke he heard his own voice use English for some reason.

"Take the mask off now. Come on. Take the fucking mask off."

He wasn't angry. He'd just had enough. He didn't want any more of their games. That should all have been left back there, in the city.

"I have a gift for you," she said, he could hear an odd kind of smile beneath the mask.

"I'm not interested. I'll be on my way."

The eagle flapped its wings and hopped forward.

"You should go, Herr Fox," said the eagle with its deep voice.

"I think you'll be interested. Come with me. It won't take long."

"Take off your mask then. Demi is it? Mond even? I was never quite sure."

"Very well."

She took off the mask. Her face was one he didn't recognise. A woman in her twenties with a pretty oval face and cropped black hair.

"Don't look so surprised," she said, "You've not always been wrong. Sometimes it was Demi. Other times it has been other people. We're all Dr Pest. Come on, follow me."

She put the mask back on. Fox stood where he was.

"The car?" he said.

"No-one will touch it."

She nodded down the road from where he had come. Then whistled. A couple of masked men holding rifles came out of the woods and then disappeared back in. The eagle took flight disappearing over the treetops.

Fox followed her into the woods, rising ground that was thickly covered in trees, but she threaded her way through all this as though there was a path. When she looked back to see if he was keeping up Fox saw the face of the medieval doctor, the one who comes to your bedside when you have the plague and offers nothing but prayers and quackery.

"We're nearly there."

As she said this he recognised where they were, coming at it from another angle but there, as the trees thinned through the bare branches he could see the clearing and Mond's summer cottage. Outside there was a van parked. The one he had used to get into the castle with Mond.

"You're giving me the van? I don't need the van."

"No," she said.

They stood outside the cottage and she reached into the pocket of her jacket.

"Here," she said.

She handed Fox a playing card. It was a picture of a mechanical man looking a lot like the Tin Man from the Wizard of Oz. He had a fixed smile showing a metal grill for teeth. Over his shoulder he carried a bag on a stick and he was striding ahead looking up at something unseen in the sky, while just ahead was the edge of the cliff that he was about to stumble over.

The card had a banner with its name on across the bottom.

Le Mat.

The Fool.

And yes, Fox checked, there was a tiny piece torn off the bottom right hand corner.

"Victor's card," he said.

"Yes."

"You keep it. I'm done with it all now."

He handed it back.

"The card isn't the gift," she said. "The gift is inside. The gift is waiting for you behind the door. It's all wrapped up and waiting. Bob is dead. We executed him for the murder of Victor who was, at least technically, a member of the Masquerade. The murder of Olympia, of a civilian is more problematic…"

Karl would have had the card.

From her holster she drew a machine pistol and held it out to him.

He said nothing. It was quiet but no-where is ever really silent. Always in the distance is the sound of birds, or the crack of a fox as it steps on a bed of fallen twigs. There was now, another sound, a rhythm just at the edge of hearing.

"Take the gun. A head shot. Finish it."

Would it be that simple? To open the door and pull the trigger. Would that really finish anything? Hans Hofner still lurked inside him, always ready to run through his dreams. Did Fox imagine, from behind the door that he could hear the steady tick tock of an ultraclock heart and that by ending that anything would be better?

"No."

There was no ticking. He couldn't have possibly heard ticking though the door, or could he? Yet the other noise…the rhythm he had heard, a swishing, another type of heartbeat, a beast of the forest depths he couldn't fathom. But no, it was up in the air. He turned and looked up.

"Helicopters," Dr Pest said. "The Northern League are coming. They're gambling that the Provisional Government won't use the Eirni. They'll reinforce the Renewal Society and provide aerial cover for them to retake the city. There are almost certainly ground troops on the way too. I really should get back to Genesia shouldn't I? So the sooner we get this over with the better."

She didn't sound like she was in a hurry. The helicopters grew louder.

"You're going to lose aren't you," said Fox.

"They make take the city but they won't capture the people. We will take off our masks and so be in disguise."

"Just words."

She thrust the gun towards him again.

"This isn't words though is it? Finish it."

But Fox was already finished.

***

Fox and his dead lover drove on. As they drove something registered with Fox, the memory of the life-bug leaving Hans Hofner with its flight plan. It was a mystery he hardly dare contemplate. Better to just go on the way Parsifal had told him.

They crossed into the Diesel Lands a few hours after the road left the forest behind. It was the old industrial belt from the last days of fossil fuel intoxication. In the decades that followed armies had fought over the remnants and added their own debris. Now it was a landscape of wrecked cars and lorries, great ponds of dirty water cracked with rainbows of spilt oil. The buildings were ruins, blasted brickwork forming shapes just suggestive of what they might have once been, factories and warehouses, petrol stations and repair garages. There were truncated tower bocks of neo-Brutalism that had been the apartments of workers.

Here and there Fox and Olympia passed the remains of someone, skeletons in uniforms or blue overalls. From abandoned vehicles Fox siphoned petrol with a piece of tubing he'd found in the glove compartment.

"It's all right," he told Olympia, "We'll soon be there. You'll soon be home."

Early out on the third morning they discovered that there were still people living out there. There was a little township of corrugated iron shacks built against the huge wall of what had once been a football stadium. Part of the terracing inside had been bomb and Fox saw inside as they drove past, an allotment of vegetables on the pitch where the players had once run around.

They didn't stop there. The people looked mean, mostly just staring at them as the car approached and withdrawing into their shacks before the car reached them. Only two people didn't do this. A little boy and girl who stood in the road staring at the car so that Fox thought he would have to brake before a woman in grey rags came out and hustled them away, slapping them both for dallying.

A few hours after that he pulled into another settlement. This one abandoned. There was a fuel stop, some bottles of landfill gas and Fox took these. Then drove past a strip of bars and a casino with a dead neon sign on top.

Then, later that day they saw the sign for Okraj, fifty kilometres. The wreckage of the Diesel Lands went on but now the wrecked cars were replaced with wrecked locomotives, great diesel engines that had had their guts ripped out by scavengers. They sat on rusting rails that converged in a great line of tracks that ran beside the road as Fox and Olympia came into Okraj.

Already Fox could see their goal. Beyond the town the line of the Carpathians was perhaps another fifty kilometres away. They would be there by the end of the day.

CHAPTER FORTY

One of the old monk's cells in the ruined monastery called Harmony. On the wall a painting had been recently hung, Castringius's *The Lascivious Orchid Inseminates the Embryo*. There was a small bed with rough grey blankets and a single pillow. Next to this a bedside cabinet on which was hurricane lamp, its glass blackened with use.

These cells, in the residential part of the monastery, numbered over two hundred. The ground and first floor storeys led out onto covered cloisters, one cloister above the other to form a loggia, the columns and shadows looking out over the central yard of the monastery where the onion-domed Church of St Basil stood in the centre. On the other side of the yard, the cloisters ran around to meet the ancient Romanesque Tower of Clouds, with its crenelated battlements. The tower was so called because of the interior frescos depicting Daniel 7.13, the vision seen in the clouds, the Son of Man, revealed at last as not only sinful flesh but also in nature divine, the son of God. The frescoes were added to the main hall of the tower in the nineteenth century when the walls were re-plastered, the technique of fresco being to paint onto wet lime plaster.

The Church of St Basil also contained frescoes. These depicted the history of the world, which begins in a garden with the fall of man and ends at last beyond the days of Anti-Christ in the advent of the Holy City. All this foreseen by John, out on his island in the Aegean.

There was a well plentiful in fresh water. There was little to eat in the monastery but then for a long time there had been no-one there to eat it and the fresh vegetables and fruits that had once been gathered from the gardens outside the walls were now rotted. All that could be found were canned goods. A guest would not starve but might grow tired of tinned meats, beans, soup.

The monastery was once famous for its library, which contained a collection of over three hundred medieval manuscripts in Latin, Greek and Old Slavonic.

Adjacent to the library was the scriptorium. Here for about two centuries before the coming of moveable type, the monks would produce manuscripts, not only for the monastery library but also for other religious houses and sometimes secular princes who possessed either piety enough to desire them for devotional purposes or ostentation to want them as treasures to display. The lecterns were no longer extant.

On the desks instead were a number of specialised machines for the playing of a particular type of recording. These recordings, audio, visual, immersive, were accessed via virtual reality headsets and played on devices with an orifice designed for their particular media. Next to these were mechanical typewriters, some with paper still in them. Other typewritten pages were scattered. These transcripts, attempts to render the complexities of life-bugs into prose, read like nonsense, a scrabbled joke book, odd images, non-sequiturs and contextless descriptions. But perhaps God would have been able to decipher them.

Occasionally a scarab would fly through the monastery and come to rest, waiting on the desk of the scriptorium for auditor who would now never appear.

This was Ammut then. This was the obliteration that Kardos had been terrified of. Not a hybrid beast ready to devour but just the endless piling on of debris, abandoned papers across the floor, bugs with nowhere to go.

After the first time Fox never went to the scriptorium.

***

The Church of St Basil dominated the inner courtyard. Miraculously the interior with the aforementioned frescoes had survived. Beneath the church there was an extensive crypt where the tombs of the monks from the late medieval period through to the early twentieth century resided. The rear of the crypt gave access to the catacombs, a series of low tunnels that had been an ossuary since the foundation of the monastery. Within niches in the walls were the skulls of monks sitting on piles of bones, cushioned by dust and cobwebs.

As well as buildings given over to devotion and the cells of the monks there were also more utilitarian structures. Near the main gate was a set of stables and it was here that decades before Oxenstierna had set up his laboratory. The stables were extensive including rooms for wagons and

Oxenstierna divided them into a series of room to his particular requirements, a construction and engineering project of huge proportions.

The entrance led to a gowning area and then into decontamination where there was a shower and waste disposal unit. Beyond this, corridors led to the four work areas, the wet chemical lab, the horological workshop and the two ultralow noise and vibration labs with their isolated airflow and deep foundations. These labs were used for nano-fabrication and the furthest one included the nano-incubator where Olympia had been born along with her nervous system. The rest of her had been fabricated in the horological workshop.

Her body was the product of a technology that began centuries ago reaching peaks with the mechanical clocks and the early automata and then the creations of the eighteenth and nineteenth century masters Vaucanson, Jacquet-Droz, Cox and Merlin, and Von Kempelen.

Her brain and nervous system were something entirely new.

The lump of silica Fox had seen in the Castle was an early version of an ultraclock's brain.

An accumulation of cantor dust. Oxenstierna's great discovery. Oxenstierna created what he called a recursive gear. The physical embodiment of the sort of algorithm that creates fractal spaces in topology. The type of shapes created, at a nano-level had, mathematically, zero value and infinite space. That rock, that lump of dust, is honeycombed with tunnels and paths, shapes within shapes. Too small to ever be seen. In practice infinity could never be attained but it did allow Oxenstierna vast areas to let loose his nano-scale clockwork devices, and together they created something he said was as perfect as a human mind. The cams and barrels of the clockwork are pinned. The pins are resettable can be moved from in to out positions and these positions constantly change to control the actions of other similar devices linked to them. Multiply this throughout the vast space available and you get an idea of the amount of processing power available.

"Think of it, Herr Fox, in the infinitesimal spaces of the cantor dust are the equivalent of whole cities of clocks."

Oxenstierna's aim had been to build a computer that would be resistant to digital decay. Not knowing how the decay was mutating he decided that data would not be encoded using variances in electronic voltage and that even quantum state computers might be susceptible since the decays itself was likely some kind of weapon aimed at all extant systems.

Thus the material of the original clockwork computer and the subsequent clockwork brains would be electrically inert, based on nano-scale mechanical switches and assemblers.

The power would ultimately derive from the clockwork mechanism that operated the body on the macro scale. In the end they were not so unlike human beings who depend, in the end, in the oscillations of a heart.

**

Fox and Olympia arrived in the evening as the light was beginning to fail. The monastery was

451

above the road, up a broken trail that was half path, half a stair, made of jagged rocks. Fox wondered later how Oxenstierna had managed to get all the equipment up for the laboratory and assumed he must have had access to helicopters or else the whole process had been much more laborious involving packed donkeys.

Fox struggled, clambering without being able to use his hands as he carried Olympia. As it was almost dark the monastery became a silhouette looming above. Fox stumbled and rather than drop Olympia he fell to his knees, pain shooting through his legs. He got up and took a few more steps carefully feeling the ground with his feet.

Something came from the monastery, gliding on an air current and tacking the wind. A light. It was a sphere but with a bird in its centre. It hovered above Fox and he tried to get a better look at the bird but staring directly at the light hurt his eyes. It illuminated the way so that he could reach the monastery without falling again. At the top there was open ground, shapes beyond this, the sphere of bird light showing what might be fences or trellis with trailing plants. A path led through this, not jagged rock or broken earth now but flagstones worn smooth by footfall after footfall.

Before they reached the open gates of the monastery the bird flew ahead and hovered over them so that Fox walked beneath it and everything outside the pool of light was darkness. Then ahead other lights came, other birds speeding out of the shadows of the columned cloisters. They swirled about in the air like the beams of searchlights.

Across the courtyard someone was coming. He walked with confident strides. He had an almost art-deco elegance, smooth and in the light the colour of gun-metal.

"Victor?" Fox said.

"No. Victor is my brother. I am Monet Same. Welcome to Harmony."

***

They were his birds and the others that had come to Genesia in recent months were his, along with the beetles and other bugs.

"I need to see Oxenstierna," Fox had said.

Monet Same led Fox into the church and told him to lay Olympia out on the altar.

"He can help her," Fox said, "Parsifal told me. The dead can rise. She can be made new again."

Fox said variations of this over and over, babbling as they stood there in the church. All around the frescoes were being animated by candlelight. The way the candle flickered and wavered touching the bare chest of Adam, the bosom of Eve, washing over the emerald scales of the servant.

Oxenstierna was dead.

Even as Fox took this in other thoughts were occurring.

"But you...you could..."

Monet Same told how he had made those birds and bugs. But the bioluminescent birds were his first venture beyond the strictly clockwork. Oxenstierna had taught him much but he hadn't yet mastered the final art of creation, the fitting a body with a personality.

When Oxenstierna had come here he had found the scriptorium of the life-bugs in much the state it was in now. The scribes, who transcribed the tapes into the great book that would be sent to God, were gone. The pages of the book were there, in pieces, wrecked. But still the scarabs came, bearing the life-bugs, the essence of personalities, soldiers mostly. Oxenstierna took that raw material as one of the key inputs into the process that had made the ultraclocks, some aspect of the base personality presumably kept but the memories gone, the violence purged, he hoped.

The brain he had built, the vast, labyrinth of cantor dust populated by tiny clockwork machines had been a type of computer. When he began to encode the next generation of such devices with memories from the life-bugs he created something entirely new.

"What is it that makes us what we are?" Monet Same asked.

Oxenstierna did not harvest the individuality from the life-bugs but rather some essence of what it is to be a person. The possibility of being a person. The personality came later, fashioned by the bodies they were given, their faces, then their relationships to one another and the world.

This was all explained to Fox over the first night and again over the days that followed. He would walk with Monet Same through the shadowed cloisters, they would sit at a table while Fox ate.

At first only part of Fox listened, because Olympia was beyond hope, and Olympia was

454

revealed as something other than what he had known her as, the remnant of another's life had gone to forge her.

"Who was she?" he once asked, "Who was she before she was Olympia?"

He could hardly bear that some essence of her was like the soldiers he had known. Like Kardos. There might have been some redemption if she could arise again, could take his hand and be charming, and naïve, and knowing, and all the things that Olympia had been.

"Who was she?"

But Monet Same did not know.

Fox began to assist the ultraclock. Standing with him in the horological workshop, learning some of the rudiments. And later they would go through the laboratories and Monet Same, with Oxenstierna's notes and journals, would talk about how they might go about reconstructing the great work.

Out in the courtyard Fox watched the life-bug scarabs fly to the scriptorium. Usually there were only one or two a day, sometimes a few more. Then one day, the first warm day for longer than he could remember, a swarm of them came, perhaps fifty, then more, then hundreds. The same the next day. Then no more at all. He wondered if the war in Genesia had come to some violent climax and whether that meant that soon he might see a ragged trail of ultraclocks moving across the lands towards him. If Parsifal had survived. If his message had had any effect. The ultraclocks would be coming home.

www.ingramcontent.com/pod-product-compliance
Lightning Source LLC
Chambersburg PA
CBHW011401010726
47495CB00009B/2721